New York Review of Science Fiction

"A fascinating cast of characters involved in a richly complex situation. . . . Her people are convincingly real. . . . Traviss has created a vivid assortment of alien races, each with distinctive characteristics and agendas. . . . She brings a rare combination of insight and experience that will greatly contribute to our field."
James Alan Gardner, author of *Expendable*

"Karen Traviss [takes] space voyagers, warring extraterrestrials, and alien/human interactions, and [gives] those tropes new life."
Locus

"Stellar."
Jack Mc Devitt, author of *Deepsix*

"In Shan Frankland, Karen Traviss has created a tough, interesting, believable character."
Gregory Frost, author of *Fitcher's Brides*

"A writer to watch. . . . Traviss takes what could have been a rote collection of characters (marines, cops, religious extremists) and slowly adds depth, complexity, and color."
BookPage

Books of The Wess'har Wars by
Karen Traviss

CITY OF PEARL
CROSSING THE LINE
THE WORLD BEFORE
MATRIARCH
ALLY

KAREN TRAVISS

ALLY

An Imprint of HarperCollins*Publishers*

This is a work of fiction. The characters, incidents, and dialogue are drawn from the author's imagination and are not to be construed as real. Any resemblance to actual events or persons, living or dead, is entirely coincidental.

EOS
An Imprint of HarperCollins*Publishers*
10 East 53rd Street
New York, New York 10022–5299

Copyright © 2007 by Karen Traviss
ISBN: 978–0–06–088232–7
ISBN–10: 0–06–088232–8
www.eosbooks.com

First Eos paperback printing: April 2007

HarperCollins® and Eos® are registered trademarks of HarperCollins Publishers.

Printed in the U.S.A.

10 9 8 7 6 5 4 3 2

For Jim Gilmer, the man with the compass.

Acknowledgments

My grateful thanks go to Bryan Boult for critical reading, and to my editor, Diana Gill, and my agent, Russ Galen, for keeping me in line.

ALLY

Prologue

The Temporary City, Bezer'ej, Cavanagh's Star system: interrogation room

One down, one to go.

Shan Frankland had two ways of tracking Lindsay bloody Neville: to let the Eqbas find her by scanning the sea or by squeezing information out of Mohan Rayat and doing the job herself, like she always had.

Lindsay had to be found before she did something stupid.

I should have shot her when I had the chance and when she could still be killed. The second *chance, fuck it. And Rayat, too. Christ, I'm getting slack.*

Rayat watched Shan walk around the room without moving his head. She knew when someone was following her in their peripheral vision by the fixed stare ahead and the blink rate; but Rayat didn't blink.

He was a spook. He was trained for this. Sod it, she'd *make* him blink. She was a copper, so she was trained for it too.

"So where do *you* think she's gone?" Shan asked.

Rayat didn't move a muscle. "No idea. It's a big ocean, and Lindsay's an unpredictable woman."

"You wouldn't be shitting me, of course."

"Would I have turned myself in if I was colluding with her?"

Shan thought of a few scenarios where he might have done just that. She wouldn't trust him as far as she could spit in a Force Ten. "You tell me."

"I've seen what this parasite can do and it scares me."

"So have I. " *C'naatat* had kept her alive through a shot-shattered skull and drowning and even drifting in the vacuum of space minus a suit. *Scared? You have no idea, chum.* She paused in front of him and folded her arms: he sat at the bare table with his hands folded. "You used to call it a symbiont. You're a scientist. You're precise about terminology."

"Symbionts are about mutual benefit. Parasites are about keeping you as alive as you need to be for *their* benefit."

"It wants to reproduce and find new hosts, that's for sure."

"So you can't kill me easily. You know that."

"I know. Consider it an incentive for me."

Shan stared him in the eye until he looked away. She had no intention of giving in again to her urge to punch that smirk off his face. Whatever you threw at a *c'naatat* host, it made them stronger: the organism adapted instantly with a nifty work-round, cheating death with disturbing ease, and the host came out with a new healing adaptation. No, she wasn't going to oblige Rayat by making a supersoldier out of him. It was bad enough that he'd been infected with a strain of *c'naatat* that now knew how to keep her alive in space.

The bastard had been sent to secure the organism for the European federal government. Like her, he didn't abandon his mission just because things got awkward. She hated him with the passion you could only muster for someone who showed you the worst aspects of yourself.

"Well, you're not going anywhere now," said Shan. "And neither is Lin."

"Vengeance is a powerful focus."

"Not vengeance. Just stopping someone who takes decisions to change the course of the fucking universe at the drop of a hat. You know. Nuke an island, near as damn it wipe out the bezeri, change a whole ecology, that kind of stuff." She was getting mad now: her fists went involuntarily to her hips and she felt her jaw set. "Her and her poxy humanitarian conscience—and don't tell me she's found religion. That'd just piss me off even more. It's bad enough that she thinks she knows best every time, without her thinking she's got a hotline to God for mission tasking."

Rayat considered Shan with a benign hint of a smile. "Take the word God out of that stream of vitriol, and you might well be describing yourself."

"Nice try," said Shan quietly. "But I'm past having pissing contests with you."

He carried on anyway. "Or your wess'har friends. You all make those epic decisions so easily."

"I'll stick another one on the list, then," said Shan. For all his spook expertise at reading people's reactions, Rayat didn't know what was in her head right then, what was preoccupying her. He didn't know the decisions she'd had to make. "Either way, *c'naatat* stays here and nobody else picks up a dose. EnHaz might be long gone, but I'm not, and I'm still on duty."

Rayat looked at her with dark eyes that might have betrayed a hint of kindness had they not been his. She wondered how long her self-control would stop her thrashing him the way she had before he picked up *c'naatat*. She also wondered how many of her memories—and Ade's, and Aras's—were surfacing in this smug bastard's mind. She hoped they'd be the worst ones, like stepping out of the airlock into the void, a slower way to die than most imagined.

But Rayat didn't know all the decisions she'd had to take. She'd aborted her own child. Killing Rayat and Lindsay Neville wouldn't trouble her at all, provided she had enough explosive power to do the job. She wondered again why she hadn't done it already, when all it would have taken was one round in the head.

It struck her that it wasn't Lindsay Neville she needed to find. It was the Shan Frankland that she used to be who was missing.

1

Seguor Marshes near the former colony of Constantine, Bezer'ej: 2377

The *sheven* reared from the marshes, and suddenly it was a plastic bag dragged dripping from a polluted river and falling back into the water with a splash.

Aras had never seen that river and he'd never seen Earth. But the memory was vivid, and it wasn't his.

"I hate those bloody things." Ade Bennett peered over the edge of the skiff, rifle ready. "How big do they get?"

"Did you live near a river once?"

"What?"

"A river. A memory. It feels like yours. Plastic waste in a river."

"Maybe." Ade's gaze stayed fixed on the marshes. "Might be Shan's. We've both seen plenty of shit at home." He turned his head slightly, eyes still darting back to the *sheven*'s last location, ever the vigilant soldier. "Come on, how big?"

Aras's *c'naatat* parasite, efficiently filing recollections from other hosts, had absorbed the memory of the river either from Ade, or from Shan, their mutual *isan*—their "missus," as Ade put it. The snapshot of the humans' filthy homeworld was shared between them by an organism that adapted, preserved and repaired its host in the face of all threats except fragmentation.

"Three meters, perhaps." Aras considered the range of *sheven* he had seen over the years. They lurked just beneath the surface, emerging only to snatch prey and plunge back beneath the surface. "I saw one that size a century ago, but most of them are two meters or smaller."

"Bloody awful way to die, being digested by a bit of cling-wrap."

"But you wouldn't die. *C'naatat* wouldn't allow it."

"Bloody awful way to give the thing indigestion, then." Ade had a quiet persistence when it came to pursuing ideas. "So what would happen? Would I sort of sit there in its guts until it threw up? I mean, do they have arses? Would it shit me out?"

"You *might* infect it, of course, in which case you might remain within it." It was unhappy speculation, but nothing that Aras hadn't considered himself in the five centuries since he'd become a host to the organism. "But *c'naatat* seems to favor more complex hosts than a *sheven.*"

"I feel so much better. Thanks."

C'naatat certainly favored humans. They were hunting an infected human now; Commander Lindsay Neville was somewhere out there in the waters beyond this estuary, an altered woman living underwater with the native cephalopod bezeri. Aras now wondered if Ade had been right to infect her deliberately.

You were seconds away from doing it yourself.

"No bezeri," said Ade.

"With so few left, I doubt we would spot them now."

"It sounds like Lindsay at least got them organized."

"You're still asking if you made a mistake giving her *c'naatat.*"

"I'm still feeling like an arsehole, yes."

"If you hadn't, *I* would be down there now."

Ade's focus on the water seemed unnaturally intense.

"Shan would have gone ballistic either way. Maybe it doesn't make any difference."

It wasn't Ade's fault. It had almost been a joint decision.

The bezeri needed help of the kind only a *c'naatat* could give, and if Ade hadn't stopped him, Aras would have been where Lindsay was now, helping the bezeri salvage what they could of their shattered society.

"I think you made the right decision. I believe Lindsay Neville has found a sense of responsibility and will do as much as I ever could."

"What if you'd known the bezeri had exterminated a whole bloody race? Would you have been so quick to put your arse on the line for them then?"

"Their ancestors committed genocide. Not this generation. Nor the generation I aided in the past."

"You smelled bloody shocked when you found out."

"I was."

"Do you believe Rayat, though? He's a lying bastard. Maybe it's part of some ruse."

"No," said Aras. He wanted desperately to see the bezeri again. He wanted to confront them about it. "I believe him. It serves no purpose to tell me a lie about their past, and it explains a great deal."

"I'm not sure I give a fuck about them any more."

"Hindsight."

"Reality. They're no better than us. Maybe this serves the fuckers right. Poetic justice."

Aras had always seen the bezeri as victims. They had been the victims of the isenj colonists, and them the victims of the *gethes,* the carrion-eating humans of the *Thetis* mission. They were *collateral damage,* to use Ade's jargon.

"It doesn't alter what Lindsay and Rayat did to them," said Aras. He labored patiently through human moral logic. "Even if bezeri see no shame in genocide, their ancestors carried out the slaughter, not this generation. They didn't earn their own destruction."

"But they aren't apologizing for it, either, are they?"

"Motive is irrelevant. Only outcomes count."

"I'm still too human to believe that, mate. Motive *matters.*"

Intent was an oddly human factor. Aras knew that very well, but sometimes he slipped back into human thinking, and the wess'har and human perspectives on guilt and responsibility could never align. Of all the differences between the species, that was the one that Ade had never come to terms with. Not even Shan had, and she was a wess'har-minded human even before she absorbed the genes.

"No," said Aras. "It doesn't matter. The only thing that counts is what's *done.*"

Ade lay against the gunwales of the boat with his rifle trained on the water, a grenade launcher bolted to its muzzle. Lindsay Neville had walked ashore around here once; she might do so again. Her baby son was buried here.

"We must've just missed her last time we were out this way," he said. "I know Shan said she wanted her alive, but I'm still not sure she'll slot the bitch and have done with it."

"Then we take the opportunity if we get it." The transparent *sheven,* no more than one single, insatiable digestive tract, broke the surface of the water twenty meters ahead of them, staying close to the shoreline, where its prey—small crawling creatures—was most likely to stray too close. This kind of *sheven* was a freshwater predator of the rivers and marshes and avoided the saline water further down the estuary. "I'll explain it to Shan if that happens. She can rage at *me* this time."

Ade made a vague grunt. "It's not like the Boss to be forgiving. Maybe she's got some problem with it." He sounded more baffled than critical. "Maybe she *can't* do it to someone she knows that well."

"You once pulled a weapon on Lindsay Neville too, and never finished the task either."

"If I'd known where this was going to end, don't you think I would have?"

"No. She was your superior officer. Even if she wasn't a marine."

"Bullshit," Ade said quietly, and made no sense again. "But what I cock up, I put right."

Aras scanned the water with eyes that saw polarized light and detected the weed and movement of small creatures beneath the surface. Ade struggled with a host of unfortunate events, not just the contamination of Lindsay and Rayat—he was still grieving for the loss of a child that could never be. Aras judged this by his faint scent of anxiety at unguarded moments that could only come from unhappy thoughts.

"You have to forget the child," said Aras.

"Can you?" said Ade.

Aras wasn't sure, but he was trying.

"Shan had no choice. You know what a *c'naatat* child would mean. It would live in isolation for an unimaginable time, just as I did."

"I know." Ade's blinked for a second as he sighted up through the scope of his rifle. "But *can* you forget it? I asked a question."

"Wess'har have perfect recall."

"For Chrissakes, Aras, you know what I'm asking."

"I mourn, yes. But I know recrimination serves no purpose."

"I'm still upset that she got rid of it." Ade's voice dropped, wounded and bewildered. "It would have been good to have a kid with her."

"Think about the future for that child had it survived. Alone. Not like us. You *know* it was impossible."

"Yeah. Anyway, what are we doing yakking away like this when we're doing surveillance? Maybe we should shut up."

Aras took the hint and doubted it had much to do with stalking a target. Ade took a long, slow breath and seemed to tire of looking through the scope. He eased himself onto his knees and sat back on one heel, rifle resting in the crook of his elbow. Around them the silence was broken only by the murmur of the water and the clicks and whirrs of living things hidden in the nearby grasses.

"I *did* think about it," he said at last. "And you're right. But I really wanted a kid."

Aras wanted a child too, perhaps more than Ade understood or Shan knew. But he was wess'har, and so what was done was done, and regret was pointless. The part of him that was human tried to indulge in what-if and if-only from time to time, but he dismissed it. It was a corrosive, destructive habit.

Instead he concentrated on an Earth he recalled but had never seen, and that same human fragment of him wanted to go back there with the Eqbas Vorhi task force. The wess'har part of him, the part that knew how the Eqbas had dealt with the isenj on Umeh, preferred not to see the invasion at all. And it *would* be an invasion, even if the Australians thought they were being voluntary hosts to the Eqbas fleet.

It's going to be bloody, even with Earth's agreement.

He decided his time was better spent healing the raw pain within his own small, bizarre family than worrying about the fate of a distant planet that had caused so much death and destruction here on Bezer'ej. And there was a lot of pain to heal.

Ade changed the subject and sighted up again. He froze, fixed on something, and his voice dropped to a whisper. "Dead ahead."

Aras followed the direction of Ade's focus. "What can you see?"

"Probably a *sheven.*" The estuary was a maze of mudflats and inlets. "It's a bugger to spot transparent targets."

Lindsay was now as translucent as the bezeri, and amphibious with it. *C'naatat* tackled each host as a new project to be transformed; it never behaved quite the same way twice. They were hunting a glass ghost.

Something sparkled in Aras's peripheral vision and he jerked round. But there was nothing.

Ade suddenly raised the rifle, slow and steady. He indicated with an exaggerated nod to his right and tracked his scope. *Rushes,* he mouthed.

The sunlight caught something in Aras's peripheral vision again and he wheeled round. It seemed to be bobbing up from cover and dropping back again, too big to be a *sheven,* but it left the same visual impression. He paused. Then he began paddling with long, slow strokes to ease the skiff clear of the bank. Ade said nothing and adjusted his aim. The rifle whirred faintly as it auto-targeted.

A glistening translucent curve flashed and fell.

There was no splash. Whatever it was had fallen on dry land.

Lindsay Neville.

Ade was on one knee, finger curled against the trigger. Aras drew the paddle through the water and then he saw it for a moment: a liquid curve above the grasses, not quite completely transparent, but still far from human. Mohan Rayat insisted that Lindsay was still in bipedal human form.

"Hold fire," said Aras, just a breath of a whisper. "It's not her."

Ade held his aim, froze for a second, and then swung the rifle left as if he was targeting again. Aras stared as a glimpse of a formless, gelatinous shape slipped into the water, leaving an impression of sparkling lights and opalescence.

Ade lowered the weapon and his shoulders sagged. "What the hell was that?"

It wasn't anything like a streamlined humanoid. And it could produce light. *Sheven* didn't have bioluminescence.

But the bezeri did.

"It's a whole new problem," said Aras.

Yes, it was.

The Temporary City, Bezer'ej: Eqbas Vorhi base

"You shove that probe any further, sunshine, and you're going to be using it for a suppository."

Shan stared at Da Shapakti with as much malevolent dignity as she could muster with her legs spread apart.

"My apologies," said the biologist. The fact that he wasn't human and had no preconceived ideas about women didn't make it any easier for her. It was definitely a scene for the dingbat abduction conspiracists' album. "Unfamiliar anatomy."

"I'll bet." It was years since Shan had undergone a manual examination: even her don't-interfere-with-nature Pagan parents thought a scan was perfectly acceptable. "Haven't you got an ultrasound probe? Jesus, even I've got one in my swiss, and that's an antique."

"*Ultrasound,* as you call it, provides no cells." The Eqbas biologist brushed the probe over the surface of a sheet of gel. "I want to know how your uterus regenerates."

"Okay, give me the probe. I know the layout better than you." It looked like a glass cocktail stirrer. Eqbas technology was largely transparent and baffling, but Shan didn't need to understand it to insert it. And at least it was warm. " I check myself every day now. No uterus. It hasn't come back."

"I've made you angry," said Shapakti. He froze in mid-examination, the classic alarm reaction in wess'har. "Did you have to shout at people when you were a police officer?"

Shan gritted her teeth. Wess'har—whether they were the local population on Wess'ej or their newly arrived Eqbas cousins—had the bizarre knack of being both childishly open and uncompromisingly menacing. She'd been too harsh on Shapakti, the poor bugger. Like her, he was just a long way from home, making the best of a bad job.

No. I am home. This is where Aras has to stay; this is where Ade wants to be. I've got new priorities now.

"I did a lot worse than shout, believe me," she said. Shapakti seemed to cope with her occasionally pidgin mix of English and eqbas'u. "Sorry. I'm angry that Lindsay and Rayat are walking round alive when they nearly wiped out the bezeri. At least we've got *that* bastard even if we haven't found her."

"You want to kill him."

"They'll do for starters."

"Even though you now know the bezeri slaughtered another race in the past?"

"Would that make a difference to you?"

"No. It was many generations ago. It wasn't this one."

"Okay, I admit I've got a lot less sympathy for them now." *It's nothing to do with sympathy. You think you've been conned. You don't like anyone pulling a fast one on you.* "But I'm still a copper. If I stand back and look at the evidence, Rayat and Lin are guilty. End of story."

"Motive matters to you."

"Intent is a large part of human law."

"What will you do if you catch Lindsay Neville?"

It was a good simple question. Shapakti had a talent for those, just like Ade. "I ought to nip the problem in the bud and kill her too."

Shan tried to think of some outcome that made sense beyond wanting to smash Rayat's smirking face. Lindsay's solution seemed clearer cut: Lin wasn't going to hand over *c'naatat* any faster than Shan would, but Shan wanted to be certain. *Fragmentation.* If the risk would be around forever, it was the only answer.

"Rayat has asked for asylum," said Shapakti.

"Wess'har don't do fancy legal stuff like asylum."

"If I can remove *c'naatat* from him, then you would have no need to hunt down and destroy other *c'naatat* hosts. Then the condition could be managed if it got into a wider human population."

Shan didn't like the sound of *managed.* She wanted to hear *eradicated,* and also wanted not to be part of that eradication, because she almost liked her life now. "How long am I going to lay here like a Drury Lane whore, Shap?" She held out her hand, palm up, imperious. "Give me the bloody probe and I'll do it."

Shapakti hadn't seen a human in this kind of detail before. He certainly hadn't examined one with *c'naatat,* and he was fully suited against the risk of contamination. Sensible precaution: but Shan still felt like a leper, and an embarrassed one at that. She extracted the glass wand and held it by its midsection so that he could take the clean end in gloved fingers.

"You can't remove it from wess'har, you can't remove it from ussissi, and it looks like the thing's learned how to stop you removing it from humans," she said. *Don't get me back in that loop of wondering why I don't have another go at killing myself, if it's that dangerous.* "So I think I'll hang on to a high-yield grenade until further notice, if that's okay by you."

Esganikan Gai regarded Rayat as her prisoner to process, and processing prisoners only had one definition for wess'har—execution. Shan didn't have a problem with that, not for Rayat anyway. She recognized single-minded obses-

sion with mission objectives when she saw it. It was like
looking in a mirror.

You bastard.

She had to be clear why she was doing this. She tried to
separate the logical necessity from just hating him for nebulous, meaningless things like needing to best him or letting
his resilience goad her.

"Is this it?" Shapakti consulted the data in his *virin,* tilting the hand-sized slab of translucent composite to see the
data. Shan swung her legs over the edge of the makeshift examination table and pulled on her underpants before peering
over his shoulder. He was looking at a cutaway image of a
female human that had come from the Constantine colony's
simple library. "Here? In the pelvis?"

"That's the thing," she said, trying to be patiently helpful.
"About the size of a fist."

"You're certain it was removed before?"

"I reckon so. The doc made a big fuss about it. They don't
usually resort to surgery, but I refused gene therapy."

"Why?"

"I was brought up Pagan. My family wouldn't allow anything to alter my genome."

"And now you have a very altered genome indeed."

"Don't rub it in."

"And you're sure you removed the uterus when it re-
grew?"

Shan detached from a memory that felt like disembowel-
ment. She could hardly believe what she'd done: she'd heard
all the horror stories of how trapped people had cut through
their own limbs, and now she knew there was a level of des-
peration you reached—like the one she'd reached floating
suitless in the void—where the survival reflex took over totally and pain didn't matter.

"Yes, I'm certain," she said.

"Did it hurt?"

"I cut through my abdominal wall without anesthesia.
Of course it bloody well hurt." She stared at him, waiting
for a lecture on abortion. She didn't need one. It had up-
ended her more than she ever thought possible. "It was the

only way to guarantee getting past *c'naatat*'s defenses."

"I understand why you wanted to spare the child the life you have," he said kindly. "Just as Vijissi was unable to bear the isolation."

Thanks. Remind me he killed himself. You could always rely on wess'har to cut the crap and plow straight through the euphemism. They didn't understand oblique language. "It still shocks you, I know."

"We have no unwanted offspring." Shapakti smoothed his gel gloves over his hands. It made them look wet, and with his multi-jointed thin fingers, the effect was one of a sea creature stranded on the shore. "But then we have no offspring who would bear your burden, either."

"You have a great bedside manner," said Shan.

"It's hard to tell how upset you are because you suppress your scent."

"Just as well I can." *C'naatat,* forever tinkering with its collection of DNA fragments from other creatures it had passed through, had given her a wess'har scent signaling system. She kept her *jask*, her matriarchal dominance phero- mone, well under conscious control. "I don't want to lose my temper and end up deposing Esganikan."

"This child was Ade's."

She took it as a rebuke for carelessness. "We'd both been sterilized and we thought it was okay to copulate. *C'naatat* had other ideas."

"You think it *has* ideas? That it's sentient?"

"Just a figure of speech. Bacteria try to survive and repro- duce. But, yes, it does seem to learn and react to its hosts' anxieties." Shan stepped on thin ice of her own making: she'd taken the wess'har view of life and sentience to heart. Humans had no special rights or position in creation. "But I don't like thinking of it as something making decisions for me. *Nobody* does that."

Shapakti tilted his head on one side in that appealingly canine wess'har gesture of intense interest. Eqbas wess'har and their Wess'ej cousins might have looked different, but they both had those four-lobed pupils that made them cock their heads to get a better focus.

"This is very much a *gethes'* habit, this need to lock your-self away in your own head," he said. *Gethes:* carrion-eaters. Human eating habits appalled wess'har. "Their thoughts are still within you."

"You ought to think of me more as a human with a few bolt-on extras." Shan flexed her hands and bioluminescence danced as violet and amber lights in her fingers. She still didn't know where those bezeri genes had come from. "So, no uterus. But I don't know when it's going to make a come-back, and . . . well . . . it's affecting Ade."

"You have no *oursan* now."

"Yes. No sex. Not proper sex, anyway."

"Is that because you fear conception, or because he shuns you for killing his child?"

Eqbas were wess'har, all right. However used she was to that brusque manner, the words still stung; she occupied her-self fastening her belt and fidgeting with her handgun while she swallowed a retort.

No, I don't have a smart answer. I'm just hurt.

Shapakti held both hands over a shallow metal bowl and shook them as if he was performing a conjuring trick, and in a way he was: his gel gloves slid from his spi-dery hands and coalesced into a pool of liquid. A thought crossed her mind, one that diverted her productively from her guilt.

"One size fits all," she said, indicating the gloves with a jerk of her thumb. "You're good at making reactive liquid materials. That's the same tech you use for your ship's hull, isn't it?"

Shapakti did his baffled Labrador act. "Barrier and con-tainment, yes."

There was no delicate way to put it, but wess'har had no taboos about sex anyway. "If you can make gloves, you can make condoms." She didn't expect him to know the English word. "That's a covering you put over the *oursan'te*—to contain seminal fluid."

Shapakti trilled happily. "I understand." He held up the *virin.* "I have all human medical data here. Only one organ for both *sanil* and *oursan'te.*"

"Think of us as the economy model."

"I can make this device."

"Can I try the gloves?"

He took another bowl from the neat slatted shelves of his temporary surgery and held it in front of her. A biologist—a genetic engineer—playing doctor didn't trouble her quite as much as it had a few months ago; it made sense. He knew how to build the engine as well as repair it.

"Immerse your hands," he said.

Shan sank her fingers into a clear gel that felt like liquid on contact and crept up her hands to her wrists. Its inexorable progress over her skin made her jerk back, and judging by the wet sheen it had stopped about halfway up her forearms. It wasn't an unpleasant sensation; it just felt uncontrollable, as if it had a life of its own. She'd had her fill of that kind of thing with *c'naatat.*

"How does it know how to do that?"

"You withdrew your hands."

"Fascinating."

"It's an effective barrier."

Shan thought of the *sheven,* a carnivorous plastic bag, one huge enveloping gut and not much else. "If I hadn't pulled my hands out, would it have covered my whole body?"

"Yes."

"Jesus."

"It's safe, if uncomfortable. A complete barrier. You would still breathe, of course." Shapakti made another little trill in his throat. In a Wess'ej wess'har it was excited amusement. "But you don't need to breathe. You survived in space without a suit for many months."

She stared at the gloves, a slick glaze as thin as skin, and rubbed her fingertips together. They simply felt wet. There was no loss of sensation. It was another wess'har gizmo that would have made a fortune on Earth if they had any desire for commerce—which they didn't.

Condom. The gel was almost yelling it at her, and, God, how she wanted to fuck Ade properly again. *So is that all you care about? You're no better than Lin.*

She tried to imagine how she'd sell the idea to Ade. "No

thanks. I got used to breathing again. I think I'd miss it. How do you clean these things after use?"

Shapakti made the shaking gesture with both hands. "The coating will release itself."

Shan suppressed a mental image of Ade separating himself from the sticky embrace of the gel. It was just as well he had a uniform-black sense of humor. "And the contaminant?"

"How dangerous is it?"

"Just body fluids. It's not like it's going to make us any more *c'naatat* than we already are."

"Rinse the gel in water."

"Is that it? Nearly a million years ahead of us, and you just *rinse*?"

"The best solution is the simplest one."

"Yes, I do hanker for a napped flint and a pointy stick some days."

"But how will you exchange memories now, if you put a barrier between the *oursan* membranes?"

"We don't need to. It might be a useful trait for an isenj, but it's a pain in the arse for the rest of us." Shan shook the glove coating into the bowl with a flick of her hands that made her wrist joints crack, and watched the liquid become a gel that huddled in an oblate sphere like mercury at the bottom of the bowl. "And normal wess'har don't swap memories either. It's not mandatory in a relationship."

Shan made a mental note to carry on checking herself for signs of regenerated body parts anyway, condom or not. She was a copper. She didn't put trust in what she couldn't break into components, analyze and understand. This gel's technology was as far beyond her as the Eqbas's liquid spaceships, and she didn't do blind faith.

Locked in a small room down the passage of this underground base—hidden out of respect for the wilderness round it, not for security or concealment—Rayat was another element in her life that she couldn't trust, although she understood him far too well. She still wasn't sure which government department he really worked for; but he was a spook, and that was all she needed to know.

She was damned if he was heading back home with his prize. *C'naatat* wasn't for sale.

"Can't your clean-up teams trace Lindsay?" she asked.

Shapakti picked up the imaging device that Shan thought of simply as the glass tea-tray and stared into its layers like a haruspex seeking meaning in entrails. He had been annoyed—as annoyed as he could be, anyway—that he couldn't remove *c'naatat* from human cells as he once had. The damn thing was learning to thwart him. He made little noises in his throat that reminded her of an otter and she wondered if he was avoiding the issue in a very un-wess'har way.

But he wasn't. He was just preoccupied. "They've lost track of the bezeri. They seem to have vanished."

Shan tipped the glob of gel into a container and put it in her pocket. "I'd better find Aras and Ade, then. It's like having a couple of naughty little boys to look after."

It was a joke but she meant more than half of it, because the two of them had become a double act. The housebrother bond was as powerful for Ade as it was for any wess'har, more than just the exchange of DNA between the three of them and the biochemical bonding: Ade craved comradeship, and so did Aras. Species and trillions of miles of space might have separated them, but they had a lot in common apart from her—two soldiers, expendable and expended, who dreaded loneliness.

"If you find Lindsay," said Shapakti, "will you let me take samples from her?"

"Dead or alive?"

"Alive is always better."

"I'll see what I can do."

Shan walked out of the maze of corridors and chambers that formed the Temporary City, passing knots of ussissi displaced from Umeh by the fighting—not almost-appealing meerkats now, but irritable, anxious, pack-fighting animals. There was also the Eqbas crew working on the decontamination of Ouzhari island, around a hundred of them in this former wess'har garrison. The rest of the 2,000-strong force was split between Umeh and the surrounding camp, and they were marking time on those duties until the rest of the Eqbas task force joined them for the journey to Earth.

Shan found a sheltered spot on the shingle beach and sat in the lee of a twenty-meter long mat of some tufted lavender-gray succulents. This was where Ade and Aras would land the boat. She'd see them coming.

Umeh is not your problem. Leave it alone.

But Umeh was tearing itself apart. The Eqbas were giving them a hand in making a bang-up thorough job of it, too.

None of this is your problem. Stop looking for more fights to keep yourself occupied.

From the beach she could see the first island in the chain that ran south, about six kilometers across the channel. She realized she didn't actually know the local name for it; to her, it had always been Constantine. That was the name of the religious colony that had lived there for nearly two centuries, and so in the proprietorial way of foreign empires the island's identity had been subsumed by it. The chain of islands ran south, decreasing in size like a bunch of stylized grapes—Catherine, Charity, Clare, Chad, and Christopher, named for saints who hadn't been on hand here to perform any miracles when they were really needed.

Christopher had a local name: *Ouzhari.* Shan wondered if it would go down in history like Hiroshima or Istanbul, an icon of destruction. It had been idyllic white sand and black grass set in a vivid blue sea, but the grass was gone, and only *c'naatat* survived in the soil of the irradiated wasteland.

So the bezeri were as rotten and profligate as humans. They'd wiped out a rival race long before the wess'har came to the Cavanagh system, and—according to Rayat—they didn't feel the least bit guilty, and they didn't deny it. They seemed bullish: proud, even. Shan realized she'd been hoping that the unifying principle of non-human life across the galaxy would be compassion, and that *Homo sapiens* was the bad apple in the galactic barrel. Deep down, though, her rational self had long suspected that gang-banging dolphins and murdering chimps were just evidence that all life was brutal and opportunistic in its way, and that people by the wess'har definition of sentience—human or cephalopod, insectoid or un-cute meerkat—were equal, both in their right to life and their complete disregard for it.

But she *liked* the wess'har. They killed too, but she understood their rules: vegan, cooperative, frugal, and utterly remorseless. They didn't pick on the small and the weak. They swaggered up to the biggest bully in the playground, tapped them on the shoulder, and punched them out. That was how she did things too. She fitted in fine with the local wess'har. She also fitted in with the Eqbas wess'har, up to a point, and that was the part that worried her, because the cultural and ethical rift between the two branches was big. She watched it growing bigger each day.

They all think it's perfectly okay for me to betray my duty and help eco-terrorists, though. Normal, decent, wess'har thing to do.

If only she embraced the Wess'ej Targassati philosophy of non-intervention as well, she might have been a lot happier. But her gut still told her to do as the Eqbas branch of the family did; wade into trouble to sort things out, unasked and uninvited.

Across the channel, a pinpoint of reflection wreathed in a bow wave of white foam was heading her way. As she watched, it resolved into a rigid inflatable. Two figures sat forward, leaning on the gunwales, one the dark and heavily muscled shape of a once wess'har rendered almost unrecognizable by the changes *c'naatat* had made to him, the other a smaller blur of lovat green combats, a human male.

How will we ever get back to normal after all this?

Normal was relative; other people's normal had never been hers anyway, but the last few years had shifted it much further along the spectrum. Now she wondered if she was actually irreparably damaged by accepting that you could suck hard vacuum or cut your guts open and still carry on as if you were human. The only reference point of sanity that she had was two lovers who were as altered as she was, and probably about as well adjusted. Their shared purdah seemed a powerful bond. Now, after the abortion, it seemed fragile.

Yeah, maybe a bit of discussion beforehand would have been a good idea. But what if you'd talked me into keeping it?

It could never be. *It* was a girl, but Shan hung on to the neuter, the nameless, and made damn sure she didn't start sentimentalizing. It wouldn't change a thing. As she focused on Ade, she also made sure she didn't wonder if the kid would have looked like him. That was the path to becoming a fucking lunatic like Lindsay.

By the time the inflatable slowed down in the shallows Shan could see that neither Ade nor Aras were happy. If the wind had been in the right direction, she was sure she could have smelled them. Ade jumped out of the boat as it ran up onto the beach, and lifted its outboard clear to haul up the pebbles for Aras to step out.

Now Shan could see why. Aras was cradling something in his arms. It was a makeshift container of folded plastic, full of vegetation and soil.

He's rescued something. He's found some animal. He's so bloody soft.

Wess'har generally expressed their strict vegan outlook by unsentimental avoidance of other species, but Aras had insisted on looking after the lab rat colony he'd liberated from Rayat before surrendering them to Shapakti. He found their little paws fascinatingly like human hands. Shan got to her feet and walked towards him, expecting to see something helpless and rare in the container, something Aras wanted to nurture.

She peered in. It was just wet earth and vegetation coated in what looked like raw albumen.

"Where is it?" she said. "Come to that, *what* is it?"

Ade had that studied lack of expression that said he had bad news, but his acid scent of anxiety conveyed the real message just fine. "I think we need to get Shapakti to take a look."

"Why?"

Aras—far from the seahorse-like elegant wess'har he had been, now more a heraldic beast overlaid on a man, magical and tragic—still had that tendency to tilt his head to indicate intense interest. "I believe there are trace cells on this piece of riverbank that are from a bezeri."

Shan heard *riverbank* and *bezeri*. She was no biologist, but bezeri were ocean dwellers, saltwater animals. "What's driven them inshore? Are they beaching themselves?"

She expected more bad news about their numbers. They were down to the last forty or so individuals of a population that had already declined to tens of thousands before the cobalt-salted neutron devices scoured Ouzhari and contaminated the sea round it. They would never recover.

Aras tilted the container. Shan reached out automatically and the lights in her fingertips sparkled in a complex pattern of blue and amber pinpricks. The display distracted her briefly from the wet mess in the plastic box.

"What's in there?" she asked.

"Traces of mucus from the mantle of a bezeri," said Aras. "From the banks of the estuary."

Another dead one. They beached themselves in their thousands after the fallout hit them. "The body's still there, then."

"No." Ade folded his arms and stared down at the pebbles for a few moments. He looked up, eyes wide and wary. "It ran off."

Northern Assembly, Ebj continent, Umeh, Cavanagh's Star system: near the Maritime Fringe border

Minister Rit picked her way between rubble on the construction site and wondered when the Maritime Fringe forces would pour across the border again.

The Eqbas had withdrawn their ship and she didn't know if they'd be back. They'd agreed to help Umeh restore its ecology: her husband, Par Paral Ual, had lost his life for asking them to intervene, and she expected that sacrifice not to be wasted. Once invited, Eqbas didn't walk away, but they seemed to have walked away now, as if Umeh was so far beyond their help that they'd lost interest in reshaping it.

It was still Rit's duty to see that her husband's wishes were honored. She didn't know how to cope if they weren't.

"I expect them to come back to discuss the bioweapons," said Rit.

Ralassi, her ussissi aide, half closed his eyes in faint disapproval. "They always keep their word."

"Meanwhile, then, we rebuild." Humans, her late husband used to tell her, were prone to descend into anarchy in wartime. They abandoned their sense of community. "Are your people going to return?"

"Perhaps." Ralassi trotted on, inspecting the progress. He was one of the few ussissi who seemed not to run with the pack. "But they seem to be settling into life on Wess'ej. Whatever happens, that's home. We evolved with the wess'har, regardless of what other partnerships we might form. Never forget that."

Buildings along the route of the Maritime Fringe's abortive advance stood smashed to the first and second floors, their colored fascias blackened and peeling. Most of the fallen masonry had been cleared, at least the length of the road ahead. The dead had been taken away and cremated long before. Joists and scaffold crisscrossed Rit's field of view like a web.

Nothing in her genetic memory, no voice or recollection of her many ancestors, could tell her what move to make now. Isenj rarely fought among themselves. It had taken an external threat—the wess'har and their cousins from Eqbas Vorhi—to tip them into brief, destructive skirmishes, and then—then they paused, bewildered, and looked around at what they had done, and tried to repair it.

"We still have a tree," said Ralassi.

Yes, they still had a tree. In the crater gouged by an explosion, a *dalf* was growing in the exposed soil, soil that hadn't seen the light of day for centuries until the brief battle—if the rout of the Fringe armored column could be called that—ripped foundations out of the ground. Long feathery projections, translucent gold in the hazy sun, had unfurled from three slim stalks at the tree's head.

Esganikan Gai said it was important that the utter sterility of Umeh should be broken by a living tree planted in that rarest of things, a patch of bare soil. She insisted on it.

The humans called it a park, except parks had more trees and a variety of other plants. The *dalf* would have been better off staying on Tasir Var, where it came from; but Esganikan, in that wess'har way of hers, carried on regardless and imposed a park upon the Northern Assembly.

Rit remembered trees, or at least her ancestors did; that meant they were significant memories. Rit's ancestral memory also recalled a time when the wess'har were simply newcomers to the system, settlers with impossibly advanced technology who were happy to settle on Asht's uninhabited twin planet and trouble nobody.

"How did we live in peace with wess'har for more than nine thousand years," said Rit, "and then end up fighting so bitterly?"

"Because the bezeri asked them to intervene to throw you off Bezer'ej." Ralassi dodged a loader sagging under the weight of chunks of shattered rubble. "Had they been *Eqbas* wess'har, they would have stopped you colonizing Asht to begin with."

This was the concept that gave Rit the most trouble, this idea that wess'har felt obligated to render aid—and carry on rendering it even when they were no longer wanted. She searched her inherited memories and found no hint that any of her forebears had understood that. All they had known was that wess'har didn't attack Umeh. That had left Umeh unprepared for the aggressively interventionist Eqbas Vorhi.

"How do humans cope?" she asked Ralassi.

The ussissi aide reached out and touched the *dalf*'s fronds carefully as if expecting pain from them. "With parks?"

"With having to learn everything anew in each generation."

"They don't," said Ralassi. "They make the same mistakes each time."

"No wonder they're so possessive about information. It's hard won for them." They did learn, though. They didn't seem at all surprised by the Eqbas. "What are they doing now?"

"They seem happy to have an outgoing ITX link to Earth, even if they have to queue to make their transmissions and even though they have nothing to say."

It took one authorization from Rit to lift the block on outgoing messages. Her ministry could have done it sooner, but they hadn't, and now it had been done that day, after requests had been countersigned and permissions passed down the line. The humans thought there was some strategy to it. But they had simply been forgotten in the unfolding crisis. They didn't seem used to being a small detail in the galaxy.

"I see no point continuing the embargo," said Rit. "There's no harm that they can do, now that they're leaving."

"And now that the problem isn't humans provoking wess'har any longer. Minister, what will you do about the Eqbas?"

"I have to reach an understanding with them, of course."

"Shomen Eit says this is now an infrastructure matter, and so his responsibility."

The park and the restoration was—strictly speaking—the preserve of Shomen Eit too. Rit, whose ministry handled alien relations, was making a statement by being here at all, even if she had planted the tree because it was, technically, alien.

And that statement was that she was moving into Shomen Eit's fiefdom.

My husband died for this. He wanted Umeh to be restored. And all Eit wants is more power for the Assembly. I can't let it stop at that.

"Until he relieves me of my post," said Rit, measuring every word, "then I carry on doing my duty to the state."

Two isenj who had been inspecting the *dalf* paused to stare at her. For a moment she thought they might speak to her: unlike human politicians, isenj didn't fear their electorate enough to want constant protection from them. But they simply acknowledged her office with a rattle of quills, stared at the tree for a moment longer, and then moved away.

She waited for them to pass. "Where is our army now?"

Ralassi checked the latest deployment on his data cube. "Those who've remained loyal to the Assembly are still surrounding the administration buildings, and there are units holding out along the border."

"What would *you* do?"

"Minister, I'm not a military tactician."

"I meant politically."

Ralassi had those same spherical eyes as all the furthings—wess'har, Eqbas, human—except they had none of that disturbing wet glaze that made them look like internal organs protruding through wounds. They were matte black. Even the changing patterns of electrical activity in the cells didn't give Rit much idea of where those eyes were focused. She had met her first ussissi when she came to Jejeno as a child, and she still sought some pattern in their eyes like she did in the receptors of her own kind. She never found it. She always felt there was something unsaid when she spoke with ussissi.

"I'm not here to advise," said Ralassi carefully. "Not about direction. Execution, yes. But the direction can only come from you and your colleagues."

"Shomen Eit must be displaced."

Rit paused and waited for a reaction. Ralassi's head bobbed as if he didn't quite understand what she'd said. He did, of course: it was just that no isenj minister would even suggest a coup. Isenj were largely cooperative, their ambitions held in check by shared memories and the orderly society they inherited from their colony-dwelling ancestors. Rit could recall that ancient sense of purpose for the common good, the sense of knowing where she fitted into the greater scheme and what she had to do.

But this act was for that greater good of the colony. Defending the colony transcended the need for narrow bureaucratic order. She had to do it.

"The elections are still a year away." Ralassi's flat tone betrayed his reluctance to discuss the unthinkable. "Time for any number of crises before then."

"I didn't mean that we should wait for elections." But there was no "we" for ussissi, not on Umeh at least. "You were born and raised here, Ralassi. Do you not feel any sense of a stake in this society?"

He blinked. It made him look like the soft, smooth humans again, whose eyes were in constant movement. "This is still *not* my world. And we can only involve ourselves so far in your affairs. We serve while we can remain neutral."

So she'd be removing Shomen Eit on her own, then. She turned her back on the *dalf* and made her way back to the groundcar, still uncertain of how much support she might get from her cabinet colleagues. Ralassi trotted behind her, his silence telling her that he found her machinations distasteful. Right then it seemed not the prospect of further war that was the greatest threat to her children, but her own government—her own colleagues—seeing the Eqbas intervention solely as a chance to emerge as a global power.

A global power on a dying planet. A poor prize.

"There's no room for old politics," she said. The driver couldn't hear them in the sealed cab. "My husband wanted change, and change we'll have."

"You'll never get Bedoi's support for this. You need Bedoi to carry the whole cabinet. You *know* you do."

"Maybe I'll have the army's."

Ralassi didn't protest. It was, as he said, not his world. Rit had no grasp of what it meant to know no other home and yet not feel part of it. But ussissi, like humans and wess'har, had no genetic memory, and so they couldn't possibly have a true sense of home and heritage.

"You're not a general," Ralassi said.

"My ancestors were conquerors." She wondered if anyone had the skills needed to fight a civil war, a rare thing indeed among isenj. She searched her ancient memories again, seeking something to guide or inspire her. "All I need is Shomen Eit's influence to be removed, and a weapon that another's skills can deploy. None of us know how to use a bioweapon except the wess'har. So I have as good a chance as anyone else of using it to advantage."

"You accept the deaths of some of your own citizens are inevitable, then."

Bioagents were a wess'har speciality: even the Wess'ej wess'har could do that, despite their lack of interest in pursuing technology and their talk of respecting the "natural"

world. They could even target the pathogens by small variations between different isenj genotypes. Rit knew that, but
she wondered how reliable the weapons might be, and if it
might not be a ruse to wipe them all out.

No, wess'har weren't humans. If they were set on destroying isenj, they would have done it without a moment's
hesitation. Deception wasn't a weapon they needed to use.
She could at least trust them.

"You know the stakes," said Rit. "Our population will
soon reach the point where even the managed environment
will collapse and there'll be millions of deaths anyway. Better to manage that in a controlled way—or do you subscribe
to this view of Tass . . . Tassati . . ."

"Targassat," said Ralassi. "That only outcomes matter?
All wess'har think that, not just Targassat. Yes, I believe I
do think that as well. But you sound as if you're trying to
convince yourself, Minister."

*I am, because I'm out of my depth. But I know we can't
carry on as we are and survive. How suddenly these tipping
points come upon us.*

"I'm simply choosing the manner of their dying."

Ralassi narrowed his eyes again. "You and the cabinet."

The groundcar edged forward. The streets here weren't as
tightly packed with pedestrians as the capital, and the driver
made better progress.

Rit looked at Ralassi with renewed curiosity: why did ussissi adopt the culture of another species so thoroughly, and
yet not that of the world where they were raised? Did they
have their own languages and beliefs? What did it mean,
then, to be ussissi? She couldn't grasp a sense of allegiance
and belonging so devoid of place or genes. But Ralassi was
loyal in the sense that he wouldn't betray her. That was all.

"The human and the wess'har who have *c'naatat*," she
said. "Is it true they have isenj genes?"

"I hear they have." Ralassi glanced out the hatch of the
groundcar and leaned through it to stare up at the sky. "And
isenj memories."

It was a shocking revelation, but *c'naatat* was a strange
symbiont. "Whose?"

"Whoever captured Aras Sar Iussan in the wars."

That was five centuries ago. This wess'har, this freak of nature, had isenj memories—but direct ones, undiluted by forty or more generations, and he wasn't just any wess'har but the destroyer of Mjat, a historical figure of hate for all isenj. This war criminal had a *direct* memory, a parental memory, one generation removed and no doubt vivid and detailed. Did it change the way he saw isenj now? Did he feel anything that his fellow wess'har didn't?

She wanted to meet him. She wondered if her dead husband had. "So the humans have inherited the memory from him, and so the two I saw, the soldier and the matriarch, they also . . ."

Rit trailed off. Ralassi seemed distracted by something, cocking his head to one side.

"Stop—" he said.

Ussissi had excellent hearing. He was straining to hear something. Seconds later, a faint whistling sound became loud and insistent, and the noise of the crowd either side of the car leapt from a low continuous whirring to a few high-pitched shrieks, silenced almost instantly by an explosion that left Rit numb and tasting saline in her mouth.

Snapping sounds crackled around her, her hearing so overloaded that it left a taste in her mouth. She was looking up at the inner canopy of the ground car. It was canted at an angle, but she couldn't work out if it was the vehicle or she who was tipped on one side.

The ground shook and she tasted more deafening sounds. Screams were drowned by low-frequency thuds. Ralassi's face was suddenly right in hers, lips drawn back to reveal an unbroken reef of white, spiked teeth.

"Minister—"

"We're under attack."

"Can you hear me, Minister?"

Rit was convinced she was speaking and couldn't understand why Ralassi couldn't hear her. Perhaps ussissi were deafened by loud noises, like humans. She realized the snapping was the sound of her own quills, broken as she was thrown around the interior of the groundcar. Two goldstone beads rolled across the floor of the vehicle as it lurched into a new position, and she could see clouds of smoke with particles roiling in them.

"What is it?" she asked. "What *is* it?"

Ralassi was barely audible now.

"We're under attack, Minister. The Maritime Fringe has launched missiles."

2

He's not the God of answers; he's the God of questions. He uses the events of history to interrogate us and ask how we will live and deal with them.

Franciscan monk
speaking after the earthquake that damaged
the Basilica of St. Francis of Assisi in 1997

The Temporary City, Bezer'ej: Eqbas Vorhi ship 886–001–005–6, in disassembled mode

Esganikan Gai liked the bulkhead of her cabin set to transparency, for the reassurance of the unspoiled wilderness of Bezer'ej a glance away. Watching the output from the Umeh observation remotes fifty million miles away was somehow uniquely claustrophobic.

It was also disappointing: the isenj had started fighting again.

She watched the live images on the screen set in the bulkhead like a waking nightmare intruding on a peaceful day, a portal into what the humans called Hell. At high magnification, the sprawl of construction from one coast of the Ebj continent to the other was peppered and illuminated by detonations. Smoke spread like blooms south of Jejeno, the Northern Assembly's capital.

Aitassi trotted into the cabin and paused to stare at the image of Umeh. "They still seem unable to make up their minds whether to fight or not."

"They're unaccustomed to civil war," said Esganikan. "Their genetic memories are mainly of being a colonial power."

"Who did they fight?"

"The local wess'har. You know that."

"I meant who else. If they were a colonial power, if they

established instant communications relays across star systems, then do they have other colonies? Why haven't we come across them before?"

Esganikan considered the idea that there might be more isenj out there, breeding to destruction and pillaging environments. Eqbas had as good an idea as anyone could about the spread of species in this arm of the galaxy; but even after millennia, they hadn't charted every world. Life wasn't rare, and space was vast.

"Perhaps, like humans, their colonial ambition is on a more domestic scale." She couldn't cover every eventuality. She fought to keep her focus. "But if they have colonies beyond Tasir Var, they haven't ever come to their homeworld's aid."

"Umeh makes you indecisive, doesn't it?"

Esganikan didn't need reminding. "Except for their potential to threaten Wess'ej, it doesn't matter if the isenj species survives or not. And that makes it difficult to evaluate the benefit of intervention."

It also didn't matter which image of Umeh the orbiting remotes were relaying. Whichever of Umeh's four island continents Esganikan observed, they looked the same except, at close quarters, in the detail of the architecture: coast-to-coast cityscapes and desperately overcrowded conditions. Umeh's ecology was wholly artificial. The isenj had consumed and destroyed everything else that shared their planet except for microscopic life in the oceans. Left to its own devices, it was a dying world anyway.

Does it matter if they kill each other? Does it matter if I help them do it? They'll die sooner or later, along with their world.

"I wish I'd never agreed to help the isenj restore the planet," said Esganikan. "But I did agree, so I have to see this through somehow. Do you think the Northern Assembly will use bioweapons if we give them the capacity?"

Aitassi made a little dubious chattering noise. "They'll try it once."

"Once is all it takes."

"Perhaps leaving the weapons with the local wess'har might be a better idea."

"If the matriarchs of F'nar were prepared to use those countermeasures, they'd have done it by now. They have their own biological weapon capability. They've already seeded this planet with anti-isenj pathogens."

"Generic ones, commander. They never had the tissue samples to create more targeted weapons."

"They've never attacked Umeh so they didn't need them. They only fought isenj in disputed territory."

The wess'har had arrived in this system ten thousand years ago. If they'd looked at their isenj neighbors then, and identified them as the threat they clearly were, things might have been very different. Instead they waited until a few hundred years ago, and intervened when the bezeri begged for aid. Too little; and far too late.

That's the problem with Targassat's ideology. Don't interfere. Turn a blind eye. And this is what happens.

Shan Frankland would have called them *bloody hippies.* Apparently it meant the same thing.

"I'm waiting for Curas Ti to respond," said Esganikan. "I need to know exactly what resources she can now commit to Earth."

Aitassi didn't say the obvious, that the matriarch of Surang, Curas Ti, should have worked that out by now. Earth *mattered.* Earth was more than the homeworld of humans who needed controlling: Earth had biodiversity to lose. Species there became extinct in decades, and it would take twenty-five years to reach the planet.

Esganikan drummed her fingers on the console and the grim picture of the Ebj continent switched to another orbital image, this time a far more familiar one: Surang, her home city on Eqbas Vorhi five light-years away.

Yes, she missed it.

It was a landscape of discreet but artificial canyons and cliffs studded with terraced homes and communal buildings where the business of government and manufacture took place. Compared to the deliberately concealed architecture of Wess'ej, where the local wess'har strove to blend in with the landscape, it looked intrusive. This was the world that the followers of Targassat left thousands of years before, rejecting the responsibility that wess'har had always accepted as an ancient race: the duty to teach, enable and—if necessary—impose environmental stability on other worlds.

But we came to your aid when you asked us to deal with the humans. We were heading home, and we've been away a long time. Now you don't even want us on Wess'ej.

Esganikan shook herself out of her growing resentment of her cousins. "I'd like a quick and straightforward solution." She was thinking once again of how many years it might be before she could return to Surang and start a family of her own. "But there won't be one."

How did I get drawn into this? Why did I not just let the isenj drown on their own filth?

Another screen activated in the bulkhead, spreading from a pinpoint to form a rectangle a meter across. Curas Ti's adviser on alien ecology, Sarmatakian Ve, seemed harassed. The backdrop behind her was a room that Esganikan recognized, dominated by a wall that was a single image of world's weather systems: the climate-modeling center, in Upper Girim.

"Is Curas Ti free to talk to me yet?" she asked.

"We have a pressing problem at the moment," said Sarmatakian. "We need to divert part of the fleet we've allocated to Hac Demil."

"Hac Demil has been stable for centuries."

"This is a natural disaster. A magma explosion. They've asked for our aid to restore the atmosphere, but it'll still take months to reach them."

Unplanned and urgent: Esganikan understood the priority, but that still left her with one more world to restore that wasn't on the schedule. They hadn't even anticipated the need to intervene on Earth. "What resources can you give me to support this mission, then? Umeh can't manage its own problems now."

"You should have thought of that before committing troops to it."

"The isenj asked for help, just as Hac Demil did."

"Hac Demil has a restored ecology and thousands of species. Umeh is virtually sterile."

"The planet is dying. Now they're at war because we intervened. If we start refusing to help the willing, what does that make us? And much as I regret the decision, how can I withdraw completely now?"

Sarmatakian didn't appear impressed. It was hard to be sure of her mood without scent signals, but her head jiggled in visible irritation. "The planet won't die. *They* will. Another kind of life will evolve and reclaim Umeh in time, as it does on every other world."

The adviser had never quite seen eye to eye with traditional Eqbas policy on selecting an optimum datum line for a planet's restoration. Esganikan strongly suspected her of being a follower of Targassat's theory of non-intervention, and that would have seemed extraordinarily archaic had she not been surrounded by Targassati wess'har on Wess'ej.

You can't have the power we have and not use it for the greater good. You can't look the other way and pretend that matters will resolve themselves, because those least able to defend themselves will always succumb to the dominant and irresponsible.

Nobody said it would be easy. Life never was.

"What can you give me, then?"

Sarmatakian hesitated for a second. "I have a standing offer from the overseers of Garav that they'll commit troops to support us."

"They're . . . extreme."

"Many find *us* extreme. I realize you have unhappy memories of Garav."

"The alacrity with which they embraced environmental balance after the war came as a shock."

"Converts can be more zealous than those who convert them. But Garav forces say they can be on Umeh in weeks, so consider the offer."

"Zealous." It was one word for it: the intervention on Garav was a painstaking, difficult operation that cost lives. The ecology was too delicate and complex for Eqbas forces to pound down resistance with brute force as they might on Umeh. Esganikan's commander had gambled and led ground troops. It had been the right thing to do but it had left her dead and Esganikan in command in a split-second burst of *jask*. "How many?"

"A hundred thousand, perhaps."

Esganikan bristled. "Did you approach them?"

"They're aware of events because we remain in touch with them. They offered."

The Garav forces had experience of living in a vastly altered world and seeing the benefits. They called themselves Skavu: the newly awake. Esganikan didn't trust zeal. She preferred stable pragmatism.

But if they could deal with Umeh, she could concentrate on Earth. "How many ships can you commit to Earth now?"

"Two more if we can recruit a full crew."

Six ships were already in transit to rendezvous with Esganikan: forty thousand personnel. "We need more than that to pacify a planet of billions without unnecessary destruction. We need more environmental specialists, too."

"You can't have more. There *are* no more. Not at the moment."

Sarmatakian wasn't a soldier: she was a scientist. Esganikan was getting tired of explaining what resources were needed to do the job. Maybe it was time Sarmatakian spent some time on the *sharp end*, as Shan Frankland called it.

"Then I might have to accept Garav troops for Umeh."

"They're keen to help. I'll stand them by."

Esganikan closed the link and turned to Aitassi. "The *gethes* find our consensus odd. If only they could see us now."

"They wouldn't see this as lack of consensus."

"This is the problem with remote working. No scent. No *jask* to help us agree on matters."

"So, you're content to have the Skavu in this system?"

Aitassi knew as well as anyone what the Skavu were. But like all her kind, she walked the fine line of neutrality, culturally anchored to the wess'har but somehow able to work with other races on a dozen worlds. Humans seemed completely bemused by that. Everyone, as far as they were concerned, *had* to take sides. The neutral couldn't be trusted. It was typical of a species that regarded information as a commodity.

Esganikan's gaze shifted to the Bezer'ej grassland beyond the hull. "The Skavu are utterly inflexible, but they're efficient. I would have preferred an alternative, but time isn't on our side."

"Perhaps they're just what the isenj need. However heavy-handed they are, there's not much more damage that they could cause. A case of two extremes meeting each other."

"Two extremes don't make balance."

A patch on the deck of her cabin became transparent as she touched the bulkhead controls, giving her an aerial view south of Jejeno.

The recent fighting had left patches of reconstruction work like the stumps of decaying teeth. It was impossible to attack a section of such a crowded, complex environment without the effects being felt like shock waves all round.

Maybe she *could* make some inroads without needing to call in the Skavu. "It's time I saw the isenj ministers again."

"They still ask for access to bioweapons."

"I find their method of warfare confusing. They never seem to finish anything. They simply peck away at each other now and again."

"If you look at their history," said Aitassi, "they might have squabbles, but destruction is rarely their way of settling disputes. They have to be facing catastrophe before that reaction sets in."

"They *are* facing catastrophe. Perhaps it's happening too slowly for them to notice."

Esganikan adjusted the magnification with a flick of her fingers so that the remote brought the cityscape hundreds of meters closer. She could see movement in some of the canyonlike streets that looked like a mudslide—the heads of thousands of isenj, dark and velvety, moving in orderly procession according to strict pedestrian traffic rules because they were so crowded. The infrastructure was finely balanced: they'd destroyed the ecology of their planet and everything was now carefully managed and engineered.

Yes, isenj *were* brilliant engineers. And the trouble with brilliant engineers was that they always felt they could fix things in the end, even when the situation was beyond them.

Esganikan touched the controls and the bulkhead became opaque again. "Call Shomen Eit. I can't wait any longer for him to decide when he wants to talk about the transfer of bioweapons. Arrange a time for us to meet." The minister spoke English now, the one positive thing the *gethes* had contributed to the situation: they had a common language, alien though it was. She could have called Shomen Eit herself, but it was usually Aitassi's role to interpret, and bored ussissi troubled her. "We've never walked away from a request to restore a planet. The isenj can only save themselves by reducing their population. There's no other option, and they know it."

Earth was the priority. She *had* to keep that in mind. Earth had biodiversity—thousands, even millions, of different types of people to save, from insects to large carnivores. *Gethes* might not have seen their fellow Earth species as people, but that was a lesson they would have to learn in time.

There was a skittering noise along the passage: a ussissi in a hurry, a small one. Aitassi turned. It was one of her male youngsters. He dropped down onto his four rear legs to approach her, head lowered, clearly very excited about something.

"Hilissi's baby's here!" He almost bounced. "Come and see!"

Aitassi gave him a quick nip on the ear that might have been more annoyance than playful matriarchal sparring with a juvenile of her pack. Ussissi took their family with them when they traveled. Eqbas didn't. Only a handful of her crew even had families: the time dilation involved in missions made it a single-status navy by necessity. The males maintained the integrity of their DNA by medication rather than the natural way by *oursan*. They too wanted to go back home and start their lives.

It was no way to live. Service life was a great sacrifice. The one benefit—a dubious one—was that the compressed passage of time on board ship and the frequent periods of suspension meant an apparently extended life. The invasion and restoration of Garav was generations ago: for Esganikan, it was only ten years. It gave mission personnel a unique perspective.

I might even know how Shan Frankland feels in due course, seeing all I knew long dead.

"I have to go," Aitassi said, appearing softened by the news. "It's Hilissi's first. She's very pleased."

The ussissi disappeared down the passage, Aitassi trailing the excited youngster. Esganikan thought it was cruelly bad timing. The last thing she needed was a reminder that she had to put off having her own family for many more years.

I have to complete the Earth adjustment mission first. I can't go home until I've done my duty. What kind of isan *shirks her duty? Can do,* must *do.*

She was running out of time. Even Earth wasn't in quite the same hurry that she was. She switched back to the remote's view of Umeh to remind herself that the Northern Assembly and the Maritime Fringe weren't quite one sprawl of building any longer. There was a space, naked soil, the fabric of the living planet as it had been: a bomb crater that had exposed earth that hadn't seen light in centuries.

They'd planted a tree there. It was what the carrion-eating humans, the *gethes,* called a park. The tree had to be imported from Umeh's moon of Tasir Var, but it was a real tree, and it was growing.

Nothing else had grown on Umeh in living memory except food plants sealed in enclosed hydroponic houses and fungus vats.

It was a start. Some things might happen late, but they happened in the end. She hoped her life would mirror the tree's.

Bezer'ej: Nazel, the island called Chad by the *gethes*

Lindsay Neville was getting impatient with Saib. The bezeri elder lurched along the shoreline, occasionally trailing a tentacle in the water as if he didn't believe he could survive out of it.

She stepped in front of him so he could see her bioluminescence. Lights signals were strictly line of sight, and she had to treat him like a deaf man, making sure he could see her before she communicated.

Light signaling was second nature to her now. She could even add a tone to it: this time it was exasperation, staccato pulses of red between the patterns of meaning. *You're not going to die, Saib. I gave you the parasite.*

Saib was perpetually sullen. She wondered if he'd been a happier creature before the bombing. *If we can't die, then why can't we return to the sea? What difference does it make?*

You can *die if someone detonates an explosive next to you.* Lindsay had taken everything from them when she let Rayat con her into deploying cobalt-salted bombs. The one thing she could give them was the ability to defend themselves from terrestrial creatures. *Take control of the land and secure your future. The isenj nearly wiped you out. So did we. Don't let that happen to you again.*

Saib paused, sparkling with pinpoints of gold and green light. It was his equivalent of muttering to himself. *We,* he said. *We. Look at yourself.* He inched along the shore like a translucent elephant seal, casting some of his tentacles forward to pull his bulk and pushing behind him with the others. *What are you now? What are we?*

It was like the constant niggling low-level argument with Rayat. *Survivors,* she said. *And you agreed to it. I didn't drag you ashore, either.*

There were forty-four bezeri left alive. *C'naatat* was all that could preserve them. The only ones left of breeding age were from one family, and they'd been resigned to extinction until Rayat literally walked out of his imprisonment and Lindsay decided that she might embrace something that looked like a higher purpose. It had taken a lot of effort to infect them with her own tissue, but she'd done it.

The altered wess'har was out hunting, said Saib. *I saw him.*

You mean Aras? Wess'har don't hunt. She decided they'd need to learn new words like *vegan. They don't eat flesh or use other creatures.*

The human soldier was with him, Saib said. *He had a weapon.*

So they were looking for someone. Maybe it was Rayat. Shan would have shoved a grenade down his throat in a heartbeat.

Was it Ade Bennett? Lindsay asked. *The one who brought me to you?*

Yes. I thought they had seen me, so I returned to the water.

Lindsay stopped and blocked Saib's path. *C'naatat* might have made her unrecognizably amphibious, but she still felt that jolt of alarm. *Did they see you or not?*

I don't believe they did.

If they see you moving ashore, they'll know you carry the parasite.

And then what will they do? Saib's tone was pure contempt. *Punish us? Kill us?*

Lindsay thought of Aras, and then Shan. *Maybe.*

Saib shimmered amber. It was the light pattern the signal lamp had never managed to translate, but Lindsay understood it clearly now as a special kind of anger. He was a respected elder, suddenly without authority and being challenged not only by a female but an alien—and an alien chimera, at that.

He inched towards her but stopped when she stood her ground. *You worry too much. Wess'har have always tried to protect us. They won't attempt to kill us.*

Shan Frankland will, though, said Lindsay.

Saib seemed unconcerned. *She said she would defend us.*

They really didn't understand the woman. They had no idea. *She drowned in the empty part of the Dry Above to keep the parasite from spreading,* Lindsay explained. Did he understand spacing? He certainly understood drowning in air. *If she can face taking her own life, taking yours won't be a problem, will it?*

Saib always had to have the last word. *You might not understand her as well as you think.*

Ice water ran down Lindsay's back. She had a brief, awful thought that some previous host of *c'naatat* was telepathic.

She couldn't cope with that, she really couldn't. *She's fanatical, Saib. You have no idea.*

Saib didn't seem convinced. *She pledged to protect us. She hardly knew us, so she had no other reason other than inner voices that drive her.*

It was an astute assessment for a squid.

Lindsay stepped back to let Saib lumber on along the beach. She fell in behind him, watching the wobbles and shock waves in his mantle and wondering how long it would be before *c'naatat* adapted him fully for terrestrial life. Whatever the parasite was, it had intervened to save her and Rayat from being crushed and drowned on the ocean bed; and it had taken *seconds* to call up unknown fragments of DNA to do the impossible and protect Shan from cold hard space. Turning a squid into an ambulant land animal wouldn't stretch it at all.

But *c'naatat* was unpredictable. She knew that now. She looked through her own hands—gelatine, water, smeared glass—and wondered why she was still shaped like a bipedal human and not some amalgam of forms. Aras was like the regular wess'har once, they said, one of those long, lean, gold seahorses; now you could mistake him for a large human at a quick glance in poor light.

But Shan and Ade still looked much the same. Whatever *c'naatat* did, it responded to a voice Lindsay couldn't hear.

She stopped and put her fingers to her neck. Ridges like keloid scars ran from under her ears and jaw to her collarbone—or at least where it had been—and down her rib cage.

Gills. She had *gills.* Lately the realization would occasionally hit her anew, shocking her for a moment.

It was okay. She could handle this. She could cope. She would *make* herself cope. Humans started out with gills during gestation; no big deal, nothing alien at all. She took a long slow breath and concentrated on the next second at hand, no further in the future than that, until she had control of herself again.

In a way, it was easier turning into a cephalopod than living with being Lindsay Neville, destroyer of bezeri and

mother of a dead child. There was life in it. From a benchmark of death she could use *c'naatat* to create new life, of
a kind.

Rayat despises us for our past genocide, said Saib. She
could see his light signals from any angle. *And you don't.*

No, she didn't. *You didn't slaughter the birzula personally.*

Saib paused. *I don't feel sorry that my ancestors did.*

Lindsay found that harder to handle. She heard Shan's
voice telling her not to apply her human morality, shabby
thing that it was, to alien cultures. Humans had no examples
to set the galaxy.

And I helped Rayat detonate cobalt devices, she said. *I
didn't intend for any bezeri to die, just to stop anyone getting hold of the parasite. But I was responsible. This is how
terrible crimes are committed.*

Saib gave a little shudder that reverberated through his
bulk. *Rayat said the wess'har will hate us for killing all the
birzula and hunting our prey to extinction.*

Lindsay had no idea where Rayat was, and the bezeri no
longer seemed to care. They'd wanted both of them for punishment—death, inevitably—but they settled on servitude.
Then they seemed to lose interest in vengeance and tolerated
their two human prisoners as servants. She couldn't square
that attitude with an intelligent species that had destroyed
another in a deliberate, unapologetic act of genocide. But,
as Shan always said, aliens didn't think like humans. It was
hard enough to fathom or predict the actions of her own kind,
let alone intelligent squid.

Saib teetered at the edge of the water. Lindsay moved to
one side of him and gave him a nudge to steer him back to
land.

*If you don't try harder, you'll be confined to the sea for-
ever.*

Saib grumbled gold again. *We're from the sea. Is that so
bad?*

*The parasite can make you fit for any environment. Give
it a chance. See what change can bring you.*

Can we have mates again? Saib asked.

Lindsay shrugged. *You can certainly try.*

My female's long dead.

Then take another, Saib. See what happens.

Saib seemed to consider the idea. Perhaps he didn't fancy any of the remaining elderly females. He must have had some inclination to try a new way of life, or he wouldn't have agreed to be infected with *c'naatat*; but maybe he didn't really understand what it did, even if he'd seen Lindsay and Rayat change from air-breathing, vulnerable humans to aquatic creatures that could survive in deep ocean and eat any food in a matter of seconds, minutes, hours. *C'naatat* was instant evolution.

Where has Rayat gone? asked Saib.

Lindsay wondered if the bezeri could work out the real threat from Earth. *He's trying to get back home. He wants to give the parasite to our government.*

To make soldiers that can't die?

Either Rayat had discussed *c'naatat*'s potential, or Saib was an astute tactician. *More or less,* said Lindsay.

Very dangerous.

Rayat was dangerous too. *It's called* c'naatat. *It lives on Ouzhari, nowhere else. We tried to destroy it to stop humans getting hold of it.*

But you *got hold of it. You have it.*

Saib, I asked *for it, so I could serve you as punishment.*

The old bezeri shimmered. *Your regret makes you weak.*

Rayat referred to the bezeri as Nazi squid, and when Saib made comments like that then Lindsay could see exactly what he meant. When the first Earth mission had killed one of the bezeri infants and faced retaliation from the wess'har, she'd seen them as helpless victims. She knew now that they'd been as brutal and exploitative in their own context as any human society.

But that didn't make her innocent. And it didn't give her any purpose for her interminable future.

"You have to learn to speak," Lindsay said aloud. She found she had to make a conscious effort to suck in air; speech was a habit you could lose when your body had changed so radically. Her bioluminescence mirrored her words. "Sound's more efficient than light on land. I know you can do it. You made the sound *leenz* under water."

Saib was as stubborn as they came. He really was a grumpy old man, but she took heart in his willingness to be infected with *c'naatat*. Bezeri were creatures of extreme habit. It was their unshakeable fixation with their spawning grounds and territories round Ouzhari that put most of them in the fallout zone when the bombs were detonated.

It was also what had led them to total war with the birzula over hunting territories. Bezer'ej was a big world with big oceans; but the bezeri wouldn't move. Their azin shell maps were their history. Their mindset was all about place.

And Saib was as hard to shift as any of his kind.

"Come on, you cantankerous old sod," she said. "Try."

His bulk shook like an angry jelly. The sound that emerged was more of a belch than a word, but it was clear enough: "Leenz-*eeeee*."

"There you go," she said, and didn't translate into lights this time.

She walked on, trying not to think about how she remained upright and rigid when she could see only opaque structures like cartilage in her forearms and legs. If the bezeri came ashore, though, what would they do? They had no history of technology of the kind that relied on wheels and heat and metal. They made stone implements. They bred organic vessels from plants. They wrote in sand pictures or etched symbols in stone and shell.

They were Paleolithic. They needed to undergo a whole industrial revolution—or grab the trappings of another civilization and make it their own.

And they'd found no other survivors.

Saib didn't like to be seen to give in too easily. He muttered again, sparkling orange light. *We can hide in the sea.*

"The sea didn't save you from me, old man."

"Leeeenz-*eeeeeee.*"

"Clever. Keep it up."

He shuffled, scattering pebbles. Any other huge sea creature would have struggled to move and found its organs failing without the supporting buoyancy of water, but *c'naatat* seemed to be taking care of that.

Lindsay was as adrift as he was now. She had nothing except her belt and a few tools: no data, no knowledge, and no skills beyond the basic survival techniques she learned as a navy pilot. She was newly reduced to a primitive, just like the bezeri.

Perhaps the Eqbas would help. But as soon as the bezeri asked for knowledge of land-based technology, it would be clear to them what had happened. And Lindsay had no way of knowing how they'd react to the news that *c'naatat* had spread into new hosts.

Nobody knew, not even Rayat. If he'd walked ashore, he'd have headed for the Eqbas as his best chance of escape. Would he guess that she would infect the bezeri? He did all he could to avoid it himself. Maybe he hadn't been lying. Maybe he really *did* think the parasite was a disaster waiting to happen if it ever got off the planet. In the end, he was just like Shan: they were both cold, obsessive, soulless bastards. Lindsay was better off without him.

"Home," Saib said aloud. The sound was rasping, like a human's vocal fry. "Home."

"You want to go home?" Well, *c'naatat* was getting into gear with something, then: language. "Or are you asking if this is home?"

Whatever Saib meant, the answer defeated him. He shook visibly. Gold and scarlet light burst from his mantle in neon-bright outrage and frustration, and he lumbered into the shallows, thrashing tentacles in the water. She knew all the nuances now. She waded after him and slid into the sea. Her lungs didn't protest any longer. Her gills parted, open gashes of red mouths, and the sea felt like soothing relief as it engulfed her.

You've got time, she signaled. *Time is one problem you don't have now. Take it easy.*

Back in his preferred element, Saib shot into deeper water and picked up speed, pumping water behind him. If he didn't make the transition as the dominant elder, none of the others would.

You can train us to be an army, then.

Ah, so he *was* thinking it through. He just didn't want to lose face.

I believe I can, Lindsay said.

The Dry Above is a better place to fight, is it?

Yes. She had his interest now. *Because your biggest threats will be land animals like humans.*

Lindsay saw a future Bezer'ej that wasn't a disputed territory for wess'har, isenj and humans to fight over. She wondered if she was going insane. Who needed most to be on dry land—them, or her? But she had a vision now, and she was going to use that to put things right.

All she'd done was bring two native Bezer'ej life-forms together, *c'naatat* and bezeri. It wasn't the same as infecting a human never meant to be here. And Shan Frankland wasn't so rigorous about eradicating *c'naatat* from the human population when it came to her precious Ade, either: she let him live. The knowledge that the bitch had some areas in her life that weren't governed by her inflexible brand of justice gave Lindsay some sour comfort.

Saib persisted, pausing to drift with the current, tentacles trailing. *But why can't we just go deep? Who would find us? Who could kill us?*

You still have to eat, said Lindsay. *The isenj killed their own oceans. If they get a foothold on this planet again, they'll kill yours too. They almost did before, remember?*

She knew that Saib remembered, all right. Or at least he recalled the azin shell maps with their exquisite designs of colored sand that recounted the time the isenj had claimed Bezer'ej and caught *c'naatat*. They bred. They bred in their millions, and they didn't die until Aras and his troops destroyed them: male, female, young, old, soldier, civilian, no quarter given. Shan had fallen for a war criminal. Lindsay wasn't sure if that was ironic or inevitable.

Millions of us died, said Saib. *Filthy isenj. Filthy polluters. We called the wess'har to drive them away.*

For a moment, Lindsay had an uncharitable thought that the bezeri might have been in decline anyway because of their ruthless hunting. Perhaps the isenj only accelerated the process. It was odd how her picture shifted simply from discovering their history.

Did the wess'har know what the isenj had done? She assumed they didn't.

Daylight faded into soft green light above her and the sounds of the ocean and its relentless weight enveloped her again.

Dominate the land, Saib. Lindsay thought of all she could teach them: every scrap of her naval training required hardware and technology of the kind the bezeri couldn't make. And there was none on Bezer'ej to plunder now, not even the human colonists' mothballed ship. The wess'har restoration process had reduced nearly every artifact to its component elements. *That's the only way you'll get control of your future. Hold the Dry Above.*

You dream, said Saib.

Lindsay's spirits sank further with each meter she moved away from the sunlight above. Her own ability to cope with the last few weeks under water stunned her and she tried not to think about it too closely in case reality crowded in on her again and it all came unraveled in screaming, water-choked hysteria. As long as she didn't think her resolve had come from Shan's borrowed genes, she was fine: that was her ultimate fear. She didn't want those memories and attitudes smuggled in with *c'naatat* through Ade Bennett's blood. She needed her courage to be her own. It was all she had left.

Shan must have struggled for sanity like this when she was floating in space.

Lindsay seized that. If Shan could take it, then so could she.

Get your people together, Saib, Lindsay said. *Tell them that they have to get used to the Dry Above.*

The Temporary City, Bezer'ej: biohazard lab

"This is too fucking weird for me."

Shan hovered at Shapakti's elbow, and for a moment Ade saw the detective she must have been in her police days:

harrying the lab for forensics, grimly impatient, working something through in her mind that showed in the twitch of muscle in her jaw.

He had to say it. It was a boil to be lanced: *you infected Lindsay and Rayat, and now look what's happened.* Just when he thought Shan had forgiven him, he was back in the shit again. "So . . . what if it *is* an altered bezeri, Boss?"

"No idea," she said wearily. "How do you track a creature that can go anywhere? And what do we do when we find them—shoot them? And what if it's a *sheven* instead? Jesus H. Christ. What a fucking mess."

Ade glanced at Aras, who stood quietly in the corner of the laboratory watching Shapakti with his head slightly to one side like he was lost in thought. Aras raised his eyes from the bench Shapakti was working at and met Ade's stare. He shrugged—just a micro-movement of the muscles, nothing more. Then he lowered his head a fraction. *I don't know and I wish I did.* Ade understood right away; they were so well attuned now that he didn't have to ask.

"Aras, I need an answer," said Shan.

"To what question?"

"If the bezeri are infected, what options do we have?"

"If you're asking if infected bezeri represent a risk that I would feel justified in removing, I don't know."

Ade thought about the bezeri's recently revealed history— overfishing and genocide, very human sins that he understood pretty well—and knew what was going through Shan's mind. It was going through his too. *They'll do it again.*

"They don't have a history of being environmentally responsible," Shan said quietly. Shapakti peered down at the glass tray, head cocking left and right. Shan wasn't giving him a lot of room. "Not a good start, is it?"

"A few weeks ago," said Aras, "you wanted to save them."

"A few weeks ago, they weren't bloody *c'naatat*." She was starting to get that shutdown look, turning back into a Superintendent Frankland about to break bad news, talking to necessary strangers. "And I didn't know they had form for being environmental vandals."

Her next request would be for a grenade that could frag a four-meter heap of gel. Ade knew it.

"Look," said Shapakti. He could switch to English with more ease than Ade could manage wess'u. "Observe the cells."

When the biologist tilted the tray a little, Ade could see that it was actually an image like a microscope display. It looked like tiny radial hairbrushes scattered between a mass of tangled wires and misshapen lumps.

"Shit," said Shan. "*Shit.*"

"What is it, Boss? Is that *c'naatat*?"

"It is, isn't it?" Shan was staring at the display, not at Shapakti. "That's what you showed me on Ouzhari."

Ade allowed himself a moment of distraction. He'd expected to be underwhelmed when he finally saw *c'naatat,* but he wasn't. It astounded him. As Shapakti increased the magnification, it unwound into brushes within brushes like a fractal. It was infinite. It was like looking at a galaxy and seeing it break up into stars and worlds.

"But what's the host?" asked Aras. He didn't seem amazed. Maybe he'd seen it before. "Is it bezeri or *sheven*?"

Shan stepped back from leaning over Shapakti, shaking her head, mouth set in that position that showed she'd thrust her lower jaw forward. It usually preceded clenched fists, a sudden turn on her heel and a fast march towards the nearest door. Ade edged slowly towards the exit to head her off as casually as he could.

"I don't know which is worse, immortal predators or bezeri," she said. "That explains the lights. You think Lindsay came ashore and a *sheven* grabbed her?"

"It's bezeri," said Shapakti. He tilted the transparent tray and the image enlarged several times. Icons that Ade couldn't begin to identify appeared in a row on the right-hand side and Shapakti tapped at them with long spider fingers, summoning up more cell-like images. Ade hadn't even seen him insert any samples. It was incomprehensible technology. "There are distinctly bezeri features as well as *c'naatat,* isenj and human."

"No *sheven*?" said Shan, as if that would make matters

worse than they already were. She was right, though: it
would. Those bloody things were everywhere already, and
giving them extra superpowers was bound to end in tears.
"You sure? Because the last thing we need is them chomping
on wildlife here and spreading it further."

"It's a native organism," said Aras. "But it hasn't spread
here. It hasn't infected native carnivores, and if it could do
that easily then I'd have seen evidence of it by now among
flying species like the stabtails."

"Bezeri are carnivores. Omnivores, anyway."

"But they only caught it through a human vector in the
marine environment. I rarely guess, *Shan Chail,* but if I
didn't infect them by accident in five hundred years, then
this may well be the result of a deliberate act, the same way
that Rayat and Lindsay acquired bezeri characteristics."

It was just the thing to make Shan blow a gasket. But she
settled for going white and angry instead. "If I find she's
pissed around with the ecosystems here, I might lose my leg-
endary patience."

Shapakti looked up for a moment. "But you have none."

"I know. It's humor."

"Oh." Shapakti pondered, head cocked. "Do you think
she's foolish enough to infect them deliberately?"

It begged the obvious answer. Shan gave it: Ade winced.

"Two out of three *c'naatat* hosts in this room have done
just that," she said, "and they're both a lot smarter and a lot
more disciplined than Lindsay fucking Neville."

"Intent makes no difference."

"Oh, it does. It makes me angrier."

Shapakti switched topics with surprising tact, or maybe
it was just that wess'har habit of darting from one topic to
the next. "There are many structures in the cells that cor-
respond to nothing I have on record. There might well be
sheven elements in this and many other things. But I *can*
say that this is very similar to the bezeri material we've
gathered."

Shan stood with fists on hips, seeming to have forgotten
the door. "Okay, let's scope the worst nuclear accident here.
We've got *c'naatat* bezeri material ashore. That's two new

problems—bezeri contaminated with *c'naatat,* and bezeri ashore."

"Bezeri always did come ashore," Aras said quietly. "They used podships to explore the beaches. You've seen the memorial to the first of them who did this and died in the attempt. They can survive out of water for a brief time, if you recall what happened to the beached infant Surendra Parekh found."

Ade did, and Shan did too. Ade wondered if he'd look back on that incident one day and see it as the point at which human-wess'har relations really went to rat shit. Silly cow, Parekh: she thought the beached bezeri was dead. It certainly was after she'd finished with it.

Shan didn't deviate. "Yeah, but they didn't bloody walk ashore and stroll around with a picnic lunch, did they? You said you saw a large gelatinous shape moving around in the marshes and going back into the water."

"Yes, *isan.* Something has changed."

"I'll say. Walking bezeri. *C'naatat* bezeri."

Shan turned for the door. Ade risked stepping in front of her.

"Where you off to, then, Boss?"

She looked him in the eye, all hostile out-of-my-way ice. Then her expression softened as if she'd suddenly recognized him in a crowd of strangers and was glad of it.

"If you ask Rayat if he knows the time, he'll just say yes." She edged forward half a pace, impatient. "I want another chat with him just in case there's something he forgot to tell me."

"I'll give you a hand."

"Ade, I'm not exactly new to interrogations."

"I just don't want you getting upset."

She almost smiled, but put her left hand firmly on his elbow to steer him aside. "You're too nice for your own good sometimes, you know that?"

Ade knew that. But he also knew he had his father in him, and that—given the opportunity—he could make Rayat wish that he could die. He let Shan pass and watched her stride down the passageway, longing for her to drop the act and show how broken she really was by what she'd had to do.

She *had* to be grieving. He needed to comfort her, to feel some kind of bloody use for a change. When she was out of sight and he turned his attention back to the lab, Aras was staring at the specimen captured in the tray, oblivious.

"Infection control is a difficult thing," said Shapakti, jerking Ade back to the here and now. "If we assume the worst, then—"

Aras didn't take his eyes off the tray. "*Shan Chail* will always assume the worst."

"Then the worst," said Shapakti, "is that the bezeri become infected and that they spread *c'naatat,* and eventually destroy the ecology of the planet. But there are few of them, and it may well be possible to stop the spread."

Aras wasn't prone to outbursts. Apart from his raging grief when Shan died, he was almost mild mannered in that oddly bipolar wess'har way, patient to the point of being dull and then flipping without warning into a ruthless killer. Ade knew. He'd tracked isenj troops with him: and wess'har really didn't take prisoners.

"What has it all been for?" Aras asked. There was an almost infrasonic rumble in his voice, right on the threshold of Ade's hearing. "The last five centuries, *what has it all been for?* What do I have to do now, *kill* them? After defending them for so many years?"

He turned so sharply that his long dark braid whipped around almost horizontally as he stormed out. Ade's instinct was to go after him. Shapakti held out a restraining arm but stopped short of grabbing Ade.

"It's snowballing." Ade wasn't sure what he would say to Aras when he caught up with him. *Yeah, you went into exile for them, and we kicked off a war over them, and you executed your best friend because of them—and now we might have to kill them.* It was all turning to shit and Ade knew he'd played his part in getting it there. "How do we stop this, Shapakti? You got any ideas?"

The biologist seemed mesmerized by his specimens. In another chamber, the two macaws he'd recreated from the gene bank started screeching at each other, their flapping wings making *fut-fut-fut* sounds. "When we can define what we want to stop, Ade Bennett, then we can proceed," said Shapakti. "But that also depends on what the bezeri do next."

"It'll end in tears."

"What?"

"Just a saying."

"It may end in culling."

A wess'har could use the word *cull* without any connotation of an animal at the top of the food chain pulling a gun on one at the bottom that was just a bit too inconvenient for its tastes. It still meant dead. Aras faced the prospect of seeing the bezeri wiped out again, *really* wiped out.

It must have been a bloody nightmare to think about that after all he'd been through for so very, very long. Ade debated who needed him most right then, and decided that out of the two of them, Shan was probably coping better.

Ade went in search of Aras.

3

We have complete choice as individuals: the only decisions we can take are our own. And yet so many species use the state of being an individual as an excuse for inaction, helplessness and irresponsibility. No situation is so overwhelming that action is pointless.

TARGASSAT OF SURANG,
on taking action

F'nar, Wess'ej: February 2377

Every world that Eddie Michallat knew was already full of crazy bitches, and nobody needed another one.

He watched the news from Earth with one hand pressed to his mouth. He hadn't even noticed he'd done it. On the screen on the wall, part of the stone itself, a woman called Helen Marchant urged governments to intervene with troops to stop the clearance of replanted forests for agricultural use.

"Stupid cow," he muttered.

"Why is *cow* an insult?" asked Giyadas. She was a child, but young wess'har seemed simply to be undersized adults hungrily absorbing data. She was catching up fast. "*Stupid* should suffice."

"Is this my daily lecture on speciesism, doll?"

"I'm interested."

Eddie ruffled her mane, tufted hair that ran in a stiff brush from front to back across her little seahorse skull like a Spartan's plume. "I'm just being rude about her, that's all."

"So by comparison with what you think of as an inferior species, you insult her. And you also make her not human, and so not worthy of respect."

"Thank you, Jeremy Bentham."

"Is that an insult too?"

"No." Eddie laughed; these days Giyadas was his only source of humor. He slipped his handheld out of his pocket and fingered in *Bentham*. "Read that." Damn, she was just a kid, wess'har or not, and sometimes he worried that he was burdening her with too much adult crap—adult *human* crap. "Try some *felicific calculus*."

Giyadas read intently, long muzzle tipped down so that her chin almost rested on her chest. This alien child could read his language, but he hadn't a hope in hell of reading hers or even speaking it: he couldn't manage the overtones that gave wess'u its two distinct and simultaneous voices. It rendered him illiterate. For a journalist, that was as near to hell as he might ever come. Giyadas viewed his ignorance with a grave patience that bordered on pity.

And Helen Marchant carried on calling for war to save the forests.

"She *is* mad, you know, doll."

"She only wants what the Eqbas have done for generations. This is not *mad* to us."

Marchant was a clever nutter, then. She'd once persuaded an antiterrorist officer called Shan Frankland to become an ally of her eco-guerilla movement. Knowing Shan, that must have taken some doing. Eddie didn't underestimate Marchant one bloody bit.

Giyadas studied the handheld's cream matte surface as it filled with text and images. She looked up, head cocked to one side, crosswire pupils flaring into four teardrop lobes. Eddie didn't find those bright citrine eyes quite so alien now.

"This Bentham shares many of Targassat's views," she said.

"Yes, he was one of the great liberal reformers."

"How could he be?"

Giyadas was the equivalent of maybe a seven year old human kid now. Eddie still measured his words, and got them badly wrong every time. "Well, at the time, people didn't see the world that way. Women and anyone who wasn't white didn't have rights, the rich ruled, and animal rights were unheard of."

"I meant that he said those things nearly six hundred years ago by your calendar and little has changed among the *gethes* since. So he is *not* a reformer. Intent is nothing. Only action matters."

I'm debating utilitarianism with an alien child 25 light-years from home, and she's winning. Wess'har logic was hard. "That's true, sweetheart."

"Gethes don't learn, do they, Eddie?"

"We never seem to." *The wess'har can take out one of our warships with ten-thousand-year-old tech. The Eqbas can scour whole planets.* "And we don't have long to change that."

"Are you all right, Eddie?"

Yeah, I'm fine for a man who's watching galactic war unfolding. "Never better, doll."

"We know this is hard for you. You're doing *very* well for a human."

Talking squid. Talking meerkats. Talking spiders. Seahorse aliens with two voices and two dicks. And they're the normal ones compared to Shan and her menagerie.

"I try," said Eddie, and gestured to her for his handheld. "For a monkey boy, I'm not doing so bad."

The two crazy bitches, Shan and Helen, should have been dead by now, of course, and they weren't—Helen Marchant because she'd been on ice for the best part of seventy years, and Shan because her *c'naatat* parasite wouldn't let her die. Jesus, it was so easy to think that now. But once he'd seen one immortal, he'd seen them all.

Marchant—small-boned, bobbed light brown hair—was in full flood, addressing a rally on population control.

"We'll go to war over oil, over water, over fish stocks and over any religious or political ideology you care to name." She had that quietly reasonable tone and benign, rarely blinking gaze of all really dangerous demagogues. "But we won't fight to preserve the planet. It's all we've got—and that *has* to be worth military action."

Eddie responded with the frustration of a journalist who hadn't had a crack at a ripe interviewee. "You're going to get all the military intervention you want, doll," he muttered.

"In about twenty-nine years, when the Eqbas show up with a frigging task force."

But Helen Marchant was talking about here and now—as it applied to Earth, anyway—and she was urging the Pacific Rim States to intervene to stop clearance of restored forests for human use.

Earth, short of land and swamped by inexorably rising seas, needed the space for people, which it was still producing at a brisk rate despite all the evidence that it was a bad idea. The wess'har—whether the militarized Eqbas or the agrarian Wess'ej variety—didn't give a shit about humans. Marchant would get on with them just fine, if she was still alive when they reached Earth. They could purge the planet together.

"Why don't you interview her?" asked Giyadas.

Marchant was 25 light-years away. It was definitely a case of doing it down the line. "Because everyone else has. What could I add?"

"You know a lot more than she does. You could ask her better questions."

"You really have got a journo's brain in that little head of yours, haven't you?" Giyadas was ferociously smart. Perhaps all wess'har kids were, but he didn't have that much contact with the rest of them, and he chose—yes, almost like a doting dad—to think of her as exceptional. "Besides, I can't call her up any time I want to. The UN is still controlling access to the ITX link."

"Controlling who hears things doesn't change what's said. *Gethes* need to learn that."

"Well, seeing as we had to scrape up chunks of *Actaeon* last time we pissed off the wess'har, everyone's understandably cautious."

"Do you miss your friends?"

Damn, he'd almost forgotten *Actaeon.* Sometimes the memory ambushed him. Barry Yung, Malcolm Okurt. They were nice blokes one minute and dead naval officers the next. The wess'har had a very clean sense of reprisal. *Actaeon,* the best technology that Earth could manage, was fragmented by three missiles whose design was ten thousand years old.

Our best is their equivalent of a stone axe.

"I didn't know them well enough to really miss them," said Eddie. "But I remember them, and I still think it's a bad thing to die so far from home."

"I agree." Giyadas ran spidery, multijointed fingers across the soft fabric keyboard and screen that made up Eddie's edit suite on the road. "Everyone should return to the cycle of life in the place where they were born."

"Good point . . . Giyadas, what are you doing with that?"

"Making a record."

She wasn't playing with his kit. She was *editing*. She really was. He was fascinated to see what she might make of the footage the bee cam had recorded on Umeh.

"What have you done, then, doll? Show me."

She held the screen between her fingertips as if she was showing off clean linen. Eddie leaned forward and touched the icon to roll the footage. It was the attack on the Maritime Fringe armored column as it rolled over the border into the Northern Assembly, jarringly disjointed and—he thought— full of flash frames. It ran for exactly one minute. It was one short clip after the next with no apparent judgment exercised on shots or sequences. It was chronological, though, so she could certainly follow a time code.

"That's very good," he said. Well, she'd mastered the technology even if the visual grammar left a lot to be desired. Not bad for a little kid. "Want me to show you how we'd do it?"

"Like this?" she said.

Giyadas laid the screen back down on the table and began working her fingertips over the surface again at high speed. She was utterly fixed on it. Her pupils snapped open and closed, flower to crosshairs and back again, and her head tilted to get the best focus. She seemed all movement; wess'har were usually remarkable for their lack of fidgeting. Their controlled motion could look glacial to a human, even more so when they went into that freeze reaction when startled. Eventually she paused.

"This is how humans see the world," she said gravely. "Look. Am I right, Eddie?"

It certainly wasn't how Eddie would have cut it.

She'd spliced together a perfectly lyrical sequence that showed none of the carnage—the body parts and isenj rushing for cover—but only the aerial shots, explosions and billowing clouds of dust and flame. At first he thought she'd spotted that some images wouldn't be shown because they were too graphic. It was a sensitivity that came into fashion and waned again from time to time. He hadn't explained it to her; but she'd seen enough somehow to know that what made it to air was a fraction of what was shot.

"Yes, we have to be selective sometimes," he said. Was there anything about her other than her size that made her different from an adult wess'har? He was damned if he could see it. "Blood and guts upset the viewers."

"You don't understand." It was a comment, not a rebuke. "I meant that *gethes* don't see beings involved in these acts. When you look at something, you remove all that doesn't affect you. You see what you need and feel, nothing else. You see nobody else."

Giyadas had a way of slapping him down without intending to. She had that external perspective that he believed all journalists needed, while he now struggled to maintain his own professional distance as he veered between intensely partisan feelings and brief forays back into detachment. But Giyadas really *could* stand outside humanity: she was an alien.

Eddie paused and took the verdict like a man. He was used to it. "Do we do *anything* right, doll?"

"I don't know if you're wrong or right, only that you're different, and you don't behave the way we do, and we choose not to do what you do."

"Is there any point to Esganikan restoring Earth, then, if humans can't behave right?" At times a voice told him he was insane to attach any importance to the world view of a child, but most of the time the other inner voice said that this was the raw wess'har heart, and a bloody good guide to their attitudes. The adults would have said exactly the same thing; unfiltered, undiplomatic, and blisteringly honest. He thought of the isenj and Esganikan's view of them as numbers to be reduced. "I know the Eqbas aren't quite the same as you, but they're still wess'har. Would you wipe us out?"

"Not all of you."

"That's nice to know."

"The woman you called the cow sees the world as we do. Shan does too. There seem to be many."

"How would you choose? Who's guilty? Who's not?"

Giyadas tilted her head to one side very slowly as if trying to work something out. "Who lives extravagantly with no thought of balance? Who kills other beings without provocation? Who eats carrion?"

"Probably a few billion people."

"Then they'll answer to the Eqbas. As well as those who let the *gethes* contaminate Ouzhari."

Eddie always felt like a kid edging across a frozen pond at this stage, desperate for the adventure but dreading what might happen. "They might be very old people by the time the Eqbas get there. Is it worth punishing them?"

"What difference does age make?"

No statute of limitation on war crimes, then: that was much the same as human morality. He felt a slight cracking and the threat of breath-stopping icy water. "Okay, Rayat and Lindsay set the cobalt bombs. Why are the people who *authorized* it guilty too? Wess'har logic says that they didn't carry out the act. Intent doesn't matter."

"Does Rayat have orders? Like Ade? Orders he has to follow?"

Eddie considered what he knew of spooks. "Yes. More or less."

"Then the person giving the orders knew that, and so is guilty."

Eddie pondered the thought process. He'd moved from cracking ice to a maze from which he might not find his way out. Wess'har seemed to regard those given orders as mere buttons to be pushed, and yet they also regarded following bad orders—orders they considered immoral—as worse than giving them, because of the redemptive chance to refuse, and prevent the act.

And yet they didn't hold the Royal Marines responsible

for helping Lindsay transport the bombs to Bezer'ej. They hadn't taken part in setting them, and—Barencoin had told him—they'd reminded her that nuking Ouzhari wasn't within the rules of engagement.

Giyadas stared at him, pupils snapping. Eddie stared back, not quite seeing her.

Then it dawned on him: responsibility was about *proximity*. It wasn't just about breaking the chain of events.

"So, the government that had *Actaeon* carry nuclear weapons wasn't responsible."

She considered that for a second. "No. Where would this end if it was? *All* humans would be responsible. And *all* humans don't have the ability to prevent this. There's always a line to draw."

"Do you understand why we don't get it?"

"I know you don't think like us."

"We're going to have to learn."

"We might try to think like you, too," said Giyadas. "But as we've made up our minds about what we think is the right way for us to behave, that would be no use."

She gave him a very adult nod and walked off, every inch the matriarch she would be one day. Just when he thought he'd nailed the wess'har mindset, there was one final twist that jerked it out of his reach again. *Face it, Monkey Boy, we're always going to be wrong unless we behave like they do.* They didn't even agree with the Eqbas side of the family some of the time. He could see that Earth's diplomats were going to crash and burn on the first day.

Shan thought a lot like a wess'har long before she'd been pumped full of their DNA, even if she didn't hold with their line on guilt. No wonder she liked it here. She wasn't an alien like she'd been on Earth. He sat back in the makeshift seat he'd built out of crates and suddenly understood why Shan had spent so much time building a sofa 150 trillion light-years from home. He scrolled back to the first package Giyadas had edited, running his fingertip over the reactive pigment embedded in the smartfabric, and replayed the sequence.

It was a moving screen print, just like the marines' chameleon camouflage battledress that detected the terrain and mimicked it. Once, the technology had provided trivial but fascinating shirts that played movies. Like the organic computers grown into the marines' palms, and the implants that gave them head-up displays in their eyes, it was all technology from the entertainment industry.

As are we all: a distant diversion for the folks back home, aliens in your living room.

Eddie watched.

The sequence was a glimpse into the wess'har mind. Giyadas had cut the shots together scrupulously: every angle, every scene, every separate shot was included in some form, even if it was wobbly and canted. It was a representative sample of what the Eqbas fighter's on-board cam had recorded during the bombing run. The steady shots had been cut proportionally too: effectively, nothing had been omitted. Wess'har had a literal eye. They saw the world as it was.

"We're fucked," he said aloud. "Fucked, fucked, *fucked.*"

Eddie got up and walked through the maze of interconnecting passages that made up Nevyan's home and led to the terraced walkway circling the caldera that housed F'nar. The wess'har's warren-dwelling heritage was visible in the way they'd cut into the natural landscape, lining the bowl of the dead volcano with row upon row of terraces and tunneled homes. That alone was spectacular enough; but the most extraordinary aspect of the city was the uniform coating of nacre that covered every smooth surface. Ashlars, paths, doors and the roofs of the small buildings in the basin were all covered in the natural pearl fecal deposits laid by the surprisingly drab *tem* flies that swarmed in hot weather.

It was, as Shan put it, only insect shit. But it was exquisite and magical, and there was never a day that Eddie didn't find it mesmerizing. The city changed constantly as the light varied: it was an iconic view, a studio backdrop, a souvenir shot, the essence of F'nar. Just as Surang on Eqbas Vorhi was a billowing cityscape of sinuous, almost organic-looking buildings like an outcrop of exotic fungi, F'nar was a wedding cake in a near desert.

Shit, I even see *in headlines. Another gulf.*

He was five light-years from the Eqbas homeworld and

twenty-five from his own. He thought of Surang, and wondered how he could ever go back to Earth now when there were so many new things to be seen and discovered closer to—

Home. Yes, *home.*

The thought didn't shock him half as much as he expected.

The Temporary City, Bezer'ej

Shan stood opposite Rayat. She folded her arms, feet slightly spread, the width of the table between them.

"Okay, Superintendent." Rayat was annoyingly calm, but if he thought he was going to provoke her, he had another thing coming. "Decided my fate yet? Experimental subject for the removal of *c'naatat,* or grenade practice?"

"Don't piss me about," she said. She never thought she could tire of anger, but she very nearly had. "I don't suppose you recall seeing any infected bezeri during your stay down below, do you?"

She caught a whiff of acid. Rayat had reacted; it was the scent equivalent of a surprised flinch. He might have been posed for a poker match, but he didn't know how to control his skin chemistry like Shan did. Whatever scrap of her he'd inherited with *c'naatat,* he hadn't mastered that one yet.

"I take it you found one, then."

"Possibly."

"I took a lot of care *not* to contaminate them. The only tissue contact either Lindsay or I had was with a cadaver."

"You're sure."

"I introduced some of its mantle tissue into open wounds to encourage *c'naatat* to develop bioluminescence for signaling." Rayat held out his hand to Shan as if offering to shake it: green light danced under the skin. Shan had her facial muscles locked into I-don-t-give-a-shit, but her hands responded whether she wanted them to or not. Green light sparkled in her fingers, making them look backlit as they rested on her sleeve. She glanced at them and they stopped.

It troubled her that she didn't know why they did it or how she could control it consistently. "How did you get *your* lights, Superintendent?"

That was a mystery too. She hated mysteries. "Free with a dose of seawater, I expect."

"Extraordinary, bezeri signaling. Photophores and light-producing cells combined. Bright colors even in daylight. You can imagine the applications in bioengineering—"

"That's fascinating, but we've got a bezeri strolling around on dry land now." She managed to resist the bait. He was slipping if he thought he could rile her by pressing the old EnHaz buttons. "Anything you want to tell me?"

"Well, Superintendent, if it's strolling, it's probably Lindsay Neville."

"Aras said it was large and shapeless as far as he could see."

"She's let herself go a little."

"Look, maybe you get a hard on from verbal fencing, sunshine, but it doesn't do a thing for me. What happened?"

Shan didn't move a muscle, and she didn't blink. She counted to six before Rayat leaned back slightly and looked away, but it might have been a maneuver rather than a concession. Rayat was as much of a gamesman as she was.

"Last time I saw Lin, she was still humanoid in shape, but composed of gelatinous tissue," he said. "Human-shaped bezeri."

"How come you're still a Rayat-shaped arsehole?"

"You know *c'naatat* doesn't produce the same result twice. Look at you and your . . . family, for a start." He gave the impression of being genuinely fascinated by it. "Are you aware of *toxoplasma gondii*? Protozoan that alters rodent behavior and makes them easier prey so it can continue its reproductive cycle in predators."

"I am," Shan said. "And, yes, I've wondered if *c'naatat* influences me. We all have. So Lin wants to be a bezeri. Or *c'naatat* wants bezeri to take up hiking. Or maybe both. Right now all I want to do is to gauge the size of the problem. You say there's forty-four bezeri left, one complete family and the rest too old to breed. Right?"

"Correct."

"So many of those are now carrying *c'naatat*?"

"When I got out, none of them were."

Shan leaned a fraction closer. "Aras has had contact with bezeri for centuries, and they never picked it up from him, and they never got it from me, either, so they're not easy to infect. So what's Lindsay been up to?"

"She seems to feel she has to be their savior to atone for killing so many of them. Their numbers won't ever recover now. They have no breeding population."

"Oh, I can do Lindsay logic."

"So can I, alas."

"She's saving them the permanent way, isn't she?"

"Maybe she hasn't infected them all."

"Lindsay likes her lists and rotas. She'll have lined them up and doled it out at roll call."

"The risk probably isn't as serious as it looks," said Rayat, clasping his hands and resting them on the table. "They weren't a breeding colony, Superintendent. One family with fertile members, and they don't inbreed."

Shan hesitated for a painful split-second that Rayat couldn't see. She wouldn't bank on the infertile ones staying that way. She certainly hadn't. "They're still a risk."

"They aren't about to disperse across the galaxy. They're very territorial for a start. There might be a risk to the ecology here, but the problem's quarantined."

"Good to see your approach to risk assessment hasn't changed since Ouzhari."

"But I don't know what happens if *c'naatat* carriers are confined to an environment indefinitely."

Shan knew, or at least Aras did. It was why he and his troops wiped out the isenj colonies here. The combination of the natural isenj breeding rate and a zero death rate had been an environmental disaster. With the bezeri's penchant for hunting to extinction, the critical thing was to make sure they didn't multiply into billions.

And only a few weeks ago, you were still hoping you'd find more of them so they could breed and repopulate. Life's fucking ironic.

"Are you listening, Superintendent . . . ?"

"I don't have any police rank now, actually."

"That seems to make no difference."

"I'd appeal to your sense of responsibility if I thought you had one, and hope you'd help me avert another disaster."

"I don't want this to spread any more than you do, Shan."

Shan. Jesus, he was trying to be chummy. She hated people using her first name unless she bloody well said they could. "And I'm not playing games now. If *c'naatat* can be reversed at will, then it's even more dangerous because it's fully exploitable with no apparent downside. So it stays here. The Eqbas *can* remove it, can't they?"

"Never tried a live subject," said Shan. She didn't believe in miraculous conversions. She'd seen way too many that corresponded with a prisoner's desire to get out of the shit she was about to unload on them. "So I'll make decisions based on what I *know.*"

She never stopped to ask if it was her responsibility; everything just *was.*

"I wouldn't have deployed ERDs on Ouzhari if I hadn't been serious about asset denial."

"You talk a good game, Rayat, but you missed out the bit where you busted a gut to try to get a sample back to Earth."

"Initially. But I know what it can do now. And I don't like it."

"You still went back to Constantine to see if there was an intact ship."

"Yes. But I'm stuck here now. Like you."

Smarmy bastard. It was just another feint to get in position to ship a *c'naatat* sample back to his FEU bosses. *Thetis* was due back in a few months to evacuate personnel from Umeh Station, and if he didn't have his eye on a ticket home that way, then he really was going soft.

"One more time." Shan was sure she could beat it out of him eventually, but maybe there was nothing in there after all. "How would you describe Lindsay's state of mind when it came to *c'naatat*?"

Rayat looked genuinely thoughtful. "The squid messiah, as Eddie might say. Don't worry, she's not working with me."

Shan knew that. Lindsay had no motive for getting the damn thing back to Earth. She was wallowing in guilt and repentance, and maybe even acting out what she would have wanted for her dead kid.

"She came ashore to get a few keepsakes from her kid's grave, though."

Rayat either shared Shan's concern or was acting brilliantly. "You think she'll come back for the rest."

"Perhaps." If the Eqbas couldn't follow traces of the bezeri in the ocean it meant they'd gone deep, or moved on—but bezeri didn't move on. They clung tenaciously to their territory. They killed to keep it, too. "Something came ashore here, anyway."

"You know you might have to hunt them down and destroy them."

"Is this going to be some attempt at justification?"

"No, just wargaming. If they spread it, how do you track it? And when you track it, how do you destroy it?"

"That's my problem," said Shan.

Inside her jacket, in a pocket that nestled just under her left breast, she kept her last grenade. It was a guaranteed way out if she ever needed it. It was also the best weapon she had to take out a *c'naatat* host. Rayat wasn't worth hanging on to for scraps of information, and this was the best—and possibly last—chance she'd get she remove one more problem.

He's not your prisoner.

He's no threat right now.

You could cause a roof collapse.

Shan glanced around the small chamber, applied a little rudimentary physics, and decided to chance it. A voice in her rational brain said none of that crap mattered and that Rayat was a complication she should have dealt with a long time ago.

"Time I got on with it," she said. "Goodbye."

It struck her as odd how that persona took over without argument. The Shan Frankland who shut the door behind her and took out the grenade for priming was a creature of rational calculation without a hint of dread, doubt or guilt, and it wasn't the first time she'd taken the decision to eradicate a pain in the arse without the process of law. It wouldn't be the last, either: she knew that. The grenade, a little curved slab of drab composite with a cap like an antique lighter, sat in her palm as if it had always been there. She flipped the cap up with her thumbnail to set the blast pattern. The pin was a thin strip that swung through ninety degrees, and once it was pulled clear and the pressure on the cap was released, two sections inside pulled apart, broke a sac of reactive gel, and started the impossibly short chain of a detonation.

Pin, door open, throw, close. Or was it door open, pin, throw, close?

Shit, she'd never drilled for this. One quick demonstration from Ade, and that was it. How hard could it be? She grasped the strip and eased it to the correct angle, thumb holding the cap closed again. Her left hand felt for the door. In her right palm, the small grenade felt reassuringly heavy.

It'll be a mess. I'll have to clean up. Can't let anyone uncontaminated risk it.

She'd done worse.

One, two, three. . .

The faint scent hit her just as she began to lean her weight against the door, and it stopped her for a fraction of a moment. That heartbeat was enough for someone a lot heavier than her—Esganikan—to shove her away from the door, and hard.

The grenade skidded across the floor.

She had five seconds.

It might have been her own training or it might have been Ade's, but she flung herself full length along the flagstones to grab the grenade and snap the cap tight shut in one hand. Her heart pounded. She counted. This time, she really wanted to live. She *did.*

. . . three, four, five.

Nothing happened. Shan exhaled and eased herself onto her knees with her left arm, her right hand clamped tight around the grenade. The pin was a fiddly bastard to reinsert. She slid it back to its closed position and wondered if the thing was stable now. She'd have to ask Ade. *Shit.*

"Give that to me," said Esganikan. She held out her hand imperiously. "I want Rayat kept alive."

"Piss off," said Shan. She got to her feet. "I should have done this ages ago."

"Shapakti said you would do this."

"Shapakti's going to get what's coming to him for grassing me up, then, isn't he?"

If Esganikan wanted to take the grenade from her, she'd have to fight her for it. The two matriarchs stood facing each other, angry and wary. Shan could smell it, the faint scent of tropical fruit. The last thing she needed now was to oust Esganikan from her position by accident. It was a job she didn't want.

Don't react. No jask. *Don't. Don't . . .*

"I want to continue the tests." Esganikan loomed over Shan. "Especially now we have infected bezeri. We need to be able to remove it."

"And that makes it a tactical weapon, not a guaranteed own-goal. Rayat was right about that." Rayat was right about a lot of things. "It's Rayat's mission to secure it."

"So you make a habit of this game with grenades."

Shan had pulled a pin before, but that was *different.* That was to make Chayyas see sense and not punish Aras for infecting her. This time—*this* was vermin control. "Maybe you should too. You'll regret not finishing off that bastard. Let me do us all a favor."

"I want him alive."

"You can test it on *me.*"

"Removing *c'naatat* might kill the host. I need *you* alive too. I *knew* you would try this, and I forbid you to try again."

Forbid was a challenge Shan would never normally refuse. She tensed to punch Esganikan out of the way, but there was enough common sense left in the Superintendent Frankland persona for it to pin down the angry animal called Shan and tell it that she absolutely could *not* provoke a *jask* reaction by going for Esganikan.

You can't *depose her. You can't plunge her mission into chaos, do you hear me?*

"Good timing, then." Shan felt her shoulders sag and the ache of dissipating adrenaline working through her muscles. She hated that unspent fight reflex flooding her system. It would leave her edgy for hours. "So Shapakti told you where I was going."

"I asked him."

Less than a minute. I shouldn't have wasted time talking. "So what are you going to do about the bezeri?"

"Evaluate the risk, which means tracking them." Esganikan put one hand on the door to Rayat's holding cell. Wess'har didn't lock doors and they'd had to improvise with a bolt at Shan's insistence. "And if we judge them a risk, we'll remove them. If they show no signs of making a serious impact on the environment, then we leave them be—as we do you and your males."

In a human it would have been a bitchslap. In an Eqbas, it was simply an explanation. But the fact that she, Ade and Aras were seen no differently to a bezeri was a reminder that brought her up short: not just because it was sobering to remember she was a biohazard, but that she'd done the unthinkable and separated herself from . . . the *animals*.

That's not me. I never thought that way. I never have.

Perhaps it was a bezeri voice in her, or even an isenj one. She didn't like to hear it." I can't do much without your teams to help me track them."

"You need do nothing. The most useful thing you can do for us is to use your unique asset of being a human police officer."

"What, rattle a few door handles?"

"Your networks on Earth. You can activate the humans most likely to cooperate with the adjustment of Earth."

"I'm nearly eighty years adrift. I don't have a list. Helen Marchant should be doing that for you."

"She says that *you're* the most powerful icon for them. You recovered the gene bank. You're the—"

"Then get a bumper sticker. That works too."

"What?"

"Doesn't matter." This was what Shan had dreaded in her EnHaz days: the lure of vanity, the prospect of heroism muddying the waters of her motivation. *Please, please, if there's one wess'har trait you can give me, you bloody thing, it's not caring about motive.* "I can't do this. I can't be a martyr."

"In the years between now and our arrival on Earth, humans motivated by you can prepare the ground and make the adjustment much, much easier."

"For you?"

"For Earth."

"Since when did you discover public relations?"

"I work with what humans are, and humans are persuadable with nebulous things. They can do great things with inspiration. The Christian colony crossed star systems to save terrestrial species on no more motivation than the belief in a supernatural being."

The Eqbas had discovered something of spin, and that was a very un-wess'har thing. "You've been hanging around with Eddie a little too much."

Esganikan's hand pushed against the cell door. She was going inside, and that made Shan uneasy because she wouldn't be around to keep an eye on Rayat. "You can help."

"I'll think about it," said Shan.

She thought. She thought as she walked away, forcing herself to breathe evenly. *C'naatat* hadn't seen fit to smooth out her adrenaline reactions and she still occasionally stopped breathing, a legacy of her months floating in vacuum. Ade hated her doing that and would nudge her to make her breathe again, like he was making sure she wasn't dead and that she really had come back to him. It disturbed her, too: she distracted herself wondering what the parasite did to oxygenate her tissues in those periods. But the thoughts that Esganikan put in her mind were insistent.

I don't want ties to Earth. I have to forget it. I've done my job and this is my home now, and, Jesus, have I got enough problems to occupy me here.

If she succumbed to the Saint Shan ruse, then how did she explain away Eddie's report on her nobly British I-might-be-some-time walk out the airlock? How could she be a dead saint and still give pep talks to the faithful? What had that stupid bitch Marchant told people already?

C'naatat was a crazy story, and like all reports of reality, people generally believed what they wanted to believe and ignored what didn't fit. Perhaps she'd been dismissed as a myth already.

I never ignore what doesn't fit. My whole working life has been about looking for it.

It was one more reminder that she didn't fit on Earth. She found she was already picking her way through a patch of tufted lavender grass a few hundred meters from the Temporary City, too preoccupied to notice how far she'd walked. Scattered across the land, the disassembled bubbles of bronze and blue metal habitats that would coalesce into a compete warship on command looked like exotic puffballs.

But it was normal now. *This* was normal. Her *ménage à trois* was normal, and her alien friends were normal. Even *c'naatat* was now normal. Earth was not.

Shan took in the unspoiled wilderness and knew exactly why Umeh needed to change or die. It wasn't logical thought, because there were no laws of the universe that said grass and biodiversity were inherently better than concrete and one lonely species, but she believed it. And you had to believe something, to make a moral choice, or you'd be nothing.

And having choice, must make it.

She'd made hers, and Marchant could find another saint. Or a bumper sticker.

Shoreline, five kilometers from the Temporary City

Aras let out an irritated hiss. It was a typical wess'har sound and it surprised him: for a moment he was a human standing outside watching himself and wondering what this creature was. He waded into the water waist-deep and searched, irrationally angry at betrayal.

This isn't me. This isn't wess'har.

The sensation was fleeting. He considered the fact that he might be changing again, edging closer to being human, but there was none of the characteristic raised temperature that accompanied the peak of *c'naatat*'s genetic rearrangement.

C'naatat had done a long and thorough job of remodeling him, apart from his way of seeing the world. Aras wasn't usually aware of it, but Ade told him he was just as "bloody rude and crude" as any normal wess'har. But a lasting sense of betrayal was a human thing, one he'd tasted all too recently when Josh Garrod—friend, almost family—had done the unthinkable.

It doesn't matter. The why *doesn't matter. Deal with the* now.

But the bezeri hadn't told him about their past crimes, and while his wess'har heart said only actions mattered, his human element was bitterly hurt by the deception. The bezeri had never been his friends like the humans of Constantine, but he'd certainly been their guardian, and had he known what he was guarding, then his actions might have been different.

It was thousands of years ago. It was long before wess'har came to this system. You can't punish their descendants for thoughts.

They were here, he knew it. The bezeri had always been fond of this bay; it was his regular landing place from Constantine on his trips to the garrison at the Temporary City, the spot where bezeri pilots would pick him up in their podships and take him across the strait. He waded around, looking for familiar lights rising up to meet him. He could see nothing.

And Ade had given his signal lamp to Lindsay. Even if Aras found a bezeri, he couldn't talk with them. He had no bioluminescence; he didn't even have the random flickering in his hands like Shan had.

But Mohan Rayat could speak in lights. The *gethes* who nearly wiped them out could talk to them, and he couldn't. Shan called this kind of thing *irony*. It tipped Aras over an edge he hadn't known was there.

He hammered his fists on the surface of the water, thrashing foam into the air. "Come and face me! We died for you!" he screamed. "My *brothers*. My *friends*. Everyone I loved. We fought for you, and you're everything we despise. I killed Josh for *you*. Come and face me—"

Aras felt his breath sobbing from his chest as if it was

another life escaping. It was grief. He knew grief: he'd raged briefly like this when Shan was taken from him, and it felt every bit as physically agonizing and unbearable as those terrible days. And he couldn't stop it. It erupted, and with the grief came a spewing torrent of other unbearable emotions that he could hardly identify and that threatened to choke him unconscious. He found himself sinking down into the water onto his knees, and he was back in a world that he rarely visited, a world that now only reminded him of having his head held under water by his isenj captors.

You spread c'naatat *among wess'har. Who are you really angry with?*

The bezeri weren't who he'd thought they were. It shouldn't have mattered. But it did, and he couldn't stop it mattering. The sea pressed on him and carried distant sounds. He could see well even in the depths, but he found he was staring into a void that suddenly seemed as empty and hostile as space.

He scrambled upright, struggling against a wave as his head broke the surface again and he was back in thin, noisy air. He shivered as he flopped down on the beach and sat with the water draining out of his clothing.

The crunch of pebbles behind him made him inhale involuntarily to check the scent on the air. *Ade.* He didn't turn around and sat contemplating his folly and ill-defined betrayal.

"Jesus, mate, you're soaking." Ade squatted down beside him and stared into his face, forcing him to look him in the eye. "What happened?"

"I'm waiting for the bezeri."

"To . . . shoot them?"

He'd thought about it. "To talk to them."

Ade swallowed as if embarrassed. The lump at the front of his throat bobbed up and down. "You might have a long wait."

"I haven't gone insane."

"I didn't—"

"You have the tone of someone reasoning with the unstable."

"Sorry. But you don't have a signal lamp, do you? I gave it to Lindsay. So you can't understand each other."

"Rayat said they were starting to understand English."

"But how would they reply, though?"

Aras had no idea. Emotions rarely overtook him but they had now. He was raging, and he knew it. Ade simply waited with him, squatting back on his heels and finally sitting down with his knees pulled up to his chest, arms folded around them.

"You're right, they know we're here," said Ade. "They always did."

Aras kept his gaze on the water. He was at the right angle to see the shallows, and after a while he saw what he first thought was reflection on the sea, and then realized was speckled blue light.

It was a bezeri, a large one, and it moved closer inshore.

Aras scrambled to his feet and walked down the slope of shingle. Ade followed him, reeking of agitation. He seemed to hate arguments but had no trouble fighting wars, and the shared memory reminded Aras that rows between his parents led to his father beating his mother, and then Ade and his brother. He was conditioned to dread argument.

Aras stood ankle-deep in the water, staring down at the bezeri, wondering if it could hear well enough, let alone understand him.

"You never told me," said Aras. He raised his voice. "You—never—told—me—you—killed—everything—else."

The lights danced, still blue, then suffused with green.

Aras plunged into the shallows so he was alongside the huge gel mantle, and the bezeri backed off a meter.

"Do you understand me? Do you?"

Ade waded in after him. "Aras, steady on—"

"Get back, Ade." Aras pushed him away. He started shouting and felt no embarrassment. "Can you hear me, bezeri? Are you the same as your ancestors? Do you regret killing the birzula, hunting everything you could find? *You* destroyed your world. *You* did it."

The lights froze for a moment, and the surface of the water broke as a column of gel reared up, draining foam. The bezeri literally stood on the sand of the shallows. The part above the water was taller than Aras. Yes, this creatures had *changed.* That meant only one thing.

"Shit, that's *big,*" said Ade.

Aras stood his ground. He was so angry he didn't care what it did to him. He couldn't die, and neither could the bezeri.

"I wasted lives on you!" Aras yelled. It wasn't true: the isenj had still needed stopping, bezeri or none. "It was for nothing . . ."

A stoma opened in the glassy mantle and Aras heard an intake of air, a wet slurping sound like a human sniffing loudly.

"This . . . our world."

The sound was like hearing imagined voices in a wind, enough to recognize but still fleeting. Ade had a tight grip on Aras's arm as if to pull him back.

"Your ancestors—"

"We . . . not sorry . . . thanks . . ."

The stoma shut in a wet slap, and the bezeri flopped back into the water, splashing Aras as it spun in the shallows and shot out towards the ocean with a powerful jet of expelled water that nearly knocked him off his feet.

Ade kept him upright, a fierce two-handed grip on his arm. "Easy, mate."

"It can speak."

"*C'naatat.* Well, that proves it."

"It regrets nothing. It learned *nothing.*"

"I know. I know." Ade was dragging him back to the shore, with that same patient, soothing tone he used when Aras was sobbing and grieving for Shan. "Doesn't matter, mate, it doesn't matter at all now."

They stumbled up the beach. Aras turned and looked back at the sea and then sank down on his knees. Ade grabbed his face in both hands and made him look up.

"Aras, *look* at me."

"And Josh—"

"Aras, shut up and *listen,* mate." Ade changed before him: a voice that had to be listened to, eyes impossible to avoid, the embodiment of certainty. "Not *wasted.* None of it. The isenj had to go. Josh had to pay. There's more to this planet than the bezeri. You didn't waste a single life, believe me you *didn't,* and I've been there, remember. I've lost my mates, I've lost men under me, and I *know* the difference between pissing away their lives and having to spend them. Got it?"

They'd swapped memories. Aras knew what Ade had seen and done. "Why does it feel so terrible, after all these years?"

"Aras, I asked if you understood." Ade gave him a little shake, hands still clamped to each side of his head. *"Say it."*

"It . . . it was not wasted. We had to act."

"You had to protect the planet."

"I did."

"Good." Ade let go and then hugged him fiercely. "It's been a shitty year all round. Too much all at once, mate, that's all. Shan, the bombing, the war, now this." Ade was so utterly reassuring that Aras let himself believe him. Ade *knew.* "Let's go home. Fuck the bezeri, and fuck everything."

"This is still my—"

"You did a five-hundred-year tour of duty. I think that's enough for anyone." Ade stood up and actually hauled Aras to his feet. He wasn't a big man even by human standards— Shan was taller—but he could somehow shift Aras. "Come on. Let's catch up with Shan. That's what matters, the three of us."

Aras walked back towards the Temporary City with him, not speaking, but seeing Ade in the new light: as a sergeant, not just a soldier, but a man who could hold a squad together and get them through the unimaginable. Aras had been a soldier too. The bond with Ade was precious to him in more ways than he'd imagined. He still seethed inside, but Ade had taken the edge off his agony and now he felt foolish at his outburst.

"I should have had better control," said Aras. "I apologize."

"I've done worse," said Ade. "And shit myself, as well.

Besides, you got some intel out of it. We know the bastards
have metamorphosed."

Bastards. The bezeri had now been relegated into the
catchall of the unwelcome along with Rayat, the FEU and at
least some of the isenj. Ade knew how to compartmentalize
the world to cope with it.

Aras would do that too, then. He was no longer the bezeri's ally. And until he heard them say that they regretted
their past, and that their future would be different, then he
couldn't rule out being their enemy.

The Temporary City, Bezer'ej: holding cell

"I heard," said Rayat, arms folded. "Why don't you just
let her do it?"

Esganikan looked him over, trying to see what it was that
made the usually controlled Shan Frankland descend into
rage when she saw him. There might have been scents and
minute gestures that irritated a human female, but Esganikan
couldn't tell. Rayat simply appeared to her to be calm and
almost amused. That might have been the trigger. He wasn't
showing deference.

"Is that a *bluff*?" asked Esganikan.

Rayat's brow puckered briefly. "No, just that it's inevitable."

"You've given up this plan to acquire *c'naatat* for your
government to use." She sniffed the air. He was pungent
with human sweat, underlaid with that sharp scent that might
have been fear or anger. Human scent signaling was far more
blurred than a wess'har's. "This is a radical change."

"I've seen how dangerous it is, and I can work out what
we'd do with it," Rayat said wearily, as if he'd repeated it too
many times to Shan.

"You could have done that *before* you became infected."

Rayat looked up at her, eyes wide and finely lined at the
corners. His hair was streaked with gray. Shan said he was
younger than she was, but he didn't look it. "It was something
to be quarantined for safety then," he said sharply. "Once you

can remove it, it becomes a viable weapon. *That's* the difference. And you're working on removing it, aren't you?"

"We are. You know this."

"My apologies. That was rhetorical." He pushed his fingers through his hair and gave his head a little shake. "*C'naatat* has its downside in its current state. You can use it to keep people alive and make them adapt to any environment. Fantastic. Miracle cure, a means to survive in hostile environments—medicine and the military would welcome it. But it's also an incurable disease that spreads relatively easily in humans and that would create population chaos. *Nobody dies.* I could give a long list of all the disasters inherent in a growing and pretty well immortal population, but I don't have to, do I? The wonder cure has its curse. An incentive not to use it. Take the curse away, and it becomes usable with the deceptive appearance of no consequences."

Esganikan listened patiently. She made adjustments for human motivation and saw his point. Humans didn't accept that it would always be a curse for them. They would feel they could *get away with it,* as Shan put it, that the problem would be someone else's.

"Are you pleading for mercy in some oblique way?"

"Sorry?"

"This is why you irradiated Ouzhari. Asset denial."

"Removing temptation, yes. But forget mercy. You know what I am?"

"A spook."

"You understand the psychology of my profession."

"That you accept risk of death."

"That's one way of putting it."

Esganikan had been warned: he was *a slimy bastard,* Shan said, and would attempt to manipulate her into doing his bidding. She tilted her head a little further to see every pore and hair on his face, to search for lies.

"Do you want to go home, Rayat?"

He let out a breath. "Of course I do. Everyone does, don't they? You do too. This isn't home for any of us."

It isn't. It'll be years before I see mine again. "You can't go home until we can remove the organism. That could be a very long time indeed. Are you ready for that? Is that why you say I should let Shan kill you instead? Like the wess'har troops who took their own lives rather than go on?"

Esganikan wished she hadn't sent Shan away. The woman could read the signals from Rayat: she couldn't. He raised his eyebrows and his lips parted, but it meant nothing to her. She'd never seen the expression on Shan's face and so she couldn't match it to a state of mind.

And Shan had warned her he could feign emotions anyway. Normal humans did that a great deal, so a c'naatat-infected human might even be able to feign scents. Shan could suppress hers totally.

"The good thing about c'naatat," Rayat said slowly, "is that at least you *can* wait for the cure. The thing it buys you is time."

Esganikan felt those words were different. She weighed them carefully and saw the germ of an idea.

"Shapakti is a diligent researcher," she said. *Time. I never thought I was greedy, but time . . .* "He'll make progress, I know. He managed to remove it from human cells once, but the organism adapts."

Rayat looked suddenly interested. "I have my theories."

"You're a scientist by training. Shan told me so. You might help him."

"The lab rat puts on the white coat, eh?" He made a little snorting noise, gazing in defocus towards the light shaft. "Good old Frankland. I'm a pharmacologist, actually. Easier to train a scientist as a spy than to train a spy to pass himself off as a scientist."

"Yes or no?"

"Yes."

"You really do believe it's too dangerous for any human to possess."

"At every level. Wess'har might have the moral fiber to use it sensibly, but humans generally don't."

Esganikan looked into his face for a few more moments but Rayat said nothing further. He didn't even appear uncomfortable at her gaze: no licking of lips, no blinking, no little twitching movements. She thought of Shan's advice on resisting Rayat's manipulation, and decided that so far she had only given him a stay of execution, and something to keep him occupied while Shapakti worked on a consistent and non-lethal method of removing *c'naatat*.

I don't want to slaughter the bezeri. And I also want to be certain that they're environmentally irresponsible before I have to.

She didn't enjoy killing. If humans thought that wess'har killed without caring, they were wrong.

But dead, as Shan put it, was dead.

Esganikan walked back along the passage that sloped gently up to the exit, catching the faint remnant of Shan's scent on the air: no emotional state, just that waxy human smell blended with wess'har female musk and a woody freshness. Shan kept her anger to herself.

Wess'har could use *c'naatat* wisely, and humans couldn't.

C'naatat bought Rayat time.

He was manipulating her. He was trying to flatter her, and to get her to take him home, where he could deliver his prize.

He wouldn't go home, then. She'd make sure of that. But if he thought he had insinuated his wishes into her mind, he'd taken her for a stupid malleable *gethes*.

All he had given her were ideas. She wouldn't give him a way home.

4

Pacific Rim UN delegate Jim Matsoukis has called for those responsible for authorizing the bombing of Bezer'ej to stand trial for war crimes. The Federal European Union denies sanctioning the attack and says those responsible were handed over to the wess'har.

Matsoukis attacked the denial as "not just a lie, but a lie that'll have repercussions for everyone on the planet." He added: "If the wess'har authorities are still calling for us to punish whoever authorized the bombing from this end, then they know something we don't. And why deploy a ship with cobalt bombs unless there was an acceptance that the FEU might use them?"

FEU space vessels routinely carry nuclear ordnance including ERDs—"neutron" bombs—and cobalt devices for emergency sterilization of biohazards in orbital laboratories. Cobalt is banned for weapons use by international treaty.

BBChan update, February 2, 2377

Chad Island, known in the bezeri language as Nazel

"I don't care," said Lindsay.

"I hurt," said Saib.

"Hurt is better than dead. Keep moving. Where's have you been, Keet?"

Chad was an island of stony coastline with rock pools like the shores of Constantine, not a textbook idyll like Ouzhari, its southernmost cousin in the chain. There were no icing-sugar beaches giving way to dunes tufted with glossy black grass: it was a silver gray island that looked less magical and more plainly grubby when Cavanagh's Star—Ceret, Nir, whatever—dipped behind clouds. Lindsay tried to imagine the geology that created the variety of shorelines as she coaxed Saib and Keet inland and further away from the sea. They inched up the exposed sand between the outcrops of rock, sliding through gaps with an audible wet sound like someone peeling off plastic gloves.

"Seeing the Aras," said Keet.

"What?"

"I see Aras. I tell him, not sorry."

Lindsay stopped dead, furious. "I told you to steer clear of the Eqbas camp. You idiot. Don't do it again." There was nothing Aras or anyone else could do about the bezeri now, but she felt advertising their changed physiology was a bad move anyway. "You took the lamp? Where is it?"

"No, I speak!"

Brilliant. That'll get back to Shan in no time. Ah well. "You stay away from the mainland and the Eqbas patrols unless I say otherwise. Understand?"

Keet lapsed into silence, and as he moved he looked uncannily like a sulky teenager scuffing his heels in protest.

"No change," he said.

"You don't *want* to change, or you *can't* change?" She stopped and confronted them, still mirroring her spoken words in light signals. *Learn, damn you.* It was a real speak-and-show lesson. The two elderly bezeri settled in heaps of translucent mantle and exhaled like air escaping from a tire. "Look, I can live under water. And you're moving across dry land and you're *talking.* You're making sounds. *C'naatat* will do whatever you need it to do to keep you alive."

"Want to," said Keet sullenly.

"Take back this planet. Defend it."

"With forty?"

"Forty's all you need if you're immortal."

She turned and walked towards the fringe of brilliant yellow and amber mossy bushes that marked the edge of the beach. The moss formed mounds that were waist high in places and looked soft and insubstantial until her arm brushed against one and it scratched her.

Doesn't matter. You're indestructible—more or less.

"Hurt too," said Keet behind her.

But they still followed her, through the rigid moss bushes

and into heathland dotted with coppices of chocolate brown stubby trees with trailing branches that appeared to grow back into the soil. The ground beneath her feet felt slightly spongy. She paused, remembering the bogs on Constantine with their shifting organic roads, mats of vegetation afloat on quicksand and constantly, dangerously changing. Indestructible or not, she didn't fancy testing her new powers of recovery in liquid mud populated by God only knew what kind of creatures.

"Go careful," she said. "Follow where I tread."

Saib made that deflating tire noise again. "I see redness."

"What?"

"Hot moving redness."

Lindsay came to a careful halt. She felt she was on a rolling deck, which might have been her imagination, but if she was on saturated ground then she was going to be wary. She turned to look at them: Saib had settled back on the ground in an awkward way that reminded her of an elephant, two tentacles braced on the ground in front of him like forelegs.

"Something you can see that I can't?" She had plenty of their visual enhancements but maybe she didn't have them all. "What is it?"

"In the heart."

She was getting used to their idiom now. The lamp hadn't shown the subtle detail of the bezeri language, and now she wondered if she was experiencing it or if they were already slipping into a blend of all the linguistic concepts that previous hosts had donated via *c'naatat*.

"Your heart," she said carefully. "Your mind. Your brain?"

"Not now, and not mine." said Saib. "Long before. Where is it?"

Long before. Memory. And not *his* memory, obviously: someone else's. *Hot moving redness.* Fire.

There was no getting away from Shan Frankland. Saib was reliving her memory of facing a riot and having a petrol bomb—not petrol, but the name had survived—smashing against her riot shield in a cascade of flames. She'd talked about it: that, and the gorilla. The bloody woman could agonize over abandoning a caged gorilla but had no problem turning her back on a dying baby. *My son.* The fact that Shan had been right not to save his life with *c'naatat* didn't make it hurt any less. And the bitter irony of her own actions wasn't lost on her.

"It's fire," she said. Aquatic creatures had no concept of it, of course, but maybe they'd seen smoking hot vents on the sea bed. "That's genetic memory kicking in. You'll have all kinds of memories that aren't yours. It's a characteristic of the isenj."

"Are isenj always angry?"

"Not that I noticed." Lindsay began to think about an amalgam of a reactionary, genocidally inclined Saib and a fists-first-questions-later Shan. It wasn't pretty. "That'd be Shan Frankland again."

But maybe that was what the bezeri needed, a dose of ruthless pragmatism that went beyond self. Shan got things done. She'd changed the course of entire worlds, for good or ill. And the last of the bezeri needed that obsessive focus badly if they weren't to become the galactic equivalent of unicorns.

They're immortal, barring detonations. Why the hell make them do all this? And what happens if they start breeding again?

"This *Frankland,*" said Saib, almost chewing the syllables. "Explain who is in my mind."

"Your people saw her. The one who brought the dead child back to you."

"The one who failed to keep her promise to defend us."

For some reason that stung Lindsay. She had no idea if it was species loyalty kicking in or if there was a bit of Shan too near the surface in her now. "All she had to defend you from was me."

Saib said nothing. Keet made a loud noise like a fart and heaved himself into a strange loping movement, propelling himself along by throwing two tentacles forward and then swinging his bulk between them like a man on crutches. He didn't seem remotely afraid of the unknown terrain and even if he didn't know where he was going, he was moving with purpose. That was encouraging.

His tentacles seemed to be changing and becoming capable of rigidity. That was *c'naatat* in action. He was evolving before her eyes, as she had before his. *I'm used to this. Where's it all going to end? What am I going to become?* She had a moment of heart-stopping clarity and the sense of loss almost overwhelmed her. Raw survival was a wonderfully erasing, focusing thing but she didn't have that to distract her any longer—and she never would again.

She centered herself on a goal. It had always worked before. It had to work now.

"Here's what you do," she said. Keet was moving faster now and she had to break into a trot to keep up with him. Each time he grounded between swings his translucent bulk shook like rolls of blubber. "You rebuild your civilization ashore. You build it here, and you concentrate on developing technology to defend yourselves. That's why I brought you ashore."

"Yes, so easy," said Saib from behind her. The steady *thud-thud-thud* of his movements was slower. He was keeping pace with her. "From nothing, we invent. Forty of us, none of us scientists, none of us land engineers."

"You're speaking, and you're speaking English. That's two things you couldn't do a month ago."

"What shall we eat here?"

"And you're getting fluent."

"What is to *eat*?"

"Everything. *C'naatat* can help you digest anything at all. You saw me live on seaweed." Saib didn't need sympathy: he needed to get a grip. "My species made the transition from the sea to the land once. Without bloody *c'naatat*, too, so stop whining."

They were hunters. They'd hunted other aquatic species to extinction. Lindsay didn't know what animals lived on Chad that would take their fancy, but the bezeri were as bad as humans when it came to exploiting their planet. And she knew the wess'har and their Eqbas cousins well enough by now to know that they wouldn't take the bezeri's near extinction as a plea in mitigation if they wiped out any more species. They'd "balance" them. It sounded like a euphemism, but it was literal. You killed: so you died. Maybe a dose of Shan, and Aras, in them would temper that. Maybe they'd avoid being "balanced."

"Eqbas will protect us." Keet loped between the trees and a shaft of bright sunlight caught him, illuminating his flesh. For a moment he was a lump of ice studded with debris, and then his color changed completely, instantly, inexplicably to an opaque mottled brown like camouflage. He blended into the landscape, his lights silent, until he burst into a vivid green display of pure panic.

He was screaming. Under stress, he defaulted to light signals. Lindsay ran up to him.

"*C'naatat* does that," she said, voice calm, lights a soothing violet. She wondered if the camo could now adapt to any environment like the chameleon battledress the Royal Marines wore. "Take it easy. However it makes its decisions, it's decided you need camo for a while."

"I am not me," said Keet. *"I am not me!"*

They'd taken the decision. They'd agreed to be infected, and she was certain they'd understood the full implications. If they hadn't, it was too late now. It's was irrevocable. And she had no explosives, no certainty of ending it for any of them if they decided immortality wasn't all it was cracked up to be.

"You'll be okay," said Lindsay. *But will I?* "It gets easier. I've seen it. Shan was okay, Aras was okay—you remember Aras, don't you?"

"I remember what Aras remembers," said Saib. He edged forward, sounding like water slopping around a tank. Keet was slumped in a heap, tentacles twitching, a beached cephalopod again, not a brave pioneer. Saib stretched out a translucent limb and placed it on his comrade's mantle. In seconds the flesh became the same mottled brown. "He remembers *us*. I know how we appear to him. And others like us once changed color."

Saib used the past tense. Lindsay wanted to be sure that wasn't just a slip in an unfamiliar language.

"You mean the birzula. The ones you wiped out."

"Yes. Much like us. But color changers."

It was the kind of thing Rayat could have explained to her. She knew enough about photophores to understand they weren't all that different from the chromatophores that made terrestrial—no, *Earth*—squid change color.

She was looking at a *genuinely* terrestrial squid now; a cephalopod that had walked ashore and become—however reluctantly—a land animal. That should have stunned her. It didn't.

"What's upsetting you?" she asked Keet. Saib seemed resigned to the changes, sitting in a Buddha-like heap without a trace of bioluminescence. He was now totally mottled brown and opaque. "Is it that your body's changing or that you're like the race you killed?"

It was probably too complex a question for Keet; she wasn't sure how she would have answered it herself. He levered himself up and swung off in the direction of a clearing, looking for all the world as if he had moved that way all his life. No wonder he was scared. She'd been scared, too, when her body and even her mind didn't feel or look like her own any longer.

If you thought about *c'naatat* too much, it was worse than being dead. You were a tenant in your own body. You could be kicked out at any time.

But not if you're Shan bloody Frankland.

Lindsay tried to center herself and conjure up that degree of certainty—of blinkered arrogance—that enabled Shan Frankland to take *c'naatat* in her stride and make it serve her. It was in her somewhere. The parasite had passed through Aras, and Ade, and Shan, picking up genetic material along the way. Something of all of them—memory too—was there within her for the taking, and if she could force the bloody thing to express the genes for photophores to give her bioluminescence, then she could wring some extra willpower out of it too.

Lindsay and her entourage of evolving squid followed the course of a stream inland. It wasn't the image of a glittering naval career that she'd dreamed of as a young cadet.

Keet stopped. Saib shook to a halt next to him. They were now in a clearing fringed by taller trees, bulbous purple-brown columns almost like fungi but with a fine mesh of drooping branches coated in glistening dark red leaves. They were sticky to her touch. When she withdrew her hand, a soft resin pulled out in thin weblike strings and left her smelling of sickly-sweet decay. Unseen life rustled and moved in the undergrowth and when she glanced up, a stabtail was circling high overhead, pursued at a distance by a flock of some small flying creatures she hadn't seen before.

"We can never go back," said Saib.

"Actually, you *can* go back." She hoped she was right, but she had no real idea of how *c'naatat* behaved in different species. Did anyone? No, not even the wess'har, and they'd had more experience of it than anyone. "Because the parasite will keep changing you. If you want to go back into the sea, fine. You'll adapt right back to it. But you're going to give this your best shot."

She tried hard to stay in her own head and not slip into the external view, perhaps the combined views of the others known and unknown within her that she was finding all too easy now. A gel woman, bioluminescent and amphibious, chatting to walking, talking squid. That was her reality. She fought down panic. Shan wouldn't panic. Shan would *organize* them. She'd give them tasks. She'd galvanize them.

"You start here," said Lindsay. "It's as good a place as any to build a town."

She was asking an aquatic civilization to move to a new environment and start over again from the hunter-gatherer level.

It was that or hide in the sea and hope nobody else invaded. There was only one way to defend the planet against off-worlders, and that was on land. You couldn't build weapons underwater. You had to engage a terrestrial enemy on their own terms.

Defend the planet. Whose thoughts were those?

"We call this place the Unwanted Dry Above," said Saib.

"Nothing like a positive approach, is there?"

"We will ask if others want to make the journey." Saib understood sarcasm well enough, but he also knew how to ignore it. "If others want this disease."

"I'll ask them." It was harder to contaminate someone than she'd thought. Blood, or whatever passed for it in her circulation now, was hard to extract when you healed almost instantly, so she'd steeled herself to slicing more chunks out of her skin and pressing it into cuts in their mantles. "Can you contaminate each other? You can spread it by copulation. It would be easier."

Saib and Keet never said a word or flashed a signal. But they were staring at her, as much as a cephalopod could.

It struck her that Shan would never have said that.

"If any of you are partners, that is," she added.

If you're going to live among them forever, you have to treat them the way you treat humans. You're still thinking of them as animals.

"We lay eggs, when young," Saib said at last. "We spawn—when young."

"Okay," Lindsay said. "We'll do it the hard way, then."

It paid not to think what an insane situation she was in. She wondered where Rayat was now. If he'd run into the Eqbas, they'd have filleted him already. But it was probably better than falling into Shan's hands.

She hated to admit it, but she missed his encyclopedic knowledge, and—spy or not, arrogant bastard or not—she missed *him,* because she was still human at her core. If there was anything else to hang on to, she hadn't identified it yet—but without another human around, she would *have* to.

Saib stretched out a marbled brown tentacle and it lightened into shades of clear amber pinpricked with gold lights. He seemed to be marveling at it.

"Too late to save my child," he said.

"Too late to save mine, too," said Lindsay.

Jejeno: cabinet rooms, now the crisis center for the Northern Assembly government

"If the Eqbas crippled the Maritime Fringe, then they didn't cripple them enough." Minister Shomen Eit held court in the cabinet room, silhouetted against the long window with palls of black smoke beyond him, a portal into another world. The artillery barrage was getting closer. "Are you quite well, colleague?"

Rit, still shaken and battered from the blast, was determined she would be *quite well* even if it killed her. She knew what she had to do now. Minister Nir Bedoi was the only other cabinet member who had managed to get to the offices. The city was in chaos. It took very little to disrupt and paralyze a city as impossibly crowded as Jejeno, and the Maritime Fringe and its allies had launched ground-to-air missiles that had struck at least seven of the tallest residential towers in the heart of the city. There was nowhere to run. The emergency relief teams were finding it impossible to move around.

"I'm bruised." Rit's broken quill shafts gave her an odd crawling sensation in her skin. Ralassi, close to her side, watched Shomen Eit with baleful concentration. "I'll survive."

"Where are your sons?" asked Eit.

"On Tasir Var. I left them there for safety and I'm glad I did."

Eit missed them: Luot and Shimev, all she had of her late husband. They had his genetic memories, and she didn't, so now their lives became more important than hers because what mattered, what defined isenj, was the continuation of the memory line, and they had both hers and Ual's.

She wanted a radically different future for them from the moment she'd stood studying the *dalf,* the tree that should never have been. It triggered truly ancient memories. Remembering was a complex act for isenj, layer upon layer of events arranged in a hierarchy of importance coexisting with the day-to-day recall stored in the secondary brain. She recalled what mattered most to her bloodline, across millennia. Memory defined a people.

And now she recalled trees.

"The Fringe clearly managed to salvage a great deal of armament," said Shomen Eit. "The Eqbas aren't thorough."

"They destroyed enough to stop the rest of Umeh threatening Wess'ej, colleague," said Rit. "The Eqbas will finish what they started."

And finish you.

Bedoi, who had been watching the aftermath of the missile strikes in the city from the window, turned sharply and set his beads rattling. "They've abandoned us. And three-quarters of our defense forces have deserted or joined the Fringe. Now we're at the mercy of any nation that wants to overrun us."

"Who is 'us'?" Eit moved from screen to screen in the crisis center and from his ever-so-slightly raised quills he looked like a leader who feared defeat. "This isn't our nation at war. This is its government utterly isolated and its population divided while invaders swarm across out borders, and are even welcomed. This is anarchy."

Rit's memory had suddenly become not just recalled images but also emotions. She was in a comblike grid of chambers, moving towards a brilliant white light and then tumbling down a steep incline and righting herself before rushing with many others towards a tapering column of packed earth, deep brown and peppered with small openings. She was enraged. She wanted resolution. She wanted destruction. Whatever was in that mound was a threat to everything she valued.

In her memory, she rushed to overrun and wipe out a rival colony of proto-isenj in a world of open spaces and vibrant plant life.

In the here and now, she resolved to act to protect her young. Even knowing that this was a primeval swarming reflex to defend the colony at times of crisis, she allowed it to steer her, just as it steered the troops attacking Jejeno and the civilians who turned their backs on their government to side with an enemy.

Survival advantage. That was all it was, the usually orderly and formal isenj tipping suddenly into violent chaos to reestablish an equilibrium.

"I think we should negotiate a settlement," said Bedoi.

"If they want one." Shomen Eit wouldn't stay away from the window. It was a strange, impotent display of anxiety when the most important data on the state of the city was on screens around him in tidy collated displays, not in the vista beyond. "We allowed the Eqbas to land, and so there's nothing to negotiate."

"We can still negotiate," said Bedoi. "Agree we made a mistake. Offer to help rebuild a credible fleet." He had always been torn between total war on the wess'har and accepting their assistance, Ual had told Rit. It was visible now. "If our way of life needs a drastic change, maybe it's to deal with the wess'har once and for all, by concentrating on regaining the military power we once had."

Rit said nothing. If you were a minister whose office came from exploiting an ancient law that let you take your husband's duties, nobody expected glittering strategic debate from you anyway.

Shomen Eit considered Bedoi for a few moments and seemed suddenly impatient with him. "The only target they have is those of us in government, colleague, because the population that survives will join them anyway. Then they'll embark on a noble, suicidal and very, *very* short war against the wess'har and Eqbas—after they've rebuilt a few fighters. No, this requires something more intelligent. But I agree that the radical change is needed—we should have followed our instincts. Let's see what we have to offer them in terms of matériel."

"That means diverting resources from environmental management. It'll cost health—lives."

"So will allowing the Eqbas to remodel our world the way they see fit."

"You're the one who asked them for targeted biological weapons."

"Perhaps that's another capacity we need to develop for ourselves."

Rit felt the push from her ancestor, the rattling quills unheard for eons urging her to protect the colony. The transition from dutiful wife to politician with her own agenda was effortless and immediate.

"Ralassi," she said. "I can't do anything more here. See if we can find a route back to my chambers."

Shomen Eit turned on her sharply, beads rattling and shimmering. "You're walking out when you should be coordinating the defense of this nation?"

"I can do nothing here." *But I can do plenty elsewhere.*

"Your *husband* had a sense of duty."

"It killed him, too." Rit resisted the bait. "And it's a poor excuse for an argument to remind me that I'm a widow and that I only hold his office through a loophole in the law."

She gestured to Ralassi and moved towards the door, imbued with a confidence that had nothing to do with her own life's experience and everything to do with an ancestral memory of an alpha warrior in a primitive colony mound who knew what had to be done to save the future.

The street-by-street fighting had now spilled over the Northern Assembly border. Slow going, hand-to-hand fighting in a shattered, tight-packed maze of streets: she had time. She had to act now.

"You betray this government by abandoning your position," said Eit.

Rit wondered if he was going to attempt to bar her way, but he didn't. Ralassi must have thought so too, because his lips were pulled back in that precursor to a serious threat she'd seen once or twice before. Like isenj, ussissi had a capacity for suddenly snapping in extreme situations and plunging into violence.

They said ussissi always became one united creature, a superbly coordinated mob when they attacked, but Rit had never seen it, and her memory told her that none of her ancestors had seen it either.

The doors closed behind her. In the long stone-lined corridor outside, shellfire seemed distant. The clerical staff were still at their posts, collating information being sent back from utilities and hospitals, and they didn't need a cabinet minister to implement a disaster plan. Isenj were orderly. They were planners and engineers. They could always stave off a crisis.

And that is our weakness. Sometimes, the crisis has to happen to restore sanity. Sometimes, we have to start over.

"What are you planning?" asked Ralassi. He was the last ussissi left in the building as far as she could tell.

"Call Esganikan Gai."

"Without consulting your cabinet colleagues?"

"Yes. And without consulting them again, I'm also asking her to invade Umeh."

Ralassi's beaded belts, strung over one shoulder, slapped and cracked as he walked. Rit wondered if the ussissi penchant for beading had come from contact with isenj culture. If it was, it was the only element they'd borrowed. He said nothing for a few paces and then slowed to a halt.

"You remind me so much of Minister Ual," he said. "But be sure you've thought this through, and not simply continuing a flawed plan out of love and duty."

"I have," she said, and thought of her sons and what she had to do. "Now find me a quiet and secure place where I can call Esganikan Gai."

Ralassi made no comment, neutral and unjudgmental again, and trotted off down the passage with his claws skittering on the polished pale blue stone. There was no stone like this left for quarrying, just the composite recovered from endless rebuilding over millennia. In Rit's ancestral memory—now painfully raw and fresh, kicked into higher conscious levels of her recall by the crisis—she was suddenly aware of how fast, how *geometrically* overcrowding had accelerated so that one year Jejeno seemed a busy city and the next it was noticeably oppressive. It was long before she was born.

I know what I think. This isn't my instinct to kill to protect food sources for my young. This is rational, this is seeking a new solution because none of the others work.

Rit made her way down the passage to a chamber where staff were coordinating rescue teams. They acknowledged her with clicks and whistles and went straight back to their tasks.

She approached one of them sitting at a desk with a planning map in front of him that covered the whole desk.

"I have a request for you," she said quietly.

"Yes, Minister?"

Rit reached out to the schematic of the south side of the city and tapped it until the scale changed and the southern border with the Maritime Fringe appeared. Then she focused on the junction of roads that had been obliterated by an explosion in a previous attack, and that was now a park.

"Speak to the emergency authority in this area," she said. "And make sure they protect the *dalf* tree there."

"A tree . . ."

"A tree," she said. "And one dearly bought."

F'nar, Wess'ej: agricultural zone

". . . and the general asks him what his ambition is, and the squaddie says, 'To get the brush before those other two bastards, sir.' "

Jon Becken straightened up from his spade to receive his applause, one arm held wide and a silly grin on his face. The Royal Marines' detachment—five of them, if Shan didn't count Ade—roared with laughter and went on hoeing the soil between the rows of onions. If they didn't grow it, they didn't eat it; life here was uncomplicated, but the marines were trained to live off the land, so vegetable gardening represented an easier break.

Shan and Nevyan strolled between irregularly shaped crop bed, carefully designed to harmonize with the wild landscape. They were contained in a nearly invisible biobarrier to maintain an Earthlike growing environment.

"I didn't hear the rest of the joke," said Nevyan.

Shan shrugged, thinking of Aras. "Just as well."

"So why did you leave Bezer'ej so soon?"

"There's something I haven't told you."

Nevyan emitted a faint whiff of acid irritation. "You used to be open with me, my friend."

Yes, I did. "Lindsay's infected the bezeri with *c'naatat*. There's something wandering around on land and Shapakti's taken a look at the cells it left. And one of the bezeri seems to have acquired the power of speech."

Nevyan froze for a moment and Shan found herself a few paces ahead of her. She stopped and turned.

"Speech," said Nevyan.

"Yes, apparently it told Aras it wasn't sorry for the bezeri's record."

"This is appalling."

"Nev, I tried to go after Lin, but I'm dependent on Esganikan for transport, resources, everything."

Wess'har didn't bother to control their tempers, but Nevyan almost tried. "Dealing with infected isenj on Bezer'ej was hard enough. Now we have to deal with *c'naatat* hosts who could be anywhere on land or sea."

Deal with. So Nevyan had defaulted to worst scenario too. The bezeri had fallen from grace in an instant, and it had nothing to do with their shameful past.

"We might not have to eradicate them."

"You mean kill. *Say* kill."

Shan had thought it over a thousand times in the last all-too-brief days, searching for the clear line that divided black from white. "Okay, if they don't breed, they're just a tragic anomaly. If they breed or spread *c'naatat,* they're a problem."

"*C'naatat* never spread accidentally among Bezer'ej native species. When non-native life arrived, it spread."

Large, mobile hosts. Aras had said that once. *C'naatat* liked them. Like any organism, it sought the best vector for reproduction. Spacefaring aliens were as good as it got.

"It likes difference," said Shan. That wasn't very scientific, but she took a guess that *c'naatat* assessed potential hosts and latched on to what it didn't recognize as the locals. "It likes novelty. It's a collector of foreign DNA. Look at me, or Aras."

Shan held out her hands and they rippled with bezeri light. Nevyan reeked of agitation. "I don't care what Esganikan wants. I have to assess this."

"That means taking a team back to Bezer'ej, and the bezeri don't want you there now."

"The bezeri may no longer be in the best position to judge," said Nevyan, "and none of the other life-forms under threat from them can ask us for help as they once did."

Shan watched the delicate fence between Targassat's philosophy of non-interference and the old Eqbas doctrine of policing collapsing before her eyes. She searched for her own line, and failed. *And having a choice, must make it.* Targassat had made hers, and Shan would too.

"If they're not breeding now," said Shan, "there's no telling what changes will occur in the future. I think we have to wipe them out."

The suggestion of genocide slipped out as easily as any decision she'd ever made. Shan felt it lock into her memory as a moment she would be able to recall in photographic detail for the rest of her life; she was staring almost unseeing at the marines in their dusty lovat green T-shirts and combat trousers, their conversation a murmur on a breeze heady with coconut-scented weeds and pungent onion, and she knew that any of those smells or sights or sounds would trigger this moment in her again. It wouldn't be a happy memory.

Is it because I see the bezeri as animals? Would I do this if I believed they were people? Is this even my thinking at all?

For a woman whose self-awareness was as solid and brutal as a steel bar, genetic memory was a cruelly unsettling trait. But her rational brain said, *Yes, stop it now, stop it before it gets worse than you can imagine.* Aras was thinking it too.

Nevyan held her hands clasped in front of her. "We could ignore this. The bezeri will never trouble us. But others may yet arrive to trouble them, as the *gethes* did."

Genies like the promise of eternal life didn't get shoved back into bottles that easily. Nevyan was right: it wasn't just the ecology of Bezer'ej. It was the lure and value of *c'naatat* too. There was almost an inevitability that other off-worlders would come after it, just like humans had.

"But if we kill them, I'm still around. So are Aras and Ade. I'm the root cause of all this contagion."

"And you're my friend," said Nevyan.

Shan groped for the line again and couldn't find it. She felt nobody expected her to, either, as if spacing herself was so unutterably noble that it relieved her of all future obligation to do the right thing. It didn't. It just showed her how easily it could be done again if she really wanted to.

She didn't.

F'nar was beautiful. The whole planet was magical, and this was her home, and she didn't want to die. The bezeri must have felt the same way. As choices went, it stank, and Shan knew she could no more reconcile the reality of controlling *c'naatat* with the morality of who should have been forced to surrender it than she could reconcile human and wess'har ethics.

"Shit," she said.

"And Rayat?"

"Word association, eh?" Even now, Nevyan could still make her smile. "Shapakti's using him to find a way of removing *c'naatat* and leaving the host alive."

"If that could be done, it would relieve us of the burden of destroying the bezeri."

"And make it a viable weapon. At the moment, it's still carrying a WARNING: MAY CAUSE GLOBAL DISASTER sticker."

"We have no way of knowing if it can be done, and when, and in that time—"

"Are we talking each other into genocide, Nev?"

"That might be your word for it."

"We've still got some way to go. We have to find them first, then work out how we kill what we find."

I killed people I felt were a problem to society, and had others kill them. I've been here before. It's only a matter of numbers.

Motive didn't matter. Outcomes, always outcomes. Shan's morality hadn't shifted. She'd just started applying it more widely.

She stood in silence with Nevyan and watched the marines for a while, then turned and walked slowly back towards the pearl city and a late lunch with an increasingly distressed Aras, and an Ade who was definitely—and touchingly—playing the morale-boosting sergeant to him.

Nevyan's sense of burden was tangible. She was still just a kid, not really ready for all this crap. Was anyone?

Shan wondered how things would have turned out if she had told Eugenie Perault to stuff her mission and gone home. She had no way of knowing if anyone else would have made the situation unfold differently, and she was past the stage of thinking she was the only person fit for the job.

"There's never going to be a return to normal, is there?" she said.

Nevyan dug her hand into the front pocket of her *dhren.* "Life is in constant change, but we rarely notice it."

She took out her *virin,* the communications device that Shan had never really got the hang of. It was pulsing with color and images that Shan couldn't see clearly from the side angle. But she could certainly smell the agitation and anxiety rolling off Nevyan; the young matriarch held the *virin* in both hands now, moving her fingers over it as if lathering a bar of soap, and suddenly sound emerged from it.

"Nevyan Chail, we have unauthorized ships approaching Bezer'ej."

Had the isenj more of a fleet than the Eqbas had thought, or had elements of the Eqbas task force turned up ludicrously early? It couldn't be a human fleet. Shan took out her swiss and opened the link to Ade without even thinking. Something in her head said *emergency* and she switched over to autopilot.

"What ships are these?" said Nevyan. "Why are they here?"

"They speak eqbas'u, *chail,* and they say they're Skavu. They've come to back up Esganikan Gai's Umeh mission. They say they are her allies."

5

*If an injury has to be done to a man it should be so severe
that his vengeance need not be feared.*

NICCOLO MACHIAVELLI, 1469–1527

The Exchange of Surplus Things, F'nar

Aras could smell the excitement rolling off the marines—including Ade. He wasn't sure if that was the correct
interpretation of it, but they smelled strongly of humans who
wanted very badly to go somewhere and do something. They
watched the screen set in the wall of the Exchange as if totally oblivious to everyone else in the hall.

"This is a bloody funny way to run a briefing," said Ismat Qureshi. Eddie Michallat sidled up to her: it had long
been obvious that he found the marine attractive but he appeared to do nothing about it. Aras thought that was a wasted
life, and humans had such a short span that it saddened him.
"Like having your comcen in the supermarket for everyone
to gawp at."

It was more than that. Nevyan was having a heated discussion with Esganikan via a communications link, and with
the risk of *jask* removed, they were both expressing their
anger fully. The hall smelled of mangoes, and nobody—not
even the ussissi packed in between the curious wess'har
who had come to watch their leaders argue—could miss the
pheromonal signal that Nevyan was the dominant matriarch.
The other senior matriarchs of the city—Nevyan's mother
Mestin, Chayyas and Fersanye—stood behind her but said
nothing. Shan kept her scent locked down and stood beside
the marines with her arms folded, jaw muscles clenching and
unclenching.

"Who are they?" Nevyan demanded. "Who are the
Skavu?"

"They're from Garav, a world we restored several generations ago. It's two months from this system." Esganikan had the tone of someone who felt she was owed a little gratitude. "They became enthusiastic converts to a balanced way of life."

"After a war?"

"A war I fought in, yes. They became allies, and I need personnel right now."

"And I need to know more about *them*."

"They're dedicated and they're thorough. They don't compromise."

It sounded like euphemisms a human would use. Aras watched Mart Barencoin close his eyes for a second and mouth something that looked like *Oh shit*. The two engineer-trained marines, Sue Webster and Bulwant Singh Chahal, turned to look at him and their expressions matched his; dread.

Nevyan—a head shorter than most matriarchs, built more like a male—persisted with her onslaught. "Why did you not warn us they were coming? Why allow them to simply arrive in this system unannounced?"

"I was told they were weeks away," said Esganikan. "And they announced themselves. You want the isenj problem addressed? Then this is how I do it. I accepted their offer of assistance."

"When? You told me nothing of this."

"I took the decision a matter of days ago."

"The Skavu must have embarked many weeks ago to have arrived so soon, long before you accepted their offer, which makes them *overconfident* of their welcome."

"But they're here, and they have a job to do, and they'll obey my command."

"How many troops?"

"In this wave, ten thousand."

Nevyan hesitated. "They can't be billeted here."

"No, I plan to accommodate them on Bezer'ej."

"That's impossible. The Temporary City was never designed for those numbers."

"Nor was it designed for two thousand of my troops,

either, but you made no complaint about that when you summoned us." Esganikan's face filled the screen, cutting off the top of her bobbing copper-red plume. Aras couldn't argue with her logic, but he shared Nevyan's alarm at a wholly unknown race being pulled in as support in a system where there were already too many tensions. "I'll vouch for the Skavu. I'll keep them under control, and I guarantee they'll do no harm to Bezer'ej. They are *not* your problem. They've come to deal with Umeh, and they won't trouble you."

The screen went blank. The marines, Shan and Eddie all reacted as if they'd been slapped in the face. They seemed to think the abrupt end of the conversation was rude, but Esganikan had no more to add. Nevyan, however, clearly did. She spun around and beckoned to her ussissi aide, Serrimissani. "Get data on Garav. And see what the other ussissi know. Do the isenj realize these troops are here?"

Most wess'har who'd paused to watch the exchange between the two matriarchs dispersed and went about their business, depositing produce they didn't need so that others could use it, and selecting what they needed from others' bounty. Drama or not, life went on. Some stopped to talk to Nevyan and the other senior matriarchs, then went on their way.

"I'd say the Skavu are a bit too keen," Shan said. She made an annoyed click with her teeth and examined her thumbnail in a rather un-Shanlike way. "Converts can be a pain in the arse. Can't stand a born-again zealot, even if they're on my side."

The marines were ominously silent but their bearing and scent said they were, to use Ade's phrase, *up for it*. There was a crisis; and they were bored, and trained precisely for times like these. For men and women who had been dismissed from their jobs, it gave them renewed focus. Ade and Eddie turned to Shan almost at the same time. Aras had begun to dread each day now, waiting for the next escalation or brand-new problem that accompanied it, and recognized the irony in a *c'naatat* worrying about the future.

Ade glanced at him, checking again, and patted his back.

He winked. *It's okay. It'll all be okay.* He'd taken over Shan's role of pretending things would be sorted out, and illusory as it was, Aras still welcomed it.

"How about the isenj?" said Jon Becken. "If I were them, I'd be shitting myself right now."

Barencoin snorted. "What, more than if the Eqbas had just razed a few of your cities to the ground and were prepping bioweapons? How much more shit can they possibly have left?"

It was none of Aras's business, but the Skavu—whatever they were—would be on Bezer'ej, and centuries of commitment to protecting the planet was impossible to switch off however betrayed he felt. What would the Skavu make of the bezeri—or him? An uneasiness echoed in him and he listened carefully to it, unsure if it was his own fear or an ancient isenj voice embedded in his genetic memory.

"The isenj react badly to the new arrivals," he said. "As *gethes* would. The fact that they can't be more doomed than they already are has no bearing on their emotions."

"I can't say I blame them," said Shan. "Where does this leave Umeh Station?"

"Yeah, I'm feeling nervous about them too, Boss." Ade's pupils were dilated and he swallowed a couple of times. The rest of the marines were looking at him as if waiting for direction. Whatever the court back on Earth had decided, Ade was still the sergeant, the pack leader, and it was a bond that wasn't easily broken. He had that certain quality, just as Shan did: when things went wrong, he stepped in and provided leadership. "We have to get the civvies out, at least. It's too unstable over there. The station wasn't designed to withstand a war going on outside the front door and if Jejeno's utilities get hit, the dome's systems can't keep up cycling power and water for that many people. It's way over capacity."

"A direct hit would ruin their entire day too," Barencoin muttered. "If the Eqbas withdraw their top cover, the dome's a nice big symbolic target."

"Come on, we've established refugee camps before," said Webster. "Just get someone to say the word. Let's get them out. It'd solve a lot more problems than it causes—keep all the Earthbound personnel in one location."

Aras had expected some of the Umeh Station party to want to stay, given that they'd taken a fifty-year round trip and abandoned everything to come to the Cavanagh system. It was a measure of the precarious situation on Umeh that there had been no argument about withdrawing. Now it was an evacuation.

"Okay, Devil's advocate," said Shan. "How are we going to support a few hundred extra bodies here when the colony on Mar'an'cas can barely feed itself? We can't ship in supplies. They can't forage or live off the land. It's not like disaster relief on Earth, Sue."

"Then they ship out with all the supplies they've got," said Webster, "and if the colonists remember all that Christian guff about helping those in need, we might manage it. If we need to. Nobody's taken that decision yet."

Shan chewed it over visibly, then swung around looking for Nevyan. She was in a huddle with the matriarchs. "Okay, let me see if Nev will change her mind about having more humans on her turf. Wait one."

Aras called after her. "We should ask Deborah Garrod's permission too."

"It's Nevyan's planet," Shan called back. "And if she says no, Deborah's view doesn't matter."

Chahal and Webster began sketching out plumbing schematics on a ragged sheet of hemp paper. They were engineers, something Aras regularly overlooked because he saw only commandos. They didn't just kill enemies. They provided humanitarian relief too. Aras had found that an odd combination until Ade explained something called "hearts and minds." Aras and his troops hadn't been much interested in the hearts or minds of the isenj colony on Bezer'ej, just their eradication.

Now he found himself thinking of eradicating the last of the bezeri, and that thought was getting persistent. It was a human one: he tried to measure it against the wess'har need for balance.

This isn't wess'har. This isn't wess'har at all.

"So, Sarge, is the missus going to let you out to play when we go to Umeh Station?" Barencoin asked. "Or are you grounded?"

"If you go, I'm going." Ade glanced at Aras. "You up for it too, mate? I know it's Umeh—"

"You should ask Shan."

Barencoin frowned, his permanent dark stubble making him look what Shan called *a right thug*. "So she's got your balls in her handbag, then. They'll be nice and safe there."

"It's called manners, Mart. Y'know, consulting your wife." Ade watched Shan walk back towards them, wistful adoration on his face for a moment. "Well, Boss?"

Shan shrugged. "Nevyan's not ecstatic, but she says yes, if we have to—it's Mar'an'cas."

"Okay, then I want to take the detachment over to Umeh Station," Ade said. Shan said nothing, or at least her mouth didn't. She simply stared eloquently. "It's my job, Boss."

Aras rallied to his house-brother. "I don't doubt the detachment's competence, but I fought the isenj and I want to go too."

Shan held her swiss in a white knuckled grip. Its status indicators flashed blue and the bioluminescence in her hands mirrored it as if answering. "You've got Esganikan's top cover. You don't need my permission, either."

"I ask anyway." Aras glanced at Barencoin, inviting comment if he dared. For a moment, he felt himself back in a larger family again, establishing the pecking order of the males. "You're always concerned for my welfare. I don't want to cause you concern."

"Aras, do you *seriously* want to go to Umeh?"

Over the years, a mix of curiosity and wanting to face his demons gripped him from time to time, but now he wanted to be with his brother, with Ade, because he was walking into a war. The time was right—inevitable.

"It might help to walk on Umeh among isenj who regard me as a monster." He didn't have to tell her the rest, but the watching marines needed explanation. He knew they discussed his time as a prisoner of war. "It can't make my memories worse, but it might temper them."

He was the Beast of Mjat, slaughterer of innocents, war criminal. And a scrap of isenj within him yearned to see home: he'd learned to live with that voice without heeding it. He saw himself as none of those things, and yet he knew they were all him.

"Okay," Shan said. "Can you spare time to talk to Deborah with me first? I need to sweet-talk her into accommodating the evacuees, and I don't do sweet-talk well."

"We can secure Umeh Station first," said Barencoin. "Then you join us."

"When we're done with the colony, we'll get a shuttle to Jejeno."

"Shooting might have started, and wess'har craft don't have Eqbas shielding," said Barencoin.

"I've been shot at on a routine basis, Mart. I know the drill." Shan glanced at the marine. "What is this, a testosterone epidemic?"

"Just anxious to do our jobs," Barencoin said. "Might be dim and distant, but we were sent here to provide protection for a civilian mission."

"I do vaguely recall *Thetis*, yes . . ." For all her sarcasm, Shan never seemed to lose her patience with the marine, even though he was what Ade called *in your face*. Respect for the detachment gave her a tolerance she rarely showed to others. "Just remember that you can die, and so can Aras and Ade, if the explosion is enough to fragment them." Her expression was oddly benign. "I came here with six marines, and I want six alive when it's time to go home. Okay?"

"We need transport," Ade said. "Makes sense if we go in with the Eqbas. *We* being the detachment."

"I'd better talk to Miss Sunshine about your first-class seats, then," said Shan. She walked a few paces away and then turned to Aras, hands in pockets. "Are you coming, sweetheart?"

They walked a few paces and then Shan turned round, went up to Ade, and kissed him unselfconsciously. That wasn't typical Shan, and certainly not in front of Ade's comrades.

"In case I'm not around when you have to ship out," she

said. "Just in case. No swanning off without saying goodbye, never again."

Ade blushed on cue. The marines looked blank in that studious way that said they didn't think the usual chorus of ribaldry was going to be funny this time. Shan turned around as if she'd suddenly realized where she was, and walked off briskly, eyes fixed ahead. Aras followed her out of the city, through the alleys at the bottom of the caldera's bowl and towards the landing area to collect a shuttle.

"Should have taken the freight tube rather than fly," she said. The network ran underground, stark carriages for moving material and produce between cities without disturbing the surface. "But it's a few hours we don't have—"

"Ade will be fine. You needn't worry."

"Okay, I didn't get to say goodbye to you before I ended up doing an EVA sans suit, and I didn't get to say goodbye to *either* of you when you went on your half-arsed let's-see-who-can-sacrifice-himself-first mission to join the bezeri." Shan rubbed her hand quickly across her nose, but she wasn't crying. She wasn't the weeping kind. "And I'm never going to risk that again. Not now. We think we might get separated—we part right. Okay?"

Aras nodded. Shan wasn't good at intimacy and it burst out of her sporadically, as if she wasn't sure how to use it. "There will be an end to this cycle of trouble, *isan*, and then we have no reason to be apart. And we'll savor boredom."

Shan paused as if sizing up the idea. "I like the sound of boredom, actually. It's a novelty in itself."

Aras flew the small shuttle to Mar'an'cas. He hadn't piloted a vessel in a long time, and his body recalled being a pilot and that he was good at it. Shan peered out of the cockpit's wraparound shield and seemed absorbed by the canyons and winding rivers that gave way to forests and eventually to coastal plains, where the island of Mar'an'cas sat staring back at Pajat.

It was just a gray rock. It seemed hard to believe that anyone could live there.

"Y'know, I've never flown over anywhere on Earth so unmarked by people," said Shan.

No roads, no scattered towns, no big cities, no iconic buildings: it was the polar opposite of Umeh in every conceivable way. Aras still felt restoration would be wholly beyond the isenj. As he brought the vessel lower, Pajat emerged suddenly in the curve of cliffs, as dully gray as F'nar was frivolously pearlescent. "This is not a world for architects."

"Maybe the Skavu will approve. Christ, it worries me that Esganikan didn't know they were showing up so soon."

"You seem to think the Eqbas should be omnipotent."

"Well, it's disconcerting to think that a million-year-old culture is as prone to bad communication, under-resourcing and getting in over their heads as the chimps back home."

"There is no such thing as continual improvement. Just change."

"Maybe I should adjust my expectations. I'm just glad I insisted on splitting the gene bank and keeping one in reserve."

Aras set the vessel down near the beach. They sat in silence, listening to the ticking of the airframe as parts cooled.

"Five years," said Shan. "It'll all be behind us. The colony, the Eqbas, Umeh Station, everyone—on their way back to Earth. Umeh—well, on the mend or a blank slate. We won't know what to do with our time, will we?"

Shan didn't mention the bezeri, or the Skavu. Aras also wondered what they might be doing in five years' time. Shan was still thinking like a creature that died within a hundred years, but it was early days for her.

"What did you have in mind for the gene bank?" he asked.

"The spare?"

"If the Earth adjustment fails, you won't commit your last resource to a second attempt."

"No, I'll hand it to the Eqbas. Perhaps they can create a terrestrial environment minus *Homo sapiens* and give every other bugger a chance." She nudged him with her elbow. "It's too big for me to think about. Right now, I'll settle for getting the colony to take on the Umeh evacuees. Tick 'em off the list one at a time."

"This is an escalating problem."

"Here's the trick," said Shan. She swung down from the cockpit. She actually seemed more cheerful today: she hadn't mentioned the abortion for a while, and she wasn't fretting openly about Rayat and Lindsay. "You reach a point where there's so much shit coming down the pipe that you can't worry or panic any longer because you have no choices to make. You just deal with what's immediate. Tactical rather than strategic level. If tactical gets too much, I default to operational. Does that make sense?"

It was police jargon. "No."

"Basically, you do what you can."

She strode down to the shallow-draft boat on the beach. Nobody else went to Mar'an'cas. It was there for them alone. Aras followed her example, and thought of his list, the *tactical* things he might do to stem the feeling of being buried in chaos and unbidden memories.

Do what you can.

He settled for accepting that his five-hundred-year vigil to keep Bezer'ej from being despoiled again had failed.

From there, things could only improve.

The Temporary City, Bezer'ej

Esganikan Gai had expected the call sooner, but the isenj were no longer working together globally. The Northern Assembly, millions of miles away on Umeh, had finally detected the Skavu fleet.

"Minister Shomen Eit wants an explanation," said Aitassi. "I didn't tell him it was too late to debate about this."

Esganikan wondered whether to tell him that Minister Rit had already asked for her immediate intervention, but the internal power struggles of the Northern Assembly cabinet didn't concern her. "If Rit intends to remove Shomen Eit to ensure the restoration goes ahead with some degree of cooperation, that will be a bonus."

There was nothing the isenj could do about it either way. Their long-range systems still fed back data, but their strike capacity was gone. In the command center cut into the rock of Bezer'ej, the Eqbas crew paused to watch the exchange. Humans, Shan said, didn't conduct critical meetings in front of an audience. Esganikan couldn't see why; the more people who saw it, the better informed everyone was, and the more chance they had to make a useful contribution.

But *gethes* didn't work that way. Earth was going to be hard work in more ways than one.

"What is this, Commander?" Shomen Eit appeared on the screen, agitated. Esganikan wasn't sure if raised quills meant anger or fear, but this certainly wasn't a relaxed isenj on her screen. The cabochon beads of green gems that tipped his quills rattled, making his gasping delivery of English harder to understand. "These look like Eqbas ships. Are you sending more support, or are you invading?"

"They are Skavu," said Esganikan. "From Garav." Did isenj have any knowledge of the system? It was so close as to be next door—a few light-weeks—but that didn't mean they had ever had contact with each other. "Garav is—"

Shomen Eit seemed to expand. His quills were now almost 90 degrees from his body. "We *know* about Garav," he said. Every word was sucked and exhaled through a hole in his throat, bypassing his own vocal system. "We have seen what you did to Garav, and many other worlds. Minister Ual was keen to show us the evidence to justify why we should cooperate with you."

"The Skavu can help you restore your planet once we give them the means."

"You give them ships and weapons, they wipe us out. Yes, I understand."

"They don't want conquest. They want balance. I don't have the troops to fight street by street with your enemies. So choose, Minister—I can deal with your planet very rapidly from orbit, or I can give you land forces who'll do a more considered job and isenj will survive."

"But they will not be under *our* command, will they? All other states are at war with us, and that small problem has to be resolved before I can worry about planting more *trees*." Shomen Eit did a very good job of spitting out the word for a creature who wasn't using lips to form sound. "So tell me what your Skavu allies can do that's *helpful*."

"Minister, your domestic affairs are your concern. What do you plan to do? Surrender?"

Shomen Eit was silent for a moment. "I have a number of options. I may have to capitulate and accept enemy terms."

"Which are?"

"As before, sever all ties with off-worlders, and join the rest of the states to rearm and remove the wess'har from this system once and for all."

"And you want Asht—Bezer'ej—back too."

"We have indeed had this conversation before."

"And your colleagues across Umeh know that you have no hope whatsoever of launching any credible assault on Wess'ej, and that once you start down that path, we will remove you from this system." Esganikan had her misgivings about Tasir Var. "Is your satellite's administration involved in this?"

"In the event of war, we would expect their full support."

"I have no more patience left, Minister." Esganikan couldn't take any more of the indecision and maneuvering. There *would* be a clear course of action at the end of the day. "Here are your options. Cooperate globally—reduce your population by three-quarters. Cooperation between the Northern Assembly and us—reduce the global population by three-quarters. Unite, declare war on Wess'ej and attempt to invade Bezer'ej—we will exterminate you all. Choose."

Shomen Eit said nothing. Without eyes to focus on or scent to guide her, Esganikan felt unsettled. But the choice was made: the Northern Assembly couldn't get cooperation from the rest of Umeh, so its only option was to stand alone and accept Eqbas military intervention.

Nobody would choose to fight in those circumstances.

The Northern Assembly could survive with a single choice, and its neighbors would not.

Esganikan felt time dying; every day now, she was more aware of the empty minutes and the time she would never be able to relive. It was more than impatience. She felt robbed.

It was time to decide. The choice was obvious. "You

agreed to our restoration. We offered you nonlethal methods of reducing your numbers. I have no more time to give to this when I have other worlds with more pressing needs."

Shomen Eit was completely still.

"Then," he said, "I regret that I must join my fellow isenj and prepare for war."

The communications officer, Hayin, following the English conversation with difficulty, bent down to catch a translation from Aitassi. He bobbed up again and tilted his head in amazement. "Insane," he said.

Esganikan had almost expected it, given the isenj history of fighting when guaranteed defeat. But it still surprised her. It was, as Hayin said, an insane choice.

But they had made it.

"Then we have nothing further to discuss," said Esganikan.

She closed the link. Nobody offered an opinion. The command center was silent except for the occasional tick of monitoring systems and the sigh of air from the vents.

"For a race of engineers, they appear extraordinarily unable to grasp reality," she said.

"I think the Skavu made up their minds." Hayin ran his hands over the console and checked channels. "What happened to Minister Rit?"

"Either she's been forced to abandon her coup, or she'll contact us very soon."

At least Esganikan had a clear objective now. She'd never done the full erasure of a world before: there had been so very few in history. She might need a little advice and information from Surang, but she had the bioweapons, and it was simply a matter of organizing their distribution and delivery.

Then she could focus on Earth, on talking to the Australian hosts, refining and modeling the Earth mission. There was surprisingly little time left before the main task force reached the rendezvous point: less than five years, during which she also had to ensure Bezer'ej wasn't heading for disaster. *Infected bezeri. A complication, but not a disaster, not caught this early.* "At least the Skavu's journey won't be wasted."

The mood in the command center was somber, and she understood that. She looked around at the disappointed faces, and inhaled the agitation scents she expected. Nobody enjoyed erasing a planet. It was an admission of defeat for professional restorers, and it also meant billions of deaths.

"In generations to come," she said, trying to soothe them, "we may have a world on which to revive the Earth gene bank. Shan Frankland doesn't trust humans to look after the first one well."

"Full erasure and repopulation has only been done once," Aitassi said.

"Depending on how the Earth adjustment mission goes, it may have to be done *twice.*" Esganikan walked to the door. "I was wrong to try to reconcile two objectives. Security for Wess'ej and Bezer'ej were the priorities, the isenj request for help distracted me. Isenj will resent wess'har as long as they exist. Their genetic memory ensures it. I apologize for my lack of clarity."

The air group commander, Joluti, opened the link to the Skavu fleet and stood waiting with an expectant expression on his face. The silence of the command center vanished and was filled by the hum and trill of voices.

"You still haven't spoken to them yet, *chail,*" said Joluti. "Now would be advisable."

"They're far too keen," she said. "I should talk to Canh Pho. I haven't had a conversation with the Australians for some time."

It was simply the past demanding too much attention. The past couldn't be changed, and so had to be learned from and then put away, and only allowed to touch the present if it could improve it. Memories of the war on Garav didn't improve Esganikan's present day at all.

"And Shan Frankland has called for you twice," Hayin said. "She wants to know if we can transport the personnel from Umeh Station. Under the circumstances, we must."

Shan. There was always that bright obsessive light in her face that was also in the eyes of the Skavu. They might find some common ground, but they would need to have *c'naatat* explained to them carefully, and be ordered not to interfere.

"Yes." It was one less complication to consider on Umeh, anyway. "Tell her she has to be ready to do it as soon as we've briefed the Skavu."

Sooner or later, she had to face them again. Perhaps this was how Aras Sar Iussan felt when he met Minister Ual. It was hard to look at the present and not see the faces from the past.

"You want them to land?"

Esganikan thought of infected bezeri, and discussions not had with Earth, and work not done, and more time wasted. At least she hadn't taken any casualties. The list of tasks was growing and intertwining. Yes, the Skavu might be a blessing after all. She let herself feel guilty relief.

"Give them permission," she said. "And deploy a remote to look for signs of the bezeri on land."

She wandered the passages of the Temporary City to ease the kinks in her muscles, passing groups of ussissi who had far too little to do at the moment before seeking refuge in Shapakti's laboratory. He was huddled over a table deep in conversation with Mohan Rayat, apparently oblivious to the ear-splitting screeches of the two macaws who had been penned temporarily in one half of the room with a sheet of mesh. They liked company.

"Umeh has declared war on us," she said.

Rayat looked up. "Will you notice?"

"I don't do this lightly, Doctor." Did he even understand what it meant? "They'll all die."

Rayat blinked. Shapakti was watching him, not her, evidently fascinated.

"You believe in clearing the decks, then."

"You have seen the condition of Umeh?"

"Oh yes. I was at Umeh Station for a while. Until Minister Ual had me abducted with Commander Neville so he could offer us to placate the wess'har." Rayat pushed a pad of composite towards Shapakti. It was covered in symbols: they seemed to be exchanging writing systems. "Don't forget that Ual traded us as war criminals for Wess'ej's help to make Umeh a nicer neighborhood."

Rayat didn't reveal information randomly. He wasn't the

chatty type, Shan had said. Esganikan needed to discuss his future with Shapakti when the current operation was finished.

"You appear to be a man in demand, then," she said. "You seem to be working."

"I'm very motivated to remove this parasite," said Rayat. "As long as I carry it, I'll always be something of a commodity."

At least Shapakti smelled content for the moment. He missed his family: he was one of the few Eqbas here who had one, and he would have been home long ago had his survey ship not been diverted to go to F'nar's aid. It was good to see him distracted by something that he relished.

"It's remarkable to work with a scientist from so different a world," he said. "We make a good team."

"I won't delay you, then," said Esganikan.

"I'll never be short of time." Rayat grinned, an expression that always seemed hostile and predatory. "You know, if *c'naatat* had been something humans could have used responsibly, it would have been very useful for deep-space missions. Imagine. No longer confined by our lifespan." He turned back to the sheet of eqbas'u lettering, showing no sign of being a man either on a military mission or worried about his future.

Esganikan thought over his comment as she walked back to the command center.

I know what you're doing.

You want to interest me in c'naatat *for some reason.*

Esganikan tried hard to grasp human motivation but without an interpreter—Shan, Eddie, even Aras—she could only make wild guesses, based on the oblique nature of human speech. Rayat was more oblique than most: he would try to fool her. She had no idea why or how.

But he was pushing her towards something.

She'd work it out. She would do it herself, too, with no help from Shan. She needed to understand humans better before she reached Earth, humans who weren't almost wess'har in outlook, like Shan, or completely open, like Ade Bennett.

When she stepped into the command center, Hayin was waiting anxiously, wafting agitation. He tapped his console and pointed at the main communications screen.

"She's been waiting," he said. "I told her you would be back soon."

Minister Rit's distinctive amber beads shimmered on the tips of her quills: her ussissi interpreter, Ralassi, was at her side.

"Commander," he said. "The Minister urges you to think again. Help her remove Shomen Eit, and restoration *will* happen."

The island known as Chad, now called the Dry Above Where We Do Not Wish To Be

Leaving the ocean for the land wasn't a matter to be rushed.

Lindsay wondered if she'd placed too much faith in *c'naatat*'s capacity to transform. She watched Saib, Keet, and two of the more adventurous bezeri who'd accepted *c'naatat* via a lump of her blood and skin, struggling with the novel concept of construction ashore.

She hacked away at branches with one of the razor-edged pieces of hard slate, finding it tough going. Chad's vegetation didn't behave like trees on Earth; the large plants were remarkably similar to the *efte* trees of Constantine island at the top of the chain, whose trunks made of layer upon layer of core like a mille-feuille pastry. They grew as fast as fungus and at the end of the season their sticky, silver fronds and flosslike seed-bodies drooped to the ground and the whole tree decomposed and rotted down to liquid, leaving a dark patch in the soil that sprouted again the next season.

It was a useful tree. The Constantine colonists set aside time in autumn to gather the peeling bark and harvest the trunks before the annual rot set in, and turned the fiber into everything from fabric, twine and paper to felted material and hard laminate bonded with the natural glue from the *efte*'s own seeds. Maybe this plant would be the same. Lindsay peeled off long strips and considered weaving a shelter rather than building one from timber.

"Is hard," said Keet.

"Not hard enough, I'm afraid." She rapped the strips with her knuckles, producing silence. "Let's rethink this. No rigid structures."

"Mud," said Keet.

Lindsay stared at his mottled dark mantle, looking for recognition of a person. *Will that be me one day? Will I find that attractive?* "Yes, you're used to mud."

It was like talking to a haiku. Did he mean the wood needed to be hard, or that the task was difficult? Was he saying he preferred building from hardened mud or that they could use mud here?

"Wattle and daub," she said, thinking aloud.

Saib and the others—Carf and Maipay—swung on crutch-legs between the trees and broke off stalks, mimicking her attempts to cut branches. Maybe if she showed them, they'd get the idea and make a better job of it than she could. Her camping skills ran to field exercises and pilot survival training. Bezeri were highly skilled engineers and artisans, and it wasn't beyond them to learn the technique—or even devise a new one.

Lindsay sliced strips of *efte* bark into wide ribbons and laid them on a clear patch of soil as the warp and then wove narrower ones through them as the weft. It made a loose lattice, and she beckoned the bezeri over to see it.

"Weaving," she said.

Then she pounded soil and water in a large shell to create mud, and smeared it across the woven strips. Their collective gasping and belching of air indicated either surprise or revelation. Saib was a sudden kaleidoscope of deep purple and amber lights pulsing across his mantle, easily visible in the dappled shade of the clearing.

"We understand," he announced in that grave, bubbling voice. "We do this."

Whether it was a statement of intention or an indication that bezeri knew how to weave, or that they used wattle and daub techniques—and how their hard mud cities underwater were made, she had no idea—wasn't clear. All she knew was that the four of them began clambering over the vegetation, pulling down branches and fronds, tentacles thrashing.

It became clear very soon: they'd worked out how to build shelters, although their solution was more spider than squid. They began stringing the branches they could reach with strips of bark, knotting them together with rapid and remarkably precise tentacle movements and lacing them across spaces. The structure began to look like webs.

Carf—still translucent, with none of the dark mottling that marked Keet—shuffled to the base of one of the trees and launched two tentacles into its branches, getting a grip and testing them. Then he hauled himself aloft, hesitant at first and then climbing the tree, which creaked under his weight and bent slightly. He settled near the top and appeared to be looking around at the view.

"Far," he said. "Far and clear. And *bright*."

Lindsay tried to imagine how brilliantly lit and sharply defined the word of the Dry Above was to them after a lifetime moving between filtered sunlight and pitch black. Their ancestors had risked death, sometimes with the certainty of it, to beach themselves to gain glimpses of the dry land and report back on what they could see. Bezeri could flop onto dry land by riding a strong wave and usually get back to the water, but the further they went, the more likely they were to be stranded. It was a hostile environment, a world of strangeness and novelty, not one to be lived in. It was like space to them. Now they were walking unaided in the unknown void, and still alive.

Just like Shan Frankland.

Lindsay imagined those who beached too far inland and knew they had undertaken a suicide mission. They would have light-signaled their information back to those waiting and watching in the shallows. She imagined them not panicking and screaming green in their final moments, but relaying all the impressions they could before they died, thinking it a worthwhile sacrifice.

They were just curious. They never knew they'd have to do this for real one day.

The four bezeri were mixing mud now, slapping it on the mesh of woven bark and working it smooth with a skill that told her they were expert plasterers. So this was how they shaped their mud cities. They'd made the transition, although it was one they didn't have ambitions to make. It wouldn't be long before others decided to choose *c'naatat*, if only to stay with the last of their comrades, and then they'd be able to begin building a new civilization. For all she knew, *c'naatat* might even make them fertile again. It seemed able to fix pretty well anything.

"You know what we're going to do?" she said. Three of the bezeri stopped weaving and plastering, but Carf seemed obsessed with his task and worked feverishly. "We'll go back to Constantine and find the memorials your ancestors erected on the beach. The ones to the memories of the land pioneers."

"Memory of the First, Memory of the Returned," said Saib. Those were more or less the inscriptions on the rocks they'd made and somehow moved up the incline to the beach to mark the places where the first bezeri explorers had left the water—one to die in the attempt, the other the first to return.

"Exactly. Maybe you need a memorial here, too. To the Changed. Except you'll always be alive to see them."

Lindsay wasn't sure if they fully understood that *c'naatat* would keep them alive indefinitely. She wasn't even sure herself, because despite the prodigious feats of repair that the parasite had managed so far, the most she knew was that Aras had survived a little over five hundred years. Whether that boded immortality or not—she'd take that as it came.

The bezeri *were* changing before her eyes, though. Their bulky bodies were wobbling less each time they thudded to the ground, as if their mantles were strengthening and thickening, making them more rigid and more suited to a land animal. They were getting faster and more agile. Even Saib could loop his way up a tree now, looking for all the world like an obese glass gibbon.

Lindsay was so absorbed by the spectacle of tree-climbing squid that the two years of misery on this planet had been pushed to the side of her mind, if not to the back. She stood back to contemplate the mud-daubed orbs of bark webbing they'd strung from the trees: no, not spiders—these reminded her of warblers and their little basket nests threaded precariously on reeds. It was a truly bizarre image.

I've seen the birth of a new civilization. Now that's something. That really is.

It occurred to her that the unspoiled clearing was now very spoiled indeed, with broken and crushed undergrowth from the bezeri's clumsy progress and the debris of their first construction attempts. This wasn't an idyll that the wess'har would admire. They built discreetly, anxious not to be seen, never wanting to intrude too far on the natural landscape if at all. She'd started to change the face of the planet itself, and it was a dubious honor.

It didn't matter that the bezeri came from a line of genocidal conquerors. They'd paid their debt by being nearly exterminated not once but twice—once by the careless pollution of the isenj colonists here, and then . . . then by her and Mohan Rayat.

Where are you now, you bastard? I hope the Eqbas beat the shit out of you before they found a way to kill you. They'd never let you live.

But Rayat didn't matter now. One thing that Lindsay knew she needed in order to stay sane was a mission, a focus, and now she had another one. There was always something she could add to the list.

I haven't thought of David.

Guilt pinched at her gut, and it was true. She could now go for most of a day without thinking of her child. When you wanted nothing more than for the pain to stop, it was disturbing to find that when it did, another crushing emotion waiting to take its place. But she had a real base now, a place that she would inevitably have to call home: she'd make time to retrieve the rest of the stained-glass gravestone on Constantine, exhume David's body, and bring him here. Then she could have closure. *Then* she could have a point in the day that she kept for him, neat and controlled, so that the rest of the day could be for the living she had to do, and she wouldn't feel she had robbed him of existence in her memory as well.

She walked out of the stand of trees and onto the open

heath—pale, gray and taupe vegetation dotted with small spindly brown bushes—to look back at the new settlement. If the bezeri went back to the sea tonight, that was fine. They'd be back on land in the morning, she knew it. And then she had to come to terms that this wasn't just colonization, replicating old towns in new lands, but a whole evolution, the transition from aquatic life to terrestrial; then they had to move from paleothic to industrial as soon as they could, so they'd never be anyone's victims again.

They or we? What am I now, and what do I have to be to feel at home with them?

She was wondering how much of her resolve was thanks to the legacy of Shan Frankland that *c'naatat* had brought with it, and comforting herself with the thought that it probably was all her own, when the ground beneath her feet felt softer. She thought it was wet and looked down to see mud oozing up between her toes; and then she fell, or so she thought. She was standing, though, still upright but lower, and she realized she was in bog, and sinking. She flailed her arms instinctively for a moment until her survival training took over.

I can't drown. Just have to stay calm. She was doing well to get that far. *Should have learned from Constantine— should have looked for the firm ground, the mats of vegetation, the organic roads.*

There was a routine for this, she knew. She thought of Ade Bennett, once her utterly reliable Royal Marines sergeant, and how he'd rescued Sabine Mesevy from a bog much like this.

Lindsay was still rehearsing the procedure in her mind, remembering to work her way onto her back and spread her arms and legs as if floating, feeling the thick slurry of vegetation sucking at her legs when she tried to lift them, when something as glittering and as glassy as she was caught her eye.

She glanced at it, and realized that *sheven* were more widespread than she imagined. She screamed, wondering why the sound emerged as rippling green light.

6

The question is not can they reason, nor can they talk, but can they suffer?

JEREMY BENTHAM (1748–1832) on animals

Mar'an'cas island, Wess'ej

Shan squinted against the spray flying from the bow of the skimmer and decided that island penal colonies probably looked the same anywhere in the galaxy.

It was a far cry from the bucolic Constantine colony. She recalled landing on Bezer'ej in her biohaz suit, scared of bringing contagion to an isolated world, and marveling at the incredible color and variety of natural life around her. But Mar'an'cas was as gray as the sea on this overcast day, and she knew it would live up to that image when she landed. She'd been here before. She hoped they'd improved the sewage arrangements since then.

Aras steered the skimmer with distracted ease, holding one hand above the control column occasionally to correct the course. Shan knelt at the bow, one hand on the gunwale to keep her balance.

"You're not worried about going back there, are you?" she said.

He glanced at her as if he'd been lost in thought and suddenly realized she was there. "Why should I?"

"No red carpet."

"They can't harm me. Last time, they seemed less hostile."

"Doing a bit of forgiving to get them into heaven, no doubt."

"Forgiveness is hard. I can't criticize them for what I can't do myself."

Aras never pulled his punches. Not even a century and

more living among humans and a solid dose of human genes had curbed his wess'har frankness. She waited for him to go on, but he didn't.

"What can't you forgive, Aras? Me?"

He jerked his head around sharply. "The bezeri."

"Because they didn't tell you their ancestors were mass murderers and general arseholes?"

"I shouldn't be influenced by that, because later generations aren't responsible."

"Welcome to the illogical world of human prejudice."

Shan had her own bias, she knew. She couldn't remember quite when she'd started disliking the colonists, but she had. It made no sense; they were ecologically responsible, they'd have been totally harmless without Lindsay bloody Neville and that bastard Rayat, and they were taking the gene bank back to Earth after generations of keeping it out of the hands of scumbag corporations. The only thing that made her different from them was their imaginary divine friend.

I know you don't exist, because where I've been, I'd have seen you. I wish you did. A bit of justice, a few thunderbolts and smitings, and we wouldn't be in the shit we're in now. That's what we need God for.

"Are you all right?"

Shan wiped spray from her face. "Fine."

"Your lips were moving. You're arguing with someone again."

"It's okay," she said, embarrassed at the lapse. "Not the first time. Won't be the last."

Aras ran the skimmer up the shingle beach, passing through the invisible biobarrier that puckered the skin on Shan's arms, and she tried to jump out with Ade's nonchalant ease. Again, she failed and splashed into the shallows, and despite all that she'd endured the discomfort really bothered her. *It's just wet boots. You sucked vacuum for three months, for Chrissakes. You got shot in the head. You cut your own guts open. Get a grip.* She squelched up the beach, wondering for a moment if she'd picked up some genetic contamination and that *c'naatat* had once passed through a bloody whining civilian.

Deborah Garrod, hair flying in the stiff breeze, stood at the top of the shingle bank with a battered padded hemp coat pulled tight around her.

"How are the parrots?" she said.

Deborah—impossibly thin now, a little doll of a woman—was clearly still very taken with Shapakti's blue and gold macaws, the only higher animals he'd resurrected from the gene bank to see if it could be done.

"Squawking in eqbas'u." Shan smiled as best she could. "I still can't see how he'll ever release them into the wild when the task force reaches Earth."

"You'd be amazed what's possible."

Don't say with faith. "Amaze me with your capacity to find room for between three and four hundred extra bodies, then."

"Oh." Deborah only blinked. She held out her hand to Aras and grasped his arm with all the joy of seeing a precious friend again, rather than the man who had decapitated her husband. Shan never ceased to wonder at the gamut of human reactions. "That would be Umeh Station."

"The situation's getting too risky in Jejeno. We're prepping to evac."

Shan cast a discreet eye over the temporary camp. It still looked like a holiday resort that had chosen a very bad location but had decided to tough it out. Blue and green jacquard-type fabric tents flapped and snapped in the constant breeze, a comfort provided by the matriarchs of Pajat. She'd had never seen a calm sunny day here.

"How many, exactly?"

"Three hundred and sixty, last count," said Aras. "An engineer died—a heart attack."

Shan wondered how the station would deal with the body. It was a pragmatic copper's thought and she was glad to see some of her old self making a comeback. *Do what you can.* "I thought they had three hundred."

"They didn't include all the service personnel in the tally they gave the isenj."

"How can you *not* have an accurate head count in a sealed environment?"

"Are you worried by that?" asked Aras.

Deborah was almost forgotten for the moment as they crunched up the pebbles and picked their way through the sharp bristles of airforce blue tufted grass. "I don't like unknowns. I don't like not knowing how many bodies we have over there." *No, not "we." Not your problem.* "I'll do my own tally when we get there, then."

"No matter," said Deborah. "It's temporary. A few years at most before we go home."

So it was *home* now. But Deborah had been born on Bezer'ej. So had her mother, and her grandmother, and a few more branches back up the tree if Shan could be arsed to count them. The woman adapted fast: nothing fazed her, not even a twenty-five-year journey to a world she'd never seen—not even being widowed and dumped on this miserable rock. Shan found herself mentally scoring the shit points, comparing Deborah's traumas to her own to see if she was coping as well as the colonist.

And Aras killed her husband, decapitated him in front of a crowd of colonists. Jesus, did Deborah see him do it? I never asked.

Aras walked a little ahead of them through the paths between the carefully aligned rows of tents as if letting the two women have space to talk.

"Nobody's ever returned from extrasolar deployments to Earth except from flight missions and orbitals, and they've only been gone ten years or less," Shan said. "Nobody's come back from a colony before. Not born off-world, living among aliens, separated for generations. Are you going to be ready for this?"

Deborah actually laughed even though she had nothing much to laugh about."Of course I'm ready for it," she said. "We've spent our lives here preparing for this. That was our mission, to keep the gene bank safe and wait until the time was right to return it to Earth and restore the world God gave us."

She always said that kind of thing with such utter sincerity that the hair on Shan's nape prickled. Deborah was a real frontier woman, the kind who could feed an army with two dead rats and a cup of flour, the essence of no-nonsense pragmatism: but then she'd go off into this strange realm of the unseen and unproven with such a plausible manner that Shan had to stop hard at the edge of that cliff to avoid plummeting with her.

Motive doesn't matter. Just actions. Don't argue with her.

"Does this feel like the right time to you, Deborah?"

"When the only civilization that could resurrect the species in the bank shows up, and also happens to be able to return us to Earth, and make those events happen, what does that tell you?" She looked at Shan as if she was a slow child who needed extra help to cope with big ideas. "It feels like the only time to me."

Shan felt her lips part and an involuntary exercise in logic start to form on them when Aras glanced casually over his shoulder and said, *"Bar'hainte, isan."* Don't do it, wife: shut it, Frankland.

She heeded the warning. The macaws had *really* done the miracle trick for Deborah. Shan, who saw the pearl of F'nar for the insect shit it really was, and found the reassuring but unlovely reality in everything, knew she would never see the miracles that Deborah did, just wretched causality.

"You're probably right there," Shan said, catching Aras's eye on the next glance. "I never asked, but if the Eqbas provided the means to recreate living specimens from the genetic material, does that mean you didn't have that technology when you embarked?"

"No."

"That's . . . unusually optimistic."

"We knew that it would be available in the future when the time came to return."

"I see." Shan bit her lip. *How can people be competent enough to plan a deep space mission, but so completely fucking naive that they gamble on technology turning up out of nowhere?* "Well, that's a bit of luck, then, isn't it?"

Shan reminded herself that Deborah had never locked a door in her life. Yes, she *was* bloody lucky. On a cosmic scale, it was a trillion-to-one shot . . . no, the gene bank had *caused* the chain of events that eventually brought the Eqbas Vorhi into the game. God didn't shape events like that. If he engineered all those deaths and the intervention of an army that made Genghis Khan look like a day-tripper, instead of just thunderbolting some environmental sense into mankind the Old Testament way, then God was a sick bastard. She couldn't be bothered to believe in a sadist.

The discussion faded into silence. They walked through the camp, and Shan decided she'd have staggered the lines of the tents to stop that bloody wind being funneled through. The site was clean and tidy, but the smell of shit still pervaded the air.

"Is that your composting system?" she asked. "Because if you're having trouble with the latrines, the marines can help you out there."

"Both," Deborah said.

On either side of the path there was little activity in the tents, as if the place had been abandoned. There was nobody around to hurl rocks at Aras or call her a heathen murderer anyway, and she realized the copper in her had expected it because she had relegated these colonists to the status of a mob. It was only when she passed beyond the tent city that she could see the colonists busy in the fields.

Fields was a generous word for the land. It wasn't a fertile place. It was a rock.

Somehow, though, they'd built up soil and enriched it in a matter of months. The transparent composite tunnels rescued from Constantine and the *Thetis* camp were hazy with blurred greenery and shapes of beige-coated people working in them. The visible soil looked respectably clear of stones. It must have taken the colonists most of their waking day to transform this grim rock into something approaching a viable farm is so short a time.

Shan wandered past Aras and picked her way between shallow furrows that were speckled with emerging green leaves. Broad beans: she'd grown them too, and hoed onions on Constantine, and broken up frozen lumps of soil during the brief months when she thought her days would be spent with Aras in exile with a bunch of Christians she liked but—as a Pagan, lapsed or otherwise—she could never truly identify with.

She stared down. Ade would be annoyed at her for getting mud caked on the boots he'd gone to such lengths to find for her. She hoped it was mud, anyway.

"You're going to wait until the Eqbas fleet shows up in a few years, or are you heading back with *Thetis*?" she asked.

"The sooner we start, the better." Deborah walked over to Aras and patted him gently on the back. Shan didn't like that familiarity, innocent as it was. "So we wait for the faster ships."

"So . . . you're sure you can handle a few hundred extra mouths for a while."

"Yes, but it would be better if they have dry supplies they can bring too."

"I bet Ade's got that in hand." She'd check anyway. She didn't believe in *surely*. "Remember all these people are useful—fit, competent, craft skills too. They built a biodome. They can earn their keep while they're here."

"I was sold already, Shan. We can't turn away people who need refuge."

Shan had forgotten the persuasive power of Christian duty. But it seemed a dirty trick to exploit their commandments. Aras just tilted his head and gave her a sad doglike look that could have been anything from adoration to relief that she hadn't started arguing theology with them. His scent, or as much as penetrated the fecal stench of fertilizer, was blandly content but his preoccupied expression said otherwise. She really had got out of the habit of filtering out farming smells in F'nar. Wess'har processed sewage in very different ways.

"Okay, Deborah. Thanks. We'll ship out all the solar kit that we can lift, too." Shan squatted down to admire the seedlings battling through the dark soil and decided that she'd spend more time with the crops back at home when the situation settled. No: sod it, she'd start as soon as the evacuation was completed. Having endless time was no excuse for wasting it. "It'd be really kind if you could keep the Booties busy here for a while too."

"Booties . . . oh yes. Marines. Certainly."

"They weren't welcome last time, I recall," said Aras quietly, his tone always the more pointed for being mild. "Which is a pity."

"I'll make sure they're treated courteously this time if they come."

Aras walked over to the composite tunnels, squelching mud along the margin of the field. He leaned inside, ducking his head, and then came out again almost immediately.

Poor sod: he missed all this. A life he'd shared with the colonists for generations had ended abruptly and brutally. But then it had ended that way for Josh Garrod, too, and Shan suddenly missed him even though she hardly knew him. What a stupid, senseless waste: what a fucking inexplicable thing for a level-headed farmer to do, to decide that a microscopic organism was the work of the devil and so it was okay to help some spook nuke an island to drive out the demon. Medieval, irrational, superstitious.

That was why motive still mattered. Sometimes it was an early warning system for lunacy.

And I frag an infected bezeri, and what does that make me? Shan sought the line between what she might do and what Lindsay had done, and couldn't find anything other than the range of collateral damage. It was one of those fragile moments when she had a real insight into the impossible nature of ethical logic, and that it was an Escher staircase that apparently led somewhere but couldn't exist.

"Where are Lindsay and Dr. Rayat now?" Deborah asked. Shan flinched: it was an inevitable question but the timing felt like telepathy. "We do still pray for them."

"Lin has . . . changed a lot. And living with the bezeri, we assume. Rayat turned himself in. Wasn't cut out for being a valued member of squid society."

"What are you going to do about him?"

Shan wished she knew. He should have been fragmented into hamburger by now. She'd never had problems about killing in the past, not like normal coppers, and she was sure she didn't have any now, not when she could still taste the pulsing rage rising in her throat when she'd set about kicking the shit out of Rayat on a cell floor. She'd have killed him then, all right, *shit* yes. Something had diverted her. Something had dulled both her motive and her anger.

It was always about justice.

"He says he now believes *c'naatat* has to be kept out of human hands," she said. "But as he's a pathological frigging liar, who knows? Esganikan's left him with Shapakti to play with. I hope he shoves a few probes up his arse while I'm away."

Deborah looked down at her feet for a second, and Shan remembered she'd never sworn in front of the Garrods. "Apart from your views on deception, you're more alike than you think."

Perhaps I'm hoping Shapakti really will *do some useful research on removing* c'naatat.

"He's certainly persistent," said Shan.

"He believes he's serving his state."

So he ended up nearly exterminating a genocidal race. If I was Deborah, I'd see a bit of divine intervention there, too.

"Everyone in a war does," said Shan. "Still doesn't mean there aren't two sides of the story."

If Deborah said *forgiveness* next, Shan resolved to swing for her, even if the woman was half her weight and a lot shorter. That was fine for *her*. She could tell herself any lies she wanted about days of reckoning and turning cheeks and all that shit, but Shan looked at the here and now, and at Aras. At that moment, he erased everything around her: he held his head tilted slightly on one side in that wess'har gesture of curiosity, dark braid coiled into his collar, so alien and lonely and guileless that she wanted to forget the bloody colonists and the Umeh crew and, *yes,* even the gene bank, and protect him—ferociously, totally, without reservation. It was a powerful and ambushing emotion. It was as strong as anger. Nothing had ever trumped her rage before.

I forgot you. I forgot who you were. I forgot you were the last thought I had as I died.

But she wasn't dead, and Aras had his own anguish. She walked the few meters to the crop tunnel and slipped her arm through his, pulling him away as discreetly as she could. He looked puzzled, head tilting further, but followed her.

"'Bye, Deborah," Shan said. "I'll be in touch, but expect the evacuees any time."

"Can I ask for a favor?" That was unusual for Deborah. "Is there any chance of an ITX link? I'd like to make contact with the churches back home."

Normally Shan would have automatically heard the ringing of unspecific alarms, but Esganikan was right: it made no difference now what humans said to Earth.

"Certainly." *I'm going soft.* "Can't promise you'll get through the queue for the portal at the Earth end, but I'll get you the kit."

"Giyadas would enjoy showing you how to use it," said Aras. "The matriarch's child."

Shan had promised her a visit to Mar'an'cas to see the *gethes* in their unnatural habitat. Good old Deborah: she'd keep the marines busy and amuse Giyadas. That was worth paying for with an ITX link.

Deborah left them to walk back through the camp on their own, as if confident that none of the colonists they might run into would embarrass her by being overtly hostile. There were no baleful stares this time, and few people out and about to deliver them. The sound of running feet behind her made Shan spin around and her hand was already reaching down the back of her belt for her 9mm when she checked herself on seeing someone she recognized.

"Shan!" A woman called Sabine Mesevy—Dr. Mesevy, botanist Mesevy, former payload Mesevy—came pounding up to her with a package in her hand. "Shan, wait."

Shan dropped her arms to her side, wondering why *c'naatat* didn't override that reflex to draw a gun. "It's been a long time, Doctor."

Mesevy, hair scraped back and pinned, rough brown working clothes showing signs of fraying, thrust the package in Shan's direction. She'd found God back on Bezer'ej, a more likely location for a Pauline revelation than Reading Metro.

"Here," she said. "I never did it. I never thanked Ade for saving my life. This is for him. Pickles."

"I'm sure he'll love that. Thanks."

"I'll never forget him."

But she'd done a pretty good job at the time. Ade had ignored his own fear—fear enough to make him shit himself and throw up—to haul her out of bog with a *sheven* on the hunt. Maybe time spent in quiet prayer made you realize why you were still breathing and who you owed your life to.

"It was quite a feat," said Shan. It was the moment she found she wanted a modest, earnest, slightly awkward marine sergeant called Adrian Bennett, and was embarrassed by her own human weakness. "But those blokes free-fall from high orbit, so all in a day's work, eh?"

"Thank him for me."

"Will do."

Shan wasn't managing *gracious* today. She could do it with a following wind but these days the impatient, tactless wess'har component of her was ganging up with her own lack of diplomacy to vent her frustration about things she couldn't even name. She shoved the hemp-wrapped jar in her pocket and strode on towards the shore with Aras at her heels.

He went to push the skimmer back into the water, offering no comment as she took out the jar and examined the carefully tied bow of *efte* twine.

"I find Deborah's attitude to you totally—unnatural," she said at last.

"Why?"

"Because if anyone harmed you, I'd kill them. That's all there is to it." She stepped into the shallow draft vessel and settled down in the stern. *Don't upset the trim.* "Just imagine faith that strong."

"Strong enough to take *you* twenty-five light-years from home without consciously knowing why?"

Aras could never quite manage a human smile, but when he was amused or pleased it was obvious. He beamed, for want of a better word, radiating satisfaction for a moment. Maybe it was the relaxation in his facial muscles and some infrasonics she'd ceased to notice consciously. The skimmer moved astern at his touch and then came about to head out of the rocky cover and into open water.

"I knew why I took a one-way ticket," she said. "Suppressed Briefings are conscious, whatever people think. The drug stopped me recalling the information until I came across the right trigger, but it's not like having no intellectual proof of something."

"Do you still resent Eugenie Perault for sending you on this mission under false pretenses?"

"They were only false for her, sweetheart. I found the gene bank and it's going *home*. Well, part is. I wouldn't sleep well if we didn't have a duplicate."

Aras paused. "I miss Josh."

He was suddenly back to his unsettled self of recent weeks. It hadn't been a good idea to bring him here; and that didn't bode well for a trip to Umeh. It was heartbreaking to hear him say it.

"Don't start beating yourself up," said Shan. "Whatever we know now doesn't change the fact that he played an active role in detonating nuclear devices. There's no way I can color that innocent."

"My pain is that I'd do the same again even though I also regret it. And you?"

"And me . . . what?"

"Would you step out the airlock again?"

It was the kind of grand gesture that beatified you and didn't require an encore. She was conscious of the grenade in her jacket pocket. But the fact that she *could* finish herself off properly gave her a whole new layer of moral dilemmas that almost no other human would ever experience.

Her job was to keep it that way. It always would be.

"It's easier to do that than to shove someone else out into space." She edged up to the bow and stood to put her arm around his waist. *Sod the trim.* The skimmer rocked briefly: they couldn't drown, so it didn't matter. "And that tells me that I care more about you than solving the *c'naatat* problem once and for all."

"The soil-dwelling *c'naatat* organisms survived the bombing, and now the bezeri are infected. Killing me and Ade would solve nothing."

"I was actually saying that I love you two and I'd rather

take my own life than yours, uncharacteristically mushy as that might seem."

"I realize you find it hard to express emotions."

"I'm fine with anger and being pissed off."

"It was an act of kindness to allow the colony an ITX link, too."

She hadn't asked Nevyan. She ought to, she knew. "No reason to refuse. I'm buying goodwill."

The colony's homebound transmissions were no different from Eddie's broadcasts, and she didn't vet those any more. She hadn't any idea of the full content that he filed to BBChan daily except that if it was controversial, he'd show her first.

Eddie had always understood the catalytic nature of reporting, that it shaped and changed as much as it stood back and observed. In some ways, he had a harder job than she did. Her purpose was usually effortlessly clear. In a world of gray areas, she had always been able to find black and white, until she came to the Cavanagh system.

"The colonists are harmless," Aras said. "If all humans lived carefully because they were afraid of eternal damnation, then Earth would have no problems."

"You must have some God-bothering genes in you, sweetheart."

"God, real or not, drives many humans, so I take it into account."

Shan wondered if God drove Helen Marchant, whose family link to devout Eugenie Perault she didn't know about until Eddie told her. Helen, whose arse she covered and whose terror operation she shielded because—copper or not—she thought it was moral.

And I still do.

Yes, maybe it was time she returned her message.

And thank you for Helen.

That bitch Perault hadn't slipped *that* into her Suppressed Briefing. Shan always had the feeling that there was still more data to be triggered and unleashed, an itch at the back of her mind that she couldn't scratch, but it was probably her wounded pride at being stiffed for once by a politician.

"Bastard," she said, and meant pretty well everyone.

F'nar: Nevyan Tan Mestin's home

There was a fleet of new aliens in the system and nobody would ship Eddie Michallat out to see them.

He was furious. He wasn't sure why it aggravated him, because nobody else was going to get the story either: he was the only journalist in 150 trillion miles.

He went in search of Shan or anyone he could cajole into taking him to see the Skavu. The insistent inner voice that told him that News Desk would rip him a new one if he didn't get the story had suddenly emerged again, long after he'd been certain that he didn't give a shit. What were they going to do, fire him?

From this terrace level, he could see Ade and Qureshi heading towards the Exchange. They were prepping to evacuate Umeh Station: the Skavu would be deployed on Umeh. His journo logistics connected the dots and he set off after them. Where there were marines, there was the promise of transport.

"Ade!" he called. "Ade! Hang on, mate!"

F'nar's acoustics made his voice echo around the bowl of the caldera. For some reason it embarrassed him, even though the wess'har were as unselfconscious about noise as they were about venting their unedited thoughts or copulating. Ade and Qureshi stopped dead and turned to look at him.

Eddie took the narrow steps down the terraces a little faster than was sensible and stumbled, missing the next step and suddenly seeing a hundred-meter drop looming as he grabbed a pearl-coated post to stop his fall. His gut rolled. It was a bloody long way down, and wess'har didn't have balustrades on the walkways.

Qureshi cupped her hands in front of her mouth to shout back at him. "Take it one step at a time, Eddie . . ."

"Ha fucking ha."

Ade looked unamused when Eddie caught up with them, his heart still hammering.

"You don't bounce like I do, Eddie. Remember that."

"Yeah, thanks, Mum." Embarrassment was worse than injury and lasted longer. "Are you heading to Umeh?"

"There's some crap going on with Rit and Shomen Eit. He declared war on Wess'ej etcetera etcetera etcetera, daft bastard, Esganikan loaded up for Armageddon, and then Rit said she'd depose him and everything would be hunky-dory."

"Jesus. From our political correspondent."

"Didn't you know?"

"No, I didn't, Ade. No bastard tells me anything."

"Either way, they're banging out of Umeh Station." Ade dropped his voice as if he was talking to an idiot. "You know they meant *complete* extermination, don't you?"

It had always been an option. Eddie had got used to it. He tried hard to get *un*-used right away. "Hunky-dory means three-quarters of their global population dead, Ade."

"Northern Assembly—one; every other poor isenj—nil," said Qureshi.

"I want a lift, then. Got to record this for posterity. And the Skavu."

"Not my call, mate. Try asking the Boss."

"Okay, if I give you my spare cam and you run into any Skavu, can you crank out a few shots?" Sod that. A mass evacuation was something News Desk always liked. It made more sense to viewers than dead squid and spiders; they could relate to humans in jeopardy on the extreme frontier of space. "But I'll kiss Shan's arse for a flight out there."

"That's *my* job." Ade winked and held his hand out for the camera. He'd done it before: dead bezeri on irradiated beaches, a place where Ade could walk and come to no harm. "Done."

"Seen images of any Skavu?"

"Yeah."

"And you didn't grab a file for me?"

"Christ, mate, we're busy."

"What do they look like, then?"

"Closest I can get is . . . I dunno. Izzy?"

Qureshi stared into mid-distance for inspiration. "I suppose if you crossed a ussissi with an iguana, you might get close. Two legs. Which is handy."

Ade seemed animated. A proper mission had really

pepped him up. "The ussissi say they're total gung-ho ma-
niacs. Militant green doesn't even come close. Loathed and
feared in the Garav system, which they've gone through like
a dose of salts."

Eddie saw *story* on one hand and *massive threat* on the
other. His body, marinated in adrenaline, strained at an
imaginary leash and made him forget the *threat* bit. "At least
they're on our side."

Qureshi's bergen looked heavier than she was. She hitched
it higher on her back and fiddled with the webbing. "I never
assume that much," she said. "Just that they probably won't
be trying to kill us."

"Where's Shan?"

"She went over to talk to Nevyan."

"Good."

"Don't push your luck. She's got one of her stroppy
moods on."

Eddie had noticed. He'd also noted that neither Aras nor
Ade were especially chipper either, and he speculated on
some marital rift. How they made that kind of setup work he
had no idea, and he wasn't about to ask. Ambushing Shan for
a favor looked less predatory now, though, because he could
stroll into Nevyan's home any time. He lived there, after all.
He picked up his pace—carefully this time—and made his
way along the terraces, pausing a couple of times to check if
he had an ITX link through to Jejeno. There was no connec-
tion. He swore and hurried on.

Eddie walked into the passage, whose roughly circular
skylights cast columns of early morning sun into the gold
flagstones. He still didn't know how the wess'har could
route daylight below ground and into tunnels as easily
as some fiber optic system. But there was always time to
find out, and Jejeno and the Skavu were far more pressing
topics. The buzz of voices—in English—were Shan's and
Nevyan's.

Eddie stopped and listened, but he wasn't eavesdropping.
He just didn't want to interrupt at the wrong time. Two alpha
females, each capable of killing without a backwards glance,
weren't to be annoyed.

The voices stopped for a moment. Eddie knew an awkward silence when he heard one.

"You would tell me if you wanted me to know," Nevyan said. "But so far, you haven't."

"What?" Shan's tone was defensive.

"I can smell it. You know I can. You lost the child."

Shan's pause was long. *One, two, three, four . . .*

"I couldn't keep it. You know it would have been a disaster for so many reasons."

This time it was Nevyan's turn at silence. Eddie could imagine her freezing in that lizardlike way that wess'har had, a perfect seahorse statue for a few moments. His mouth was instantly dry and his brain told him he'd misheard. *Child.*

"Knowing *c'naatat*'s capabilities, I can barely imagine how you destroyed it."

"You have a way with words, Nev."

"I won't judge you."

"Bloody glad to hear it. I got a queue forming for that."

Eddie wasn't sure if Nevyan understood. He thought he did. "You must have . . . suffered greatly."

"You've still got the *Christopher* archive. Really handy trick that humans have. When we're desperate enough, the pain gets blanked out mostly."

Eddie put this hand over his mouth and realized his pulse was pounding. It felt exactly like the moment when he'd been musing over a precious cup of coffee back at the *Thetis* camp on Constantine island—when things had seemed much simpler—and felt a blast of cold revelation: Shan Frankland had *c'naatat*.

Not everything that had happened since had been a consequence of his pursuit of that story, but too much was.

Jesus H. Christ. Shan hadn't just got herself knocked up, just like Lindsay Neville, whose lack of iron discipline she despised—she'd aborted it herself.

This was a Shan he didn't know. There were too many shouldn't-have-beens for a start—her age, brutal common sense, circumstances—but most of all there was a sense that she wasn't some icon of invincibility after all, but a woman with frailties and trials like anyone. *That* was it: he never thought of her as a woman. She was Shan Frankland, and she happened to be female. When the world was divided into male and female, rich and poor, old and young, good and bad, or whatever category he chose, there would always be a single slot marked *Shan Frankland,* untouched by any other benchmark.

He was aware of the coolness of the stone through his shirt. His mind darted, thought to thought: Aras's, Ade's, whose kid? He fought prurient curiosity, as he always had, not because he felt he owed Shan better than to speculate on the vagaries of her sex life with two-dicked aliens and chimeras, but because it stopped him thinking about his own lonely celibacy.

"I'm sure they would discuss it with you," said a voice at waist height.

Eddie was so startled that he let out an involuntary grunt of surprise and jerked upright away from the wall. Giyadas looked up at him with cross-hair pupils that flared instantly into black petals.

"Ah," he said, utterly ashamed.

"Shan was carrying an *isanket,* but she removed it," said Giyadas. "And I understand her reasons."

Shan and Giyadas stepped out into the passage, and Shan's expression was now one of the copper who could—and would—do *anything* to you now that the cell door was locked and nobody could hear you. Primeval panic gripped his gut.

"Hi, Eddie," said Shan, voice flat, eyes that dreadful dead gray of downtrodden snow. "Haven't seen you in a while."

"Punch me out now," he said. "Get it over with."

"I'll take that as an apology." She had an extraordinary capacity to switch off, but he'd seen split-second glimpses of the raw psyche buried deep beneath the casing. He still treated her as a human who could be hurt. She glanced back at Nevyan. "Ade's going to Umeh with the detachment now, and Esganikan's committing a section of ship to pick them up. If you want to go, get a move on."

"Can I come?" asked Giyadas.

Shan's expression was pure pain for a heartbeat and then

vanished. Eddie had an impression of a face looming suddenly under the thick glassy ice of a frozen river, mouth open in screaming panic, and then swept away by the hidden current beneath to leave a lifeless calm behind again.

"When we get the rest of the humans settled in, yes." Shan was all instant, unexpected patience that made sense now. "Then you can compare the difference in their attitudes."

Nevyan went back into the main room and Giyadas disappeared after her, evidently satisfied. Shan made for the main door and Eddie followed her at a respectful distance. They emerged onto a terrace dappled with reflections from the nacre covering every flat surface. The air smelled of damp vegetation—not grass, not soil, nothing remotely like Earth, but vividly alive—and the throat-catching spices of someone cooking *rov'la* nearby.

"I'm really sorry," he said helplessly.

Shan kept walking, but not at her usual brisk march. "Try knocking in future."

"I meant about—well, the baby."

"Thanks. Everything's fine now."

"The hell it is. I should have realized something was wrong. I thought you were upset about Vijissi topping himself."

"That as well. Any more happy highlights from the last year you'd like to remind me of?"

"If there's anything I can do, ask."

He meant it. He'd veered between reverence and fear of Shan over the last few years, but sometimes he admitted that he liked her because there was something both admirable and tragic about someone who not only couldn't be bought or intimidated, but who was also prepared to die as often as it took to defend some ideal. She was an obsessive hunter and a vengeful enemy, and the conscience of the world. Consciences were never meant to be comfortable.

"Okay." She did that displaced punch action, shoving her fists deep in her pockets as if she was stopping herself from using them. "Thanks. I know you mean well."

She still could say *fuck off* a hundred different ways.

"What's happening with Lin and Rayat?"

"I don't think you want to know, Eddie."

She was right. It would only plague him. He asked anyway, because it was in the fiber of his being to want to find out. "Try me."

"I know where Rayat is and you don't need to worry your little hack head about that. Lin—Christ only knows where she is."

"Who knows about all this?"

"Not the detachment, so keep your mouth shut around them until further notice."

"Is it a problem? I mean, a *real* problem?"

"Don't worry. Esganikan will sort it if I can't."

Eddie considered what *sort* meant, and knew. He followed Shan all the way to the end of the terrace to the first flight of treacherously narrow steps cut into the rock that linked the terrace to the levels above and below. From the top, it was a curved cliff face, two hundred meters to the floor of the caldera, filled with curved and irregularly shaped pearl-coated buildings like bubbles in a cup. It was one of those moments when he tried out the feeling of never seeing the city again, and he didn't like that at all.

"So are you going home when *Thetis* shows up?" Shan asked. She looked him in the eye, a slight frown puckering the skin between her brows, and there was no hint of its being a suggestion to piss off. "Or are you waiting for the main task force to swing by?"

"I don't know. Can't wait seventy-five years to get there, so I'll probably catch the later express."

"Time to make up your mind, then," said Shan. She looked down into the basin of the city and for a moment he wondered how many of her prisoners had had nasty falls during her police career on Earth. There was always that edge of violence glittering in her, even when she was being humblingly noble. "I know. I'm a bitch today. Sorry. You've been a good mate to me and those two buggers, and I know you've got a job to do. I'll miss you when the time comes."

Shan turned away from the steps and walked away, arms swinging. *Those two buggers.* Ade and Aras: his mates, the blokes he'd shared a house with when she was dead, the only friends alive in his universe right now. Everyone else he once worked with, drank with, and argued with was either dead or close to it back on Earth now. Time dilation and chill sleep were a permanent exile, even if you went home in the end.

I'll miss you.

Eddie felt tears sting his eyes, observed that Ade was correct—she did at least have a nice arse on her—and went back to grab his bag.

Funny. He'd shared the house with Ade and Aras after Shan was declared dead, and he thought they were close. He still thought they were close when she was found alive. He was hurt to find they hadn't told him about the baby.

He wondered if they really trusted him at all, or if he was just the tame hack who had his uses.

Eqbas Vorhi ship 886–001–005–6: preparing to debark in Jejeno, Umeh

Esganikan Gai admitted disappointment—to herself—that she wasn't erasing every isenj from the face of their utterly despoiled planet.

She didn't dislike the isenj. She'd just steeled herself to thinking that at least the issue would be resolved, buying her time, and then it was unresolved. There was a chance. Rit's coup had to be tested.

It was the contrast that brought it home to her, the stark comparison between Bezer'ej—wild, unspoiled, rich in life—and Umeh, a planet so destroyed that there was no natural, uncultivated life on the land, just a solid sprawl of buildings and a single *dalf* tree imported from the isenj moon of Tasir Var.

She glanced down between her boots through the transparent deck of the ship as it passed over the center of Jejeno. The city was both a tribute to isenj engineering skills and an indictment of their stupidity. The forest of asymmetric towers—bronze, brown, copper, tan—and narrow streets created endless canyons. Shapakti said that it was an echo of isenj origins as termite-like animals living in giant mounds, but Esganikan had seen almost identical soaring buildings in the images of Earth. It was how greedy species built: it showed space was at a premium because they had filled it and out-priced it—yes, she understood Earth's economy now, she understood it *very* well—and they didn't care about the intrusion on the landscape. It was a statement of their contempt for all other life.

It was one thing that reassured her about Australia as host nation for the landings. They built underground now. It was the relentless daytime temperatures and fierce storms that motivated them, and not environmental modesty in most cases, but motive didn't matter. Outcomes did.

The six soldiers who had insisted on being brought to Umeh Station to do their duty, as they put it, were clustered on the port side of the bridge. Apart from Shan Frankland's *jurej*, Ade, they spoke no eqbas'u and waited in silence to be disembarked.

Ade was learning slowly, but Shapakti said that was normal for humans with their poor language skills.

"Teh, niyukal hasve?" Ade's speech was more wess'u than eqbas'u, but the crew liked him for his unselfconscious honesty. He managed to make himself understood, but sometimes he did something that the other marines called *crashing and burning*. This was such a time. The bridge crew stared at him. "Did that make sense?"

Hayin, the communications officer, felt compelled to try out his English. "You say you want closeness."

Barencoin, the big dark-haired marine, and the small female one called Qureshi laughed loudly. "Keep your mind on the job, you dirty bugger," Barencoin said.

"I thought I was asking what range the shield's got." Ade squatted with his rifle across his knees, staring down at the cityscape passing beneath them. "As in how much ship do they have to leave behind to provide cover for the whole dome area."

Hayin flicked the magnification in the deck to give Ade a better view of the faceted transparent dome of Umeh Station, and he flinched as the image beneath him snapped into larger scale.

The damage to the dome was visible. A large opaque patch had crazed but not shattered, and twisted debris was still sitting on the panels.

"That was done when, exactly?" she asked.

Ade consulted the *virin* clipped to his pouch belt. "Yesterday. Bit too close for comfort."

"You know what they say about glass houses," she said to Mart Barencoin.

"What, that you shouldn't whip out your cucumber if you live in one?"

The other marines laughed. "You're hilarious," said Qureshi. "For a man who's only got a gherkin."

Hayin appeared not to understand the joke. Esganikan decided to ask Shan later for an explanation of the comic value of vegetables. Her English was now fully fluent, but some nuances still evaded her.

"You can just set us down by the perimeter, ma'am," said Ade. "We'll be fine. We're not under fire. If we were—well, we've all done that a few times."

"If I didn't provide some cover for you, then I expect your *isan* would have serious objections," said Esganikan. "We have enough resources to leave a ship section to shield the dome."

"When do we get to meet the Skavu, ma'am?"

"You don't need to."

"I'd *like* to." Ade was quietly insistent, and his scent was very wess'har, very much the dominant male in the pecking order. "We may have to fight alongside these blokes or work with them at the very least."

There were just six Royal Marines. Perhaps their presence reassured the humans in the dome, but Esganikan couldn't see how a handful of troops with basic weapons could make a difference if Umeh Station came under attack. They could make little difference to the evacuation, either. But she did understand their compulsion to do their duty. Hers was taking her more than fifty years out of time, to Earth.

"Very well," she said. "I'll arrange for you to accompany one of their patrols."

Ade brightened visibly. "Thank you, ma'am."

"I want Eddie to remain in the dome."

"Yes, ma'am." Ade didn't ask why. Eddie would. "What do I need to know about their command structure?"

"They rank themselves in order of who will die."

The marines stared at her, their identical expressions—very slight frowns, lips slightly parted—giving them almost a family resemblance.

"Well, it happens that way with us," said Barencoin. "Only we don't plan it that way."

"Educated guess, or is this a . . . well, suicide squad?" Ade asked.

Suicide squad. It was a fascinating term. "If there's an need to die to achieve a mission, then they have a numbered sequence of personnel. Commanders tend to go first."

"Works for me," said Becken. "Bit extreme, though."

Ade shrugged, but he looked uneasy. "Not unknown back home."

"Not with a bloody numbered ticket. Gentleman's understanding, maybe."

Esganikan decided to introduce the marines to the Skavu gently. She wasn't sure how to explain the cultural gulf. "They are extremely rigorous about environmental policy, and intolerant of infringement, and they will kill to enforce balance."

"Best thing is to meet them," said Ade, and his comment had a finality about it. "If they're going to be in our backyard for the next few years, then we need to get to know them *properly*."

Esganikan went to break the news to Eddie. He was in the aft section of the ship as it was configured at that moment, using his remote camera to record images of the fighters forming from the hangar deck material and coalescing with it again. It fascinated him. Joluti had left him in the hands of the air group staff because he wanted to see it demonstrated so many times to *get all the angles*.

It was basic technology, unchanged in years. Esganikan wondered what the reaction would be on Earth when she broke out sections of the ship on landing, if Eddie hadn't tired his audience of the spectacle by then.

"So what can I cover?" he asked. "Where can I go?"

"Umeh Station," said Esganikan. "The combat zone is closed to you."

"Oh."

"The Skavu aren't used to *embedded journalists*. That's the right term, yes?"

Eddie looked about to argue, chin lifting slightly, but then he lowered it and nodded. "Okay. Onboard footage?"

"Perhaps." How much carnage did he need? "Stay with Ade Bennett. There's nothing new for you in this phase."

"Are you going to deploy bioweapons?"

"I'll assess the situation after the Skavu have begun the assault on the Maritime Fringe."

"Can you estimate how long you expect this to last?"

"Possibly weeks. The more dust that bombing throws into the atmosphere, the more remediation work we have to do. Bioweapons make less impact, however much the idea repels humans."

Eddie looked down and put the back of his hand to his mouth, knuckles against his lips. He looked deep in thought for a moment. When he looked up again, his face seemed to have sagged slightly.

"I don't know why this doesn't shock me any longer," he said. "Because it bloody well should."

He turned to summon his bee cam with a gesture and closed the small ball in his palm. Esganikan indicated the forward section of the ship and waited for him to notice that he was being sent elsewhere.

"Join the marine detachment," she said.

Eddie gave her a mock salute of the kind the marines used, hand to brow, and left the hangar. Joluti knelt down on the gantry to rest and surveyed the deck below.

"The Skavu are in position. They aim to cut off the Maritime Fringe forces just before your squad enables Minister Rit to take control."

"How far inside the border is the Fringe now?"

"Thirty kilometers."

"Untidy."

"Yes, there'll be heavy Northern Assembly casualties.

There's nowhere to move civilians in this kind of infrastructure."

"Then we'll deploy the bioagent as soon as possible. It won't be tidy, but the more Fringe genotypes we can wipe out without bombardment, the better."

"You know what the Skavu will do."

"Oh yes. I know that very well."

There were plenty of Northern Assembly citizens—and even troops—who opposed their government now. Even the bioagent tailored to the Fringe's majority genome wouldn't target all those resisting the restoration. Esganikan said the internal politics of the isenj were irrelevant, but it still made her uneasy.

"With Earth," she said, "we have time to select those who want to cooperate. No crude lines across a chart. We can select those who can sustain the planet responsibly."

"Is that what happened with Garav?"

"No. The Skavu seemed to be culturally prone to radical conversions."

Joluti got to his feet again. "Then let's get this done," he sighed.

The engineered pathogen would take a few days to work through the target population. Rit didn't have that long. If she couldn't hold the government together, then the erasure option would follow. Esganikan returned to the bridge to begin transforming Umeh, and paused at one of the screens that showed a view of the hangar bay hatch. Sleek bronze fighter craft formed from the body of the ship, configured in this sortie to seed clouds, were slipping out of the hatch at regular intervals that almost created a strobe effect in the field of view. She turned to watch through the transparent bulkhead section as they streaked south towards the Fringe.

I want this to work. I'm tired of slaughter.

She hoped this would be the last world she ever had to restore by global destruction. It was as well that worlds needing such radical measures were very, very rare.

"Aitassi," said Esganikan. "Call Minister Rit."

The minister had progressed a great deal in terms of confidence and sheer audacity since Esganikan had first met her in Umeh Station to discuss a kinder, slower way of reducing the isenj population with contraceptive agents in the water supply. *They could have done this without conflict.* But if they'd had that foresight, she wouldn't have been here in the first place.

"All the cabinet members are in the main government offices," said Ralassi, turning back and forth to interpret. Sometimes he paused and seemed to be arguing with her, but it was hard to tell by the tone. He might simply have been annoyed, as ussissi frequently were. "Seven of them. They have not yet replaced Minister Rit with another. She asks you to remove them so she can declare herself head of an emergency government and formally sanction your intervention."

Isenj liked their bureaucracy tidy. "Then let me be certain what she now means by *remove*."

"Eradicate."

"I thought so. We have no facilities for prisoners and experience tells me the minister would be unwise to hold any."

"Are you ready to begin?"

"As soon as the marines have been landed."

"When will you begin seeding the clouds?"

"We already have."

From the tracking remote, Esganikan could see the fighters, now configured as armed payload vessels, in formation above the cloud layer cloaking most of the coastal strip that made up the Maritime Fringe. Once dropped, the crystals containing the pathogen would result in heavy rain within hours, coating the city-packed land beneath, scattering contaminated water droplets to be inhaled, disrupting the biochemistry of every isenj in the region whose genome had certain key alleles, and causing massive internal hemorrhage. In hours, they'd sicken. In days they would all be dead.

Esganikan could do this to the whole planet if and when she wished.

"Minister Rit says that was premature."

"She said she intended to use the weapon."

"She wanted to deploy it at a time of her choosing."

"We understand how to do these things. This is the best time for her." Esganikan turned to Hayin and inclined her head in a mute signal to be passed to the pilots. *Drop the payload.* She'd done this before, on more modest scales. She never took it lightly. "The effects should be seen in four hours, if she'd like images from the remotes to make her point to the rest of her administration. There should be dead and dying visible to the cameras by then."

Ralassi's silence on the other end of the link was palpable shock. It seemed he'd spent too long among isenj if he didn't recall that wess'har—the ones he knew, or the Eqbas—were literal and not given to shows of *brinksmanship,* as Shan called it. Eventually he exchanged high-pitched chatter with Rit.

"The Minister says she understands and will operate from her chambers in the north of the city until the situation is stable enough for her to appear in public."

"We may be able to add some emphasis to her words."

"You have still not agreed who will have control of the universal pathogen."

"No, but I do have it, and I *will* deploy it if need be," said Esganikan.

If she did, there would be no isenj to worry about any longer, not on Umeh anyway. She could let the nanites loose to scour the planet and break down every last thing the isenj had created, and their corpses along with their works; then the phased remediation systems would finally move in to cleanse what couldn't be broken down—some of the heavier metals—and then the planet would be left fallow.

"If you did that, what would follow? Tasir Var—"

"We would need to eradicate all isenj on Tasir Var, too."

This would take generations. Esganikan looked down, found herself standing on an opaque deck, and passed her hand in front of the controls to make it transparent so she could truly look at what she was eradicating. A dying world: then she was doing it a kindness, putting it out of its misery as a catastrophic meteor strike might. A living world, full of talented beings whose desire to expand made them inventive: then they would expand too far, as they already had, and she was prolonging the agony of others.

The chatter continued while she waited.

Ralassi finally responded. "Minister Rit says her sons are on Tasir Var."

"Then she has a good reason to ensure this is managed efficiently."

· "Minister Rit agrees and says she'll speak to the nation after the transfer of power has taken place."

"Then we'll land troops immediately and secure the government building. The minister can identify her chambers to us so we can put a defensive shield around that too, assuming she won't operate from this ship."

Consultation took place. "She says she must be seen to stand here," said Ralassi.

Esganikan glanced at the chronometer displays in the bulkhead. It was to focus on the time the operation began locally, but she could also see the time—and date—for Surang, nearly five light-years away, and it hit her hard to be reminded how much time had passed since she left. She was a veteran spacefarer; she still had that feeling of hurtling towards the end of her life, rootless and with nothing truly to show for it except restored planets in which she had no personal stake. She wanted her *time* back, time to make her choices and live a life where she could afford to be *late* and days could be wasted.

Shan didn't have to worry about such things now, and for a moment Esganikan envied her again.

"Then we begin," she said. "Deploy the shield. Landing party, stand to."

Chad Island, Bezer'ej

Lindsay reassured herself with the knowledge that she couldn't die—not easily, anyway—and kept as still as she could.

And she fell back on her naval training, which had taught her that she would get out of this okay as long as she did what she was trained to do, and booked a day for panicking later.

Shit shit shit shit shit. . .

The *sheven* floated like a tall iceberg breaking the surface of the bog, almost totally transparent with a fine lace of fibers shot through its mantle. It was shapeless, a sheet of glass-clear stomach tissue, ready to plunge down upon anything in its path to envelop and digest it. It was motionless except for a faint rhythmic shiver.

Maybe movement triggered it: vibrations in the fluid of the bog, changes in light levels firing visual cells, sound waves pressing on its skin, whatever it took to locate prey. Lindsay's eyes, adapted by the heritage of previous *c'naatat* hosts in ways she didn't yet fully understand, saw the variations in its density as echoes: yes, *sounds,* but silent ones that pressed on some place within her jaw.

There might have been seven-eighths of the creature below the surface if the iceberg analogy held true. With two meters of flesh rearing above the bog, that would make it immense. She opened her mouth slightly out of some alien instinct and got a return sensation of a single, almost uniform concentration of density beneath the surface where the *sheven* sat. It felt like a smooth granular paste in her mouth. *Am I echolocating? What am I using here?* Whatever it was, it told her that there was little if anything of the *sheven* hidden from her visual spectrum.

It was still a six-footer. Just two meters of stomach, and a means to move it around and make more *shevens.*

C'naatat or not, she didn't need to deal with that right now. *C'naatat* didn't mean immortal, either. Aras Sar Iussan was the last of the *c'naatat* troops. That meant the others had been killed by fragmentation. Maybe other things worked too—not the vacuum of space, because she'd seen that trick fail, and not drowning or shooting or crushing, because she'd seen those fail too. But digestion could be another matter.

Still. Very still.

"Leeeeenz . . ."

Saib's vibrating breath of a voice carried from the direction of the clearing behind her. She didn't dare turn to look and take her eyes off the *sheven*.

"Sssshhhhh . . . "

"Leeeeeeeenz . . ."

"Shut . . . *up* . . . " He didn't understand *hush*. She kept her gaze fixed on the *sheven*, a bizarre heraldic beast frozen rampant on a vert field, watching the pulse-like shudder that shook its whole body, wondering how the hell she could move if it came for her. The cold wet slime of the bog held her and there was nothing rigid to push against to get clear in a hurry even if the viscosity wasn't holding her.

"Leeeenz . . ."

The *sheven* wasn't reacting to sound. Saib was loud now, enough to trigger it to attack if that was its method of location.

Body heat? Light, movement, vibration? Scent?

Saib was a big creature, three or four meters, and as he swung between his front tentacles in that crutch-walk, the saturated ground shook each time he landed. The *sheven* had to be able to sense that. Lindsay, focused on picking up every detail and thinking her way out of this, could no longer feel fear or work out how long all this was taking. At each swinging stride, the *sheven* started to flinch rhythmically.

Maybe it's confused—prey signals coming from one direction, vibrations from another. . .

"Leeeenzzzzz . . ."

"Stop. *Don't move*." She whispered as loudly as she could, then slowly raised her hand and signaled in light: *it's dangerous, it's a predator.*

Saib, still defaulting to his bezeri core in crisis, heeded the lights and stopped. She couldn't see him. She only heard more distant thuds and rustling, and then what she could only describe as wet noises as a sensation built up in her throat and jaw that said *large, near, moving this way.*

The *sheven* reacted. It stretched higher, rearing into a glass column, and held that position for a few seconds. At that moment Lindsay's body thought for her. She rolled sideways just as something shot over her head and punched hard into the *sheven*, sending it flying into the air in a wet panicky flapping of membrane. Then all hell broke loose.

Lindsay knew the bezeri's hunting past, but she'd never seen them in action.

Saib, Keet and Carf landed in the bog like depth charges, tentacles whipping, and she was plunged down into the bitter, dark slurry of sodden vegetation by thrashing bodies. The light went out and she inhaled mud, churning roiling cold gritty paste that tasted sour and dead. Not even drowning could have prepared her for the terrifying sensation of solid material clogging her mouth and nose.

She struggled, forgetting all the drill about bogs and quicksand. Somehow her clawing fingers grabbed what felt like a root. She hauled herself up with an effort driven by pure animal panic, and suddenly her head was in air again and she went into convulsive coughing. Around her, the wrestling, struggling bodies registered as fluctuating spaces deep in her jaw. Then they stopped. The noise of churning water faded.

As she wiped the stinging mud from one eye, she saw Keet and Carf sliding across the surface of the bog, pulling a transparent sheet between them. It was the *sheven,* and— dear God, it was much, *much* bigger than she thought.

Six or seven meters of clear film stretched between them. The two bezeri clutched the eagles in their tentacles as if they were holding a blanket under a tree to catch fallen apples. Was it dead? It was more of a flat sheet than an iceberg now and there were opaque patches scattered across it. When Keet slumped onto the relatively solid mat of grass at the edge of the bog, he twisted the *sheven* slightly as he moved, and she could see it was slashed and scored clean through in places.

Carf eased out of the bog after Keet, still gripping one edge of the *sheven.*

"Good struggle," he rasped. "Good, good struggle!"

He rippled with a spectacular full-spectrum light display that ran in concentric pulsing rings from purple through to scarlet. Ecstatic joy: Lindsay had never seen that before. Only the bezeri instincts that *c'naatat* had scavenged and cultivated within her told her that was the meaning, because they'd had no delight to express since she'd known them.

Carf let go of the *sheven* and it flopped to the ground with a slap, not moving. Keet hung on to his section. Lindsay, still struggling to get purchase on solid ground, felt a rough leathery grip on her arm that snaked around her shoulder and waist and yanked her bodily out of the mire with a loud squelch that would have been comic in other circumstances. Saib dumped her unceremoniously on the ground. The other two bezeri were inspecting the dead *sheven,* batting at it with the tips of their tentacles like curious cats.

Then it twitched.

Saib *pounced* on it. There was no other word for it. He arched into a fluid shape and pinned it down with a stabbing tentacle. Keet and Carf reacted like crazed sharks. In seconds the bezeri were ripping the *sheven* apart with tentacles and tearing into it with their beaks.

Lindsay watched, stunned.

Why? Why does this surprise you? They're predatory cephalopods. Like Humboldt squid.

The image of gently graceful creatures shimmering with magical, ethereal light, victims of profligate isenj and rapacious man, had vanished forever. These were hunters, killers, highly intelligent carnivores. And they *liked* hunting.

Maipay appeared from behind her and loped across the ground to join them: "I see from the high! I see from high tree!" He'd watched the attack. They were now a pack. They were transformed.

They were *eating* the bloody *sheven.* She thought of boiled tripe, the nearest example she had to an animal that was one giant stomach, and felt queasy.

C'naatat meant you could eat anything. She'd develop a taste for vegetation, she decided.

Carf stopped in mid-rip, ribbons of transparent gel in his maw. "Stronger, much stronger! Like we were young! So *fast*! Again, young! See size of food!"

Lindsay got the idea. They were elderly bezeri given an astonishing new vigor by *c'naatat*. They could hunt like younger ones. And this was exactly what they cherished: large prey, the kind of size that they hadn't seen in generations and that was immortalized in their azin shell records

and maps, exquisite sand-art in vivid colors sandwiched
between two paper-thin transparent sheets of shell. They
recorded the large aquatic animals that they'd hunted to
extinction. They lived on ever smaller animals and mobile
anemone-like creatures.

Lindsay wandered away, treading with renewed care, and
found a stream to rinse off the caked mud. When she came
back, the four bezeri were leaping around the surface of the
bog, which stretched further than she had thought, splashing
and rummaging in the pooled water like demented raccoons.
They were flushing out *sheven*.

"Thanks for hauling me out," she said, but it was to herself. They were oblivious to her again.

The pack spent the afternoon hunting in a blaze of rain-
bow lights and fantastically athletic leaps, throwing *sheven*
clear of the bogs and standing water like an orca tossing a
seal from the sea to make its kill. They were pure savage
joy, glorying in a rediscovered primeval heritage. Occasionally one let out a burbling sound almost like a growl, but for
the most part they were silent and the only sound was the
splashing of water that drowned out the clicking, whirring
background of Chad's native and unseen wildlife.

"You eat?" called Maipay. He held out a shredded skein
of *sheven* flesh. "Chewy."

"I'll bet," said Lindsay. "No thanks."

Damn, they were happy. They were the last of their kind,
and now also the first—and they were *happy*.

They must have eaten their fill, or grown tired, because
they finally came to a halt and swung up into a nearby tree to
drape themselves over the branches like misshapen Venetian
glass leopards watching the ground beneath.

Saib had taken on a distinctly peacock blue cast to his
mantle. Lindsay got up and walked beneath the branches.
She looked up.

"Time to get on with more construction," she said. "Will
you bring the rest of your people ashore now? Do you think
they'll see the benefits? The need?"

Saib looked down at her, idly swinging one tentacle. It
was a bizarre spectacle.

I'm a amphibious gel-woman and they're glass arboreal squids that hunt like big cats. What will we be tomorrow?

"Yesssss . . ." It was an exhalation of air but she could have sworn it was also a sigh of contentment. "Here we can be what we were and are. Hunters and builders."

The bezeri were assimilating the comprehension of English faster than the spoken language. But they were talking, and she was talking with them. She noticed that her light signals continued involuntarily now, a kind of punctuation to the spoken word . . . no, she *knew* what this was. This was the wess'har element in them, the genes from Aras that had passed to Shan and then to Ade and to her and finally to the bezeri. This parallel use of bioluminescence and sound was an analog of the wess'har overtone voice, the stream of two different sounds like khoomei singing that formed wess'har speech.

Rayat would have enjoyed this. He was a lying bastard spook who had duped everyone, but he was still a scientist; these bezeri, evolving into land predators before his eyes, would have fascinated him. She missed his knowledge. The company of an irritating know-all right then would have been . . . fun, someone to share this extraordinary afternoon.

"Come on. Work. Chop-chop."

Saib slithered down the trunk and dropped in a heap, his tentacles coiled for a moment in a way that made her think of a giant python dropping to the ground. Shan had told her that human brains groped for patterns all the time and aliens evoked ever-shifting animal images to cope with the unknown. Lindsay was working through the whole zoo today.

"Leeeeenzz, you are right," said Saib. "This was a good thing to do, to make us move from the places we love. We know now. The Dry Above is *also* ours. We can be what we were again."

Lindsay had brought them ashore to be better able to defend their planet from further invasion. But they'd found that coming ashore restored something from their cherished past, their peak as a hunting civilization. Maybe both would work to the world's advantage.

Even so, she couldn't help hearing Rayat's voice again,

taunting her when he worked out that the bezeri had a shameful past in which they exterminated another intelligent species. *Genocide,* he said. *Nazis.*

She'd given the bezeri a new terrestrial existence, a home on land.

Rayat would have called it *Lebensraum.*

7

Umeh Station's geodesic dome had taken more than a few hits on its peak. On closer inspection, Ade saw long seared skid marks on some of the panels where hot debris had rained on them.

"Jesus H. Christ," said Becken, and craned his neck to look up. He'd never experienced the liquid technology of an Eqbas warship before, and he'd certainly never strolled into a war zone where he didn't need armor. "Talk about insulated from reality."

"That's what a million years' head start on Neanderthals gets you," said Ade.

Qureshi feigned a concerned I'm-interviewing-you expression that Ade recognized as Eddie's, and turned to Barencoin. "How do you feel about that, Mart? As a Neanderthal spokesman?"

"Piss off." Barencoin almost suppressed a smile. He liked his knuckle-dragging reputation, and knowing his academic credentials Ade could easily see him as a clever kid who had to act the grunt at school to be accepted. "I discovered fire last week."

"Steady on," said Chahal. "It'll be the wheel next."

"He'll burn out at this pace. Mark my words." Qureshi glanced behind her. "Come on, Eddie, keep up. Don't want any dead embeds on my watch."

Eddie, his bee cam hovering at head level, was staring at the city of Jejeno beyond. He must have seen enough bombed cities in his life, but his expression said he still found it distressing. Ade only saw the things he needed to see now—the positions that might still harbor snipers, the booby-trapped buildings, the pieces of your own people that you needed to recover and treat reverently. No, that was other wars and another world. There was nothing like that here.

Isenj moved amid the rubble, carrying and cleaning up, trying to rebuild, a sea of spike-quilled black eggs tottering on spidery short legs; weird wide mouths and no visible eyes made it harder to think *people*. Eddie was disturbingly good at snap classification of anything he saw to give it some familiar label. Isenj were spiders with piranha mouths. That worked fine for Ade.

People.

You've got a bit of them in you. Your *people.*

The metallic blue blob of liquid ship that had shuttled the detachment to the surface peeled off the concrete apron surrounding Umeh Station's geodesic dome, and lifted above it to join a detached section of the main warship. It still cast a huge shadow over the city. Becken watched, hand shielding his eyes against the sun, until he couldn't tilt his neck any further. Around them, a shimmering haze like a mirage on a hot road marked the boundary of the defense shield that radiated from the ship.

"Jesus, is this war of the frigging worlds or what, Ade?"

Mothership. Fuck yes, it's a mothership. Just like the movies. Ade kept a wary eye on the visible boundary of the shield. The detached vessel that would stay on station above the dome swallowed up the shuttle like coalescing mercury, blue vanishing into the bronze casing like a brief explosion of color from a firework. As the mothership hull moved off, Ade could see the separate shield that the remnant generated over the dome as far as the moatlike service road. The ship was a clean elongated oval again, uniformly bronze from stem to stern, its midline picked out with a pulsing band of red and blue chevrons.

Eddie's right again. Upturned glass. Who's the spider now?

"Amazing," said Becken. "Those things are totally brammers. Why do they change color?"

"No idea." Ade—*c'naatat* or not, Eqbas-shielded or

not—didn't like standing around in a hostile zone without cover like a spare prick at a wedding. "Maybe it's all to do with how they melt or something. Makes you feel primitive, doesn't it?"

"It's not like the OSLO training we had, is it?"

The old, old slang for an incompetent comrade—Outer Space Liaison Officer—had fresh life in the Extreme Environment Warfare Cadre of the Royal Marines. Ade recalled belting a mouthy infantry pongo who dared address him as OSLO in a bar during one particularly drink-fueled run ashore. Only your oppos, the men and women who earned the right to wear the narrow black strip with discreet silver stars next to the COMMANDO shoulder flash, could call you that. It was fucking *sacred;* it was not for the mouths of lesser mortals. It meant you could free-fall from orbit and fight in zero-g and do any bloody thing needed to secure a space station or orbital platform.

Now, coming up forty years old, Ade felt embarrassed for starting that fist-fight. But he'd been seventeen then, full of testosterone and still getting his rage at his father out of his system. It had seemed the right thing to do, and cemented his reputation: a good bloke in a scrap, his mates said, nice and quiet until you pushed him too far. Ade never backed down once he started.

And here he was, just playing at dicing with death. It was a picnic. Eqbas tech alone meant a Girl Scout could do the evacuation.

Gutless little bastard, his father's voice whispered. *You need to toughen up.*

"Let's sort it, then," said Barencoin. "Do we have to bang on the airlock hatch and give 'em the secret password, or what?" He tapped his palm to activate the bioscreen again, its audio link embedded in his jaw. *C'naatat* had rejected Ade's implanted enhancements early in the game as some amateurish attempt at what it could do so much better. "Oi, you lot in there—did you miss that spaceship? Come on. Open up. The Royals are here to add a bit of glamour to your tawdry lives."

Umeh Station looked a lot different from the last time

Ade had been here a few weeks ago. *Shit. I had Shan for the first time in the machinery space below ground. Funny, the way you think of places having meaning.* The station had always been a mess, permanently untidy in the way of places that had temporary facilities for too many people and jury-rigged systems squeezed into any available space. Now it had the air of a house being stripped before moving day. It looked raw and broken.

Crew and civilian contractors seemed overdressed although the place ran hotter than planned. They were wearing and carrying the things they wanted to hang on to in the disruption. They couldn't take a whole dome with them.

"Waste of taxpayers' money," said Becken. "How many billions to ship this out here? And we just dump it like gash."

"The isenj can make use of it," said Webster. The engineer in her saw utility in everything. "It could be a hothouse for any plants they try to reintroduce. I could stay here and sort that after the evac."

"Sue, they've got one poxy tree in a bomb crater. That's today's wildlife show from Umeh. *One tree.* Good thing they don't have any dogs."

Ade cut in. The sooner they got working, the sooner they shipped out again. "Mart, Jon, you talk to the navy and get the numbers, loads and other manifest stuff they need to have. Sue, Chaz, you check what hardware they're planning to ship and make sure it's the stuff they actually *need* most on Mar'an'cas, not just commercial shit that the companies want back in one piece. Survival takes priority."

"Can we enforce that?"

"'Course we can. We booked the taxi. Christ, Sue, we're not even Royal Marines any more, not technically. We're just heavily armed civilians with an Eqbas army backing us up."

"And we've been court-martialed already."

"Would you argue with us?"

"Nah."

"Shall I go and piss people off?" said Eddie. "I mean, if there's something I can do, I'll roll my sleeves up, but if not . . ."

"See what you can scrounge, mate." Ade spread his hands in invitation. "You're a natural resource investigator. If it looks handy, and it's not nailed down, take it for a walk."

"Organic, inorganic?"

"Food. Life's little comforts. That's the stuff the wess'har can't provide for us."

"You'll be amazed," said Eddie, all sinister promise, and wandered off looking deceptively earnest.

Ade cocked his head at Qureshi to follow him and the detachment split up, disappearing to places they knew better than he did after their stay here. He headed for the cluster of command offices on the north side of the dome. An impressive climbing plant had spread across the stays of the roof and gave the interior a pleasant filtered light that made the place feel like there should have been a coffee bar and a designer fashion store nearby. But the stacks of pallets, the loader bots and the other telltale signs of a research outpost gave the game away.

There was, of course, still the banana tree.

Ade paused as he walked past the planter. It was a circular tub, pale blue blown composite, and—as made sense in an environment where everything had to earn its keep—all the oxygen-producing plants it contained were edible. The ridged and polished jade leaves of the dwarf banana veiled a developing hand of fruits; around it, there were dwarf-stock limes, miniature papayas and pineapples. The thought of them was more arresting than sex at that moment. He had to retrieve those bloody things somehow.

Shit . . . that's a fig tree over there.

Qureshi was almost telepathic. "And I'll grab the bloody chilies," she muttered. "We're going to be here for a few more years until the main Eqbas force shows up, so we might as well enjoy it." She elbowed him discreetly, nodding in the direction of another planter. "Pomegranates, range fifty meters . . ."

"I'm on it."

Ade imagined presenting Shan with the spoils. She always put on that I'll-eat-anything stoicism and she never complained, but he saw how she relished little treats, and he desperately wanted to appease her, even though there was nothing more tangibly *wrong* between them than an emotionally traumatic event that affected them both.

I can't even tell my mates. I can't share it with them.

Nobody in the detachment had any secrets. Most of them had lived in each others' pockets for years: they were the closest he had to family before Shan came on the scene. Every tragedy, annoyance and observation was shared. But not now.

"You reckon they can make that ship shielding on a small enough scale to be individual armor?" asked Qureshi.

"You've been playing too many kilbot games, Izzy."

"Seriously. They must have a power generator. That'll be the only limiting factor, whether it's portable or not."

"They're a million years ahead of us. No 'must have' about it."

"Wouldn't half make our jobs a lot easier. Stroll up a beachhead, bimble into enemy fire, take no notice . . ."

"Won't *be* our jobs when we get back to Earth."

"You said *we*."

"*You.* Habit."

"We'll be a century or more out of date. That's serious skills-fade even if we were still in the Corps."

"You'll be alien specialists. You know how many people in human history have lived with aliens? Stayed in their homes? Eaten with them? Fought alongside them, fought *against* them? Just us. When the Eqbas show up, that's going to *count* for something."

Qureshi reached out and rubbed a leaf that filled the air with an intense lemon scent. It was a herb of sorts. "Yeah, but someone will want to sign us up to fight *them*."

"This isn't about having a paycheck when you get back."

"No. You know it isn't. It never was. It's about the shame of being kicked out for something we didn't do."

"I told you, Shan said Esganikan would put in a request to set aside the findings."

"Yeah, if Commander Neville was still alive, maybe the bitch would have testified."

"Her word won't count for much now." It was out of his

mouth before he could even check himself, and he felt his face burn immediately.

Qureshi just looked at him as if she'd touched on a sore subject, and continued. "Rayat, too. All the serious witnesses are dead."

Ade quit while he was ahead. He was a compulsive blusher, so she'd have taken it as embarrassment. He hated lying. He hated trying to keep his various stories straight, and if anything proved that honesty was the best policy, it was this. Lies destroyed everything.

He tore his gaze from the plants set to be liberated and pushed open the door to the main office. Lieutenant Sophia Cargill stood with her arms folded, contemplating a white-board on the wall. She reached out and touched the reactive surface, deleting a set of names from one section and dragging them across to another list, then writing a new list with her fingertip. Pigment leapt into life at the change in surface temperature and the words SANITATION DETAIL emerged on the board in a ghostly delayed hand. It was all too biblical for Ade. He paused, almost expecting to see LIAR appear next.

"I'm glad you're here," said Cargill, still preoccupied with the roster she was drawing up. "Fleet got back to us an hour ago. Director of Special Forces wants to talk to you."

"Sorry, ma'am?" Shit, he dropped right back into being know-your-place, deferential, reliable Bennett—Adrian J., Sergeant, 37 Commando, 510 Troop EEWC, number 61/4913D. It was his whole adult life in one databurst of a line. "What for?"

"It's need to know, and apparently I don't." She had that faintly irritated tone of a woman who'd done a bloody hard job that nobody sitting safely on their arse in CINC Fleet Main Building appreciated. "You might hang around until I get a link set up."

Qureshi caught his eye and she didn't even need to raise a brow to convey *shitty death*.

"Will do, ma'am."

"Don't have to. I have no jurisdiction over any civilians not on this list. That means you." Cargill made a circle on the tote board with her finger and dragged another block of scrawled text to another position. She was playing loadmaster, working out the sequence of evacuation and who would be tasked to carry out the jobs on the day of the airlift. "But thank you. You didn't have to front up, not after what's happened. You don't owe the FEU anything."

"It's about the Corps, ma'am, not the government," Ade said quietly. "We'll always owe the Corps." He liked to make the point. "With your permission, we'll start removing a few essential plants."

Cargill's face creased in a brief smile. "See the duty maintenance manager in block nine alpha and tell him I gave you instructions to do it. Whatever it is."

Cargill was all right. Ade and Qureshi went in search of the manager, commandeered tools and empty storage drums, and began digging up fruit trees. It was amazing the kind of things he ended up doing as a Royal Marine. In the general ebb and flow of bodies trying to strip a structure for a fast exit, their pillage of the shrubbery went unnoticed, or at least nobody tried to stop them. Eventually Eddie showed up with Sue Webster. The pockets on Eddie's vest and his battered messenger bag bulged with promising cartonlike shapes.

"What you got, Eddie?" asked Qureshi, hardly looking up from the delicate root ball that she was easing out of the soil. "Any good rabbit?"

Eddie had the glow of satisfaction that must have been familiar to his hunter-gatherer ancestors. "Curry concentrate. Cumin and coriander seeds. Pepper. Saccharin. Rice, ration-prepped *and* seed grain. Coffee, cocoa powder and oatmeal."

He might as well have said he had all the gems of the Orient. "That's bloody good rabbit, Eddie. All donated?"

He grinned. "More or less."

Ade wrapped the banana's root ball in composite sheet and secured it before sliding it into one of the small drums. "See how bloody fast we plummet into anarchy."

"I'll stick a pig's head on a pole later and we can dance around it in primal abandon."

"You're a natural born baron-strangler, mate."

"What?"

"Good at taking advantage of hospitality."

"I'm a journo. We do that."

"I'm glad you're on our side."

Eddie's knuckles showed white as he kept a ferocious grip on the straining strap of his bag. "Yeah, I am. Looks like you're liberating a few assets yourself."

"Doing a bit of jungle training. Identification and utilization of native tropical food plants for survival in the field."

"Uhuh . . ."

"Nicking the fucking banana tree."

"Ah, the endless possibilities of the English language . . ."

The next challenge was to find a secure holding area for the plunder while they awaited extraction. Sticking it in a quiet corner with Mart Barencoin was probably the best option to stop some other bastard trying to walk off with it. They were discussing the logistics when the Regulating Branch chief jogged up to them, and they instinctively formed a protective circle around the growing pile of looted items. The man was a "crusher," the ship's police.

"Your Boss is on the ITX, Royal. Cleared the bloody office out too, so make it snappy."

Ade found himself reaching without thinking for his beret and slipping it two-handed onto his head. "Come on, Izzy. Let's see what he's got to say for himself."

"Her," said the chief. "It's a *her.*"

"Can I watch?" said Eddie.

"Yeah, why not?" Ade heard a faint alarm bell, the kind that made him a witness who wasn't in uniform. "Keep your trap shut, that's all."

Qureshi didn't seem bothered. Eddie was a tame embed as far as she was concerned. Cargill held the office door open with an emphatically blank expression. "Screen's on standby. Green key, when you've got yourself looking all lovely. Call me when you're done."

Ade closed the door behind her and gestured to Qureshi and Eddie to stand out of the range of the cam. He did it without thinking again, but it wasn't his Royal Marines drill that was driving him—it was Shan's legacy in his genes, and he knew it as surely as if she'd tapped him on the shoulder. He settled himself at the console, then removed his beret to fold and slide it under the shoulder tab of his shirt.

This had better be a fucking apology.

He pressed the green key. The screen switched from the pale blue UN holding portal to a tidy desk dominated by a female brigadier—not a marines officer, but one in army drab. She looked like she could even take on Shan and last a few rounds: spare, cold-eyed, maybe forty, and with short blond curls that weren't remotely girlie.

"Yes ma'am," he said. "Bennett, ma'am. Former Five-Ten Troop."

There was always several seconds' delay even with the instant relay of the ITX. The last relay of the entangled photon link was a little way from Earth and had to limp the last leg at light speed. Ade counted.

"Brigadier Harrison," she said. "I see the service might have dispensed with you, but you haven't dispensed with the service."

"Is that what you wanted to discuss with me, ma'am?"

"Yes. We need to do some administrative resolution if you're all returning to Earth at some stage."

Here we go. Ade avoided catching Eddie's eye even in his peripheral vision. "You'll have to be specific."

"The Defense Ministry reopened the case. The senior Judge Advocate feels that the hearing was wrongly convened and that the finding of guilt can't stand."

Ade chewed the words carefully and extracted a faint and grudging flavor of apology from them. It was a start.

"What does that mean exactly, ma'am?"

One, two, three, four, five . . .

"That you may be eligible for reenlistment with your good names intact, with no loss of privileges."

He waited. Qureshi and Eddie, leaning against the wall behind the screen, were doing a good job of holding their breath. The pause was far longer than the delay on the ITX router.

"Ma'am," he said at last. "What's the condition attached?"

Harrison lost her glacial detachment for a moment and the quick compression of her lips said she was reluctant to tell him.

"My intelligence colleagues tell me one of their number is still in theater and he hasn't reported in for some time. They'd like to talk to him."

"Dr. Rayat? No need to be discreet, ma'am. Everyone knows he's a spook, including the Eqbas."

Shit. He'd used the present tense. That was no big deal for Harrison, but Qureshi thought Rayat was dead. *Oh shit.*

"Very well, and I make this offer on behalf of my colleagues, who appear to be above me in the food chain these days . . . find Rayat, and we can discuss your futures."

"They want him back."

"Yes."

Shan would have been proud of him. "Do they think he's misbehaved, or are they just worried for his safety?"

"One never knows with the intelligence community."

"Very good, ma'am. I'll report back as soon as I can."

"Please do, Mister Bennett."

Ade killed the link before Harrison got the chance to. The silence hung over the room, building like a storm.

"*Mister* Bennett, my arse," Ade muttered. "Don't try to psych me, missus."

"Oh shit," said Eddie. Ade willed him not to say the *c'naatat* word in front of Qureshi. "That does it, then."

Qureshi folded her arms and shrugged. "What do we do, dredge up the Rayat bits and bag them? Do you remember where you dumped him?"

"How badly do you want to be reinstated, Izzy?"

"Pretty badly, if only to avoid having *war criminal* on my résumé. Won't proof of death do?"

"How do we prove that?" Jesus, this was getting stupid. Ade couldn't keep it up much longer. First rule: you trusted your mates and they trusted you. You watched each other's backs. Arses were covered. You'd put your life on the line for them because they'd do the same for you. Armies ran on that simple act of faith and personal trust, and if you didn't live that principle, you weren't just fucked—you were scum.

"Izzy, go and round up the lads and find somewhere private we can talk. This is messier than it looks."

Qureshi paused for a second then walked out without a word. Ade wrestled with reality. Eddie stood next to his seat and put on hand on the back of it, leaning slightly over him.

"You can't tell anyone about Rayat. Or Lin. They haven't asked about her, have they?"

"Eddie, they won't want Lin back in the shape she's in now."

"I thought she was alive."

"She is. She's just changed a lot."

"Oh God."

"*C'naatat* does that."

"What happened?"

"Christ, Eddie, she's been living under water. Use your imagination. It's not her I'm worried about. It's that bastard Rayat."

"Do you know where they are?"

"Maybe."

"Ade, I've known about this since Christmas and I haven't said a word. I learned my lesson with Shan. Do you reckon they know about Rayat?"

"How could they? He hasn't had any comms access since he caught the bloody thing." Ade couldn't recall if Shan had explained exactly how Rayat and Lin had acquired *c'naatat*: as usual, Eddie had put two and zero together, made an intuitive leap, and worked out that there were now two more carriers. Ade wasn't going to fill in the details. "And he isn't going to be handed over to anyone, so we're stuck. Problem is . . . look, I have to tell them. I can't do this to them. They have to know why I can't deliver Rayat."

Eddie straightened up and adjusted his bulging pockets. "And you've got no guarantee that the Ministry's going to keep their promise. Jesus, if they want him back—it'll be between twenty-five and seventy-five years before they get their hands on him. Nobody who can sign an authorization is going to be around then, and even if they make you all Major-Generals with knobs on today, what's to say that'll be honored when you get back?"

"*They*," said Ade. "When *they* get back. I'm not going. You know I can't."

"What a fucking mess."

"Not if they'll forego their chance to get back in."

"What else are they going to do?"

"You reckon any Earth government is going to argue with Esganikan 'Read-My-Lips' Gai? There's another way to do this."

"Yeah." Eddie began counting off on his fingers. "One, tell them he's dead. Two, wait until you get back to Earth and challenge the verdict in the courts. Three . . ."

"You've got a three, have you?"

"Give me time."

"You can't cover things up forever, least of all with people you're close to."

"You've never had an affair, I take it."

"Fucking right I haven't."

"You think Shan tells you everything?"

"I know she does." Oh yes. *I was pregnant and now I'm not.* She could have kept it to herself, but she couldn't live with the secrecy. Sometimes people unburdened themselves to share the shit, and sometimes they just did it because it was right at some instinctive level. "And . . . well, sex with *c'naatat* carriers . . . okay, we share genetic memories. If an event is big enough and bad enough, you can't hide it."

Eddie looked as if he was going to bite back with some cynical disbelief, but his expression sagged into sad realization. "You're a matched pair, you two. Bloody scout's honor, I-might-be-some-time, death before dishonor."

"I like honesty. It's easy."

"I didn't say it was wrong. Just that you're an endangered species. Ade, you've got to discuss this with Shan. You *have* to."

The door swung open with some force and Sophia Cargill loomed in the doorway.

"I hate to interrupt, gentlemen, but shift it, will you? Got work to do."

"We're gone," said Eddie.

As they walked across the open plaza in the center of the

dome, Ade marshaled his thoughts and he fumbled in his pouch belt for the *virin,* the wess'har communications device that he was only just beginning to get the hang of. He tried to get a link through to Shan, but the sequence of finger positions defeated him and he slowed to a stop to concentrate on it. He ended up getting the Eqbas ship on station above him.

"I must speak to *Shan Chail,*" he said in his best wess'u. "I have a problem."

"We'll contact her," said the bridge officer. "Did you understand that? We . . . will . . . call . . . her."

"I understand." *Just about.* "Tell her it concerns Rayat."

Eddie stared at Ade as he slid the *virin* back in his belt.

"You can do the two voices." Eddie sounded envious. "That's amazing. I've tried for months to do it."

"It's the genes in me," said Ade, embarrassed. "It's nothing clever."

Ade began walking again, dodging bots and small loaders. He wondered if Cargill had a realistic view of how much the Eqbas were prepared to transport, and how much the colony on Mar'an'cas could deal with. But that wasn't his main problem right now: he had to decide how to make things right for his detachment, the men and women who were his personal responsibility whether they were still technically marines or not. They'd do no less for him. Wherever Qureshi had found a secure space, she'd spotted him because he heard a sharp whistle and looked around to see her beckoning to him from a service area.

There was a time when all he had to do was glance at the living computer grown into his palm to see the vital signs of the whole detachment, all of them linked through the bioscreen system implanted in them—data, communications, health monitoring, the works. Even Lindsay Neville had one. Now *c'naatat* had purged him of it and all the implanted links in his eyes, ears and organs, another reminder that he wasn't really one of them any longer.

Sometimes there wasn't much difference between being surgically loaded with battlefield data systems and having an alien symbiont. Either way, it separated you from those who didn't have it.

The detachment was holed up in a storeroom. Chahal was making a careful examination of the bagged plants, pressing his finger into the soil and trickling water into the drums from his ration bottle.

"So, Rayat's arse for our honor," said Barencoin. He sat on a cupboard, swinging his legs idly. "Shame the fucker's dead. Why didn't you tell them that?"

"Because we need to discuss this," said Ade.

"Nobody will remember us anyway by the time we get back to Earth. It's what we do to survive when we get home that matters."

Sue Webster—solidly unflappable, rosy-cheeked, endlessly cheerful, and very adept at silent kills with her fighting knife—swatted him across the knee as she edged past him. "Mart, what difference is your employment history going to make when the Eqbas show up on Earth, eh? Think about it."

"The adventure ends one day, mate," said Barencoin. "We've all got maybe sixty or seventy years to fill when we get back. But we're from another age. Earth's an alien world to us now. You've got this illusion that we're still part of it because we can watch the fucking telly and check our bank accounts when we can get a link out. But we won't fit back in. We never will."

Sue shook her head in mild exasperation. "You saw what was happening to this planet when we dropped below the cloud cover. It's doomsday. All change. New order. Might be paradise, might be hell. Won't be the same as it is now, though. Job prospects on Earth are going to be the last of your worries."

"So if we found Rayat's decaying remains and waved them in front of the ITX cam," said Becken, "then the Boss Spook says that's nice, thank you very much, we just wanted to know what happened to him out of curiosity so we can update our pension mailing list, and you're now back in business, no hard feelings. Yeah? Is that the size of it?"

Ade glanced at Qureshi. She was silent, sitting on a table with her arms around her knees. He could almost see the replay in her brain, the way she was reliving the conversation from the time he shut the door and started taking to Harrison. Maybe it was his guilt, which was always willing to stand a double watch, that made him think she was slowly working it out.

Chahal joined in the involuntary head-shaking. "Whatever they say now, in twenty-five or thirty years' time, none of those promises are going to mean shit."

Becken snorted. "That's one thing we *can* bank on."

Ade wanted clarity. He got it with Shan and now he expected it from everyone. "So what do you want me to do? Use the lever we have, such as it is, or tell them to fuck off?"

"We don't know what they want."

"Find Rayat."

"Well, he's in the Cavanagh system. He can't be anywhere else. Job done. And that takes us where, exactly?"

It bought Ade some time. He could *seek clarification*, a nice Shan-type phrase that didn't translate into calling Harrison a spook-puppet.

"Do you want the finding of guilt overturned, or do you also want to continue serving?"

There was a pause. The marines all looked at one another. Ade could guess: they knew what they really wanted—for life to go on as if the last couple of years had never happened—but they didn't understand the price, or if the bargain would be kept.

Qureshi found her voice at last. "Let's find out *exactly* what they want us to do. Because they know something that we don't. Rayat had something they want, or he did something they need to check on, or whatever, but they need him."

Ade teetered on the edge of doing the right thing, the decent thing, because if he couldn't trust special forces troops with this information—if he couldn't trust comrades—then he couldn't rely on anyone, and he didn't want to have that same cold mistrustful core growing in him that he'd felt at the root of Shan's memories.

"He's not dead." Ade blurted it out. "And they *can't* possibly know if he's dead or not."

"Aw, shit . . ." Barencoin was instant anger. "You fucking *liar,* Ade. You told us he was dead. And Neville too. You said you handed them both over to the bezeri."

"I did." No point dragging Aras into it. It wasn't the poor sod's fault there were two extra *c'naatat* on staff. "He's not dead, and neither is Lin."

"But Bezer'ej is loaded with human-specific pathogens. The wess'har answer to asset denial. And the sea's a bit damp, yeah? Am I understanding you right?"

Sometimes Barencoin's chain of logic was so like Shan's it was painful, right down to the language. "You got it."

"So either the pathogen is bullshit, or those bastards have got *c'naatat.*"

I should have just said I lied and that I'd chickened out of killing them. I could have done a good job of that. Really convincing. "It's a cock-up all round."

"This just gets better with every passing day, doesn't it?" Barencoin slid off the cupboard and strode slowly around the room, rubbing his face with both hands. He was one of those very dark blokes with pale skin that showed permanent five-o'clock shadow, and combined with his aggressive body language it made him look like a bad-tempered pirate on his day off. "Eddie, I notice you didn't call your news desk to hold the front page or whatever shit it is you do. You knew?"

"Yeah." Eddie sounded utterly unmoved. Ade realized that he'd probably come up against some real bastards in his career and an angry Barencoin wasn't going to make him back down. He didn't even give in to Aras when he was throttling the life out of him. "But if you've seen one *c'naatat,* you've seen 'em all. Old news."

"It's not fucking funny."

"Since when did you become the environmental conscience of the FEU?"

"It's another layer of shit we don't need. You bloody *sure* they don't know he's got a dose?"

Ade had now had enough. "No, they don't. So shut it. And they don't know about Lin either. Rayat's just dropped off their radar and they want to know why. And now you know that if the next thing they want is for us to bring him home in exchange for clearing us, the answer's no can do."

"Christ."

Chahal and Webster just stood up and got on with packing the food and plants into crates they could lift between them, and everyone seemed to have run out of things to say. Eddie patted Ade's back and bent down to give Qureshi a hand wrapping plants.

You've done it now. And Shan's going to go ballistic.

Ade knew that as soon as he left the room, they'd start arguing, and saying what a shit their sergeant had turned out to be, and how they'd trusted him. Right then Ade didn't give a toss about the Corps, or his honor on some record at HQ, but that he'd fallen from grace with people who weren't just friends or co-workers or any of that civilian shit, but were brothers and sisters in a way that maybe even Aras wasn't.

That was his honor: the respect and trust of his mates. *Sorry* didn't begin to cover it. He felt desperately alone and wondered what had happened to his solid dull common sense.

And it still wasn't over. Now he had to face Shan again. He'd lost too much ground with her already and she'd tear him up for arse-paper for letting anyone know about Rayat and Lin.

"I'm going to wander around and see what else I can lift," he said, and as Eddie went to follow him he held up his hand to indicate he didn't want company.

"You going to ask Harrison a bit more?" said Becken. "Work out what their game really is? Because if they know he's got a dose, or that they can get it anytime from Ouzhari, then there'll always be some bastard trying to get out here to grab it. Shan said that, didn't she?"

Becken didn't have to add that Shan took the airlock option rather than hand the parasite over to Rayat and his spookmasters. It was one of those ironies so huge that it had almost lost all meaning.

"I'll wait a few days." Ade shut the store door behind him and wished that *c'naatat* hadn't given him any more useful extras, because his hearing was acute now, as acute sometimes as Aras's. Before he moved out of range, the last words he caught were Ismat Qureshi's.

" . . . whatever happened to good old Ade?"

Good question. He didn't know either.

He hadn't even told them that the bezeri had a shabby history of genocide, and that at least one of them now carried *c'naatat*. There was only so much of his own inadequacy and bad judgment he could dump on them in a day.

Call me back, Shan, he thought. He'd face the consequences of his own actions, but reassurance from someone who believed in him would have been good right then. *Jesus, woman, I need to hear your voice.*

Private apartments of Minister Rit, Jejeno

"They'll come for you," said Ralassi. The ussissi's tone was weary and matter-of-fact. "They'll kill you."

"I haven't revealed my intentions." Rit checked her communications logs to see that the message to her sons had been received at the Tasir Var relay. She wanted to reassure them that she was safe if they heard more reports of fighting in the capital. "Shomen Eit has no idea what involvement I have with the Eqbas. I plotted with nobody."

"That also means you have no allies either, Minister."

"Winners always have allies after the fact," Rit said. "And fortunately I have no need of them before it."

"But how will you hold a government together in the aftermath of this? The Eqbas can't be at your side forever. At some point after they withdraw, the army will turn on you."

Rit's apartments were the top section of a tower to the northwest of the Northern Assembly parliament building. Her privilege gave her that most sought-after of things, an open terrace set in the asymmetric roof that sliced across the top of the tower at an angle. At this height she felt safe enough to open the doors onto the roof and take a few steps outside to get a better view of the cityscape. In her private home, she had no access to the monitoring network that would have shown her the movements of troops and the status of utilities and traffic across the country. She had to rely on what she could see, hear and smell from this high tower, and the height of the surrounding buildings meant she had almost no view of ground level.

A dozen distant palls of gray smoke rose up from the forest of towers and canyon-sided multistory blocks; muffled booms punctuated the ever-present murmur of city sounds that reminded her of the ocean on Tasir Var. Umeh's moon was a world with a few remaining forests and open land where no buildings had ever stood. It was the reason she had her children educated there, and why she was happier leaving them in the school than bringing them to Jejeno.

If that wasn't an admission of the need for drastic change on Umeh, then nothing was. Umeh wasn't a place she wanted to raise her sons. Ministers and the wealthy from all four continents sent their children there if they could, and saw no irony in the fact that the world they shaped and created wasn't good enough for their own offspring.

I see it now. Ual saw it long before me.

Now she understood her husband's willingness to risk everything to break the cycle of profligacy before it was too late.

I never understood it. I never supported you. I took on your legacy grudgingly. But I know better now.

Rit felt a pang of curious envy for the hybrid humans who could absorb each other's memories through the parasite they carried. Ironic that it was an isenj characteristic, and even more ironic that it had entered its first wess'har host, the Beast of Mjat, when he was wiping out isenj communities on Asht.

"Minister, come inside," said Ralassi. "The shelling is random. There's no point testing the law of probability."

"I can't see the Eqbas ship."

"It's probably too far south. And there's no telling what it looks like at the moment—it could be broken up into hundreds of smaller vessels. Fighters, landing craft, whatever they require at that moment to carry out the task."

"How do they do that?"

"I'm not an engineer, Minister. But wess'har have had responsive material technology for tens of thousands of years. Their ability to reshape matter is unrivaled."

"And not only inorganic matter. Genetic material too."

"Combine the two, and there's little over which they don't have control."

At that moment, those were the most reassuring words Rit could hear rather than the most alarming. She took one last look at the glittering facets of the city skyline and imagined what might be happening in the Maritime Fringe. Five hours ago, Esganikan Gai's ship—or ships—had started dispersing the pathogen that would attack only isenj with certain genetic markers. By now, the first effects would be noticed.

"Minister . . ."

"Very well." She closed the terrace doors but left the shutters parted. When the Eqbas ship came back to Jejeno, she wanted to see it. At times like this, she wanted something that Earth had and Umeh didn't: a universal broadcast network. She'd seen it. She knew that Eddie and his kind provided information that anyone could see and hear. If she'd had this now, she could have observed what was happening across the planet, without any need to know government contacts in other nations.

She picked up one of the small gray data cubes that stored network information and dropped it into its slot in the communications console, a child's puzzle with smooth shapes that fitted into only one hole. The image that emerged on the screen was one of a list of terminals she could reach. Each showed its own onward connections, red lines connecting to symbols.

"This is what is wrong," she said. "We follow chains. We connect, like we were still colonies communicating one to another. Networks touch and share information, but there is no . . ."

"Big picture."

"Is that the phrase?"

"It's what Eddie Michallat calls it."

"We need a single source of images and information, that anyone can reach directly." She needed to spend more time talking to Eddie. Her husband had found his insights useful, in some cases essential: whether Eddie knew it or not, his advice had played a part in creating the cataclysmic events she was now watching. Ralassi said knowing that would appall him.

Doesn't Eddie know that every action we take changes the world in some way? How can he think he exists in a separate state of being?

"You have a terminal, Minister." Ralassi tapped the screen and cycled through a few network portals—Rit noted her access to all the government ones had now been revoked—until one of the many BBChan streams of information appeared. "Minister Ual perfected his spoken English from this channel. He found it educational, if baffling. Would you like me to activate the translation?"

"Yes, but I meant that I would like a similar source of information of our own." She imagined Ual here, watching the activity of far-distant humans and learning their language, alone and lonely while she was with the children on Tasir Var all that time. "Wess'har understand all this?"

"Some speak English. Eqbas are learning it too. They plan to visit Earth."

"Visit. As they *visit* here?"

"Their objective is the same wherever they go. You know this."

Rit settled in front of the screen. The image was hazy—humans detected only a limited visual spectrum and their transmitted material was proof of that—but it was a window on a civilization that was less like hers than she'd thought.

And they made no mention whatsoever of anything other than their own world. The stop-start war on Umeh didn't appear, even though humans should have been interested to see what awaited them when the Eqbas *visited*.

Earth looked wonderfully rich, though. Images of a devastating storm showed giant green trees with feathery crowns not unlike the *dalf*'s, and large open areas with foliage, and clean gray-blue oceans whipped by white foamy waves.

An ancestral memory in Rit recalled seas like that. She felt she was operating largely on the impulses of that memory now as it guided her in a crisis.

"Anyone on Earth can see this, yes?"

Ralassi had seen it all before and appeared bored, "If they want to. There are many information conduits like this, and some require payment."

"But everyone knows these are available. They don't have to inquire, or rely on contacts to help them locate information that's not easily found."

"Yes. In fact, BBChan and the other providers of this material go to great lengths to tell humans that it's there and invite them to see it."

That was the difference that fascinated her.

Isenj were as much driven by the genetic memory of their lineage as they were by new daily experiences. They lived within those social networks. Those networks cooperated, but . . .

"It's very repetitive," said Ralassi. "The information is all very similar. Not only similar, but actively repeated."

It might have been tedious for Ralassi, but for Rit it was still a striking novelty. It wasn't about people and situations she knew. It should have been utterly irrelevant to her. But it wasn't. This was now her future, and—more to the point—her children's future.

Rit waited. Across the city, at the cabinet offices, Eqbas troops were landing to secure the building.

They could have tired of the discussions and launched the universal pathogen that would kill every isenj on the planet. But they hadn't, and had taken a more difficult option to preserve isenj. Oddly, it gave her hope. Hidden in what others would see as a holocaust was actually something . . . *positive* that she never expected.

The traditional enemy, the wess'har—Eqbas or Wess'ej born—had changed its stance.

Wess'har were not immune to negotiation as everyone believed. Some of them could be *persuaded.* The wess'har couldn't be driven out, but if they were open to persuasion— they could be peaceful neighbors again, just as her husband had dreamed.

8

A legal battle to decide who owns the largest and most complete terrestrial gene bank in history has begun in the international courts. The Federal European Union today lodged a claim for ownership of the Christopher mission collection, taken from Earth nearly three centuries ago and due to return with the Eqbas fleet in 2406. The FEU claims that the bank was created by European geneticists and should be returned to the control of Brussels for safekeeping. Australian premier Canh Pho described the FEU bid as "bizarre opportunism" and said the gene bank was an international resource that his country planned to defend from commercial exploitation.

BBChan 557, March 2377

F'nar, Wess'ej, underground storage complex: Day one of the Umeh invasion

"They never learn, do they?" said Shan.

The future of Earth sat in industrial refrigerators in the tunnels under F'nar. Like all miracles, it could be reduced by observation to the measurable and mundane, and Shan preferred things that way. There were enough wild cards in life already without adding conjuring tricks. She even knew how people rose from the dead: it was a parasite, not divine intervention.

Nevyan stood watching her in the same indulgent way she did with Giyadas, as if Shan was just getting the hang of reality. "Esganikan Gai is hardly likely to respond to a court order to hand over the gene bank when the fleet arrives."

"I never saw her as respectful of bureaucracy, somehow." Shan pressed the seals of the freezer unit to reassure herself they were still locked, and reminded herself she had no technical expertise whatsoever to verify anything. She was just indulging in a nervous tic of ownership, checking the bloody thing like it was a kitchen appliance and not an ecology worth fighting wars to protect. "You know what surprises me? That even now I'm still stunned by how *stupid* human beings are. Here's one of Earth's two superpowers thinking that a court order is going to make an alien fleet—hundreds of thousands of years more advanced than theirs—hand over *anything*. What do they use for brains? What in the name of God do they think the Eqbas are?"

"Why God?"

"Nev, it's just a phrase. I'm asking a real question. How can humans be that insanely blind to reality?"

"If you've been the dominant species for millennia, how can you suddenly accept that you have little significance in the scheme of things?"

"It's whistling in the dark. That's what we call it. Mindless activity to stop yourself feeling scared."

"The time scales involved in this are beyond them. One thing I've learned about *gethes* in observing them is that anything more than a few seasons in the future is never going to happen."

"You said it."

This was the original gene bank, the one that the *Christopher* mission had gambled billions of euros and a human community to send as far from Earth as it could to protect it until it was safe to return not only animal material but also all the unpatented, unregistered food plants that no corporation owned or controlled. It was Earth in a kit, copyright God, free for use without alteration, the holy shareware of life. The loony God-botherers had succeeded and Shan had no doubt that even the ludicrously tolerant Deborah Garrod had allowed herself a private moment of "Up yours, heathens!" when the Eqbas showed up to complete the miracle.

Shan bloody well had. But she didn't do tolerant. And she didn't do trusting. She'd had the gene bank divided and duplicated, so that only one version of the irreplaceable collection took the risk of returning to the world whose greed and stupidity had made it necessary in the first place.

She'd hang on to the other bank here as long as it took. It

was insurance: and she'd be around forever to keep an eye on it. That made her feel better than she ever imagined possible, and for a moment she almost saw Deborah Garrod's delusional God-logic pointing out that *c'naatat* had an enabling purpose in all this too.

Fuck you, Eugenie Perault. You never banked on me pulling it off, did you?

The jumble of emotions ambushed Shan and she shook them off. "This is what I hate about genetic memory," she said. She motioned Nevyan out of the compartment and closed the hatch of the chamber behind them. "You get mad ideas. You have to learn not to listen to the voices."

"I watch you with concern."

"Am I that different now?"

"No, and that's why I'm concerned. Events should have tempered your zeal."

Nevyan walked ahead of her along the dimly lit tunnel that led to the surface, her mane of tawny hair bobbing with her rolling gait. Shan pondered on her observation in silence until they emerged from the tunnel and stood in the cool night air of F'nar. The clean clarity of it still caught Shan unawares sometimes. When she looked up into the sky, the stars—constellations she was now beginning to recognize—were more vivid than anything she'd ever seen from Earth. They were almost as harshly bright as they'd been in the uninterrupted vacuum of space.

Shan could think about that more frequently these days without reliving the terror and pain. It heartened her. She was getting used to the long, long term perspective of *c'naatat*.

It's only pain. Everything passes.

Her swiss beeped for attention as soon as they moved clear of the tunnel entrance. "Bloody thing," said Shan. "I think it's on its way out." Everything else passed on in the end, even this little gadget that she'd carried all her adult life. She flipped the key and found a message waiting from Ade. "Still, not bad going for an antique."

"Livaor could repair it for you."

"He did a great job even getting an ITX link into it, but I think it's just getting too old." Maybe she'd part with it for a few days if Livaor could give it a stay of execution. "Ade's going to think I'm ignoring him."

"He's very anxious about your view of him."

"He doesn't have to be."

"You still refuse him *oursan*."

Nevyan's unflinching wess'har pragmatism about sex and bodily functions didn't sting Shan as much as it used to. "Actually, no. Shapakti came up with a mechanical solution to the problem. The sex situation is back to normal, more or less, except there's no exchange of genes."

"Your reproductive system has regrown *again*?"

"No, it hasn't. I check every day." Shit, what if the swiss's penetrating scan was playing up too? "I just can't take the risk again."

"This is very sad."

"Most humans manage to get through life without swapping genetic memory, Nev. So will we." Whatever Ade wanted probably wasn't urgent. He'd have called Aras by now if it was. She pressed the *return* key, tiny and worn smooth by owners long before her, not minding if Nevyan heard an intimate conversation. "Come on Ade . . ."

He must have been clutching his link to his chest. He answered immediately, voice shaky.

"You're going to be angry, Boss."

Oh, shit. Ade, don't do this. "What is it?"

He took an audible breath. "I had to tell the detachment that Rayat and Lin are alive."

Relief flooded her; stomach first, then legs. She'd imagined something worse, formless and unguessable. "Okay. Why?"

"It's okay?"

"They're bloody special forces. I'm sure they can handle surprises and keep their mouths shut. You're right, I should have leveled with them from the start. Anyway . . . why?"

"Had a contact from HQ, offering to reinstate everyone if we could find Rayat. Are you *sure* you're okay about this?"

"Yes. Look, why the interest in Rayat now? You reckon they know what he's carrying somehow? If it's Eddie—"

"Eddie's not the problem. I don't know if they do know. Just that now they can get on the ITX direct to Cargill, they're interested again."

"Well, it's an embarrassment to lose a spook. I can see how they'd want to tick him off the list. They're not personnel you can write off if they go AWOL."

"Thanks, Boss."

"What?"

"I thought you'd kill me." There was almost a little sob in his voice. "I really thought I'd done it this time."

Was that what she'd made of him? Shan felt ashamed that Ade was still scared of her reaction. It told her more than she wanted to know about herself.

"They had to be told," she said. "I'm sorry if that's the deal. Tell HQ he's dead. I'll provide the body if they insist."

"You're serious?"

"I'm serious. And you trust those fucks in Spook HQ to honor that deal, do you? Call their bluff."

"The brigadier said the verdict couldn't stand whatever that is worth."

Nevyan was watching her face intently. Wess'har had no concept of intrusion, no human habit of looking away and pretending they couldn't hear a conversation taking place right next to them. Shan tried not to feel spied upon.

"Ade, that's not a pardon. Everyone knows the court-martial was a diplomatic trick to appease the wess'har for what happened on Ouzhari. It didn't work. When the Eqbas reach Earth, they'll be able to get the FEU and all their shitty minions to do anything they tell them, so let the detachment know it'll be put right, with or without Rayat."

She meant it. If this was fear for their futures, the marines didn't have to worry about that. Earth wasn't only going to be a much-changed place for them when they returned: it was going to change out of all recognition for *everyone*. And if this was about reputation and honor—she understood that, she certainly did—then she'd get Eddie to write them a new history. He could do that just fine.

Ade was silent for a moment. There was no time delay on this ITX router.

"You still there, Ade?"

"Okay, Boss, I'll tell them that."

"Sit tight. Tell you what, I'll come over for the evacuation. *I'll* talk to them."

"I'll do it. I'm still their NCO. Even if I'm not exactly their most trusted buddy at the moment."

"Tell them I made you keep it quiet. I did, remember? They ought to understand that. Orders."

"I'd never lied to them before."

It was a forlorn little boy's comment. As always, it pushed the button that made her want to defend him and punch the shit out of anyone who so much as looked at him the wrong way. She was millions of miles from him. Impotent protective anger blinded her for a moment.

"It's Mart Barencoin, isn't it? Give him a message. Tell him I'll be there, and I want a chat with him."

"Boss—"

"Tell him, Ade."

"Okay. You can't always make things right for me, you know that?"

I'll die trying. "I'll see you soon. Don't take any shit, okay?"

Shan shut down the link and dropped the swiss into her breast pocket. Nevyan was still watching, head tilted, clearly baffled by the exchange.

"Honor is a curious concept," she said, and began walking briskly towards the steps that led up the terraces. "This is part of your problem with lies. Would you come to eat with us tonight? You and Aras?"

Shan followed her, now able to deal with the rapid changes of topic and the twin-track nature of wess'har conversation. She was even capable of it herself now. "That would be very nice, Nev. Why lies?"

"Because humans destroy reality by willingly sharing an invented universe. What wess'har *know*, what *is*, remains unchanged. But because *gethes* lie so much, your world is unreal. You have no basis for anything you think, because you alter facts."

Wess'har logic was always a cold bucket of water over

the head, even now, even though she had their blood in her veins. "Worse than theft."

"I don't understand."

"A mate of mine used to say that you could lock things away from a thief, but you could never protect yourself against a liar."

"Indeed. *Some* of you understand, then. Lies are dangerous. Of course, the situation is made worse by the nature of human perception, which is so malleable and limited anyway. The marines' actions exist and can't be changed by opinion."

It was a nice clean-cut view of the world, and smacked of the nobility enshrined in the Rochefoucauld maxim Eddie had once sent her by way of a half-arsed apology for suspecting her motives.

Perfect courage is to do without witnesses what one would be capable of doing with the world looking on.

Yeah, that was about right. If you answered only to God or your own standards, then it was great. Eddie, of course, tried to swim against the current in the illusory river of smear, spin and stupid audiences, and had become fixated on telling the truth—whatever that was.

"I cared about my reputation once." Shan thought of Op Green Rage, and yogurt-knitting terrorist Helen Marchant, who she had an overwhelming urge to contact and call every fucking cow under the sun, although they'd parted as friends and the object of Shan's anger was her long-dead two-faced politician of a sister, Eugenie Perault. "I turned from an anti-terrorist officer to pretty well being one of them. Turning a blind eye. Leaks. Letting Marchant's people get away. I lost my good name, all right. I was busted for negligence."

"But you could just as easily have been *busted* for deliberately helping them."

"Yes."

"And you chose incompetence, which I doubt anyone believed for one moment."

"No, but they couldn't pin a damn thing on me. I'm good at covering my tracks. Believe me, I'm *good*."

"And there is your pride, Shan."

Her own motives and attitude to that loss of honor still troubled her. "I know. And that's why I decided to play dumb rather than do the whole anti-hero act. You know all that."

"I know, but you raise the matter again, and so I wonder if *you* yet know why you did it."

"Because I needed to know that I did it because it was right, not because it'd make me look heroically principled. That's why."

"If you had admitted your complicity, would that have jeopardized Marchant and her activities?"

Shan paused. She usually thought through every last angle in a situation. But she'd never considered fully confessing, and if it would have made any difference to Marchant's people. If she kept her mouth shut about one thing, she could have put her hands up to being the leak and nothing else. A prison sentence—no joke for a copper—and disgrace, versus a demotion for incompetence, and disgrace. *Jesus, was I just too scared to go to jail? I don't remember thinking that way.*

"It would have given them the legal opening to try to get a lot more information out of me," she said at last. "But in the end, it made no difference at all."

"Motives are irrelevant. You achieved the best outcome, so your anxiety about purity of intent doesn't matter."

"I'm not that wess'har, Nev. I still have to live in my own head."

"And can you?"

"As long as I don't let anyone make me Saint Shan of the Tree Huggers, yes."

"You have no control over that. You never did."

Shan had reached the stage where she had no automatic reaction to wess'har brusqueness, because it was never unkind, merely factual. They were right. Anything that wasn't true—including tact—eroded reality.

But she still wanted the last word with Marchant. "What's for dinner, then?"

"Not *rov'la*. I know it isn't to human taste. Eddie said it hurt."

"Yeah . . . *hurt* is an interesting flavor. We'll eat what's put in front of us."

"If you go to Jejeno, then I must too." Esganikan had promised to involve Nevyan and Shan in the talks, but it hadn't happened, and Shan expected meltdown; she'd have belted her one if she'd been Nevyan. But maybe that was part of wess'har tactlessness too, that both matriarchs knew they weren't playing mind games. "I need to know who my neighbor really is now. Esganikan can do as she pleases and then put a galaxy between herself and Umeh, but we remain, and she promised us we would meet the Northern Assembly to discuss bioweapons."

"We'll go in mob-handed, then, Nev. Show them how F'nar *isan've* do the business."

"We will discuss it when we eat."

There was never a time set for dinner, and Wess'har had no sense of territory and privacy like humans, something Shan still struggled to accept. They now knew to avoid just walking into her home unannounced, and that the interior rooms had doors—especially the lavatory and washroom— and that humans didn't regard the sex act as an appropriate public display of affection.

But the rest of Wess'ej still had no etiquette set for knocking on doors or agreeing times for appointments. There was *now,* and there was when you felt like it. Shan wondered how the Eqbas, the original wess'har from the World Before that Nevyan's forebears had split from ten thousand years ago, had ever developed astonishing technology with such a disregard for rule books and precise time.

The realization hit her. *I don't just like these people. I love them. They're my tribe now. I never had one before, other than coppers, other than my old mates.*

It was warmly comforting. Earth seemed like a debt she'd now paid, something to be filed and forgotten, but perhaps kept for a requisite number of years in case some record-keeper needed it for audit and examination, after which it could be erased.

But there was still the specter of Helen Marchant, and her sister, and Shan didn't like anyone thinking they'd outsmarted her. Even *dead* people.

Perault was long gone, and now she had either had her

I-told-you-so moment by going to the blissful eternity God had promised her, or she had rotted and returned to the carbon cycle like everything else. She'd cheated Shan of a confrontation.

But her sister was still alive, and still keen to speak to good old Shan, the eco-warrior's best friend.

Shan liked lists. Ticking things off them kept the fearful chaos at bay. Her list was now down to Rayat, Neville . . . and Marchant. Saving Earth's ecology was done, or at least as done as any one person could achieve

Marchant—*no, you have nothing to say to her.* Perault was the one who shanghaied her here, and what Marchant had caused her to do she'd do again tomorrow, and gladly, and so nothing needed resolving or avenging.

The best revenge on Perault had been to follow her bogus mission to the letter, and recover the gene bank for Earth.

Done and dusted. Shan concentrated on dinner.

Beser'ej: Chad Island

More of the bezeri had now been persuaded to accept *c'naatat* and come ashore. For a place they now called Where We Do Not Wish To be, they seemed to be thriving and—yes, they were *enjoying* life.

Lindsay told herself that she was supervising, but the construction of the wattle-and-daub tree houses was gathering pace without her guidance. A cluster of remarkably well-shaped globes were strung in the trees between *efte* ropes like bubbles of chocolate blown into a sieve. Bezeri were master plasterers, shaping the mud over the basket-like frameworks with impressive speed and control. It was the kind of craft skill you could excel at if you had multiple arms.

The females were still reluctant to stay in the new environment at night, but the males had taken to climbing the trees with easy grace and spending their time in the bubble-nests, sometimes sitting with tentacles draped from the opening and shimmering with light. It was only a matter of time before the whole remnant was ashore and forging a new existence.

But the sport of *sheven* hunting was definitely the most powerful draw for them. Right now she could hear splashing and thuds as one of the bezeri pursued a *sheven* in the network of streams that fed the bogland. The silence that followed said he had either caught it and was eating his kill, or he'd found something interesting to distract him. Their curiosity and enthusiasm was as intense as a kitten's.

Pili, the female who had once armed Lindsay with a stone hammer to drive off persistent *irsi*—the only aquatic animal bezeri didn't care to eat—bounced across the clearing. Her mantle was a mix of rainbow-spectrum lights and dark patches that seemed to respond to the background vegetation. For the first time in ages, Lindsay found it genuinely funny. With her collection of tools and her relentless enthusiasm for building things, Pili reminded her of Marine Sue Webster. It was easy to forget the bezeri weren't cartoon characters but hunters and—she had to accept this—capable of exterminating a rival race without too many moral qualms.

This is not your culture. It's not your ethics. And you had no qualms about detonating the bombs that wiped out most of Pili's people, so . . . get off that moral high ground.

It sounded like Rayat's voice in her head. But it was definitely her own.

"You look like you're wearing chameleon camo," said Lindsay.

"Camo," said Pili. "Explain."

"Disguise. Soldiers use it so they can't be seen."

"I need not hide," Pili said, and swung off. Lindsay watched her go, and realized the old girl was actually using a tentacle as a rear stabilizer and spring. Damn, she was almost using the thing like a kangaroo's tail.

This is evolution, fast forward.

It was the wrong terrain for a jumping animal—too many obstacles, not much open land—but Lindsay expected to see her bouncing along like a 'roo in the next day or so. She walked over to the growing tree-village and found Saib, who she still regarded as the patriarch, the Boss Fella, even if Keet did appear to be the one who was overseeing the building work. Saib was the strategist, Keet the implementer. Now they had come ashore, Lindsay was better able to see the team dynamics at work in a framework she understood.

She finally accepted she wasn't a natural leader like Shan Frankland, and never would be. The bezeri weren't looking to her for direction and inspiration anyway. If Shan had been doing this . . . no, it hardly bore thinking about. She'd have made them hide the houses and stop killing the *shevens*.

Saib turned to watch her approach, lounging like a Buddha in the shade of a tree . She could see his eyes now, definite squidlike eyes with pupils and irises, pigmented and noticeable. Eyes kept evolving the same way even here, shaped by the laws of optics.

"The wess'har have left," he said.

"What?"

"No patrols," he said. "We see no rafts. We see no wess'har."

The Eqbas couldn't have pulled out. They didn't think that way: they were cleaning up the nuclear contamination on Ouzhari, for a start. That wasn't finished yet. Lindsay suddenly realized how far out of the loop she was, and it was all down to technology. She was now literally a stone-age woman in a high-tech theater of war. She needed communications and IT. She had no way of knowing what was happening around the planet other than by seeing it or hearing it.

The bezeri needed to cover a lot of ground, a full human history of ground, before they could say they were masters of Bezer'ej and able to defend the planet themselves. They needed industry and technology.

"I have to check that out some time," she said. It was a long journey to the Temporary City on the mainland, a little further than Constantine at the top of the island chain. And it meant using a podship under water. She'd done both before. "If the isenj return—no, the wess'har would never allow that. But you need to be in a position never to need the wess'har again. Which is why living on land is important."

Saib didn't seem worried. "We live now. We have time we did not have before."

If that was a thank-you, she almost missed it. Lindsay reminded herself that she'd come to the bezeri to be executed for her role in their destruction, become their servant thanks to a strange reprieve via Ade Bennett, and now had come full circle to . . . a savior of a kind. Or maybe she was deluding herself because she wanted so badly to atone.

A little scared scrap of her still recalled praying with Deborah Garrod while she waited for her sentence, and she wasn't sure if that prayer was for her own life or for a wider forgiveness. Now that she had other people's memories in her, she could no longer be sure what her prayer was really asking, but she had an answer to it, if she chose to see it that way.

"That's good," she said. "You can take control of what happens to you now."

Saib considered the idea, slowly scratching his mantle with several tentacles. Perhaps he didn't yet understand the dual-tone language of English and light signals as well as she thought he did.

"The human who sees the fire all the time, the one from where the *see-nah-tat* comes," Saib said. "I know many of her thoughts now. I know her need to kill wrong-doers."

That was Shan, all right. "You can identify that?"

"I see all of her."

C'naatat never pulled the same trick twice. It seemed to have focused Saib on Shan's genetic memory to the exclusion of all others, and for a species needing a fanatical will to survive, it might have been a good choice. Lindsay was suddenly aware she was thinking in terms of the parasite making conscious decisions. She was glad Rayat wasn't here to lecture her on sloppy unscientific thinking.

"She had her good points," Lindsay said carefully.

"The terrible black," Saib said. "I see the terrible black and the pain now. Is the black like the Dry Above was to us once?"

Lindsay had to think about what the *terrible black* might be for a few seconds. "You mean *space*. There's no air, nothing. And as cold as cold gets."

"Her enduring is wonderful and also frightening."

That's right, get some inspiration from her. "If you want tough, Shan's tough."

"She promised to protect us from harm. This way, she has."

It took a few moments for Lindsay to realize that Saib was ascribing the gift of *time we did not have* to Shan Frankland. The thought hit her like a body blow. So soon after clutching at redemption and answered prayers, Lindsay was suddenly cast back into Shan's shadow, the also-ran, the Frankland-Lite who never quite made full iconic status. Those were Shan's last words to her before she stepped from the airlock to thwart Rayat and the FEU in as spectacular and horrifying way as anyone ever could: *Now this is how you do it, girlie. Next time you lose your bottle and you can't pull that pin, think of me. Because you'd give anything to be just like me, wouldn't you?*

Lindsay could recall every word, every pause, and the fact that Shan didn't blink once all the time she was looking into her face. That told her how deeply that taunt had carved into her self-esteem. Even seeing a haggard, weakened Shan after she had been recovered alive from space—from *space,* and that still felt impossible—hadn't stopped Lindsay thinking of those words as the ones that would be carved in eternity as her epitaph. The bitch had scarred her. She'd scarred her because it had been true.

It's not true now. It really isn't.

Lindsay didn't know if she was saying that to herself or to an absent, judgmental mother who metamorphosed into a boss that she never quite convinced of her worth.

"I suppose she *has* protected you," said Lindsay. "This came from . . . the wess'har that the isenj call the Beast of Mjat, the one your people knew as Aras and who wiped out the isenj here. And then it passed through Shan Frankland, and then to a human soldier, and then to me."

Saib shimmered with a twin spectrum of ambers and blues. "This is apt. This is right."

She didn't quite understand that. There was certainly irony in that sequence, and if bezeri understood sarcasm then they probably understood irony as well. But she had to ask, and she knew she would have to live with the answer.

"I know I did a terrible thing to your people, Saib, and nothing can undo that." He should have known her bitter shame from the memories of her *c'naatat,* but Shan seemed to have elbowed them out of the way too. "But I need to know what you think of me now."

"You have given us back real hunting. Maybe quality is better than numbers. This is good." Numbers? She tried to make sense of that. "Now we hunt!"

Before she could press further, he reared up and made for the bog, and she wondered how many *shevens* there were, and how long it would be before there were none at all.

Umeh Station, Jejeno: Eight hours after dispersal of bioagent

"Oh God . . ."

It was a woman engineer who spotted it first. She was leaning against the straight section of transparent composite that formed the base section of the dome, and then she jerked upright as if something had hit her in the back.

"Oh God, what's wrong with it?"

Eddie had been watching her for no reason other than that she was nice-looking, and that erased conscious analysis. She had a small crowd around her now. They were all looking in the direction of whatever had caught her attention. Eddie's other animal instinct, the one that sent him running towards trouble out of sheer curiosity and fear of missing something, took his bee cam from his pocket and flicked it into the air. You never knew until you got there if something was worth filming, and by then you might have missed it. He went prepared.

"It's sick," said the woman. The name tag on her orange coveralls said MORANZ. Eddie peered over the cluster of heads and saw an isenj on the service road. "What's it doing here?"

The bee cam was pressed to the composite like a nosey

neighbor, and Eddie decided against slipping it outside to get a better look.

The isenj was clearly in trouble. Slumped on its side and making futile efforts to crawl towards the dome, it was losing fluid from its mouth, the same thin yellow plasma that had sprayed over him when Minister Ual was shot standing right next to him.

It was blood. The isenj was sick, all right.

"What's it doing here? I've never seen them come close to the dome."

"It's dying," said Eddie. Rit had been warned. Genomes didn't follow borders and some of her own people might die when the pathogen was released.

"Can we do something?" The woman looked around her, as if there'd be a xenobiologist handy. "We can't just leave it there. It's trying to get help."

The crowd was growing. Eddie thought it odd that a dying isenj would head for the dome and not its own medical facilities, but people *in extremis*—and isenj *were* people—did inexplicable things. Perhaps it already knew there was nothing an isenj medic could do for it, and hoped the fur-things in the dome might have a remedy. There were isenj going about their business just fifty meters away. Each watched the struggling creature for a moment before continuing on their way. It might have been an odd reaction to personnel in Umeh Station, who were mostly trained to react to emergencies, but Eddie had seen humans walk by the injured and dying far too many times in his life to pass judgment on another species' unwillingness to get involved.

"I know what this is," said Eddie. "Don't go outside, and don't touch it."

"What?" said the woman. He could see she was thinking it was a health hazard to humans, and that was fine if it kept her from getting involved. "Maybe it's been wounded."

"It's collateral damage," said Eddie. "Somebody get Lieutenant Cargill and let her know, but for Chrissakes don't go out there."

"Eddie, what exactly is this?"

He didn't know the man who was speaking to him, but

everyone knew Eddie because he was the BBChan man, one they saw not only in the flesh but also on screen from time to time, albeit with decreasing frequency now. News Desk wasn't hot for downbeat alien disaster stories at the moment.

"Don't worry, it only affects isenj." There was no point not telling them: the isenj would know soon enough, and they were the only ones it mattered to. "It's a biological weapon. It's tailored to the genome, and it was aimed at the isenj south of here who've got certain genes in common. But the pathogen drifts with prevailing winds."

They all looked at him in a moment of accusing silence. "Haven't seen *that* on the news, Eddie," said one.

"Hard to get viewers interested in wars between spiders twenty-five light-years away when the shit hits the fan at home every day." God, that sounded callous. Eddie had just validated an ancient stereotype. All he needed now was a cigarette dangling from his lip and a press pass shoved in his hat and he'd be Cynical Old Hack, the glib bastard with no heart, intruding on grief to kill time before the bar opened. "Trust me, I've tried."

The isenj's struggles were pitiful. The death throes of any creature were hard to watch, but humans always managed it okay: they were managing it now. It was a misshapen ball of spines, more like a porcupine than anything, and its spindly legs kicked as if trying to get purchase on a slippery surface. Eddie wasn't sure how the pathogen worked, but if it was bleeding from the mouth, then it was probably hemorrhaging internally. That was a bad way to go.

"You *sure* this isn't a risk to humans?" said the engineer.

"I'm sure," said Eddie. "They've already made that particular cocktail for Bezer'ej. The wess'har know what they're doing with bioagents."

"Jesus Christ, is this their war?"

"No, but they gave the isenj here the weapons they asked for. Just like we would."

Ade appeared beside him and watched for a few moments. His distress was instant and visible. He waded into the sightseers.

"For Chrissake, don't stand there gawping," he snapped. "Would you want to be a spectator sport if that was you out there? Get back to work, the lot of you. Give the poor bloody thing its dignity."

The female engineer looked lost. "Won't the isenj send someone to help it?"

"Well, I don't see any ambulances screeching to a halt, so, no, I reckon not. Now move it."

A voice behind Eddie made him jump. "Come on folks, you heard the sergeant. Get back to work." Barencoin's voice boomed over their heads and they all swung around. "It's not nice to stare."

The rest of the marines joined him, spread out and looking like they meant it. The crowd broke up and went its various ways, although the woman engineer kept looking back for as long as she could. Eddie wondered how much of the marines' talent for showing up when one of them needed backup was a natural vigilance and how much was their linked bioscreens, but Ade didn't have one. Even if they were angry with him for not telling them about Rayat, they still functioned as a team, and they watched each other's backs. It took more than a spat like that to really split them. Eddie was glad. They were a small oasis of unshakable common sense in an insane situation. Webster commandeered a small forklift loader and took up position by the airlock doors.

Ade stared at the isenj, then slid the safety catch off his rifle. "Shit, is that the first sick one you've seen?"

"Yeah. You okay?"

"I'm fine."

"What you going to do?"

"Well, it's not going to make a miraculous recovery, is it? You know what that stuff does."

"Jesus, Ade, you're not going to shoot it, are you?"

"It's that, or watch how many hours a bioagent takes to kill it. Shan reckons the human version took a few *days*. She found that family in the church, remember. You think that's right? Let the poor bastard suffer?"

Eddie had always said he wanted someone to shoot him if he was ever in a bad way with no hope of recovery. It took a cold splash of reality, watching someone actually making that decision and loading a rifle, to show him he hadn't thought it through at all.

Ade seemed to be assessing line of sight. He looked over his shoulder a couple of times. "Bugger, I wish this wasn't in full view. Mart, see if you can grab a few blankets, will you?"

Isenj had helped build Umeh Station. Maybe this one was a former worker, and that was why it had headed this way in its final hours, as if its own kind had abandoned it and the fur-things were its last hope.

Barencoin jogged off. Ade watched for a few more moments, muttered, "Sod it," and strode to the airlock. The next thing Eddie knew, Ade was outside and standing over the stricken isenj. He stood with his back to the dome and fired three quick shots, silenced by the dome's seals, into its head. It twitched and lay still. The whole thing had taken a matter of seconds and nobody in the dome appeared to have noticed.

Ade waited for a few moments—and how *did* you check an isenj was dead?—then gestured at Webster. She pushed the loader out onto the service area. With silent efficiency. They hauled the body onto the flatbed and moved it out of sight of the dome's occupants behind an opaque panel in the wall.

Webster exchanged words with Ade and left the loader outside. Ade sat down it, rifle laid across his knees. Eddie caught Webster as she came back inside.

"Is he okay, Sue?"

"Yeah." Barencoin passed them with a couple of dark blue blankets under one arm. "He says he'll wait in case any more show up. He thinks they might." She looked at her hands with an expression of wonder on her face. "They're soft. The quills are *soft.* Springy."

Eddie thought they were be rigid. Maybe they lost their stiffness on death. "You're not still pissed off with Ade about the Rayat thing, are you?"

"I'm never pissed off," said Webster. "That's Mart's job."

Eddie stood with his hands in his pockets watching Ade

for a few minutes and realized the bee cam was still nestled against the window, recording. He snatched it back and considered going out to sit with Ade. He expected outrage or at least protest from crew who'd worked out that the isenj had been put down like an animal, but the personnel inside the dome seemed totally preoccupied with evacuation. What if Ade had put a human out of their misery in the same circumstances? But an isenj was probably like a dog to them, something intelligent and capable of being friendly that you might miss or even mourn, but not as significant as a human.

No, it better to leave Ade alone. Eddie knew him well enough by now. Even so, he hovered around the airlock for the next hour. It was getting dark and Ade couldn't sit out there all night. Eventually he relented, got Becken to scrounge two coffees for him, and took them out to sit with Ade.

He nudged the marine along the flatbed of the loader without a word and put a cup in his hand.

Ade slurped a mouthful. "Never nudge a bloke with a loaded rifle, mate."

"Safety's on. I've learned that much. You sure you're okay?"

"I'm more okay than that poor bastard under that blanket."

"We got through worse than this when Shan was gone."

"I'll live."

"Yeah. You certainly will." Ade had defaulted to piss-take mode. "Are you worried about what Her Indoors will say when she finds out you told the rest of them about Rayat?"

"I told her. She's fine about it."

"Oh. Really? Good." Eddie was relieved, and slightly surprised. Shan seemed able to forgive Ade anything, as if she'd saved up all the tolerance she should have used getting along with people in general and lavished it all on a ferocious, indulgent concentrate for Ade and Aras. He suspected they had to forgive a lot with her, too. "Mart and the others will come around as well. What are you going to tell Harrison?"

"She won't be serving in twenty-odd years' time, so I don't have to tell her anything. Shan says she'll hand over a body if she likes."

"She hasn't fragged him, has she?"

"Not yet."

"She's slipping."

Eddie meant it as a joke, but he did wonder.

It was completely quiet by Jejeno standards. Eddie hadn't heard any artillery activity in the city for a while. The two men nursed their cups of coffee in silence, and overhead the detached Eqbas ship was a dark shape against the light-polluted night sky, its chevrons a disembodied belt of neon. The chevrons were reprised at a distance. Eddie thought it was a reflection caused somehow by the defense shield until he realized it was the mothership moving slowly across the skyline.

A sudden flare of silent white light just to the north caught Eddie's eye and he stood up to look, although it was a pointless move in a city that was all towers.

Ade nudged him. "It's from the ship," he said. A second pulse of light was gone in a second. "That's the government offices. This is probably when everyone works out what Rit's done and has a major sense of humor failure."

"I can't imagine how she's going to hold this together. I know isenj aren't like us, but I don't see this administration lasting the week."

"Either it lasts," said Ade, "or Umeh goes back to the drawing board. Year zero. Now they're starting to see what an engineered pathogen can do, I think it might change enough minds."

Eddie did a mental edit and substituted the word *Earth*.

It did the trick. It certainly changed his.

9

I have to do this.

I have them in my head, and I've slaughtered them in their thousands, and even millions. I am what I am because of them. They still hate me five centuries later, and I confess that I think I still hate them. The only isenj I ever met beyond the context of killing or being killed was Par Paral Ual, and he died trying to change his world. I can't die, so the least I can do is lay all our myths and dreads to rest, and visit Umeh for the first time.

I just wish I could feel the same about the bezeri.

ARAS SAR IUSSAN
in a message to Eddie Michallat in Jejeno

Jejeno: Government of the Northern Assembly

The isenj troops manning the barricade in front of the government center in Jejeno weren't prepared for an enemy that used portable shields.

They also seemed surprised to see Minister Rit with an Eqbas escort. They shrilled and chirped wildly. Rit shrilled back.

"They want to know what's happening," said Aitassi. "And Rit has told them she plans to take over the government."

There was no room for misunderstanding. Isenj were far easier to deal with in many ways than the *gethes* that Esganikan had spoken with on Earth.

"Surrender," she said, keeping it simple. Aitassi, safe within the shield area, translated even though it was obvious that surrender was a sensible choice. "Let us through, or you'll die."

Isenj used projectile weapons. There was nothing wrong

with proven technology, but it often met its superior, equally proven. They looked at the Eqbas troops, and then at Minister Rit, but they still opened fire.

The first volley of shots hit the generated field in a brief burst of light, dropping short of their target. One round made it as far as the first of Esganikan's twenty troops and bounced against his body armor like a tossed pebble.

Esganikan hadn't learned to fully read emotion in an isenj and knew she never would, but their immediate reaction of frozen shock looked very like a wess'har's. Then they broke ranks, scattered across the street and back into the building, and the Eqbas assault team picked them off. It took less than a minute to clear the way into the Northern Assembly seat of government. Esganikan wondered how much of the army had deserted as she ran after her squad down the wide corridors of polished stone. The place seemed almost deserted.

Aitassi stayed close behind for her own safety, but there were few isenj around, just clerks at desks and monitoring screens. They paused to stare at the coup unfolding in front of them.

"What are they doing?"

Aitassi cornered an isenj as if herding it and they exchanged high-pitched chatter.

"They're crisis management clerks," she said. "This is the overnight watch—everyone else has gone home for the evening."

Extraordinary: they were such creatures of habit that they stuck to their schedules even now. With every contact, Esganikan found they were far weaker than they appeared: their air assets globally were no more than a single large nation's, and had been wiped out on the ground in a brief series of preemptive strikes. Now even the clerks had gone home. They seemed equipped only to wage war on each other. They weren't a credible enemy; they were an irritant.

"I feel this will become a saying among troops," Esganikan, sidearm in hand, carried on down the passage. "Plan for Garav, hope for Umeh."

A *gethes* would have felt dishonored for trouncing such

a weak enemy, but she was a pragmatist. She fought as a means to an end, not as a tribal ritual, seizing the advantage and feeling only vague sorrow for a once-powerful civilization still putting faith in solid but obsolete technology.

But isenj still had numbers. And unless she destroyed every dissident isenj—most of the planet, it seemed—then at some point she had to walk away and leave Minister Rit to hold back chaos with a Skavu army. She strode into the main cabinet room where she had once been an invited guest and stared at seven isenj ministers distinguishable only by the colors of the decorative beads threaded on the tips of their quills.

It was Rit's turn now. "Your former colleague wishes to address you, Ministers." Esganikan stepped back and gestured to Aitassi for a translation. Shomen Eit and Nir Bedoi spoke English but none of the others did. The *gethes* had brought one thing of use to Ceret, to Cavanagh's Star, to Nir: and that was a common language that could be learned, simple and flexible enough in its components to be adapted by isenj and wess'har for mutual use. Apart from that, all they'd contributed was chaos.

Rit walked in followed by Ralassi, and the collective raising of ministerial quills indicated either aggression or shock. It was probably both. Ralassi translated her address, and it felt like an oddly restrained revolution—a meeting of ministers reading each other polite statements instead of seizing members of the old regime and killing them.

If *gethes* on Earth were as orderly as this, Esganikan would be grateful.

Rit began her polite, reasoned power grab. Aitassi watched, occasionally snapping her teeth in impatience, while Ralassi interpreted.

"Minister Rit says we have to take a path of major change. We can't expand indefinitely. If we need any more proof after today that we can never oust the wess'har either from Bezer'ej or even Wess'ej, then it will end in our total destruction."

Esganikan was interested to note how all but one of the cabinet members moved position slightly to put more distance between themselves and Shomen Eit. She wondered what primeval defense mechanisms existed in isenj. All creatures still reverted to ancient archetypes in their moments of stress, just as wess'har did. How did creatures evolved from termite colonies behave when threatened? They rallied to the dominant individuals, to the core and future of the colony.

"You're a traitor and a collaborator, like your misguided husband," said Shomen Eit, in English. "I'll call on loyal troops to kill you."

So *that* was how they reacted. Like *gethes* and a dozen other species. Some things seemed to be universal, except among wess'har.

"Minister Rit says you have a choice of working with the new government or being executed, because she has learned that prisoners like you are a liability."

"And who do you plan to call on to carry out the sentence if I don't comply?" Again Shomen Eit replied in English, and it was clear he was doing it for Esganikan's benefit, testing how firmly she stood behind Rit. He might have thought the coup was at her instigation.

Rit turned to Ralassi and shrilled. Aitassi reacted with agitated little side-to-side movements as if ready to spring at a target. "She asks for a weapon, but I have no idea if she's competent to use it."

"Ralassi," said Esganikan, "tell the minister I *am* armed and I'll carry out her instructions."

She stepped forward and drew the hand weapon that so fascinated the human marines because it bore no resemblance to a *gethes* pistol. She'd executed Jonathan Burgh with it, two pulses to ensure he was dead because she had never killed one of his species at close quarters before. Now she held it to Shomen Eit's upper body. She knew enough about isenj anatomy now from the recent fighting to know that was an effective target area.

Shomen Eit rattled slightly, beads shivering on his quills, but he stood his ground. He smelled of decaying wood. It wasn't unpleasant.

"I had no idea you would go this far," he said, and he was

definitely addressing Esganikan, not Rit. He seemed to think this was an Eqbas strategy, and telling him otherwise would have served no purpose. "Do you understand you're destroying a civilization?"

"But you called on us to kill *your* enemies, Minister, so why do you think I wouldn't do the same for another isenj with authority?" It genuinely puzzled her. "My objective is to restore this planet. It requires a reduction in your population on a massive scale, and any isenj remaining must be ones who want to maintain a balanced ecology. The detail beyond that is irrelevant in planetary terms."

Ralassi interrupted. "Minister Rit says you must all choose."

"I can't serve in an unlawful administration," said Shomen Eit.

"The Minister says that the law is also irrelevant if there's no habitable planet to govern, and she won't imprison you to provide a rallying point for dissent."

Shomen Eit had stopped rattling. Resigned or beyond fear—Esganikan badly missed scent cues in situations like this—he wasn't going to surrender. She doubted any promises he made would last out the next few days anyway.

There was a long pause between Rit's next burst of chittering and Ralassi's interpretation, as if he wasn't sure he should repeat the words. But he did.

"Please remove Minister Eit."

Esganikan liked to be clear. "Do you mean remove or kill?"

Ralassi paused. "Kill."

It was a necessary act to clear the way for Umeh's survival and restoration. Esganikan squeezed the handgrip of the dull blue cylinder in her hand, and a deafening crack of expanding plasma filled the stone-lined chamber. She followed up immediately with a second pulse, because she left nothing to chance. The six remaining cabinet ministers were silent for a moment and then launched into high-pitched squealing.

"Minister Rit says she is now assuming leadership of this cabinet and will stand down the army—with the support of her colleagues."

It was as simple as that. Nir Bedoi, effectively the deputy leader—and having no nominal head of state didn't mean there wasn't one in reality—found his voice.

"If this is good for the Northern Assembly in the long-term, then you have my support as your husband did."

He made a move around Shomen Eit's body; staff had already come to the cabinet chamber doors to investigate the noise, and seemed unsure whether to wait to be called in or not. "But explain what's happening now in the Maritime Fringe territory, and even here. Do we have an epidemic?"

"You asked for tailored genetic bioagents," said Esganikan. "And that's exactly what we gave you. They were deployed a few hours ago, and we did warn you that there would be citizens here who shared the genetic markers found in nearly all the Fringe's population."

"There will be a remnant in the fringe without those genes, and they'll rise up against us in due course."

"In a few days, deaths will be on a scale where anyone surviving the pathogen will die either from other naturally occurring disease or from infrastructure collapse. There'll be nobody to manage the utilities. It will be academic."

"But how do we clear up a disaster on that scale, with our resources so stretched?"

It was an intelligent question, and one that gave Esganikan her own resource issues. "That's our contribution."

"What if others attack us?"

These were all the questions she'd worked through with Rit, and even Shomen Eit as recently as a few weeks earlier. "You know we have templates for other pathogens specific to your major population groups. You gave us the tissue samples, remember?"

Ralassi was translating for everyone else's benefit. This was a final, personal warning from the commander who'd enforced environmental restoration on a number of worlds, and had no hesitation in using whatever means she had at her disposal to do the same here.

"And if that fails?"

"Then I shall deploy one more deterrent," said Esganikan. "The universal isenj pathogen already dispersed on Bezer'ej.

If need be, we will erase this world and start again from a blank sheet."

Rit rattled. Her gold beads—transparent, tumbled smooth, like drops of sap—seemed to have a life of their own for a moment. She inhaled air noisily, forming an approximation of English.

"Need will not be," she said. It was a wheeze, a gasp, a breath. But it was clear. *"Need will not be."*

Jejeno, Umeh: Two days later

It had to be done, and this was as good a time as any to do it.

Aras leaned against the viewing plate as the shuttle approached its final descent into Umeh's atmosphere. It was a dismal-looking planet, all grays and ochres and rusty coastlines, and his isenj memories, seldom far from the surface, filled him with strangely mixed emotions.

His scent betrayed him. Both Nevyan and Shan reacted, and his *isan* took hold of his arm just as she had on Bezer'ej two years ago; it was as comforting now as it had been then.

"You don't have to disembark," Shan said quietly. "We'll get our business done, and then we can go straight back home."

"Shan, I *do* have to face this. This isn't about reconciliation. I want to know how *I* feel. I want to see their faces."

Did he mean that? Was there some isenj within driving him too? He didn't know, and he hated not knowing. The ambiguity had never bothered him in the past, so perhaps that dissatisfaction had come from another mind—probably Shan's.

Nevyan watched from the bank of seating opposite, flanked by Serrimissani and Giyadas. The *isanket* was growing very fast now, and needed to see her mother doing a matriarch's duties so she could understand what was almost certainly her future role too. She also wanted to see Eddie, because, as she announced gravely, he became confused when trying to reconcile human morality with wess'har ethics, and he needed *guidance*.

"You can still change your mind if you wish," Nevyan said. "We won't think any less of you."

"I can manage this."

Shan leaned so close to him that he could feel her breath on his cheek. "I can smell you're scared. They can't judge you, Aras."

"It's not them I fear," he said. "It's my ability to deal with my own reaction."

"If you hate them, fine. Don't swallow all this tolerance and forgiveness shite from Deborah Garrod. She's a nice woman, but she deals in a different reality to the likes of you and me."

"She forgave *me*. It can be done." Could he do it for the bezeri? He'd have to destroy them anyway. Motive and self-examination were a human failing and he couldn't resist its effects now. "I have to see if I can."

"I married the bishop of fucking F'nar, did I?"

"Are we married?"

"You're the one who said we were bonded."

"Ade gave you a ring."

"Okay, and wess'har just slip you a length, but out here, that's good enough."

"When you resort to vulgarity, I know you're worried."

"Of course I'm worried. You're pumping out anxiety like an air freshener."

"How would *you* see a war criminal? As a police officer, what does *war criminal* mean to you?"

"Depends on the war. Those goalposts move a lot." Shan seemed to think he didn't know she was distracting him. "How much has your thinking changed over five hundred years?"

"Explain."

"Well, if I'd been an officer in the eighteen-hundreds on Earth, I'd have had very different attitudes to crime. People were executed for stealing food. Society pretty well didn't care that kids were used for prostitution. Things that even an old reactionary copper like me would find repellent today."

"Some things are *never* right."

"That's what I like about wess'har. No pissing around with moral relativism."

"I *am* afraid."

"I know."

"I don't know why. I don't know which memory this fear comes from."

"Well, once you've done it, you'll know, and ghosts will be laid."

Shan settled against him and he clung to her arm in case she pulled it away. It was only minutes now: it would be over this time tomorrow. That was a trick Ade had taught him, a way of handling hard moments, tackling them a second at a time and knowing they would pass, seeing himself at that future point where it would all be behind him.

The shuttle finally dropped through cloud, and he caught a brief glimpse of a skyline that left him bewildered by the sheer impenetrable scale of it. There was no Umeh left, but he wanted to see the *dalf* tree. The vessel spiraled down to land within the security cordon of Umeh Station and settled smoothly. It was a moment that demanded more physical drama than a routine soft landing.

"Okay, here we go," said Shan. "I'm right here, remember."

The hatch opened and the air of Jejeno rolled in. He felt a sick familiarity.

For five centuries he had lived with the inherited memory of a young isenj caught in an air raid on an isenj colony on Bezer'ej. The city of Mjat had been erased from the map, and the map had been Constantine island long before the first humans arrived. Aras had helped erase it.

His stomach churned. It was all he could do to resist his freeze reflex. The air was thick with the scent of wet wood-land floor and leaf mold, and the rustling, creaking sounds were those of windblown trees full of insects. It seemed the ghost of a forest that had died long before the isenj developed spaceflight, ironic and epitaphic.

He'd never been here. But other memories in him whispered that it was home.

"Come on, sweetheart."

Shan nudged him gently in the small of his back and hooked her fingers in his belt. It was exactly what he'd seen Ade do to her, a little proprietorial touch that said he was looking out for her, taking care of her. Aras enjoyed the gesture.

"I assure you I can deal with this, *isan*."

"You let me know if it gets too much."

"And what will you do if it does?"

It was a genuine question, nothing more. Shan knew that well enough by now. She rubbed his spine discreetly with her knuckles. "I don't know, but I'm here if you think of anything."

The defensive shield spread like an invisible skirt from the hull of the Eqbas ship overhead and swallowed Umeh Station's faceted translucent dome. Aras could feel the slight tingle on the backs of his hands when he got close to it: it was based on the same technology that he used to contain the biosphere of Constantine colony and the terrestrial crops back in F'nar. The distance from the point where the shuttle had settled to the dome's entrance was about fifty meters of invisibly defined path.

Beyond the shield, thousands of isenj waited, watching. They were like a roughly trimmed hedge of charred thorn bushes. Aras wasn't sure what he was feeling as he prepared to walk between them. He knew it was something powerfully disorienting; but memories of other minds welled up unbidden, and picking them apart was hard.

"Steady," said Shan. She put her hand flat on the small of his back again. "Square up, *Sital*. You did what you had to do. No shame in that. Fuck 'em."

She knew. She always *knew*. This was what he'd craved for so many centuries in exile: complete understanding. Nobody knew you better than those bonded with you through *c'naatat*. Shan lived his memories.

And nobody had called him *Sital*—Commander—in five hundred years.

Aras strode forward and concentrated on the main doors of the dome. They opened. He saw Ade and Barencoin step out onto the service road, and focused on them as they walked towards him.

The near silence of the isenj crowd—faint rasps and rattles of quills, the occasional high-pitched scrapes—gave way to a crescendo of chaotic chattering. Even with so much isenj within him, Aras still didn't understand their language. *C'naatat* made inexplicable choices in the scavenged characteristics it expressed in its host.

Perhaps it knows I don't want to hear what they have to say.

But he could guess.

Here's the Beast of Mjat. Here's the murderer of mothers and children. He got what he deserved.

He saw white flame rolling down the street after each explosion, felt the wind of firestorms and heard the low-frequency thrum of wess'har bombers dropping low over the city. He could separate the memories of his victim from his own. Blood filled his mouth as he was thrown against the controls of his damaged fighter as it clipped the top of a building and tore through soft masonry. Time compressed and leaped forward. He felt the skin rip from his back in a dark room. He drowned to the point of unconsciousness.

He was the victim now. The eyes that had watched his bomb run were his captor's too. It was Eddie's editing trick of images taken from various angles to show how *different* reality could appear to be.

And some of the isenj around him remembered Mjat—not from history books, not from tales handed down, but in real physical memory encoded in their ancestors' brains five centuries ago, fresh and angry at the news they heard. This was something no normal human—or wess'har—could understand. Aras existed in a simultaneous past and present with these isenj.

I made my choice. I destroyed your filthy cities to save the bezeri. You captured and tortured me. And, without intending to, that's when you infected me with the parasite. That's when our futures changed forever.

Aras didn't regret ordering the attack even though he now knew the bezeri were no better than the isenj whose careless pollution nearly killed them.

I'd do it again.

He could hardly hear the forest sounds around him now. He could just see Ade, very upright, slowing his pace with Barencoin alongside. They were both in their chameleon DPM. fatigues, two soldiers making a visible point of walking out to greet another.

I'm a fool. And I'm not the Beast of anywhere. I shouldn't feel shame.

The first colonists tried to teach him their concepts of guilt and forgiveness and redemption, but it hadn't ever made complete sense. God, they said, could forgive if Aras repented; Aras never saw what right this God had to speak for dead victims. And how could he repent if he was prepared to do it again? Humans changed their minds. They lost control. But wess'har did what made sense. Wiping the isenj off the face of Bezer'ej hadn't been a careless error.

I will not run your gauntlet.

The crowds of isenj to either side were a dark ragged blur in his peripheral vision. He was determined not to look at them, but he'd walked through the Constantine colony after executing Josh Garrod and faced the reactions, from blank stares to a hail of stones. He stopped and turned slowly, looking directly into the crowds and seeking whatever isenj instinct was buried in his memory to help him understand their mood. No visible eyes, no range of scent, no clues. Senses within him strained for the familiar.

Just as Par Paral Ual had been on meeting him, they seemed bewildered. Aras knew what angry isenj sounded like, because the alien voices were within him. But there was nothing beyond baffled scrutiny.

He should have been dead long ago; and he shouldn't have looked like *this*. They didn't expect the Beast to look more like a human. They had no idea how to relate what they saw walking along that path to what they found in their genetic memory. It was as if Genghis Khan had returned to the streets of Otar in the form of a centaur, with no iconography to connect history's monster to the stranger—the genuine stranger—in front of them.

Aras turned a complete circle to take a long, slow look at them all, turning on his heel, as much out of curiosity as defiance. But there was nobody left to defy. This was their world and their prison, fouled beyond repair. He thought he might find some hate or contempt swirling in the part of him that had absorbed the worse human tendencies, but there was just the echo of a tormented, desperate young wess'har commander who wanted the agony to stop and for his people to rescue him.

They didn't plan to, but they found him anyway, and the odd fever that left him invulnerable seemed what he later learned to call a *miracle*. *C'naatat* troops drove out the remaining bezeri and the cordon was thrown around Bezer'ej.

It was all so long ago. He wondered why he hadn't put it behind him before: now he'd seen their world, he knew he'd done what was *necessary*.

"It's all so different," he said.

"What, mate?" Ade closed the gap between them and stood with his arms folded across his chest. He seemed to have accepted that the Eqbas shield was sniper-proof. Barencoin, always the wary and hostile one in the detachment, still had his rifle slung on its strap and his hand on its grip, checking around him in a way that seemed to be utterly automatic.

"This world," said Aras. "The buildings. The way the roofs slope at a chord. I remember them being lower and less ornate."

"Shit," said Ade. "Never rang any bells with me."

Shan gave Barencoin a friendly pat on the back. Aras thought it was commendable that she never held it against him for shooting her. Shit happened, as she was fond of saying: he was just following Lindsay's orders. She had no forgiveness in her heart whatsoever for Lindsay Neville, and it was nothing to do with her role in her decision to space herself. Lindsay was simply not Shan, and didn't make the decisions Shan would make, and so she was an emotional, weak creature to be distrusted.

"Are we going to present targets here all day, then?" said Barencoin. "We've made our point. There's sod all they can do to Aras. They know that."

Ade caught Shan's hand and squeezed it for a moment

before letting go. "It's not for their benefit, Mart. Not at all."

Aras kept his eyes fixed on the airlock doors. He had a few meters to go, and then he could begin to make sense of what he'd just experienced. The doors parted: he stepped through.

He knew what had troubled him now, and what he'd feared most.

He remembered what it was like—*exactly* what it was like—to be an ordinary young wess'har male, and he remembered the joy of simply being who he was, long before he knew that bezeri destroyed, and *gethes* slaughtered, and that he would never be a father.

10

What is c'naatat, *Commander Esganikan? Your word and advice is law to us, as you know, because you brought hope to our world when we had failed to see it ourselves. All we ask is that you tell us all we need to know.*

KIIR, Fourth To Die, Skavu Fleet

Umeh Station, Jejeno: machinery space, maintenance level

"So how many dead?" asked Mick, the duty news editor, not even looking up from his snack noodles.

Eddie had hung the smartfabric screen that displayed his ITX link on a convenient bulkhead in the quiet bowels of Umeh Station. He finally had News Desk's attention again, but it was an ephemeral thing, as fleeting as the bloody transmission window he clung to jealously, and it had to compete with a harassed editor's noodles.

"Try two hundred million."

The transmission delay added the illusion of a poignant lack of reaction. "Say again."

One, two three . . . "Two. Hundred. Million. And rising."

"Holy shit, Eddie, what are they? Insects? Who can kill on that kind of scale?"

"Once upon a time, there was a place called Eqbas Vorhi. And the Eqbas were very clever aliens, and they had frigging amazing weapons, and they were ever so good at biological warfare, persistent pathogens—"

"Okay, stow the sarcasm. And these are our tourists in a few years' time."

"I love to hear a penny drop."

"Will we understand why they're having this war?"

"Because some of the isenj don't want the Eqbas to clean up their ecology—it involves reducing the population."

"I can see how that might not be as popular as recycling."

An awful impulse from the demon that sat on one shoulder tempted him to use the footage of Ade dispatching the dying isenj; the angel on the other one reminded him there were things his audience wouldn't ever understand, and didn't need to know.

"Three minute piece, Mick?"

"Two, max."

"Can you get me a line to a green politico called Helen Marchant?" The devil had switched topics and caught him off guard. "I want to do some real journalism. Not just local color."

"Steady, Eddie. Don't burn out."

"See what you can do. I've got questions for her that none of your hobby-hacks can manage."

"Such as?"

"I remember what she got up to a century or so ago, before they froze her down." Eddie suddenly found himself surrendering to the impulse that made ordinary people rant impotently at news screens that couldn't hear them. Shan's cover was partially blown: Marchant knew she was alive, but she didn't know how. "What do you use for researchers these days?"

"You're gagging to drop a bombshell on me."

"She was a terrorist."

"You're a hundred and fifty trillion miles away from the lawsuit, so you'll forgive me if I ask you to stand that up."

Eddie had no idea why he did it, other than that he could, and because people had a right to know exactly who was urging them to action in political life.

"She's the sister of Eugenie Perault, who was FEU foreign secretary when I left Earth in 2299. You know the name Shan Frankland. She was the anti-terrorism unit officer in command of Operation Green Rage. Marchant was a green terrorist—arson, explosives, the whole shebang."

"Shame that Frankland isn't alive to stand that up."

The thin ice beneath Eddie cracked but didn't break. The impulse to flourish the final piece in the puzzle and show the true picture was almost overwhelming—impartial, evidential, cold reality. *His duty.* He overwhelmed it anyway. His relationship with truth-at-any-cost had become more complex as he crossed back and forth between the worlds of human and wess'har.

"I'd still like to interview Marchant."

"Okay. I'll get one of the researchers to line her up for an ITX window when we can."

"I'm obliged, M'Lud." Only months ago, a conversation like this had been monitored by FEU Intelligence, subject to sudden interdiction and a race to transmit before e-junctions flew across networks to silence them. The urgency seemed to have passed. "No more censor trouble from Brussels?"

"Nah. Too late. The shit hit the fan and they can't get it all back in the bucket now." Mick slurped up a whole noodle in one breath with a smack of his lips. "But it's nice that they still boost the audience stats. Hi, guys."

"Hey, I might have new aliens to show you, too." It was always, *always* stupid to tell a news editor what you might have lined up, because they all had a genetic cognitive malfunction that heard *might, sometime* as *will definitely, and right away.* Eddie would regret that, he knew. "Skavu."

"Is this something I need to tag for Natural History and Wildlife, or International?"

"Dunno. But they have spaceships."

"Do we have them on file?"

"No. The Eqbas have drafted foreign troops." *Ah.* He'd just dumped the discovery of a new alien race on News Desk. He was just getting too blasé about biodiversity. "Got work to do on that."

Eddie braced for a bollocking. But Mick didn't react. "I don't think viewers can keep up with this bloody zoo."

So Eddie wasn't the only one suffering from alien overload. "I'll save it for later, then."

He grabbed the hiatus gratefully and logged off to hunt coffee or what passed for it in the short-supply days leading up to an evacuation.

"Up top," on the ground-level of Umeh Station. It now felt as if time had rewound, and the place looked as if it was at the stage of part completion it had reached when he first saw it, not long after *Actaeon* had arrived in the system with a closed habitat intended for Bezer'ej. The station hadn't been welcome on Bezer'ej, but the isenj had wanted an alliance with humans so badly that they made room for its construction here. He'd always wondered what happened to the isenj who'd been displaced by the construction.

The place was a monument to bad decisions; the isenj had picked the wrong ally, and humans had picked the wrong fight. *Actaeon*—Barry Yung, Malcolm Okurt, all the FEU navy officers he'd known and liked, all dead. That galled him. They'd died because someone in the FEU had sent *Actaeon* to the wrong place at the wrong time to do the wrong thing. Eddie was reminded with brilliant clarity that it was his holy calling to pursue politicians for buying personal power with the lives of ordinary men and women.

"You bet," he said aloud, and wandered the plaza.

The trappings of home comfort—images from home, plants, fabrics—were all disappearing and gradually exposing the bare bones of a closed world that held Earth within in it and kept an alien galaxy at bay. He hoped the marines had secured their stash of plants and other "rabbit" they'd pilfered to ease the food situation back on Wess'ej, not that he rated anyone's chances of nicking something from a bunch of Booties. As he ambled around, bee cam drifting lazily on his right wing, he noted what bounty was still hanging around and not nailed down. He wasn't above a little alternative procurement himself.

Maybe Mick would set up a conference call with Marchant tomorrow. She could call for military action against the logging nations as much as she wanted, as long as she stood on the front line to take a bullet. He was okay with that. Maybe she'd even answer him if he asked how many people she'd killed in her eco-terror days, and how.

He realized what he'd be doing to Shan, too, and wondered if this was a line—professionally or morally—that he could walk and know exactly where he was, and why he ventured there. Around him, the milling bodies in orange and navy blue and gray were a temporary blur while his mind was on matters that were far less clear-cut than deadlines. Lack of time was a good thing: focusing, clarifying, stripping away, getting to the heart of who you were. The more time he had to think, the less he knew himself. He wondered how Shan would cope with apparently infinite time now to second-guess herself. She was one of a handful of people he'd ever known who'd spend the time doing it.

Then he was aware of a break in the blurred crowd.

Giyadas was holding court, surrounded by a small group of utterly bemused civilian contractors and a few ratings from *Actaeon*. Eddie's first thought was what the hell was she doing here, and what was Nevyan thinking to let a tiny child out on her own. He'd thought that about her wandering the alleys of F'nar, too, but wess'har weren't humans, and they never harmed each other as adults, let alone kids.

But this was a human tribe, a dangerous foreign land, and his paternal instincts welled up out of nowhere.

"What are you doing out, doll?" He pushed through the crowd in an I'm-just-being-careless-not-aggressive way that parted bodies. "Where's your mother?"

"She argues," said Giyadas. "She and Shan and Esganikan and Minister Rit."

She looked up at him with those extraordinary yellow gems of eyes, and he saw not an exotic and astonishing alien but a little girl he doted on, and who he'd protect with his life like any father would. The intensity of it reminded him what he didn't have to protect.

Eddie squatted down to bring himself to eye-level with her. The dome crew were still standing around, watching her with utter fascination. They rarely saw wess'har, and never a juvenile one who spoke eloquent English with Eddie's accent and a fluting double-tone.

"Arguing, doll? About what?"

"The bioweapons. Casualties."

Eddie wondered who was losing their nerve. Maybe Esganikan wanted to purge the lot of them. Maybe Rit did. He held out his hand to Giyadas and she took it, still with that baffled cocking of the head, because only humans seemed to hold kids' hands. He led her away from her dumbstruck audience.

"Come on, doll," he said. Let's go and find them."

One of the *Actaeon* crew grinned at her. "She's amazing," he said.

Eddie paused. "I hope you didn't say anything daft to her. She'll be matriarch of F'nar one day, with her own army. She might blow your home town off the map."

"Only if it's Reading," Giyadas said. "Shan says Reading is a *shithole,* and needs *nuking.*"

At some point, Giyadas might have discovered sly humor. Eddie would never know. She cocked her head and trotted a little way ahead of him, nearly dragging his arm out of his socket because even a little wess'har was a fearsome physical reality for a soft human, and even young females, little matriarchs to be, were used to having males trailing behind them.

Eddie knew his place, and fell in obediently.

Umeh Station, service perimeter

"You wanted to meet the Skavu command," said Esganikan. "Now is a good time."

Ade followed her across the apron of concrete, Qureshi and Chahal either side of him. It wasn't a good time, because the best time to have met them would have been when they deployed, so he could see what they were made of. The pathogen had done most of their work for them. He'd missed anything that might help him evaluate them as soldiers.

"How far have they advanced into the Fringe, then, ma'am?" Ade asked. In front of him, a small ship, like an Eqbas vessel but a slightly darker bronze, sat on the apron. It was the classic cigar minus the nightclub lights. "We're not exactly getting a lot of information here."

"You had other tasks," Esganikan said, like a slap. "They've almost cut through to the coast in places."

"Much resistance?"

"No. A great many bodies. It makes transit difficult."

Ade had to keep shifting gear to take it in. Bodies blocked roads. Qureshi puffed out her cheeks in a silent breath and mouthed *shit* at him.

"Are there *any* survivors?"

"Skavu patrols report pockets of isenj who appear to have a different genome." Esganikan stopped short of the ship and a hatch formed in the side. Ade was almost too distracted by what might emerge and he had to concentrate on what she was saying, because Esganikan didn't take kindly to repeating herself. "We estimate five percent survival rate."

Ade's lips began to form the question *what about them* and then a figure stepped out of the hatch and silenced him.

"Yeah, they *do* look like iguanas," Qureshi said.

A ramp in the port bulkhead was disgorging a squad of tall bipedal creatures with a slash for a mouth and small eyes set in folds of dark gray skin. Ade still couldn't see the iguana resemblance, apart from the loose skin at the throat. They wore loose coveralls in a dull sage green strung with webbing. What he thought was a flap of tissue across their tapered faces turned out to be a breather mask like the kind humans needed on Umeh.

Esganikan simply held up her hand and the squad came to a halt and stood waiting. Ade noted that they had sidearms like Esganikan's—a metal oval with fingergrips—and two long instruments across their backs, one almost certainly a flat sword.

Ade had only ever seen a sword once, a ceremonial one at a fancy Corps dinner, and the owner wasn't heading into the sergeants' mess. He groped for common ground to evaluate them.

"Seals," Ade muttered at Qureshi. "With wrinkles."

"Turtle," said Chahal.

It was a shame Shan has missed them. So had Eddie, but Ade decided now wasn't the time to grab a few shots for him.

They didn't look much like fanatical shock troops. That was the trouble with matching aliens to animals; the associations were all wrong, and deceptively harmless. Ten thousand of these had just helped kill 95 percent of a country's

population, millions upon millions, and even with a replicating pathogen like the Eqbas could engineer mopping up
most, they had still held a line to defend Jejeno for the first
day while the pathogen was taking effect. Ade didn't have
reports, but he knew how many millions of isenj there had
been south of him, and they hadn't advanced further.

Skavu didn't look hard. He had a feeling that wasn't any
guide to their performance.

"They don't work well with other troops, and I decided to
keep them separate from you and the wess'har," Esganikan
said slowly, as if Ade didn't quite get it. "They're all male for
most practical intents and purposes, but the species is in fact
hermaphroditic. They are rigidly disciplined and intolerant
of deviation. Are you absolutely sure you want to go on a
patrol with them?"

"I like to know who's in my neighborhood, ma'am." Well,
he'd done joint ops with worse. They needed to know a bit
about him, too, for their own safety. "Have you told them
exactly what *c'naatat* is?"

Esganikan cocked her head, plume bobbing, and wandered slowly forward, hands clasped in what looked like
prayer but was just a casually comfortable position for
wess'har of either world.

"I have," she said. "Don't worry. They don't covet it, I can
assure you. They're troubled by *c'naatat*." She indicated one
soldier standing in the middle of the five-man group. "*Skavi,*
come here."

He approached as if she was going to give him a good
thrashing, head slightly lowered, but Esganikan had that effect on people.

"Kiir, Fourth To Die," he said. His voice seemed out of
sync with his mouth movement, and it took a moment for
Ade to realize that the voice was a transcast; he looked for
the receiver and eventually spotted a thin white metal band
around the collar of Kiir's blouson that vibrated almost im-
perceptibly when he spoke. "Esganikan Gai, this is our privilege." He seemed more interested in her than in acknowledg-
ing Ade. "We will do for this terrible world what you did
for us."

Ah. Esganikan was God. They owed her. Ade pieced together odds and ends of recent conversations and realized she hadn't just fought them, she'd won and they held her in high esteem. It certainly beat being spat on as an occupying army.

Then Kiir turned his head almost mechanically towards Ade. Jesus, was he commissioned? Did Ade salute him or not? Sod it, Kiir was an alien and nobody minded a display of courtesy. Ade snapped off a crisp salute and felt the breath of moving air as Chahal and Qureshi did the same. He was on autopilot. "Sergeant Adrian Bennett, Three-Seven Commando Royal Marines, sir." No, he wasn't; not any longer. *Sod it.* "And Marine Bulwant Singh Chahal and Marine Ismat Qureshi, sir."

Kiir half turned to the four troops behind him and indicated them with a vague and unmilitary flick of his gloved hand. *Three fingers. Close enough.*

"All, Ten To Die, pursuit squad."

Ade could hear the change in Qureshi's and Chahal's breathing, and for the first time he was aware that he could smell the variations in their skin chemistry. Everyone was nervous. All things considered, nervous was as good as they could hope for. Nobody in FEU armed forces have ever been trained for first contact; 510 Troop had clocked up six sentient alien species in this one deployment.

Kiir gestured to the ship. "This patrol may require you to kill. You do kill, yes or no?"

"Part of the job description," said Ade, baffled. "Yes, sir."

"You get in. We have a neighborhood to clear."

Esganikan strode off, leaving the three marines to busk it with five Skavu and no idea of the acquaint session they were going on, except that Skavu seemed to think they might use non-lethal rounds. Qureshi still had leg pain from the last firefight with an isenj landing party. Esganikan might have thought the isenj were military wimps, but Ade judged them by close-quarters battle. He checked Chahal's and Qureshi's body armor diagnostics himself. It was set to turn rigid if so much as a pebble hit it.

"You're such a worry-guts, Ade," said Chahal.

"Chaz, I'm not losing anyone on this deployment." Ade checked his own armor. He didn't need it to survive but a round still hurt. "You're too close to going home in one piece."

At least the interior of the former Eqbas ship was familiar enough, and the three of them sat on the bench along one bulkhead. The Skavu stared back at them, grim and silent.

"You can call me Ade," he said. "Or Royal. We all answer to Royal."

However the transcast rendered *Royal*, it got a baffled frown that seemed to move the Skavu's whole scalp. Qureshi checked the calibration of her rifle.

"Qureshi, *Last* To Bloody Well Die . . ." she whispered under her breath.

Cabinet office, Jejeno: the new administration

It was a messy argument, and Shan hadn't come twenty-five light-years to sit in a meeting. Esganikan and Rit were doing most of the talking, and the six members of the cabinet who remained, including Bedoi, were very subdued indeed.

Jesus Christ, Esganikan shot Shomen Eit. She actually did it.

And . . .

And . . . a few miles across the border they can't even clear the corpses.

Humans did that kind of thing too, and with equal dispassion. It was just that Esganikan wasn't an assassin, but an officer much like herself. And the Eqbas were wess'har, and she had genes in common with them.

It was way too late to have an attack of conscience. She found she wasn't listening to the discussion but trying to match up sins again, to try to put the events of the last few days in a context on her own Richter scale of amorality.

Come on, you've done worse. Just not with heads of state. You can justify every act to yourself.

She couldn't stop glancing out the window, several floors

above the street, and checking what was still out there. The telltale heat haze of the defense shield warped the carved and vividly painted designs on the building opposite. It was a high-rise block like those that seemed to cover most of the planet: isenj liked orange, green and blue, if that was how they actually saw the colors, and the building was as richly vibrant as a tapestry. Shan took no visual spectrum for granted now. Her sudden ability to see blue objects that had previously appeared white had been the first clue that she'd been infected by *c'naatat*. For a copper, the confirmation that you couldn't actually trust your own eyes was unsettling.

And the harder she looked, the more she could see the damage. Shell impact was visible on one sinuous assymmetric tower. *Jesus, Ade, go careful.* It was all getting very close.

"Umeh is not my priority mission," Esganikan repeated carefully. She wouldn't sit down: she strolled around the room, her scent getting more and more acid. "I can't garrison troops here indefinitely to protect your administration. The Skavu are willing to stay on. This will be a *very* long-term process—many generations."

Rit's speech still sounded like nails scraped down a smooth wall. Whatever isenj component lay within Shan, it hadn't extended to language. Ralassi was doing a fine job of covering the vocal range from English—delivered in a little child's voice that sat oddly with the mouthful of nasty little teeth—to the off-the-register clicks, shrills and burrs of an isenj. Shan suddenly thought of Vijissi's suicide, unable to face a lonely future as the only ussissi carrying *c'naatat,* and felt the beginnings of an unexpected sob threatening to choke her. She pressed her tongue against the roof of her mouth and waited for it to pass.

"Minister Rit says she has alarming reports of atrocities," said Ralassi. "Skavu have used blades on citizens who weren't resisting them. And you expect these alien troops to live among us for the foreseeable future?"

Shan glanced at Nevyan, who was kneeling like a geisha at a tea ceremony. It was an incongruously subservient pose for an individual who could wipe a FEU warship from orbit with one literally ancient fighter craft and a handful of missiles. Nevyan tilted her head, pupils snapping open and shut.

So these are the Skavu, the new neighbors. Fifty million miles and Eqbas ships, even if they're they're a de-enriched spec. Right next door.

Nevyan's expression and scent spelled out concern, and Shan wondered if she felt sorry at last for Rit.

"Atrocities," said Esganikan. She stood over Rit, eliciting a shiver across all those amber quill-beads. "I gave orders to use genome-targeted biological weapons. On Earth, that's banned. If I were to fragment people with explosives, humans accept that as legal. Minister, you authorized me to do this."

"Okay, we're all inconsistent hypocrites," said Shan. "But the Skavu will be an occupying army for a long time. And Minister Rit has to choose between total extermination and the eco-jihadim out there."

Nevyan smelled agitated and there was the faintest hint of mangoes. Shan leaned across and gripped her forearm discreetly but very, very hard. Their eyes met. It was enough to stop a *jask* confrontation.

Diverted, Nevyan took a deep breath. "Can you guarantee that the Skavu won't turn to other worlds in this system, if they're that zealous?"

"They have their orders," said Esganikan, "and they would have no motive to intrude on a wess'har planet."

Nevyan rustled. Shan kept a discreet eye on her. Her silence wasn't discretion; she had nothing to add, but she was too dominant to seek consensus with an Eqbas matriarch for much longer. Her *dhren,* the opalescent white robe that all the matriarchs of F'nar wore, shifted color and was yet another incongruity, a magically beautiful garment set against the backdrop of a splendid polished stone-clad chamber while politicians and generals discussed the end of millions upon millions of lives.

Maybe the Skavu just had a tough rep. *Ade will assess them. Ade knows what he's doing.* Shan patted Nevyan's arm to get her attention and simply mouthed *Ade*. Nevyan made an irritated sideways movement of her head, but the tension seemed to be relieved for the time being.

Then Ralassi changed tack, or maybe Rit did. The ussissi relayed the minister's next argument with neutral patience. "The Maritime Fringe is largely destroyed, but there are three continents also opposed to our cooperation with you, and they've sworn to attack both this nation and the wess'har."

Esganikan kept pacing. "But none of them have effective air assets, so unless they can land troops by sea they're not a threat. They now *know* you have access to bioweapons which can destroy whole populations—targeted and replicating. They've *seen* this. Do they understand it? Do they appreciate that this is an extremely asymmetric situation? That we don't need large troop numbers or even a presence here to wipe them out?"

"Then may we have the remainder of the targeted bioweapons that you developed?"

"That doesn't address your own internal security problems. The members of your own genetic group that want you ousted."

Rit considered that, shivering amber beads rattling on the tips of her quills. "Which is why I need ongoing support, so that we may get on with restoration. But not the Skavu, unless their conduct is regulated."

There *was* a war still in progress, even if it had stopped in its tracks yet again. Shan tried to see isenj as their termite-like ancestors in the same way she saw humans as apes to understand their reactions better. Did they reach population or food crises and then swarm, attacking rival colonies? She didn't understand the stop-start nature of their conflicts. It was as if they hadn't really got the hang of fighting, and paused each time to stare in horror and wonder what the hell they had unleashed.

Esganikan, for all her propensity to take out a weapon and execute someone on the spot, was clearly trying to be patient by wess'har standards. *So I couldn't get it up to kill Rayat, and you can't quite bring yourself to commit genocide.* Shan wondered how that would play out in the adjustment of Earth. She decided not to ask about that here, but she now knew how ten thousand troops could take half a continent. It all hinged on bioweapons, and firepower was just to make emphatic points.

She wondered how that could possibly work on Earth.

"How are you going to clean up after wiping out whole populations that can't even bury their dead?" Shan asked. "I'm a copper. I used to do stuff like that. Disasters. Emergencies. Shifting casualties."

"When an area is cleansed," said Esganikan, "then nanites can be released to remediate the environment. You saw that happen on Constantine island. They erase, and resolve everything to its components."

"A whole country. A *continent*. You can *vacuum* up that mess too, can you?"

Esganikan seemed to be working out the English word *vacuum*. "Yes."

Shan might easily have been the medieval peasant asking the modern man how he expected to light his home without lots of tallow. She couldn't grasp even now how advanced a civilization might be that had built towns and cities for a million years. The fact that wess'har—whether Eqbas or their local cousins—still looked like flesh and blood, still had families, still fretted over their kids, still enjoyed food and sex and the feel of wind and sunshine, made her forget how incomprehensibly different other elements of their culture might be.

Nevyan got up. Wess'har could rise from a kneeling position to upright in one fluid movement like a dancer. She walked across the cabinet chamber and stood next to Minister Rit, then knelt to bring her eyes as level with Rit's face as she could, ignoring the rest of the cabinet. They didn't seem to have much to contribute anyway, but then seeing what happened to dissenters like Eit probably made for much faster meetings and shorter agendas. Nevyan, with that intense wess'har focus, needed to be up close to the subject of her curiosity. There were no scent signals she could fully read, and no facial expressions to interpret.

Shan waited for a reaction from Rit. Humans found wess'har aggressive simply because they had no concept of personal space and got in way too close: isenj, creatures living in close confinement, probably had their own discomfort zones.

"You know now that you can never drive us out of this system," Nevyan said. "Your species is the one most at risk. But how can you ever change? I pity you, but how can we reach agreement that you will never land on Bezer'ej?"

Rit chittered. Ralassi listened.

"She intends to put a stop to those military ambitions. The rule of ancestors' memories makes it hard, which is why many deaths are needed. Thoughts have to be killed too. Gene lines must broken. New ones with . . . *green* views must be encouraged and given precedence."

Thoughts have to be killed too.

Shan struggled to make sure she still found that sinister. The day she didn't, she'd know things had gone too far. *They needed to stamp out ideas preserved in genetic memory.* Nevyan seemed taken aback too. Her pupils snapped between cross wire and flower and her head tilted further to one side. She was absolutely consumed with amazement.

It was a radically different culture, all right.

Selectively breeding for tree-huggers.

Jesus, that sounded like a grand eugenics scheme that the Eqbas might even try. It riveted Shan, like all shocking revelations. Wess'har, who didn't care about what you believed and were only concerned with what you did, were now fumbling for common ground with isenj, whose entire existence was determined by obsolete mental images, not of the here and now and real, but of the what-was. And somehow they *were* finding it. Shan could see it on Nevyan's face, and even on Esganikan's now.

She could even smell it—a bright vegetal scent that made her think of cut grass but that was nothing like it.

"Self-selecting," said Shan. "Those who fight disqualify themselves from the gene pool."

"As a survival mechanism, it's admirable," said Esganikan. "Does it trouble you, Shan?"

Shan was certain she'd suppressed her scent to avoid the olfactory equivalent of muttering dissent in the corner. She concentrated and inhaled. Yes, she had. The wess'har trait that *c'naatat* had given her had become another external "tell" that she hid, part of the poker face she'd grown over the years to feign impartiality for the world.

"It's something my society would find disgusting," Shan said at last.

"For Umeh, is there another option?"

It was just as well Eddie wasn't here. The core of the problem was that isenj bred and expanded, and that characteristic had now put them in conflict with wess'har, Eqbas and a fanatical Skavu ally. It was what Aras had called a vermin argument. He'd had a row with Eddie about the definition, and said that humans fitted it as well as any other inconvenient animal. Shan saw not the isenj being tried even in their death throes here, but Earth: because Earth was going down the same path.

You knew that. You've always known that. You even wanted some higher authority to kick our sorry arses.

And here was the philosophy, the rambling debate over a beer, made solid and scary and full of dilemmas. Shan, unflinching when it came to loathing the depths of human behavior in the way that only coppers could, imagined the reality of culling and adjustment accurately and it still hit her hard.

Did she still feel it needed doing?

It wasn't even her choice now.

Yes, it did.

Bezer'ej: Nazel, also known as Chad Island

"There are other Dry Aboves we must see," said Keet.

A dozen bezeri lounged in the shallows on the shore of Chad, still making that transition from their ancient emotional tie to the sea. Lindsay wondered how any creature could handle a shift in niche that radical, and then she recalled that she'd done it—almost.

She'd been getting used to being an aquatic human. How long that would have lasted until she missed her existence on dry land, she'd never know.

"Not Ouzhari," said Lindsay.

"Next towards the Greater Unknown."

Ah, *north*. The sequence ran northernmost to southern tip of the chain—Constantine, Catherine, Charity, Clare, Chad and Christopher, or Ouzhari. They wanted to explore Clare. The colonists had named the islands for saints. Clare—friend of Saint Francis of Assisi, Francis to whom the incongruous Norman-style church in Constantine's underground colony had been dedicated; the stained-glass window, made partly by Aras and now gone, showed the saint in brown robes surrounded by animals from Earth and Bezer'ej.

Clare.

Clare . . . Saint Clare had *not* been martyred, but she tried. Lindsay recalled that from forgotten lessons. Clare had given up her wealth to embrace poverty, and tried to give up her life too. When she heard Franciscan monks had been martyred by the Moors in Morocco, she was set on going there to share their fate, but the holy sisters held her back. Yes, *Clare.* Lindsay couldn't help but see the echo in a well-meaning woman who thought a sacrificial, late and totally impractical gesture would save the world.

But I'm being practical. The bezeri are the last of their kind, and I had no right to wipe them off the face of the planet. I'm not a martyr. Really, I'm not.

"Okay, Clare it is." She recalled the charts: twenty-five kilometers of open water, maybe. They had podships. "A day trip."

"We feel well," said Maipay. "We feel better than before, better than many seasons. *You* give us this."

It was a fragile straw to clutch, but Lindsay needed its support. She wanted forgiveness and approval. She was prepared to accept that now, and if the outcome was positive, then—as the wess'har said—motive didn't matter.

The bezeri had almost all come ashore now and made daily forays into the water for food, but they were sampling vegetation on land, and, inevitably, they were hunting. The *shevens* fascinated them. The creatures were large, aggressive prey, they put up a fight, and they often escaped. Even the largest *sheven* couldn't seize and envelope two adult bezeri hunting as a team, and all it took was a two-pronged attack with one of them going for each side simultaneously and seizing the edge of its membrane like a sheet and stretching it. Bezeri packed a lot of muscle.

"We go," said Saib imperiously, assuming his Sahib role. All he needed was native bearers, and the image of the colonial hunter would have been complete.

The impression most bezeri gave her now was of being amorphous big cats, able to spring and leap with great muscle contractions. Some had retained their translucency and others had developed camouflage-like mottling. A dozen of them rushed out of the settlement, crashing through bushes and splashing into the surf. Lindsay braced herself and went in after them. She was used to submerging but the first rush of cold seawater into her nose and the sensation of her gills opening from slits that ran parallel with what were once her ribs was always a second or two of near panic.

Once she passed that stage, she was an aquatic creature again, using bioluminescence to speak. Once she'd clung to vocalization underwater: now it seemed irrelevant.

Once. Her transforming exile was weeks, months—not years.

The bezeri also seemed to find the amphibious transition effortless. They dived to the shelf a hundred meters out to sea where they had assembled podships and began sliding into them. The pods—translucent organic material, grown from plants—were a lot faster than swimming.

The ships also reminded Lindsay of the challenges facing the bezeri ashore if they were to become capable of holding the planet against any colonizers who would inevitably have space flight capability. The ships were powered by a natural seed pod ejection system that had been selectively bred for generations into something that could eject a laden pod ten meters or so onto dry land and get it back into the water again. The technology wouldn't be much use on land.

Okay, they're ticking things off fast the evolutionary list now: walking on dry land, talking, building settlements. The industrial revolution will have to wait. First—they need to discover fire.

Lindsay could pilot a podship, and the old skills she learned as a fleet aviation cadet came back, along with memories of training for collision repair at sea; standing in a training tank with a damage control team, slipping in fast-rising ice-cold water, trying to get panels secured across breaches in the mocked-up hull in darkness, simulating a real incident on board a stricken ship.

I could stroll that now. Cold water's easy, I can detect objects without even using my eyes. I'd be really useful as part of a ship's company.

C'naatat would be a gift for the military, and for any industry needing to send humans into hostile environments. Shan said it would get used. She'd always known: and so had Rayat.

Was he dead now? He always had a plan on the go. Lindsay worried at a vague level that Rayat would always be trouble until the day she saw his corpse and watched it rot. Nothing short of that would convince her.

She shook aside the speculation. Bezeri knew their way around the islands in pods without charts and Lindsay trailed after them, trying to tap into the natural navigational skills that were now within her. Bezeri were also more adept at landing on beaches than she was. It was a largely uncontrolled beaching exactly like the first time she'd come ashore in a pod, using simple friction to slow her, but this time she skidded a long way up a smooth sandy cove. The pod shot past the rest of the flotilla, narrowly avoiding a collision.

Lindsay slipped out of her pod in a flood of water and waited for a rebuke from Saib for her lack of seamanship, but none came. He poured from his vessel like a jar of drained pickles and slid onto the beach, leaving an indentation, and swung across to the foot of low cliffs.

"We have never been beyond here." He shimmered his happy colors—amber, blue, violet—and thudded up to the cliffs, followed by Carf and Maipay, as if looking for a path inland. Lindsay followed in the wake of churned sand that they left. "We must visit all. We must go to the furthest . . . north."

"Yes, *north,*" said Lindsay. Their rate of language absorption varied a lot, and Saib was the most articulate by far, but the others were at least speaking some English. "The mainland."

"Are there *sheven* there?"

"There seem to be *sheven* or creatures very like them everywhere." Lindsay jogged past them, and the sun cast her hazy shadow ahead of her like a glass of water, dark patches and lens-magnified pools of bright light. What she saw was still basically humanoid in shape. She wasn't sure how she felt about that. "I don't know how plentiful they are, though."

Clare's cliffs crumbled into slopes of scree half a kilometer east and Lindsay led the bezeri onto a rolling plain dotted with pockets of heath and large cracked gray boulders. The island was more like Constantine. There was the same blue-gray grasslike ground cover and spiked lavender bushes that grew knee-high. Orange foliage in the mid-distance bore a resemblance to the tree-ferns that stood as an exotic alien backdrop to the rural terrestrial idyll created for the Constantine colonists by Aras. There was enough of the familiar here to prod Lindsay's memory of a recent and almost happier time.

"You remember," said Saib. "I remember too. Your glass on the grave."

"So . . . you have some of my memories as well, not just Shan's."

Saib considered the question, drumming the tips of his tentacles on the ground. Sometimes he reminded her of a sarcastic and impatient uncle almost to the point of comedy, and then she'd remind herself of his reflexes and his capacity to take down a giant *sheven,* and the humor evaporated.

"No, this is Shan too," he said. "Thinking of the glass colors."

I have to get a grip. I can't keep resenting every mention of her. Shan had seen David's grave, of course: Aras made the glass headstone, a cluster of flowers from roses and native blooms. Did it mean anything to her, then, to surface in her memories? Whatever it was, however genetic memory functioned, Saib had expressed Shan's recollections and almost nobody else's. If he'd taken on her other characteristics as well, it would make him one very aggressive, self-righteous squid. And he had plenty of that attitude to start with.

Lindsay paused and looked up, searching for stabtails, the hawk-sized flying predators that were an occasional sight on Constantine. After a few minutes she saw something else that had been a familiar sight around the colony. It was an *alyat*, a flying relative of the *sheven*.

It was a different color: it was a vivid, transparent peacock blue. But blue or not, it was still an *alyat*. She remembered them having no color, resting in branches and looking for all the world like plastic bags scattered by a high wind. They were transparent membrane too, a single piece of digestive tract that fell on prey and enfolded it, just like a *sheven* did in streams and bogs. In terms of things you didn't want dropping on you, *alyats* beat spiders by a long way.

"Look." She pointed and the bezeri turned to follow her gesture. "*Alyat*. Flying *sheven*."

Lindsay could almost see the cogs of thought grinding as the bezeri studied the creature. It was like watching a cat at a window, chattering its teeth on seeing a bird outside. They were wondering how they could catch them. Everything that moved seem to be fair game.

She was starting to realize how central hunting was to the bezeri psyche. They'd been without large challenging prey for a long time, many generations, and even millennia if she went by the azin shell records that Mohan Rayat had learned to interpret. The prospect of the chase excited them in a primeval way.

"I have not felt so well for so long," said Saib. "I feel *new*."

And then it dawned on Lindsay: not only had *c'naatat* enabled them to suddenly find prey that answered something deep in their psychology, deep in their genes, but it had also given them all renewed vigor as individuals. *C'naatat* restored the body. These survivors of an ecologically vulnerable race were all in a better state—apart from bereavement—than they had been before the neutron radiation scoured Ouzhari. In a selfish way that humans might recognize, the bezeri remnant of forty-four had seized on what was in it for *them*. They'd been old and slow: now they were young again.

Lindsay looked at her hands, translucent gel streaked with cartilage, and wondered if *she* felt better than before. Less than three years earlier, she'd been a promising naval officer, a commander at 26, and gambling that a rare opportunity to go extra-solar in the search for the Constantine colony would end in a quick mission report on a failed dream, and 150 years out of Earth time that would nevertheless make her a uniquely qualified officer on her return. It was a huge risk. And she had no way of knowing what was waiting on a planet that—officially, anyway—nobody knew was inhabited, let alone in the middle of a war zone.

Lindsay made a conscious effort not to look back. Three years was too far, even further than 150 trillion miles.

"We will also live *here*," said Saib grandly.

Maipay ambled around, looking as if he was walking on his knuckles. "We can live *all* these places. We live where we want, hunt what we want."

Their attitude was rapacious. Lindsay wondered what the frugal and environmentally responsible wess'har would think now of the bezeri, the creatures they waged war against the isenj to protect, and who had turned out to be every bit as profligate as the despised *gethes*. Saib and Maipay loped off, Maipay occasionally using a tentacle extended behind him in exactly the kangaroo-bounce that Pili had first used. Lindsay watched them cover the ground in a zigzag pattern. Something they disturbed flew up from cover and they went charging after it, jinking and changing course like cheetahs.

Their intoxication with their newfound strength and the instincts they'd long buried was overwhelming them. The creature, whatever it was, made its escape and soared into the sky as a dark dot and vanished, leaving the two bezeri circling and excited.

They were destructive. But it was still a big planet, and its previous predation by isenj had been repaired by the wess'har so that it seemed as apparently wild and unspoiled as before. There were only forty-four bezeri, no real threat to any ecology. Lindsay could humor them. If there was one lesson she had taken to heart in the last year, it was that she couldn't use Earth morality as a benchmark with any degree of confidence.

She bent and collected sharp stones and dry fluffy plant fiber.

"Come on," she said. She squatted down and formed the dry fiber into a loose ball of kindling, then held one stone in each had. "Forget the hunting. My schedule says this is your week to discover fire."

Northern Assembly–Maritime Fringe border, Umeh

After a while, Ade stopped noticing the bodies.

The bulkheads of the patrol vessel had switched to transparency and he looked down into canyons of high-rises that looked full of debris.

The Skavu were searching for a pocket of survivors in a wasteland of the dead and dying. Ade looked up at them occasionally, just to see if he could relate to anything in those faces, and he simply couldn't tell. Wess'har had once been as alien as that, though. Perhaps he was judging too soon.

"There," said Kiir.

The vessel felt as if it was banking, but it was an illusion caused by the transparent bulkhead shifting position to the deck, exactly as on Esganikan's shapeshifting warship. Qureshi and Chahal peered through the deck and said nothing, then sat upright with their rifles across their laps staring into mid-distance.

"It's bloody millions," said Chahal, muffled slightly by his breather mask. "Jesus, that stuff covers some ground."

In some areas there was what appeared to be a black and brown velvet carpet. Had it been familiar shapes of human bodies, he wondered how long it would have been before he could shut it out. He waited for the isenj deep in him to react at some primeval level, but nothing emerged.

His higher brain could tell him, though. It said that he should have found this beyond a nightmare.

"What are we actually going to do when we find survivors?" asked Qureshi. "I mean, if they're dying, then it's—"

"I'll do it," said Ade. He'd done it once this week and he could do it again if it ended some poor bastard's suffering. "But you're picking up non-targeted genomes, aren't you? Healthy isenj?"

"Won't be healthy long with all those bodies decaying," Chahal muttered.

The patrol ship touched down in the middle of a broad street paved with bright turquoise and amber images of long-extinct foliage. Ade's brain saw shapes in the doorways as black disposal bags, but then resolved into bodies, and when the bulkhead dissolved into a hatch, the smell hit him—not the smell of decomposing bodies and shattered bowels that he knew, but something else. The forest-floor smell of isenj was mixed with something sulfurous.

Ade didn't need a breather but right then it would have been useful. He swallowed a threatening wave of nausea and stepped out of the ship. Kiir—masked like the others—stared at him and paused, as if waiting for something.

"You can breathe this air freely?"

Ade nodded, and realized that the Skavu didn't know all the little tricks that *c'naatat* could pull. Esganikan hadn't briefed them thoroughly. Maybe that was just as well. He checked the ESF670's scan for concealed ordnance—fat lot of use in a world that didn't use terrestrial explosives—and covered Qureshi and Chahal while they ducked out of the ship and took cover behind the pillars of a doorway that was mercifully free of corpses. Kiir gestured towards another building. His squad started a recognizable house-clearance procedure.

"Jesus, Ade," said Chahal. "Look. They do it almost like us."

"Only so many ways a biped can get through a rectangular gap safely."

It made the Skavu feel familiar. They knew what they were doing, and professional reassurance went a long way. Apart from the fact that they were surly bastards—or seemed like it—they were doing the basics that human soldiers had been doing for centuries, and Ade concentrated on the kinship rather than the fact he didn't like them much.

Qureshi sighted up on the roofline opposite. "I want to know what happened to First, Second and Third To Die, personally."

"Promotion must be crap."

"This is our recruiting poster, eh? Bloody space marines." She stepped backwards into a dark recess and there was a strawlike crunch. She froze. "Ade, what have I trodden in?"

"Hold still." He could guess. He leaned into the recess just to be certain it wasn't an anti-personnel device—even if isenj didn't appear to have them—and confirmed it. It was a light-colored isenj, unusual, very small, and dead. He guessed it was a child. Maybe the isenj deep in him knew. "Okay, just step off carefully."

"Oh, God . . ." she sighed.

"Jesus, they're everywhere."

Kiir's squad was making its way down the silent street, door to door. Ade never assumed anything in a foreign city, but there was nothing here, no vehicles like those he'd seen when the Eqbas had wiped out a Fringe armored column. There were no vehicles here at all, and the flat fronted buildings could have been apartments or offices. Civvies could kill you as efficiently as uniformed troops, and bloody often did, so it was a bogus distinction when your arse was on the line.

Isenj didn't seem to wear uniforms anyway.

Ade caught up with Kiir. "Sir, if you have a plan, now would be a good time to share it with us."

"There!" Kiir barked. Something black shot past the corner of Ade's eye and he swung round, rifle raised like a reflex. "This zone must be cleared."

Where the hell was he going to put detainees? "Sir, who are we—"

Kiir held his weapon two-handed in front of his chest

and fired. Ade couldn't imagine how he aimed the thing, but when he looked up there was an isenj lying on the roadway in a spreading pool of clear fluid.

Ade understood now. "We don't do that, sir."

Qureshi and Chahal backed up towards Ade, still watching the high-rises, expecting—as he had—to be dealing with snipers.

Back home, Ade had a rule book that told him how to deal with an officer who shot noncombatants. Here, he didn't even have a common moral framework with any of the species. His gut said *stop this*. But his brain said that the isenj who were untouched by the pathogen would die from disease spread by unburied corpses, and the isenj had no refugee shelters. It was an impossible choice. But he made it.

Chahal turned to Ade. "We're not doing this, are we, Sarge?"

"Fire if fired upon," Ade said. "Find some bugger dying, finish them off if your gut tells you to. Other than that—just cover the street."

And it wasn't enough. He'd seen enough combat to know the gray areas, and he'd slipped around the regs and not regretted it, but this was something he'd never seen: culling. He always thought he'd handle this differently.

But the deaths here were on a scale that was too big to process.

"If I had not been told to allow you to do as you wanted, I would have shot you for disobedience by now," said Kiir.

Ade slipped his fighting knife out of his belt. "And, sir, I'd have got up and stuck this in you to see what color you bled. Do we understand each other?"

Kiir might well have been angry but it was impossible to tell. *Jesus, we go out for a quick acquaint with the new boys and here I fucking am squaring up to the CO.* Ade didn't get an answer, so he carried on down the road, foot-patrol routine, hoping that the isenj had the sense to run.

Where? This is the end of the world for them.

Qureshi moved ahead of him on point. "Now I know," she said. "I mean, we've been in some hairy situations over the years and we bend the rules a bit but I wondered why people let holocausts happen, and what sort of bastards they are. You know what? They're like *me*."

The distinctive *crack-ack-ack* of the Skavu weapon seemed to be coming from all around them now. There were other squads operating.

"I've got nothing to lose, Izzy. You and Chaz thin out, and call Shan for extraction." He jerked his thumb over his shoulder. It was a bloody long way back across the border on a carpet of bodies. "I'm happy to slot Kiir. Life's cheap here."

There was no chain of command. Legally, none of them were service personnel now. Even if they had been, there was no war between them and the isenj. There were only rules of engagement that no longer bound them and a bit of common sense.

"Piss off, Sarge," said Qureshi cheerfully. "I'm staying. It's your turn to get shot by aliens."

Chahal was staring into his palm, checking his bioscreen. "We've got five squads within a kilometer according to the sweep. They've got ten thousand troops covering two hundred million isenj here, and they've got the time to go picking off the ones that got away. I mean, what does that say about them? Is it a sport with them?"

"Well, we either walk now, or I stop this bunch," said Ade. "Is the isenj in me driving this, or is it kinder to shoot them all rather than let them starve or die of some other disease?"

"You remember isenj stuff?"

"Chaz, don't give me that look."

"Do you?"

"I don't know."

The Skavu squad stacked either side of a gaping door, paused, and then—on a signal Ade didn't see—rushed the building. Rounds cracked and echoed: shouts, squeals, and then silence. But the squeals resonated within him. They were universal, uncontrolled, just animal pain and fear.

"Okay," he said. "I've had enough."

There was a second between could-have-saved and you-let-it-happen. And the second had *passed*. One of Kiir's squad came out and started running down the road close to the wall. Ade went in.

Oh God, Aras. . .

Aras did this once.

Ade was in the present, about to confront Skavu executioners, and also behind Aras's eyes five centuries ago, bombing Mjat because only fragmentation could destroy *c'naatat*-infected isenj. Ade's moral compass spun. That guiding gut-feel of a single right and wrong had vanished and been replaced by a thousand different ones.

It was a suicidal move even for Ade: live rounds, maybe explosives, blokes who didn't know your procedure and who didn't think like you. Kiir and one of his Skavu were systematically dispatching about twenty isenj lying on the floor, or maybe they were just making sure they were dead. Ade's sense of time disintegrated, and he felt he was spending minutes trying to decide if these were sick isenj like the one he'd shot, or healthy ones with different genomes. He could hear running boots. A pool of watery fluid was spreading on the tiles, looking for all the world as if someone had peed. But it was plasma-like isenj blood. He'd seen that before.

Eddie. Ade remembered: his spare camera. *Get me some shots of Skavu.* He clipped the cam to his webbing like a radhaz sensor and just let it run.

One of the Skavu went to walk past him, his job done, moving on to the next.

"I can't let you do this, mate," Ade said. "Once, I didn't stop something I could have. Now, I will."

No, Commander Neville, I won't help you ship your frigging cobalt bombs to Ouzhari. I won't help you capture Shan.

It was that easy. It really was. He pushed the Skavu in the chest, just a warning shove. Qureshi was behind him, Chahal to the right. One of the bezeri on the floor moved, not yet dead despite the thorough attention of the Skavu, and one of them—where had Kiir gone?—drew the long flat blade from the sheath on his back.

I'm *c'naatat*, Ade thought, and saw his dad kill orphaned fox cubs he'd hidden so carefully under his bed, and his mother getting a thrashing from the bastard, and *it could all be stopped if he just stood up—*

Ade blocked the downward sweep of the blade with his arm, no conscious effort. The liquid-armor layer in his vest deflected the stroke and the blade skidded down his arm. He heard Chahal shout, "Jesus, Ade—" and he felt no pain, but he clamped his free hand down on the blade and jerked it from the Skavu's grip. Blood—he *had* to be careful with his infected blood.

Now it hurt. The blade—the sword—had sliced along the length of his forearm. Chahal and Qureshi had seen *c'naatat* do its instant healing trick before, but the Skavu had not, and they watched in either horror or fascination as the spectacular laceration sealed itself and faded through pink to unmarked skin.

Ade held on to the sword. It was covered in blood. "Don't even think about asking for it back, *Skavi.*"

"I'm clear," said Chahal. He checked himself for blood spatter. "Are you okay? Ade, you're fucking insane."

"My shirt's buggered."

Qureshi stepped in. "Come on, Sarge, take it easy. It's not worth it. Walk away."

Ade expected all hell to break loose among the Skavu, but they were quiet, and they backed away from him. Kiir looked him over like a parade inspection. Then he took out his sidearm and shot the isenj, and resumed his staring. Ade found a pure cold slab of focused hatred that really did feel like Shan's contribution to his ragbag of genes.

"You're fucking dead, sir," Ade said quietly. "First chance I get."

Qureshi stood between the two of them, rifle held one-handed on Kiir, and flashed Umeh Station for extraction. "No offense," she said. "But I don't think we're going to play well together."

I haven't thrown up or shit myself. The rescue thing usually triggered that, Ade realized, all the helpless failures in his boyhood. *Shan's going to go ballistic.*

Kiir stared him in the eye and Ade stared back. But it wasn't some macho display, he knew. It was revelation, and fear, and disgust. The Skavu would see *c'naatat* as something to eradicate. They had a point.

Eventually Kiir turned away, and the other Skavu made no attempt to recover his blade. They backed out of the room. "Your kind," said Kiir, pausing in the doorway, "is too dangerous."

"I don't think he meant the Corps," Qureshi said. "Ade—oh, never mind."

The foxes were dead, and his mum was dead, and the isenj were dead, and Ade had saved nothing. The bezeri were dead, too, and not dead. But he felt a profound peace settling in his chest, and took out his cleaning kit to wipe his blood from a rather handy sword that had nearly removed his forearm.

Eddie's cam was still running. Ade switched it off and the three marines waited in the stinking, body-strewn road to be picked up.

11

Religions wax and wane, but there's a sudden growth in all Christian sects, fueled by the extraordinary story of the Christopher mission. In just under thirty years, a community of Christians drawn originally from all sects and denominations returns to Earth with a unique repository of genetic material from plant and animal life long disappeared from Earth. Their story is made even more extraordinary by the fact that an alien civilization will be bringing both them and the gene bank home, with plans to restore the planet's environment. "If you want miracles," said a member of the congregation at the newly reopened church of Saint Bartholomew, "then this is as awe-inspiring as they come. People see the hand of God in this, both in its sheer scale and its timing."

BBChan 557, social affairs round-up

Jejeno, Umeh

Wess'har, Ade had said, had no external testicles. But when it came to sheer balls, Aras had plenty to spare.

Eddie watched him stride down the service road that circled Umeh Station and head towards the government offices of the Northern Assembly. He was Vlad the Impaler, Pol Pot, Bulaitch and every war criminal rolled into one as far as the isenj were concerned. And their historical monster was walking openly through their city.

"You're bloody mad," said Eddie. "We could have called for a ground car."

"Mad, perhaps, but I'm not afraid," said Aras. "And I'm not ashamed."

The sobering deterrent of Esganikan Gai's warship sitting indiscreetly above the city was impressive but offered no psychological support for a man running the gauntlet of those who had wanted him dead. What they wanted now was unknown: which meant Eddie had to find out or bust.

The walk was fine up to the point where Umeh Station's precincts merged into Jejeno itself. It had never been a city where you could take a casual stroll. It was so packed with teeming isenj most of the time that pedestrian traffic had its own rules, and you ignored them at your peril. It was as packed as a football crowd and in constant movement. But as Aras walked on, with no sign of stopping or giving way, the chattering, rasping sea of brown, black and umber shapes, some jangling with beaded quills, somehow managed to part. The pace of their tottering walk slowed and there was a sense of a river being dammed and forming swirling eddies.

The last time Eddie had done anything as stupid as ignoring the traffic rules and changing direction in the wrong place, he'd caused a crush. Street crushes caused injury and death. His instinct was to yank Aras back, but you couldn't stop a 170-kilo two-meter alien that easily.

The isenj simply stopped and stared, and somehow the ripple spread and the living river froze for as far as Eddie could see.

"Shit, Aras, you don't even know where the National Archive is," Eddie called. "For Chrissakes, *wait.*"

The bee cam was already flying escort overhead and he waved it forward to cover the crowd reaction. *Are you really going to use this footage? Really?* Eddie took advantage of the wake Aras left and jogged up behind him.

Aras glanced back over his shoulder. "I *know.*" His voice, which usually had little trace of the wess'har overtone when he spoke English, suddenly had two distinct notes, as if he'd slipped back into being a full wess'har again. "I *know* Jejeno from memories."

The isenj seemed dumbstruck again: no agitation, no shrill objections, nothing that indicated anything beyond incomprehension or shock. This wasn't how notorious criminals were greeted by crowds on Earth. And Aras *was* a criminal to them, one that even the Northern Assembly politicians had demanded be handed over as recently as last year, after *five hundred years.* The destruction of Mjat, one of many colony cities erased from Asht, as the isenj called Bezer'ej, was as powerful an icon of holocaust for the isenj as Hiroshima was for humans.

They don't recognize him. Shit, they can't understand why he doesn't look the way they recall.

The thought hit Eddie hard.

Their genetic memory is a wess'har who looked like Nevyan.

But something in Aras recognized parts of Jejeno even if Jejeno didn't recognize him. He strode on, scattering the crowds. Jesus, if any isenj got near enough to catch *c'naatat*—no, it wasn't that simple to pass on except through open wounds and body fluids. And isenj had a dread of *c'naatat* that Eddie had once thought was the simple common sense of an overcrowded people, but that he now suspected was a race memory of the terrible consequences of the parasite infecting them on Bezer'ej.

The bee cam pursued Aras to the National Archive, and Ralassi met them to lead them through its corridors. He'd promised Eddie an "interesting experience" before he went back to Wess'ej, as if watching a civil war and a spot of ethnic cleansing wasn't interesting enough.

Aras had also insisted on seeing the records.

"If they've got genetic memory, why do they need records and archives?" asked Eddie.

Ralassi gave him a disapproving look with compressed lips, exactly like Serrimissani's don't-be-such-a-dick look. "Because isenj don't all have the same memories, of course. Someone has to collate them."

"Ah," said Eddie. "Good point."

The bright green corridors were suffocatingly narrow and low, nothing like the grand halls of the ministerial offices. Aras looked uncomfortable ducking through them. They followed Ralassi into a pale gray plastered chamber deep in the government complex, and Eddie found himself in a well of bright light.

Looking up, he focused on a skylight with glazing bars in that distinctively isenj organic style like vines strangling a rib cage. Then he worked out why the room needed natural light. An isenj was hunched at a desk scribbling furiously on sheets of plastic material, and it looked as if it was drawing rather than writing.

That hunched posture put Eddie in mind of a dead spider in a bathtub. He hated himself for that, but he couldn't help it. He was only a pattern-recognizing monkey himself. The isenj paused and stared at Aras, and then at Eddie.

"This is the archivist of visual records," said Ralassi. "She is an artist. I brought you here for the memory."

She. The isenj paused for a second, and might have been looking at them, but it was hard to tell. She went back to her rapid scribbling.

"What memory?" asked Eddie, whispering automatically. It was a library, after all. It was amazing how universal a setting a quiet archive room was. "I don't understand."

"You wanted to know what Umeh was like in the past. Helol Chep remembers."

"Ah, she's going to let me look through the records?"

"No, she's willing to draw you an image. What would you like to see? Her job is to communicate memories accurately when needed. Helol has one of the most exact and extensive memories of anyone in the city. She comes from a long line of great recallers."

This extraordinary transgenerational power of recall also seemed to have generated a vast storehouse of records. Isenj were natural bureaucrats.

"I wouldn't trust a human to do that," said Eddie. He struggled with the notion of verifying a genetic recollection. No wonder isenj had more of a wess'har approach to truth and accuracy. "We're all lying bastards with bad memories."

"Yes, I have heard this."

Eddie took a deep breath. "What was Umeh like before the isenj . . ." He almost used the word *overran*. There was no escaping the terminology of pest control, and the remnant of his liberal heart rebelled. "Before Umeh was urbanized?"

Helol Chep appeared to listen carefully to Ralassi's interpretation and replied with shrills and clicks. Eddie suddenly understood why ussissi became interpreters. They weren't just adept at languages; they were superb mimics in the same way that the macaws were. They could reproduce any sound. That was what Ralassi was doing now.

The artist threw herself into a new work, this time using a screen, and Eddie wondered if he was going to see footage after all. She made scraping chittering sounds as she worked. He wished he could speak their language.

"She will depict it for you."

"She's going to show me pictures?"

"She is going to *draw* pictures."

"Don't they have image records?"

"Not of the original world. They had no recording devices then. That must be obvious to anyone."

"Not to me." He imagined flickering film images of a small town that later became Jejeno and the buildings engulfed the continent. "So is this how she imagines the city was then?" He thought of all the dinosaur recreations that changed every time BBChan made a new natural history show and some scientist had a better theory. "Artist's impression?"

"No, this is how she recalls the primeval world from her genetic memory."

Primeval. Ussissi were too fluent to pick the wrong word. The isenj really did *remember*. Isenj didn't just recall ancestral grudges and their parents' memories; they could go back further. How far? No, he'd misunderstood the word. It was like a bird recalling being a *Tyrannosaurus rex*. There had to be another explanation.

"Amazing," said Eddie, still impressed. "Can they all do that?"

"Most isenj seem to have the primeval memory of the forest, yes."

Eddie stared at the isenj and wondered how it would feel to shut your eyes and see woolly mammoth and ice-covered Britain.

"Okay," he said, and motioned the bee cam to an over-the-shoulder-shot position. "Fire away."

Ralassi stepped back and the isenj grasped stylus-like instruments in her hands—both of them—and began sketching furiously on a tablet. The cam recorded the astonishing spectacle of someone sketching two-handed, cross-hatching frantically with one hand and doing long curving sweeps with the other. At this angle it was hard to get a feel for the landscape, but Eddie resisted the urge to peer over her shoulder.

After a few minutes Chep paused and tilted the tablet. The image was projected into a display on the wall and for the first time Eddie could picture ancient Umeh, even though the drawing was monochrome. He watched a forest like no forest he had ever seen take shape. Aras smelled suddenly of grapefruit, a sign he was agitated. Even a human could detect that.

Ralassi's lips compressed, just like Serrimissani in stroppy mode. "I've never seen this before. I too am curious." He inclined his head towards Chep and chittered. "She says she doesn't have an explanation, only memory. The trees captured water at the top and fed the ground."

Chep tapped with both styluses. The image flooded with colors, single tones at first and then shadowed with graduation of tint and shade.

Eddie looked at a landscape of massive tubes seen from a low angle with light slanting through and between them. Where the light penetrated the trunks, it was gently pink and red; it gave him the impression of being dwarfed by giant rhubarb. Between the stalks, tall towers of soil stood aligned in a way that suggested they were built, not a random act of nature. *Termite mounds.* Chep began adding detail, pausing occasionally and becoming motionless. Then she started scribbling again. Sometimes the strokes produced nothing that Eddie could see.

"She says it is *sirp*," said Ralassi. "You call it infrared."

So it was a color to them. He wondered how they managed to depict that in a digital image—if it *was* digital, of course; he didn't know much about their technology. Maybe the reproduction emitted it as IR. It was a real shame that humans, isenj and wess'har would never cooperate enough to share technology, because Eddie could see so many applications that would transform Earth.

He could see the destructive technologies, too. He put

them out of his mind and watched the monitor in his handheld to check that the bee cam was capturing what he thought
he was seeing.

"How long ago was this?"

Ralassi was silent for a few seconds and looked as if he
was having problems calculating.

"Six hundred thousand years," he said.

"Shit," said Eddie. The footage didn't do it justice. The
bee cam couldn't record *boggling time scales* or *this is all
from memory, folks* or any of the things that made this a feat
of astonishing, unimaginable, utterly alien recall.

A bizarre landscape unfolded beneath a canopy of purple cups and spheres. A dark shape gripped the primordial
rhubarb trunks with smaller, lighter creatures clinging to it.
Growths that looked like vines snaked up some of the trunks
and disappeared into the canopy where patches of blue sky
contrasted sharply with the amethyst cups.

"Does she miss this?" said Eddie. "Does she want to see
all this back again?"

The ussissi and the isenj chattered. "She says it would be
nice but as she has it stored in her memory, it isn't necessary." Ralassi looked at the image and blinked slowly. Eddie
almost expected him to slump to the ground in slow motion
and doze like a meerkat, but the interpreter was just considering the art. "They *are* very attached to their natural world,
you know. That's why you see the images on the buildings
and the road surfaces. They revere it."

"But not enough to preserve it, eh? They love the idea but
the reality can go hang."

"You wish me to express that to Helol Chep?"

"That would be rather rude, wouldn't it?"

"Indeed." Ralassi didn't seem as quick to snap at him as
the female ussissi. He wasn't such good company, either. Eddie decided he had a weakness for awkward customers. "And
Serrimissani tells me there are many kinds of human who
behave the same way, loving the abstract ideal while abusing
and destroying the living object."

"If you say cuddly animal toy to me, I'll scream."

"Why?"

"Not literally." *Jesus, haven't I learned by now?* "Just that the wess'har say that to me too."

"*I* say it," Aras interrupted. "Pandas—why you kept the toy and let the real animal become extinct."

"Okay, what he said. And let's not get started on cuddly rabbits."

"If I knew what rabbits were, I would avoid mentioning them." It was hard to tell if Ralassi was being sarcastic or literal. "But I understand the irony of loving what you have destroyed."

"And destroying what you love," said Aras, offering no explanation. Eddie decided not to pursue it.

Chep completed her illustration and tottered backwards to consider it. Eddie gazed on a landscape that hadn't been seen for more than half a million years.

"Now ask her for the archive from Asht," said Aras. "From Bezer'ej."

Ralassi hesitated, and Eddie wondered if it was a sign that Aras was pushing his luck. "Come on, Ralassi. Let's get it over with."

"Very well."

What could they possibly have that Aras could want, that he didn't already have in his own memory? Chep went to a shelf and pulled out a wad of drawing sheets and laid them on the desk, carefully arranged in a sequence. Eddie automatically leaned over to look, but Aras simply pushed him aside, gently but firmly enough to leave Eddie in no doubt that this was not his business.

The images were equally photorealist scenes of a town in a recognizably isenj style, but not like Jejeno. This was a mass of low-rise, wider streets. Eddie expected a burst of citrus scent from Aras, but he simply looked at the images one by one, head cocked on one side, and stood in contemplation with one gloved hand braced on the desk.

"Interesting," said Aras.

Of course: Aras had been flying a fighter on Bezer'ej, seeing only an aerial view.

"Never seen it from the ground level, have you?"

As soon as he said it, Eddie realized how crass that

sounded, even if wess'har were utterly tactless themselves and wouldn't have noticed.

"Oh, I have," Aras said, apparently unconcerned. His tone was completely casual. "I have the memories of a survivor of Mjat, remember. I know what it looks like from street level, at the height of the bombing, balls of flame rolling down the street. It's very vivid, as is the hatred he had for me, which he later expressed physically as my captor."

Eddie swallowed hard. Helol Chep said nothing. If she had responded, he wasn't sure if Ralassi would have passed on her sentiments anyway. No: he *would*. Only humans, and to a lesser extent isenj, pulled their punches out here. Eddie tried hard not to substitute human equivalents in this indirect conversation between destroyer and destroyed, and knew things he didn't feel: that Aras, on Earth, would also be a war criminal, and yet Eddie knew he was a compassionate being and someone he trusted, respected, and truly cared for.

Shan must have been through that ambiguity and conflict too. She'd come down firmly on Aras's side from the start. Ade also saw him with the acceptance of a man who had to make decisions the average civilian never faced. If Eddie had wanted a few more hard and fast lines to help him navigate through his own maze of ethics about his influence as a journalist here, he hadn't found any. He'd even lost a few.

"Better be getting back," said Eddie. "Shan will be wondering where we are."

"I've seen all I want to see," said Aras.

He inclined his head to Chep with unexpected politeness—if the isenj understood that at all—and walked. Eddie stole a moment and grabbed Ralassi by the beaded belt slung across one shoulder.

"I want to ask Chep a question."

"Very well."

"Ask her what she thinks now that she's met the Beast of Mjat."

Ussissi had no human expression, but Eddie could have sworn the look on Ralassi's face said *cheap hack*.

"I shall." He exchanged chittering sounds and Eddie

waited for some explosion of ancient racial hatred. "She says she finds it hard to understand how he can walk among isenj and not try to kill more of them."

"Ask her if she hates him."

"She says she doesn't know, and that troubles her."

"Does she hate wess'har generally?"

"She fears them now they've come to Umeh. She wants to know if Aras has been sent to finish the extermination he started, using the Skavu."

Ouch. "Tell her he only came here to meet isenj and understand them." It wasn't a total lie. "He's not like that."

Chep listened patiently to Ralassi but made no reply. Then she turned back to her records and began stacking them, returning her world of memories to normal. She'd have her work cut out remembering a single brick of Jejeno if Esganikan got down to business. She was the one most likely to finish the job started on Bezer'ej.

The silence finally weighed too heavily. "Thank her for me," said Eddie. "That was very helpful."

He went to catch up with Aras, wondering how many excuses he might have made for Pol Pot, and yet still unable to see Aras—a man who rescued drowning insects, a man who gave rats the same funeral rites as he would have given Shan, a man who enjoyed dull domesticity and doted on his wife—as any kind of beast at all.

Umeh Station, Jejeno

Ade walked through the airlock doors of Umeh Station and handed a sword to Shan, hilt first.

"You might as well make the most of being court-martialed and binned, that's what I say." He didn't do his usual please-don't-be-angry grin. "I've ballsed it up. Sorry, Boss."

Shan looked down the blade and tried not to think about what an edge like that did. She'd managed to shake her dread of what might lie behind mundane doors, but sharp objects of any kind still conjured up the inventive variety of violence that she'd seen daily as a police officer. This blade had sliced

Ade's forearm muscles to the bone. Someone would pay for that.

"I'm proud of you," she said quietly. "Don't you ever think I'm not."

He rummaged in his breast pocket and handed her a rectangle of white plastic: Eddie's backup cam.

"They're bastards," he said quietly. "The isenj don't deserve that."

But he'd put a dying isenj out of its misery. Ade had his inexplicable lines, just like her. "You told him you'd kill him?"

"Yes, Boss."

"That's my boy."

"I know it's daft to get in a ruck over shooting a few isenj when we've just killed millions, but I did."

Shan handed back the sword. It looked nobly martial in Ade's grasp, but she just looked like a psycho with it. Besides, there was always the chance she might use it. Crew and contractors stared at Ade, because news traveled fast.

"Thank God there's only ten thousand Skavu," she said. "I still haven't met one."

"You will."

"This footage is going to seriously piss me off, isn't it?"

"Oh yeah." Ade looked longingly past her. "I need a pee, and a coffee, in that order."

"You sure you're okay?" She steered him towards the heads. "Just tell me."

"No, Boss, I haven't infected anyone else. I checked."

"I really was just asking if you were all right."

"I'm fine. It wasn't a stroll in vacuum." He handed her the sword again and opened the door to the lavatory. "You can hold that, or hold something else for me."

"You're not okay, are you?"

"I am. It was just very . . . cathartic. That's the right word, isn't it? Flushes out all kinds of crap."

Ade's awkwardness was utterly disarming. "Spot on," she said. "You can tell me all about it."

Shan waited outside the door, not quite knowing how to look relaxed with a meter-long sword. She ended up leaning on its hilt like a cane. Across the sea of human heads in the dome's central plaza, she saw a bright copper-red plume advancing like a galleon and just the top of a tufted gold mane. Esganikan and Nevyan were heading her way, and Shan braced for another round of loss of temper containment. Ade came out of the lavatory adjusting his pants, and let out a sigh.

"'S'okay, Boss, I'll take what's coming."

"No, I'm dealing."

Nevyan reached her a few paces ahead of Esganikan, exuding acid. Nev was pissed off. She was reining it in, not a very wess'har thing to do with emotion unless you were a dominant matriarch who didn't want to get in a ruck with another *isan* and end up spraying *jask* all over the place— and inheriting a task force. *Good call, Nev.* The stakes were high.

"Ade says the Skavu weren't overjoyed to work with him." Shan found her arms had folded across her chest of their own accord. "I hope we're not going to have any trouble with them."

"They've never encountered *c'naatat* before and they find it troubling," Esganikan said.

"No shit," said Shan. "It troubles us all, matey."

Ade interrupted deferentially. "The word they used was *dangerous.*"

Nevyan lined up right on cue. "I need to know my neighbors can be trusted."

"It's temporary," said Esganikan. "They won't bother you."

Nevyan didn't back down. "They'll be on Umeh for decades. You know that."

"Do they *have* to do this death-squad thing?" asked Shan. First things first: she took out the cam and held it up like a trump card. "I want to go and watch this footage somewhere quiet. I'd like you to see it too."

Finding somewhere quiet in Umeh Station these days was a challenge, but Shan walked into Cargill's office and put on her you-really-want-to help-me-with-my-enquiries look, patience frayed but not worn out. Cargill glanced up from the inventories on her desk and looked resigned.

"You do need my office, don't you?" It took a harassed

officer to know one. Cargill looked past Shan at Ade. "Trust Royal to play the hero."

"He shot the isenj anyway," said Ade. "I didn't save it. And I don't know what I'd have been saving it for, anyway."

In the end, Cargill stayed and they watched the recording in grim silence. Shan was used to seeing dead bodies and pretty well every perversion and act of violence on the statute books, but it was still unpleasant, with the added twist of seeing the sword slice into Ade's arm from a horribly close angle. Everyone was quiet for a few moments afterwards. Cargill left.

"So, is that boyish high spirits, Commander?" Shan asked. "I know we've got body count of a few hundred million on our consciences already, and I'm the first to say that dead's dead, but I want to be sure we haven't imported a new problem."

Esganikan did some head tilting. "The Skavu are the aftermath of the war. It means the newly awake. Their conversion has been fanatical."

"Ah, the road to Damascus," said Shan. "I know it well. Straight on, and turn right to Hell in a handbasket. Great. Fucking eco-jihad."

"This is for *Umeh*. You don't think they need rigorous adjustment here?"

"I don't know what they need, except to stay on their poxy planet and leave Wess'ej and Bezer'ej alone."

"The Skavu will ensure that, believe me."

"You said they weren't colonial, so they'll have to weed out every isenj who doesn't believe in solar power and reusing envelopes before they can walk away and leave them to it."

"Is that an unreasonable solution?"

"I don't know. I *would* like to see the Skavu, though."

"Do you still plan to accommodate them on Bezer'ej?" Nevyan asked.

"They need a base, and Umeh will be unsuitable for large numbers of them."

"Then," said Nevyan, "you'll have to warn them of the presence of *c'naatat* contamination. What will they do then?"

Esganikan paused, looking at Ade. Shan wondered what she was mulling over. "I think they will obey my orders," she said. "So I will be explicit about where they can venture."

"Ma'am," said Ade, "a technical point. The former Eqbas ships that they fly. They're old, but that still makes them a hell of a lot punchier than the fleet that Wess'ej can assemble. I'm a bit nervous about . . . well, introducing a new superpower to the Cavanagh system."

"There are ten thousand troops with recirculated Eqbas vessels and equipment. How is that a superpower?"

"Because as far as their weapons and fleet are concerned, they are, aren't they?" Ade was doing his simple-soldier routine. The tell was the little frown that creased the skin horizontally across the bridge of his nose. "They could cream Wess'ej if they wanted to. The kit we've got in F'nar might be on a nanite repair cycle, but the basic design template is ten thousand years old. And that capability gap scares me."

"Superpowers, as you call them, want power. Skavu don't."

"I don't think the isenj noticed the difference, actually, ma'am."

Shan had to bite the inside of her cheek. *Ade Bennett, you're perfect.* She was so damn proud of him.

"You'd better be able to guarantee their behavior, then," Shan said. "Because you've dumped a well-armed army of psychopaths on us, and if they get out of hand, we might be the ones rotting in the streets."

"I *know* they're extreme," Esganikan said quietly. "My commanding officer and a third of my crewmates were butchered by them in the adjustment war, and you've seen their blades at close quarters. They were the only option I was given for Umeh. I made a mistake by agreeing to help the isenj, and I should have found another way to confine them and let them carry on their path of self-destruction . . . but I didn't."

Shan tried not to lose sight of the 200 million isenj dead. It wasn't that she liked isenj, but if she failed to find that shocking at any time, she was lost.

"Guarantee they'll leave the Cavanagh system as soon as Umeh is in a secure state," she said.

"That's the agreement anyway."

"I mean by force—*your* force—if need be. Because I'm not sure we have the assets to make sure they go."

"I'll have to speak to Surang about that," said Esganikan. "I may still be on Earth when that point is reached."

"I want to talk to the Skavu command anyway," Nevyan said. "So that we understand each other exactly."

Esganikan did a quick head-jiggle of annoyance. "I'll arrange a meeting, but remember that their culture is not one of compromise and consensus. It may not achieve results."

"Maybe not," said Nevyan, "but I'll know more about them."

Esganikan left. Shan now liked the fact that wess'har just got up and left a room when they were done with talking, with no attempt at valedictory bullshit. The three of them sat in silence for a few minutes.

"They're bad news," Ade said. "Sorry that's not a very tactical assessment, but I know shit on a collision course with the fan when I see it."

"They did restore their own ecology, though." Nevyan stood up and smoothed her *dhren,* which never needed smoothing. It was her nervous tic when agitated. "The archive that Serrimissani found for me is impressive. As long as they don't carry out genocide, the planet they take on benefits greatly."

Ade actually laughed. He didn't sound amused, poor sod, but nearing the end of his tether. She put her hand on his and he gripped it hard. "Genocide. It's one of those things you just have to keep an eye on."

At least the evacuation had been a good precaution. In a week, Umeh Station would be empty. Its crew would miss its comforts on that miserable cold dog-turd of an island, Mar'an'cas, but it was better than living next door to the Skavu.

"Come on," said Shan. "Let's see what else we can liberate from this station."

She eased herself out of the seat using the Skavu sword as

a cane. It actually wasn't that much fun as a novelty: she had a random fleeting thought about who else it had been used on. There was no telling its age. It might even have killed one of Esganikan's comrades.

"Want me to take that, Boss?" Ade asked.

He took it out of her hand with slow care. He looked like he could handle a sword.

He also looked as if, one day, he might want to use it.

Chad Island, Bezer'ej

Saib and the other male bezeri swaggered back up the shore of Chad in the late afternoon like a rowdy rugby team, flashing light and making a strange array of sounds that weren't English but more like satisfied grumbling.

If Lindsay shut her eyes, it sounded remarkably like the hubbub of a distant crowd. They were happy and full of themselves. A day exploring and hunting had boosted their morale, and it showed. Back in the settlement, more bezeri had shown up from the sea; that made forty out of forty-four now ashore. They lounged in the wattle bubbles, tentacles trailing, or wandered around the heath snapping off foliage and tasting it. Most of them seemed to have perfected the between-two-crutches walk with one or two tentacles held out to the rear to achieve more forward momentum. Pili, who'd once struck Lindsay as a little dim, was sticking with the kangaroo effect, and now seemed to walk much more upright, front tentacles held near her body and the rear ones almost acting like a tripod.

Lindsay just knew that one day she'd find her bounding around. All the bezeri seemed to be finding slightly different ways of negotiating the land, developing different pigmentation, and showing all the shades of subtle variation that confirmed c'naatat was not a single template for each species.

"Where are the other four?" Lindsay asked. She counted again. "Who's missing?"

"Guurs, Essil and their young," said Keet.

That was the only family group that hadn't gone to the spawning grounds before the ER devices had detonated. *Don't euphemize. Say it: before Rayat and I blew up Ouzhari with cobalt bombs.* This wasn't a breeding colony by any stretch of the imagination. Only the frail elderly and this one group—male, female, and two juvenile females—had been outside the contaminated area and survived. They wouldn't interbreed. It had seemed a colony without hope, and that was why Lindsay had stepped across the line she wouldn't have crossed for her own baby son in the end, and passed *c'naatat* to the bezeri.

"Are they okay?" she asked. The two daughters—"juvenile females" was too brutally zoological for the community she now lived with—concerned her. Even if *c'naatat* guaranteed survival for the group, she still wanted to see bezeri grow up. "Don't they want to carry the parasite?"

Pili headed for the beach. "They carry it. The children are frightened of the changes. They fear the Dry Above."

Lindsay had dealt with adults up to then. She could explain to them, rationalize, and argue; but even then, Saib and Keet had whined and complained throughout the process. A kid would have a hard time being told to suffocate in air for the first time, and not to panic but to endure the pain and fear until *c'naatat* adapted its body to a life on land. That was hard.

"Come on," said Pili. "We encourage them. We show them how good it is on land. All of us! Now!"

The males, still in their remarkable impersonation of a rugby team, muttered and stayed put until Pili and Lindsay ran at them. Then they scattered and headed for the shore with huge loping strides. Not even the bog distracted them this time, and the whole troupe of bezeri gradually migrated to the beach and gathered on the shoreline.

Out in the shallows, Lindsay could see dark shapes glittering with blue light. Guurs and his family were waiting, plucking up courage, waiting for the youngsters to calm down and make the first transition to air.

"Have the parents come ashore yet?" she asked.

"Yes. Only once." Pili sounded disapproving, little violet

flares in her tentacles indicating her annoyance. "They set a bad example."

"Well, we'll set a good one," said Lindsay. Everyone was watching in a line strung out along the beach, lights playing, waiting. "Come on. Let's encourage them. Show the kids how easy it is."

"Eas-eeeeeeeee!" bellowed Carf, and was the first to crash down into the water and dive beneath to circle the family. A jet of water plumed from the surface as if from a whale's spout hole and Carf came up like a cork. "Eas-eeeee!"

It triggered a chain reaction. All the bezeri rushed into the water in a mass of churning foam, elephantlike trumpeting and flashing light, and the shallows were pandemonium for a few minutes. They were astonishingly noisy. Lindsay rushed in after them, trying to keep an eye on the two small females. Suddenly they were borne up out of the sea, green lights blazing in terrified, agonized screams.

C'naatat was getting good at this. It was getting faster at specific adaptations. The children were rushed up onto the beach by the adults and surrounded while they flailed and panicked. They were clearly breathing now, even though the screaming green lights carried on in silence for some time. Essil fussed over them with maternal ferocity, coiling her tentacles around them and batting Carf away with a furious wet slap that sent him flying.

Now all the bezeri were terrestrial animals, able to live on land. Lindsay chalked it up as a landmark in the rehabilitation process.

"This is good," said Pili. "Life is good."

"Well, that's great to hear." Lindsay liked Pili's can-do pragmatism. She felt she might turn out to be a friend. Pili had already given her a stone hammer, beautifully made, for whacking troublesome *irsi*. Lindsay wondered what she might give her in return. "You seem very cheerful these days. Is this working? Is this what you want? Have I gone some way towards making amends for the terrible thing I did to you?"

Oh God, I need to hear this. I need to know.

"Yes!" said Pili. "I have a good life! Look!"

She bounded off, more like a kangaroo than ever, just lacking the streamlined upper body that Lindsay suspected would develop fast. She vanished into bushes by the bog.

Oh damn, not her as well. Always bloody hunting. Lindsay resolved to teach them to knit or something productive, and wandered after her.

"Come! See!"

It wasn't Pili's fault. This was much her instinct as Lindsay's urge to be part of a tribe. She steeled herself to tolerance. "Those poor *sheven* aren't going to last much longer if you keep chasing them."

"Come!"

Lindsay found Pili settled in a heap, tentacles coiled close to her, in the long late afternoon shadow cast by a bush. At the base of the plant there was a cluster of orange-brown shapes very like cocoa pods. The objects could have been anything

The penny dropped.

"Fruit . . ." Pili had found a new food plant. Bezeri liked novelty in their diet as much as anyone, and even they couldn't live by *sheven* alone. "That's very good. What do they taste like? Have you tried them?"

"Taste? This is *terrible*!"

"Sorry?"

"Not to taste, Leeenz! To *love*!"

"What are they?" asked Lindsay, who really felt she wasn't in on a joke.

"They are eggs, Leeenz! Mine! They are *children*!"

---

12

*I don't intend to give the Skavu access to the remaining tar-
geted bioweapons. If anyone is going to use them, then it has
to be the isenj themselves. Gethes would say we were feeding
their conflicts, but for them it fulfils the role of a life-saving
amputation.*

ESGANIKAN GAI,
reporting back to the matriarch of Surang, Curas Ti

Umeh Station, Jejeno

There was nothing the isenj could do to Umeh Station
now, but it still had the feeling of a fort under siege.

"Your crops are safe," said Serrimissani. Ade watched
a shuttle section of the Eqbas ship lift clear with the final
consignment of the plants and food that the detachment had
stripped from the station. "But I thought you were more
communal creatures than this."

"It's just a few novelty plants," he said. He had no plans
to feel guilty. This was for his mates. "Nobody's going to
starve because we've liberated a few bananas."

Ade trusted Serrimissani as much as the Marines: he
could rely on her to see that the haul that the detachment
had plundered made it safely back to F'nar and didn't get
diverted to Mar'an'cas. Nevyan's ussissi aide had a jaw like
a gin trap, and if anyone fancied their chances of getting past
her, they'd have a perforated arm or worse to show for it.

"You get to keep whatever's left on Mar'an'cas anyway,"
she said. "But your concern for your comrades is under-
standable."

She yawned, lips stretched tight over teeth like a rip saw,
suddenly foxlike. Ade always saw foxes in ussissi faces, not
meerkats or mongooses like Eddie did. He couldn't forget
those bloody baby foxes—three, enchanting little kitten-like

faces—since the ruck with the Skavu. If he let himself think about it hard enough, he could recreate that hollow, searing pain in his chest when he couldn't stop his dad taking them out into the yard and crushing their skulls with a house brick.

It's quick, and it's kindest, 'cos you can't raise 'em. Shut up crying, for Chrissakes, you little bastard.

Ade could cope with hearing that voice now. It was becoming more like a historical record, a reference, than a voice that haunted him. But his hate always found fresh wind at times like this. *If only I'd gone back and killed the fucker when I'd been trained how to do it right.* Walking away from him hadn't been enough, and never would be.

Good old Ade, everyone says. He's such a nice bloke.

"I want my oppos as comfortable as I can make them for the next few years until they go home," Ade said. "I don't need bananas."

They walked back into the dome. It was a circus leaving town. It was really stripped now, a mess of crates and flatpacks waiting to be shipped out. So they were taking the accommodation units, too. A crowd was standing around watching something in the vine-covered canopy of the dome itself, and for a moment Ade wondered if Shapakti had shown up with his macaws. But when he looked up it wasn't exotic birds making the leaves shake at the top of the geodesic roof, but Jon Becken.

"Prat," said Ade.

"He found fruit on that vine, obviously."

"I always said he was a chimp."

Becken, secured on a line, was working his way through the canopy, throwing down small dark fruits to the crowd beneath. One fruit missed the cupped hands of a crewmen who was trying to catch them like a cricket fielder, following through to take the sting out of the impact. The fruit exploded on the hard floor, scattering juice and pips everywhere.

"Bloody stupid idea, having a fruiting vine here." Ade saw the cleaning and maintenance problems of ripe, inaccessible fruit directly above a public area. He went to inspect the casualty and found it was a passion fruit; the crewman cleaned it up and licked his fingers. "I haven't even seen any blooms all the times I've been here."

"It wasn't supposed to fruit." A maintenance engineer juggled fruits in his hands with quite impressive skill. "But it's flowering, and here's the proof it's self-pollinating, too."

Blooms. Ade had a thoroughly stupid idea and couldn't stop it. "Jon!" he called. "You see any flowers up there?"

Becken hung upside down, knees looped over a beam or something that Ade couldn't see through the foliage. The cocky little sod was out to impress the women with his athletic prowess; Ade had to admit he was the better climber, and when he pulled himself upright just with the power of his abdominal muscles one of the women crew members standing near Ade actually murmured appreciatively.

"You want me to pick you thome nithe flowerth, Tharge?" Becken lisped.

"Piss off." *I don't care. She'll love it.* "Can you can see any?"

"Maybe."

"Go on. Grab a few, will you?"

"Ooh, for Shan?"

Mild public humiliation didn't dent him. He had a woman and the love of his life, someone who would never hurt him or betray him. There was nothing he'd let get in the way of that. "Those of us who are actually getting some on a regular basis do like to show our appreciation sometimes."

"Flowers? Aren't you supposed to bring her dead mice and day-old chicks?"

Ade ignored the guffaws. "You're such a fucking comedian, Jon. Just get a few flowers and I'll teach you how to be nice to women. Then you might get a shag."

"Where is She Who Must be Obeyed, anyway?"

He knew Becken was winding him up. The detachment generally liked Shan and treated her as one of their own, even if Barencoin was still wary of her in an overprotective way. He'd never approved of Ade's choice of women and thought they were all on the make.

"Getting your bloody job and pension back, I expect," Ade said.

"I won't need a pension." Becken took his weight on one arm and swung dramatically to the next exposed pole that formed part of the roof. He threw down a few more fruits and narrowly missed Ade. "But it's the thought that counts."

Becken rummaged and crashed through the woody shoots and dark green leaves, sending fragments of greenery showering below. Ade wasn't sure where Shan was, but he suspected she'd gone below to look for Aras. He was moping: but then it couldn't have been easy to come to Umeh anyway, let alone walk among the species that had demanded your extradition for generations. Ade got the feeling it proved to be an unsettling mix of anticlimax and bad memories, which was what happened when you spent five hundred years fretting about something you couldn't change. He'd be buggered if he'd waste his life doing the same. Every time he caught a negative memory floating to the surface like a turd now, he treated it like the waste it was.

"Stand from under!" Becken yelled, and the little crowd cleared. Then he rappelled a hundred meters down to the ground on his line, pure theater, but exactly what he did on the job. It always had an impact on the ladies; even a warship's company never failed to be impressed by it. Becken released the line via his belt control and it fell like a rope trick for him to coil around the length of his forearm with all the casual skill of an electrician, and secure it. "You and your bloody flowers."

Becken fished inside his shirt and pulled out four blue and white blooms with long stamens and wildly curly tendrils attached to leafy stalks. Ade took them and stared at their astonishing complexity for a few moments before sniffing them. They had little scent. It was faintly sweet, but it had a familiarity that was all about Earth and warm soil and sun-baked garden walls.

"Thanks, mate."

"I still think dead mice work better. Then they know you can provide for their demon spawn as well."

"You're hilarious," said Ade, reminded agonizingly of what might have been. Becken did a double take that told

Ade his pain had shown on his face, but the question dried on his lips and remained unasked. "Haven't you got some woman to leer at?"

"Maybe I have."

As Ade walked off with his impromptu bouquet, one of the female crew moved in and made a fuss of Becken. It was high time. Two years here without a leg-over was enough to try any marine's patience. Maybe they'd prefer being on Mar'an'cas with the colonists after all. He looked around, and Serrimissani had vanished.

In the machinery spaces and hydroponics chambers buried beneath the dome, the artificial light was cool and anonymous. The constant murmur of air handling and water systems created a soothing backdrop. Considering that this was where all the sewage was reprocessed and recycled, it was actually a pleasant place to be and the only smells were cleaning fluids and a hint of cucumber: it was one of the main crops, fast growing and engineered to contain a lot of vitamins. Ade found Shan and Aras sitting on the edge of a storage bin, contemplating an empty hydroponics bay in total silence.

Ade proffered the passionflowers and said nothing.

Shan stared at them, making no attempt to hide her surprise. Sometimes she could look almost like a kid, a real stunned wide-eyed look, but it was rare. He loved to see it. He felt he'd caught a glimpse of her soul, before the shit of her job made her a total bastard, even though he certainly loved the bastard Shan as much the innocent one.

Shan let the blooms rest in one palm and stroked the waxy petals with the pad of her little finger. "Jesus, Ade, they're beautiful. Where'd you get them?"

"That big vine's a passionflower. It wasn't supposed to fruit, either, but Jon's been up there picking it clean."

"You really are the best, you know that?"

Aras said nothing. Ade felt a hot blush starting, and even if Shan said she found it appealing he always felt stupid. He usually blurted out garbage at this point. "It's okay, Aras, they'd die anyway."

Wess'har thought cut flowers were a terrible thing, a

waste in every possible way. "I know," Aras said. "You don't have to explain to me."

"I won't be sorry to leave this place." Ade had no way of sharing memories with them now. It didn't matter, but he'd started to wonder if he was out of the loop on subtle and troubling stuff. "Can't wait to get back to my morning run."

"I'm missing my own bed," said Shan. "One night on the floor down here is fine, but the novelty wears off fast." She ruffled Aras's hair, looking like a concerned mum whose kid was running a temperature. "And it's not doing you any good being here, either. Is it?"

Ade looked into Aras's face, not seeing anything beyond those desperately sad charcoal black eyes, just like a dog's in many ways. He knew who was looking back out at him; a soldier like himself, abandoned by his masters. The wess'har didn't go back for prisoners. It wasn't out of disregard, but motive didn't matter if you were the one sitting there waiting to be extracted.

Finding out that the bezeri weren't worthy of his sacrifice, and then stirring up memories of his isenj captivity, had crushed him. Aras needed uncrushing, fast.

"Look, mate, straighten up." He took hold of Aras's shoulders and braced them for him. When he touched him he got a real sense of how massively powerful the wess'har was, the sheer weight of him, and he had a split-second thought of how that felt to Shan. She didn't say a word, and watched patiently. "If you remember how bitter you were about being abandoned, I understand. Motive matters sometimes. That's one part of the way wess'har do business that I hate."

Aras jiggled his head slightly from side to side. It usually meant annoyance. He didn't smell agitated, but—shit, this man was his *brother,* literally, sharing DNA even if it was long after the fact. Ade knew he wasn't happy. It wouldn't have been natural if he was: Ade just needed to know if there was anything he could do.

"I'm just facing ghosts," Aras said calmly. "Not for the first time. But perhaps they appear more vivid here because memories are triggered by smells, sounds . . . places."

He stared back into Ade's face for a few long seconds.

For once, Ade didn't feel uncomfortable. Then Aras stood up slowly, making Ade break his grip, and simply hugged him so hard that it hurt his ribs.

"I'm not going to fall apart, Ade," Aras said. "I can't be in a state of ecstasy all the time, much as you want to shield me from realities. But the fact that you do makes me glad to have you as a house-brother."

Aras gave a quick *urrrr,* a burst of that weird purring that he did when he was happy, and walked past Ade. Shan reached out to stop him going after Aras.

"'S'okay, Ade." She gripped his arm. "We were just talking. He's trying to make sense of it. Let him go for a walk. When he needs to talk, he knows where we are."

"Poor sod." He pulled her to him but she kept a tight grip on the passionflowers. She tasted of fruit juice. "He's not feeling guilty about Mjat, is he?"

"I don't get any sense of that, no."

"Did I make it worse by going on about the Skavu exterminating them? Shit. I mean, I felt what *he* felt bombing them at the same time that I was trying stop that Skavu fucker shooting them. But it wasn't rational. I just couldn't live with knowing I didn't try to stop it. I don't even like isenj. I put one down myself. But this was different."

"It's what I'd expect of you. No explanation needed."

"I don't pick up your memories and thoughts now, remember."

"Then I'll have to keep telling you."

"I bloody well love you, woman."

"Love you too. *Vaut le détour,* as they say."

"*They* might . . . I don't."

"Sorry. Worth the detour. Worth making a diversion in your journey. Restaurants, usually." She put her hand against his cheek and ran her thumb gently over his lips. "I actually like this life. I wondered why I couldn't just say fuck it and leave the isenj and bezeri to make whatever fate they want, and just sit on my terrace in F'nar and do matriarch stuff and get shagged senseless every day. Christ, how much more *is* there to want? The point is that I can't leave it alone here because this *is* home, and what affects F'nar affects *us.*"

Ade had a nagging need both to find a cup of water for the flowers, and to shove her up against the wall and just have her before anyone came to interrupt. "The isenj are sorted, one way or the other. Nothing you can do about it."

"I still have Rayat . . . undead bezeri . . . and your detachment's acquittal to resolve before I'm done."

"No more contact from Spook HQ, then. And it's not an acquittal."

"If I call them, I'll look desperate. They've got years to come to their senses."

"You're going to kill him anyway, aren't you?"

"If Shapakti can't extract *c'naatat* from him, I've got to put him out of circulation somehow."

"Have you really still got a hate on for him, though?" He took her hand and slid it between his legs. It was nice to have a missus who was no more subtle than he was. "What is it? Punishment?"

"He's a problem as long as he's a carrier, because I don't trust him, because he's a lying, conniving fucktard."

"You don't trust most people."

"And he's done a shitty thing to a range of wildlife, but mainly to bezeri."

"Who are nazi squid."

"Whose *forebears* were nazi squid. There might even have been bezeri dissidents who wanted to see the birzula live. Which would be like shooting Kris Hugel just because she's from the German Federal Union."

"Shan, Rayat's a total bastard. One down from the Skavu. Actually, at least the Skavu are honest."

"Ade, I fucked up."

"How?"

"I had loads of chances to kill him. I get rid of my own kid but I let that twat carry on breathing. I'll have a real job getting at him now." She fondled him through his pants. "Sorry. I made Sergeant Todger forget why he woke up, didn't I?"

Ade couldn't keep an erection while talking about executions. Funny, they always said death and violence turned people on, but it bloody well didn't do the job for him, not at all. He envied wess'har for being able to consciously control their genitals. Maybe he'd develop that with a bit of help from *c'naatat*.

He held her hand on his crotch and leaned in for another kiss. "Sergeant Todger can always be persuaded."

"Now that's more like it."

"Up against the wall, Mrs. Bennett . . ."

"How very vulgar, Mr. Darcy. Okay."

"Sorry . . ."

"Joke. Go on, put me in a better mood for meeting the Skavu."

Ade fumbled. Flowers were temporarily forgotten, and he suddenly realized what a practical garment a *dhren* might be, able to part and reform a hundred different ways, instead of tackling pants and closures.

"See, that smartgel's easy to use, isn't it?"

"Oh yeah . . ."

"Uhuh . . ."

"I miss your memory upgrade, Boss."

"You got the highlights."

"I know."

"Now, if I don't regrow certain components . . ."

"No pressure. Ahhh . . ."

"Is it like a fridge?"

"What?"

"The dick-lights." The bioluminescence had migrated to his tattoos, even the one he'd had done in a really stupid place for a bet. Shan found a luminous dick hilarious. "Do they stay on when you stick it in?"

Ade burst into helpless giggles. Shan had never shown that kind of humor before, just a withering tongue that could be funny if you weren't on the receiving end. This was just silly fun, crazy teenage fumbling sex up against a bulkhead, running the risk of getting caught, and not caring. He couldn't remember the last time he'd done that sober. Shan never had, he knew. She was born responsible: she'd never been daft, rarely been drunk, never missed a shift. Raw sensation blurred his thoughts but for a moment he could shut out a horrifically complicated world, and just be Ade, a bloke

with a girl called Shan, who was always up for it and thought
the sun shone out of his arse, regardless of how often he
screwed up.

For a few minutes, that was more than enough to put the
recent past in perspective.

Umeh Station: ground level

"You did ask, Eddie."

It was a bloody clever time to line up Helen Marchant for
an interview without warning. Eddie tried to find a quieter
corner to argue with News Desk and headed for the lower
level.

"They're dismantling the place, Mick. Can you hear?
They're evacuating to Wess'ej, because Umeh might be a
ball of charcoal this time next week."

"I know, Eddie. You want me to drive out there with
soundproofing? You're the one who's talking tough about
showing Marchant how it's done. She's waiting."

"Okay, okay." He waited by the freight elevator with his
handheld almost up to his face, but the platform wasn't moving. "Hang on, I'm taking the stairs."

He ran, and over the years he'd perfected the art of talking, running, handling kit, and listening simultaneously. He
should have been able to do a balls-to-the-wall interview at a
second's notice; he'd done it all his life, every day, the seat-
of-the-pants, adrenaline-fueled stuff that he actually craved.
Helen Marchant was just another politician—or wannabe,
to be precise—to be asked why she was such a pile of lying
crap, because that was all that interviews with her kind ever
boiled down to.

But Marchant wasn't just any old candidate for FEU regional office. She was Shan Frankland's terrorist buddy, and
he knew it, and *nobody else had the story*. The heady combination of king-breaking, the painful and very real ethical dilemma, and sheer terrier obsession had thrown him, because
what he did next would have an impact on Shan.

Shan would have said it didn't matter a toss now, and

made him do his job without fear or favor. It was never that simple, though. Maybe for her: not for him, not now.

He slammed the fire doors open and strode through the passages, now clear of storage bins and plants. It was lousy for sound, echoing and boomy, and his sound kit never quite ironed all that out, whatever the software manufacturer claimed.

"Okay, I'm clear." Eddie slapped the smartfabric screen on the nearest wall with decent light and smoothed it flat so that it stuck there at head height. Linked to the handheld and his bee cam, it was an OB unit. The system adjusted the color and light levels, and he checked the icon from the inset cam that stared back at him to see what looked like a scruffy middle-aged man standing in a nice daylit room. It was all bloody lies, even the light. "What's my window?"

"Ten minutes." Mick's hands were out of sight below the cutoff, moving over a console. Staffing levels had deteriorated since Eddie's day: 'Desk staff had to double up on technical ops. "I might as well take this live."

"Is she up for that?"

"Let's find out."

"She knows I'm calling from Umeh, doesn't she? Y'know, outer fucking *space?*"

"I did tell her, Eddie. I'll stand you by when we've got her back online and give you a cue to thaw her before I count you in."

"Add the extra seconds 'delay."

"Okay . . . I can still cue you."

Live. Eddie adjusted his shirt and smoothed his hair out of perfunctory habit. Chahal had given him a modified buzz cut that was frighteningly short but didn't make him look like someone who'd been kicked out of boot camp for failing to paint coal white. *Live* still mattered. It didn't mean quite what it used to, but it still had cachet—a swashbuckling hairy-arsedness for the journalist, and a guarantee of raw confrontation for the audience. *First transmission unedited*—that was the jargon now: FTU. Mick activated the system that placed a garish lime green FTU icon on the TX, the output channel, so that anyone watching knew this was raw footage. The audience could view this any time, and by a dozen different delivery systems from screen to implant to ether display hanging in midair, but whenever they did, they knew it was a slice of real action and not a slick package.

"She knows Shan Frankland's here."

"What?"

"She knows that I probably know what she did before they put her on ice. Because of Frankland."

"Frankland's *here*?"

"Yeah." Helen knew: Mick didn't. It was better to drop it on him when he couldn't do anything about it, like monstering Eddie for not mentioning it before. But he was still too far away to ever make his anger matter. "She's alive."

"I'm going to frigging well slay you when this slot ends. I ought to dock your bloody pay. Don't you ever hold back—"

"Piss off, Mick. I'm in a war. You're going to have pump up the scary a bit to make yourself heard."

"I suppose I'm lucky you've not flogged this story to Uno-Net."

"I'm loyal. When I die, you'll find BBChan written upon my arse." Eddie hoped his guilt-flushed face didn't make him look like a drunk. "Come on, Marchant."

"Here she is. I'll patch her through now."

The smartfabric split into screens: Mick and Eddie's reverse shot as small icons, Marchant as the major screen, and an output panel. All Eddie had to do was concentrate on Marchant. He had the luxury of Mick's assistance to cut between shots. It beat having to cut for himself and lose his concentration for a microsecond.

A sixty-year-old woman with light brown bobbed hair looked out at him from an office whose window backdrop gave him a tantalizing glimpse of Leeds. He could see Earth any time on the BBChan feed, but this was . . . live. A city he knew from its skyline, still recognizable nearly eighty years after he'd last seen it.

"Thirty seconds, more or less," said Mick.

"Hi. Can I call you Eddie? I'm Helen."

"Helen," Eddie oozed, camaraderie on automatic. He

liked formality better. "Thank you for your time. Are you okay to talk FTU?"

A breath. "Yes. I might as well get used to it, eh? If I'm elected it's going to become routine. I must say it's remark-ably *exciting* to talk to someone who's *really* on another planet"

Eddie saw Mick put his hand to mouth to suppress laugh-ter as he killed the 'Desk sound for a second.

"It's . . . er . . . been routine for me for a long time," said Eddie. "Seems like all my working life, in fact."

Mick cut in. "Okay, I give up, roll when ready."

Nearly three seconds uplink . . . nearly three seconds downlink.

Eddie switched on his other voice, the one that wasn't him, the one that Ade called his posh-arse voice.

"Helen," he said. "You've been in cryo-suspension for more than sixty years. Did you expect to wake up to a world that had learned its lessons on environmental manage-ment?"

"I'd hoped," she said. "But I wasn't surprised to find it hadn't. Disappointed—yes. Motivated—very much so."

So much for the golly-gosh excited novice; she was rent-a-soundbite. *It's live, doll, you don't have to worry about sneaky edits.* He hadn't seen her manifesto.

"So what do you now regard as your priority? You're fielding candidates in every North European constituency next year, none of them with any experience above munici-pal level. Even if you get the votes, how can you form a credible government?"

He was aware of Mick staring pointedly at him, signal-ing ten minutes and mouthing *been there, asked that, get on with it.*

"With credible policies and targets that we're serious about," said Marchant. "Clear vision doesn't require experi-ence. We've seen what experience gets us. More of the same. We don't *need* more of the same."

Yes, yes, yes. Tether the goat and watch her go for it. Eddie loaded mentally: a high-velocity round marked *Op Green Rage.* "You're committed to unorthodoxy in governance, then. You think the electorate will risk radical change in a volatile world?"

"I think they will, if they focus on inevitability in their own lifetimes, and certainly in their children's."

"Climate change didn't focus us in our day, though did it? We're from the same era, the 2290s. It was never going to happen to us either. Or the generations before. We ignored it every time."

"I don't mean climate change. I mean the Eqbas Vorhi, and they'll be here in a few decades. In *our* lifetimes. That requires radical changes in political thinking, because they won't accept our pitiful excuses for mismanaging this world. They're our second chance, one we won't deserve if we don't resolve to do things differently. I've been talking to the Eqbas. Like it or not, they decide our future, and European government simply doesn't have anyone credible in dialogue with them."

Bitch. I live *with the wess'har. Don't lecture me on wess'har. Shit, she's using Esganikan as an election plat-form, and she's sidestepped my sodding goat.*

He moved the goat into her path again. She had to take it this time. "Are you willing to prosecute FEU politicians and members of the security services who were responsible for the decision to bomb Ouzhari?"

"If elected, yes."

"You would pursue a war-crimes case against them?"

"Yes. I've promised that to the Eqbas. That was their original reason for coming to Earth, and the FEU has to ac-knowledge its actions on Bezer'ej."

"So . . . you see your role as mediator, a special pleader with the Eqbas to spare Europe. What gives you the edge with them?"

"They recognize our commitment to the planet. It's really not that hard, but I agree it is *different.*"

Click. Eddie sighted up and the cross wires rested be-tween her eyes. "I've just watched Eqbas forces annihilate an entire country of two hundred million people in a matter of days, with gene-targeted biological weapons and a few thousand ground troops—just to embark on an environmental restructuring program." Shame about the FTU: he had such stunning footage of the rout of the Maritime Fringe armored division that Mick could have dropped in. Maybe a second package was called for. "Now, can you do business with a culture like that? Do you feel you can understand a mindset that alien?"

She never even blinked. "Somebody has to try."

"Are the Eqbas aware of your previous career? Do you think there's some common ground there?"

Marchant paused longer than the ITX delay. "That I was a computer technician?"

"You were head of IT at LifeInd, I believe. Life sciences research, gen-eng, genome rights protection, all kinds of things that the Eqbas find repellent. I must ask you again if they're aware of this."

Eddie hadn't had the time to check what she was claiming in her biographical notes, let alone what she'd told Esgani-kan. She'd probably told her the truth.

"It was precisely my background in that company that finally made me a committed environmentalist," she said.

Good recovery, but not good enough. "Were you investigated at any time for membership of an illegal organization, arson, murder, and conspiracy to cause explosions? An eco-terrorist group that was the subject of a police antiterror operation called Green Rage?"

"No, I was not." No indignant outrage: she actually looked baffled. And she wasn't lying, of course: Shan had seen to it that she never got charged. "But I did know officers involved in it, because LifeInd was targeted."

Okay, muddy the waters—good tactic. Eddie dithered over a question that he would have posed in a heartbeat. Was it going to serve any purpose? He didn't know. He asked it anyway. She'd been a terrorist, and voters needed to know who they were dealing with.

"Miss Marchant," said Eddie. He didn't have detail, but he could fish. "Have you ever *carried out* acts of terrorism? Arson, assault, murder, intimidation? That weren't investigated?"

Helen Marchant was every bit as frozen as a wess'har

caught in an alarm reaction. He wondered if she had even heard the question, because she didn't look fazed at all.

Oh, she had. "I think most activists in those days fell foul of the Terrorism and Civil Disruption Act in one detail or another, Mr. Michallat, so I'd say, yes, although I'd argue with you on the nature of the breach."

Shit.

And in one answer, she'd totally fucked his interview. He didn't have any more detail to confront her with. Shan would never tell him, not even 150 trillion miles from the consequences. Eddie had blinked first; only Shan Frankland had ever managed to force him onto the back foot before. Helen Marchant smiled with genuine warmth—and that was the creepiest thing of all—and simply waited in total silence. It was the ultimate defense in an awkward interview, and he had either to come back at her with a question, change tack and look defeated, or wind it down to leave the question hanging over her, indicating that was the only aspect of her that was worth enquiry.

"Miss Marchant, thank you very much," said Eddie.

One, two, three, four, five. "We're out," said Mick.

The FTU icon vanished from the output screen. They were off-air. Eddie was now aware of movement in his peripheral vision, and he turned his head just as Shan walked up beside him, Ade at tactful distance, and simply ignored the setup. It was like Eddie wasn't there.

"Well, well, Helen," she said, voice completely devoid of emotion. "I got your message."

"Shan. Good grief, you haven't changed at all."

"Have you?"

"I'm not terminally ill any longer, so I'd say, yes. How are you?"

"Look, I'm not Eddie, and I'm not a voter, so I'll cut to the chase. Don't try to make me your rallying point for green militants, or whatever you want me to be, because I'm not returning with the Eqbas. And don't try to manipulate Esganikan, because she'll chew you up and spit you out. Okay? Now you're on your own."

"Shan, I need to talk to you."

"You just did. Goodbye, Helen."

Eddie had no idea what Mick was making of this; Shan was smart enough to know the ITX link was still open and BBChan could cache it. She just walked past Eddie and headed for the stairs. Ade followed, and gave Eddie a quick roll of the eyes as he passed. Eddie had to agree: there would be hell to pay sooner or later.

"If you ever want to continue this discussion with more facts, Eddie, please do call my office," said Marchant, commendably calm, as if nothing much had happened. "It's a pity Shan didn't have more time."

The link closed, the screens resolved into the single locked-off image of the newsroom, and Mick looked like he would have cheerfully killed Eddie if he hadn't been too tired.

"She's going to be handful if she gets elected," said Mick. "She certainly gave you one up the bum."

"Okay, I should have had a list of serious shit to put to her, but Shan won't talk. And fuck me, Mick, isn't calling a candidate a terrorist enough? Anyone else would have reacted, and *lied*."

"Ah, the superweapon, eh? An honest politician. Well, it's bloody original."

"At least all the other networks will be on her case now."

"She won't get elected, so at least we broke the story." Mick rearranged his desk and reached for a cup. "So Frankland didn't die? All that about her stepping out the airlock was bullshit, then."

No. No, it bloody wasn't. It's true. "Hang on—"

"I didn't think that was your style, Eddie. Nobody really believed the parasite crap, but the airlock was real Captain Oates stuff."

Sometimes it was nice to have the last say with News Desk. No: it was *always* nice to get the last word in.

"Mick, she did it, and she lived, like surviving the shot in the head."

"Right."

You stop right there, Eddie. It was on his lips, ready to tumble out fueled by righteous indignation, when he came to his senses and realized what he would unleash.

"I . . . left out a detail."

"Then where's the rest of the fucking story?"

Eddie had told the whole impossibly heroic tale: it was hard to top Shan's spacewalk minus a suit. Real courage and tragedy, the kind of thing that made myths look inadequate. But if he explained how it was possible, and the full range of what *c'naatat* could really do—

He'd never codded up a story in his life. The accusation that he'd made it up was the worst professional insult he could imagine, even if most people thought journalists did that on a daily basis. It utterly destroyed his self-respect.

Mick thought he was just another arsehole taking advantage of exclusive and unverifiable access to file bogus crap, and it broke his heart.

I have the proof.

It would have been easy. He could stand up the story. He could save his reputation by telling the world everything about Shan Frankland's extraordinary parasite.

The spooks know it exists anyway.

But did they need the detail, and more incentive to go looking for bloody thing?

No. Nobody needs to know about Shan. The only thing that gets destroyed is my reputation. And who gives a shit about that, or the truth?

Eddie did.

In the end, his name was all he had. But he knew what Shan would have done if she were him, because she'd done it. She traded her reputation for something she thought was more important, and she'd done it time and again. She'd even traded her life to keep *c'naatat* out of the wrong hands. The whole disaster here hinged on that bloody parasite.

No contest. Suck it up, Eddie. Welcome to the world of infotainment.

"Eddie, are you listening to me?" Mick sounded more weary than angry now. "You don't have to over-egg this bloody cake. You've done some epic stuff in the last couple of years. Just don't file any more shit like that, okay? Take a week off or something. I know it can't be easy out there."

Eddie swallowed. "It's a laugh a minute."

"Take it easy, mate."

Eddie shut the link, peeled the screen off the wall, and packed up. Marchant didn't matter now: someone else would pick up the story and start digging. But he had to tell Shan what had happened. She wasn't going to pin a medal on him.

He was halfway up the stairs before he remembered the message he'd once sent her, ashamed and contrite because he hadn't believed that she wasn't carrying *c'naatat* for a pharmacorp. *Perfect courage is . . .* Yeah, Rochefoucauld, it was.

He didn't have to tell Shan at all. This wasn't about his martyrdom. It was just something that had to be done, and it hurt, and he had to be alone with it to know he'd done it for its own sake.

Wess'har said motive didn't matter. But it did. It would have been missing the whole point.

Umeh Station

It's not worth getting angry.

Shan knew she would never call Helen Marchant and demand to know if she'd been aware of her sister's plans. She watched a crew trying to shift a seized connector on a habitat cube and concentrated on not caring.

So what if Perault had lied to her and stranded her out here? Shan had her revenge in succeeding in an impossible mission. Marchant—if she was complicit—hadn't benefited from it, and when the Eqbas showed up, she'd be irrelevant. Esganikan was talking to Australia. The FEU would be a sideshow, or maybe a whole new European forest in the fullness of time.

But it still hurt to see Marchant, for all kinds of vague reasons, but mainly about wounded pride.

"Where's your flowers?" asked Ade.

"Oh shit." She'd left them below. "I'll go back and get them."

"I'll do it. No taking it out on Eddie, okay?"

"Christ, I blew it for him, didn't I? He never told News Desk I'd survived again. They'll crucify him for that."

"Well, it's out now. He'll have to explain *c'naatat*."

"Shit. But the people who want it and are most able to get it know anyway." She couldn't believe she'd done it to Eddie. "Helen wouldn't have said I was alive either, because I was an embarrassment." She raked her fingers through her hair. "Anyway, she'll probably gain as many votes as she'll lose, because half the heads of state started their careers in terrorism. Worst thing they ever bloody did, give us ITX."

"Fruit of the tree of knowledge, eh?"

"You've been talking to Deborah."

"Nah." Ade slid his hand down the back of her belt. "Where's your piece?"

"Pocket."

He patted her hip. "I could make you a holster."

"I really did love the flowers, Ade."

"I could tell."

"You're so tolerant of all my shit. Don't think I'm not grateful."

"You scare me when you're like this. Don't start apologizing again for . . . y'know."

It just kept coming back when she least expected it.

"You wanted that kid."

"Couldn't happen. I see the reasons around me each day. I see Giyadas and think what her life would be like with *c'naatat,* and I know you did the most decent thing."

Shan was going to give him the full speech about not taking lives lightly, and how she'd promise not to be a pain in the arse about it by speculating on what their daughter would have been like at various ages. She decided to skip it. He knew her well enough. And she knew him. Ade was a refuge, always offering complete acceptance however mad she got and whatever half-arsed crusade she went off on. She'd never had unconditional love before, and she still wasn't sure what to do with it. It was like finding a lot of hard currency in the street, and being told to keep it; she'd keep worrying that someone would turn up to claim it and show that it wasn't rightfully hers anyway, and so she'd save it in a jar and never spend it, just in case.

And then there was Aras, who was pretty much Ade in a different species, with his own demons that never, ever made him turn on her. *You've got no excuses left. Just be grateful that you got so many chances at life.*

"I'll find your flowers."

Ade strode off. Shan, stinging from one of the regular reminders of her capacity for destructive stupidity, began mentally listing all the things she'd do differently now that she'd embarrassed herself again. Take Aras on a trip back to Baral, where he was born; let Ade teach her to rock-climb, and not bitch about it; and see more of Nevyan and her family.

"Here you go." Ade presented the passionflowers to her in a cup of water. "Eddie looks like he had a punch-up with his editor. Smells very upset. He's still sitting down there going through his rushes. "

"Shit. Shall I—"

"Leave him. You can't fix Aras and you can't fix Eddie. Big boys. They need time to think."

"Do you? Need time alone, that is?"

"No. I had enough time alone when I thought you were dead. I know what alone feels like." He poked one of the blooms with his finger as if he hadn't seen a passionflower up close before. "Doesn't look real, does it? Could just as easily be silk. Nature's an amazing thing."

Ade had a gift for sweetly innocent understatement. Shan wondered how she'd have reacted to him if she'd met him back on Earth, where he had more choice of women, and where her job might have been a barrier for both of them.

"I never gave Eddie his camera back," she said. She slid it from her pocket. "I'll hang on to it until I've had my little chat with Fourth To Die and his cheerful little mates. He'll be promoted to First To Die if he ever lays a finger on you again."

Ade rolled up his sleeve and examined his arm. "Amazing, isn't it? Not a scratch."

"They're scared of it, aren't they?"

"They backed away from me like I was the undead."

"Is it only humans busting a gut to get *c'naatat*?"

"I'm beginning to think it is."

Shan looked around the floor of the dome and got the impression of a busy airport. People were anxious to go: *Actaeon* crew queued for the next shuttle to the Eqbas ship, fidgeting and checking watches. Shan wanted to go too, right now. All the upheaval gave her a terrible sense of loss, and she dreaded what it would be like when the time came for everyone else to head back to Earth.

"I'm really going to miss the detachment," she said.

"Jesus, yes . . ."

"Sorry."

"I was thinking what it was going to feel like when people we know start dying and we don't."

"Christ, we've turned into a morbid pair of bastards, haven't we?"

Ade smiled. "It's being so cheerful as keeps us goin'?"

"First night back, in Finar, we have a bloody big dinner and have everyone round for game of cards. Okay?"

"I'll wear my best frock."

"Silly sod . . . "

"I'll wear yours, then."

Skavu, bezeri, Rayat. Three things to fix before she could relax. *Skavu, bezeri, Rayat.* "You've got better legs, Ade."

Yeah, she was going to miss the detachment.

13

Australia's Muslim majority says it's increasingly concerned at the rapid growth of evangelist groups. The March census shows the percentage of citizens identifying themselves as Christian has risen from 2 percent this time last year to 15 percent. The resurgence of the faith has sparked a property boom, with church groups buying up meeting halls across Western Australia and the Northern Territory. The return to Earth of a unique gene bank apparently owned by a Christian sect has angered Muslim leaders who say the resource shouldn't be in the hands of one religious group, and are asking the UN to guarantee fair global use of the bank's store of food crops.

BBChan 557: Pacific Rim local opt

Chad Island, called Nazel: Bezer'ej

They were eggs all right.

Pili celebrated with her friends and neighbors. The father to be—who seemed to be a quiet male called Loc—sat curled at the base of a tree with the air of a man who'd had one beer too many at a barbecue. Lindsay wondered if he was always quiet, or just stunned silent by the fact that he'd been senile a few weeks ago, waiting patiently for death while his civilization died around him, and now he was nearly indestructible and getting his girlfriend pregnant.

Okay, eggs. Still pregnant. Semantics.

"Leeenz!" Pili called, bouncing over to her and grabbing her with a tentacle. It rasped against Lindsay's arm. "You come over here. We sing. We sing properly."

Eggs were convenient; Lindsay recalled that the last thing she felt like doing when she was heavily pregnant with David was bouncing anywhere. "Okay," she said. "How long before they hatch?"

"Many seasons. Six."

Lindsay made that something like twenty months, if she understood them right. That was before *c'naatat,* though. She decided to keep a very close eye on the clutch. She joined the group of bezeri sitting around a pile of shellfish and the ubiquitous *sheven* shreds laid out on a huge flat azin shell platter. Shan would have been proud of her; the menu had made Lindsay turn vegetarian with a vengeance. Grazing on bark and leaves was just fine as far as she was concerned. Settled farming was next week's lesson for the bezeri, and she was looking for seeds wherever she could find them.

Right now, the bezeri were still in hunter-gatherer mode, which wasn't bad progress for the recently aquatic. And they were enjoying it.

They sang, and in the absence of learned music, they sang in light. In the dusk, the rhythmic patterns of lights swept across their mantles in synchronized waves, sometimes breaking into individual patterns, and sometimes forming one continuous pattern that spanned all the bezeri in a row.

It was hypnotic. Lindsay looked down at herself and gazed into disturbing watery ghosts of organs. Sometimes her own translucency caught her by surprise. Back on land, doing the kinds of tasks that felt almost like the relief work the FEU navy was trained for, she lapsed into being someone a little closer to Commander Lindsay Neville. That was until she saw the bioluminescence within her flaring into life and answering the brilliantly colored, ever-changing patterns of her new community.

It was like hearing a tune being hummed, and finding yourself repeating it endlessly for the rest of the day. She couldn't stop herself. And it helped her put aside the nagging imagery of a horror film, of wondering what would hatch out of those eggs, and when.

"Leeenz! Does this mean we can all have babies?" Carf was a scout leader of a bezeri, cheerful and annoyingly positive, something Lindsay never thought she'd find to say about them. "Will the babies live forever?"

Oh shit, yes. Yes, they probably will.

Lindsay saw Shan's face. It was a carefully composed

lack of expression, and it said she was displeased and that Lindsay had fallen short of her personal benchmark of excellence. Lindsay saw it far too frequently. She wanted it to leave her alone.

"Probably," she said. If she showed panic, would the bezeri react? "Do you produce many eggs?"

"If we did, *we* would also be many."

"How many?"

"Four, five."

"Ah, okay." Lindsay's marine biology primer had been full of numbers like millions. "Fine."

She did a quick calculation based on twenty couples. Did they mate that way, or were they like wess'har, polyandrous? With four eggs each, all live births, she came up with eighty, which made 120-odd bezeri, and . . . yes, they said they had to be about thirty to be mature enough to lay eggs, and then they only reproduced every six or seven years. This wasn't an instant population explosion at the worst scenario. She had years to work out a solution—as long as *c'naatat* wasn't going to fast-track that. She had time to think. She *did*. There was no point in panicking.

She settled for worrying instead.

The light-song continued for a couple of hours until it was fully dark. Then Saib lit a fire. He was very good at containing it and keeping it alight. So cephalopods had discovered fire, and Lindsay was their Prometheus, and she recalled what happened to him.

"Please, God," she said loudly. "No."

She held her head in her hands, and saw for the first time the Greek myths mocking her at every step. *Thetis,* the ship she brought here: the Nereid mother of Achilles, the demigod she made almost immortal, with one vulnerability, so like *c'naatat* that Lindsay recoiled. And *Actaeon,* the hunter changed into a stag, who wasn't recognized by his own hounds and was killed by them; a transformation that *c'naatat* could have managed with ease.

And now *she* was Prometheus, the cocky Titan who decided he knew better than Zeus, and gave mankind a helping hand with technology and art, and so pissed off the boss that his punishment was a perpetual round of having his liver torn out and healed each night. She was living one big Greek in-joke about *c'naatat*. And Prometheus's brother—she never *could* remember his name—fell under the spell of some girl called Pandora.

"Okay," she said. "Funny. I get it. Now tell me something useful. Like—"

Pili nudged her roughly, as a bezeri would do to another. "Who do you talk to?"

"I wish I knew." Lindsay stared at the plate with its dwindling pile of shellfish and gelatinous tripe-like *sheven*. "I thought it was myself, but I never know these days."

Pili and Loc were happy, and the bezeri would now survive. Objective achieved: all Lindsay had to do now was to turn them into a civilization that could repel invaders.

She didn't have a Greek myth for that.

"Leeenz . . ." Saib rumbled. "See what Maipay can do."

Bezeri liked novelty. It seemed to be so overwhelming for them that they stopped mentioning the recent holocaust, and Lindsay didn't ask why. She felt she knew. No, she *did* know: she had enough bezeri in her to feel that odd sense of entitlement that if you were alive, then you *deserved* to be, and that made you stronger. It fitted their Nietzschean mindset very well.

The bioluminescence was a harmless legacy, but the attitudes she feared she was inheriting troubled her. She wondered how long it would be before she felt this was all her right, and could think no other way, and forgot David.

"Okay," she said. "Show me, Maipay. Do a trick."

"Come to the wetland."

"Does this involve killing *sheven*?"

"Not this time."

"Good. You'll run out of *sheven* if you don't let some of them breed."

"Never run out of *sheven* now . . ."

Lindsay and a few of the bezeri males trooped after Maipay and stood on the edge of the bog, feeling the faint vibration like standing on a very large ship that only occasionally reminded you that it was moving on waves. Water that pooled on the surface reflected the light of Wess'ej, a nearly full moon.

"It is better in day," Maipay said gravely. "But I light up so you see me better."

He stood back, raised slightly on his back tentacles, and spread what would have been his arms to form a shape that reminded her of a flying squirrel. His flesh lit up in a range of blue from cyan to royal, and then he seemed to . . . thin out. She had no other words for it.

Maipay stretched into a enormous sheet of blue light, maybe six meters across, and then dived head first into the bog, and vanished into the blackness.

"Holy shit," said Lindsay.

"Is clever," said one of the males.

"Is *scary*," Lindsay said. Well, if he met a *sheven* down there, Maipay was big enough and crazy enough to eat the damn thing. "What's he doing?"

And as if on cue, a brilliant blue sheet of light burst through the surface of the bog and reared in the characteristic menacing iceberg pose of a *sheven*. He hung there, like the real thing.

"I make *sheven*," he said. His voice seemed very different, but he'd deformed his body so much that the air pockets and diaphragms bezeri used to make sound had changed shape, and the vocal tone with it. "Do I look *sheven*?"

"Like a native," said Lindsay, shocked.

"I like this. I stay this way for a while."

She had to ask. "Did you find any *sheven* down there?"

"No," he said sadly. "All gone. But more to hunt on the next dryness. On *Clare*."

Saib seemed very pleased, all amber and violet smugness as he watched the display. All that Lindsay could think was that she was again aping Prometheus with a repeating cycle, but this was not a renewed daily torture but a past where bezeri hunted species to extinction, understood that, felt no shame, and did it again.

Just like us, Lindsay thought. *When us was human.*

"I can do this too," said Saib.

They practiced like athletes. Before long, Lindsay had a multicolored lightshow of *sheven*like bezeri diving into the bog and emerging, looking like sheet lightning in an inverted night sky.

Saib reared and dived with abandon. They were so bloody happy to be alive. However much it appalled her, she envied them.

"We can defend ourselves." Saib flopped onto a patch of solid ground and gradually metamorphosed into a rounded cone to sit watching her. "One day we may build like the wess'har, but now we can hunt like *sheven,* and none will come here."

It took a few seconds for the penny to drop. Saib suddenly slid into a horizontal shape and flowed towards a tree. Then he inched up it, projecting limbs and climbing. At the top of the tree, like some excessively showy Christmas lights, he draped himself over the branches and then shook loose and glided on a long shallow path to the ground. He made the climb three more times and then on the fourth, he flew a respectable distance like an *alyat.*

"Cleverrrrr!" the other bezeri cheered, ablaze with light. "Saib is clever!"

He had found an elegant solution to dealing with invaders for the time being. He was *sheven,* and he was *alyat:* he could swim, and climb, and run, and fly. He was the ultimate predator.

Saib began trying his new trick carrying a stone knife. It wouldn't be long before there were quite a few like him.

"Saib *is* clever," Lindsay said.

The goal that she thought would take years had been achieved in accidental days. It also forced a choice on her that she'd known would come, but that had happened far, far too soon for her. The bezeri had found their own protection: to become multiform predators, adapting to any environment, and when their remarkable evolution became known, Bezer'ej *would* be avoided, Lindsay had no doubt.

She had to join them. There was now nothing else she could be.

But before she changed so much that she forgot she used to be a woman, she would visit Constantine and recover what was left of David's grave and his body.

"Let me try that," she said. "I can fly. I'm sure I can."

Mar'an'cas, Pajat coast

Aras never thought that the island could accommodate so much extra equipment, but somehow it did.

Umeh Station—personnel, everything that had use, everything that could be removed—had now been squeezed onto Mar'an'cas. The blue and green tents were pitched far closer together and the camp stretched into rockier ground. Fifty meters ahead, a queue of chattering, excited Umeh crew members snaked out of a tent.

"I think we might need to get another ITX link," said Deborah Garrod.

The ITX relay meant the crew could check bank accounts. That was one of the first things they did when it was restored. Wess'har didn't have monetary economies, but Aras felt he understood the fascination. Money multiplied if you left it in a bank for long enough. Humans could never have too much of it.

A few crew, though, were trying to send messages to living relatives and friends, twenty-five years older but still there, still waiting.

Shan's journey had taken seventy-five years. Everyone she knew on Earth was dead except for Helen Marchant. Aras wondered if she still grieved about goodbyes never said to people she cared about. There'd been a few, even if she rarely mentioned them.

Deborah surveyed the camp with one hand to her brow to block the sun. "Apart from the *Thetis* crew, we've never met anyone from outside the colony," she said. "It's no bad thing to see new faces."

"Time to start practicing socialization with the godless and profane."

"Is that a quotation?"

"No," said Aras. "That's who you'll be living next door to on Earth."

"More alien than any . . . alien."

"Do you worry at all about going to Earth? Did you not see the news on the ITX link? War, corruption, strife, crowded cities."

"I know," she said. "But that's now. When we get there, it'll be a new generation, and they'll have grown up knowing that a change is coming, one that they can't avoid."

"But you're going to land in Australia, in a predominantly Moslem country that's already worried about the rise of Christianity."

"I have faith in God to shape the path, as he's done every step of our way. No, Aras, I have no doubts."

"They think you own the gene bank, and that it's a Christian privilege."

"Well, Esganikan needs to explain that God owns it, and we're taking it back to where he intended it to be. Because I doubt that I'll be making the decisions." She stopped to watch Becken, Qureshi and Chahal assembling a habitation cube and apparently enjoying it enormously. "See? We're all transformed. The Lord does that. And . . . Aras, he's done that for you too. You faced your past on Umeh. Do you feel cleansed? Have you forgiven the isenj?"

Aras was distracted by her son, James, now a man in build, as he cut through the avenues of tents and cubes. He glanced at Aras with blank disregard, nothing more, and that summed up their relationship now: James had reached his understanding of Aras's execution of his father in a more silent way than his mother. Little Rachel, who'd once adored Aras and would run laughing to him, was nowhere to be seen.

"I can't forgive someone who's dead," Aras said. "The isenj who tortured me is in my memories anyway—I recall what he recalled. And that's both good and bad, because I understand why he did what he did to me, but I also feel he's taking away my present."

"Why?"

"I can't erase the memories, and I can't reach him to

talk about them, or do something different with the future. That's forgiveness, isn't it?" Some human concepts eluded him even now. "I also recall what I was before he captured me, and what I can never have." He stared into Deborah's face and saw wide baffled brown eyes and the faint, fine blue veins around them. "Is this Hell?"

"What?"

"As long as I live, I can't escape him. It strikes me that being trapped with your victim is the kind of elaborate punishment that your god would choose."

"It's not like that, Aras."

"I know. God is not there for me. I was only curious." No, he was disturbed, and he wanted to get back to the self he was when Shan came back from the dead, when for a brief few days—just days, that was all it was, in so long a life—all he and Ade and Shan were *happy*. "And this judgment day . . ."

"We'll all be judged, Aras, and you mustn't worry. I've wondered how the glimpse of God we get from Earth can give us a full picture of his plan, and now I've been allowed to see you and so many different species, I think that's to teach us that we *haven't* seen all that God intends to show us. And so we can't judge you."

It was—finally—some kind of acceptance that humans weren't special. "Esganikan is going to fulfill that role for Earth, Deborah. That's your judge."

"We're given more glimpses of the picture each day. Esganikan is another instrument of God's will. I can accept that."

This was the point where Aras struggled with Deborah's logic. He *knew* what Esganikan was. She was a military commander, an *isan* with special skills: she subdued planets and remade them. She was the instrument of an ancient culture—his, however distant in form and place—that wanted a balanced, fair, ecologically sustainable galaxy. There was no mystery, divine or otherwise. This was consequence and *fair play*, as Shan called it. If Deborah couldn't see God's purpose, Aras could certainly see Esganikan's.

"What if she has to kill humans as part of this plan, like she's killed isenj on Umeh?" he asked.

Now it was Deborah's turn to struggle. "Aras, we reach Earth in less than thirty years. A great deal can change in that time. Something *will* happen."

"How can you be sure?"

"Knowing that a hugely powerful army is coming that will enforce change *forces* change." She was a pattern-recognizing human: the extreme events she'd lived through were rationalized into some divine plan, but there was at least some logic in the deterrent effect of an Eqbas fleet. "It's called seeing sense."

But humans never saw sense when they were warned about impending environmental disaster. Was it worth saying that? Aras never knew whether pointing out the error in her logic achieved anything, and if something had no bearing on an outcome then it wasn't worth saying. He stayed silent. Humans called that diplomacy.

"Did the isenj forgive you, Aras?"

"I didn't ask," he said. "And it doesn't matter."

He walked off in search of Barencoin and Ade, who'd shown up with tools and were helping Webster get a bank of generators running on human waste. It was an inventive adaptation from the recycling system in Umeh Station. Webster was head-down in a square tank, legs visible over the edge, all dappled combat pants and solid boots. Rhythmic banging reverberated in the tank. Ade and Barencoin, stripped to the waist, were feeding pipes through apertures, squatting down and bobbing up to check where the alignment was. Barencoin saw him and straightened up.

"We're really cooking with shit now, 'Ras," he said, grinning. "You don't look too happy."

"I've been discussing God's plans with Deborah."

Ade bounced up from the ground and his attention was immediately on his house-brother. He gave Aras a boisterous shove that was clearly designed to meet Barencoin's standards of what was acceptable contact in adult males. There was no hug. "Just nod and smile, mate."

"She keeps saying they have thirty years to achieve some change on Earth before the Eqbas arrive."

Webster reversed out of the tank, kicking her legs to get

upright. Her face was red and shiny from effort. "Well, a bit short of that, but as near as damn it in round figures."

"She thinks that means thirty years to talk."

"Oh shit, you didn't explain relativity to her, did you?"

"No."

"If they don't sort it in the next four years, then they won't be doing much more talking until they land," said Ade. "With a big gap to catch up on."

"A place can really go downhill in that time." Barencoin picked up a sawn length of pipe and blew across it, producing a plaintive note. "I love a surprise."

"Give us a hand, Aras." Webster offered him a metal tool. "Big strong lad like you shouldn't be standing around idle."

Aras knew they didn't need his help. It was just a friendly gesture to make him feel accepted. He helped manhandle the tank into position and they spent the next few hours connecting pipes, separators, catalysts and extractors to create an impressive, bright yellow arrangement of rectangular boxes. There was, he agreed, a fundamental satisfaction in getting a job done.

"I claim the inaugural shit," said Webster, standing back to admire her work. "And I declare this shit-powered generator officially online."

"Ladies first," said Barencoin. "I wouldn't have it any other way."

Ade stood with hands on hips, looking much as he did when he first arrived on Bezer'ej. Only the bioluminescence that was concentrated around the tattoos on his upper arms, a blue backlight to symbol of a globe circled with leaves, gave any hint of his vastly altered physiology.

He turned and smiled at Aras. "We better get back soon," he said. "Shan will never forgive us if we miss dinner. Jesus, mate, I love that woman more than my own life, but she's a fucking awful cook. Just nod and smile, remember. Works with anyone."

Everyone was concerned with forgiveness lately. Ben Garrod, Josh's ancestor and Aras's first human friend, said his god forgave transgressions. Aras pondered the nature of forgiveness—acceptance, getting on with the future, not letting the past consume you—and wondered how God could take personal umbrage at so many things done to others, and why the deity had the right to forgive the perpetrator if the victims didn't want to.

It was none of his business. The more Aras thought about the concept, the more it struck him that God was the distillation of humankind's worst tendencies, not its best. God, like humans, presumed too much.

Bezer'ej: Esganikan Gai's cabin, outside the Temporary City

"We've found them."

Esganikan looked up from the image of Earth's rising oceans re-created in the bulkhead of her detached section of ship. The Ouzhari remediation team leader stood in the open hatch.

"Come in, Cilan." She gestured to him to join her on the deck. He knelt down and took out his *virin*. "So, how many?"

"All of them." Cilan projected the recording from his *virin* onto the bulkhead. "Forty-five. They're all living on dry land. It's extraordinary. They've adapted, and that confirms they all carry the parasite."

"Rayat said there were forty-four. Does this mean they've reproduced already?"

"No, we think the extra bezeri is the human female in a metamorphosed state. Look."

The images were an aerial view of the islands south of the Temporary City. Greatly magnified, they showed a clearing and a number of large gelatinous shapes moving around: and there was one much smaller figure, bipedal, and very humanoid in form. "We thought it was worth trying a search on land, and we used remotes rather than overflying the area. They appear to have built a settlement on Nazel."

"We need to monitor their movements. We can't afford to lose them again."

"That's being done."

Esganikan felt delicious relief. She hadn't experienced that in a long time, and she savored it. The bezeri could be tracked, studied, and, if absolutely necessary, eliminated. She would tell Shan Frankland the situation was now under control, and forbid her to take any action. It was one problem removed.

"Is there any sign that the parasite has spread to other species?" Esganikan asked.

"None. That doesn't mean it hasn't happened, and it would be a huge task to check every species. The bezeri are very tied to territory, though, and that means they'll probably stay in this area."

"The evidence is that *c'naatat* likes large, mobile hosts."

"We found very few native species that meet those criteria."

I could simply destroy them now.

At the moment, she had no way of removing *c'naatat* from bezeri. She would be killing them on the basis of what they might do: infect other life-forms, or reproduce to excess. She had no evidence that they could do either.

And if they can, this is my best chance to prevent it happening.

Unlike the isenj situation, the need wasn't staring at her in the form of desperately overcrowded cities on a barren planet. And the isenj weren't a species reduced to a few individuals.

Her relief at finding them evaporated and gave way to concern again. "I need to brief the Skavu on this," she said. "As long as they're on Bezer'ej, they run the risk of encountering a bezeri. I don't want any accidents."

Cilan tilted his head on one side. "I hear they're very disturbed by *c'naatat.* The story of that human soldier has spread across their fleet."

Skavu didn't have accurate recollection. They were as unreliable as humans when it came to memory and observation. But *c'naatat* was spectacular, and they were right to worry.

As long as they confined their reaction to caution, Esganikan would tolerate it.

"How's the remediation progressing?" she asked.

Cilan projected radiation levels onto the bulkhead. "We're pleased with the results so far, but repopulating the island with appropriate species will be difficult. Aras Sar Iussan believes that most of the vegetation that grew there was unique to Ouzhari."

So Mohan Rayat had succeeded only in wiping out grass, small species, and nearly exterminating the bezeri. And poor Cilan: he should have been on his way home now, along with the rest of Shapakti's party. She wondered how many of the Eqbas crew she might be able to release rather than extend their tour of duty with the Earth mission. Shapakti could continue his research back on Eqbas Vorhi, and taking Rayat with him would put the human far beyond the reach of Earth forever.

Esganikan got to her feet in one movement. "I have to warn the Skavu about the bezeri. If they were accidentally contaminated, it would be an ugly situation."

It was always better to deal with Skavu in person. She had personal authority, but she was never confident that any other Eqbas commander could carry the same weight. She found Kiir, Fourth To Die, walking along the shore and looking out to Constantine.

"This is commendably unspoiled, Commander," he said.

"Aras Sar Iussan says this was all isenj settlements before the wars." Yes, Kiir would approve of Aras. "I have to warn you all to look out for bezeri that have been infected with *c'naatat*."

He took the news as she expected.

"You want us to eradicate them? We would appreciate advice on how to—"

"No," said Esganikan. "These are the last of their kind. I want you to avoid them—to leave them alone. They've become terrestrial, so you might encounter them ashore."

"I understand they destroyed a number of other species, Commander. That makes them a threat to the balance here."

"I'm aware of that, but until I have reason to think they're a problem, I want them left alone. My crew are monitoring them."

Kiir was deferential, but Esganikan had the feeling that he was beginning to think of her as . . . sloppy.

"I had no idea that *c'naatat* was so widespread," he said. He stood at the edge of the shore and stared out to sea. "Or that you *tolerate* it."

"It's a soil-dwelling organism, so it's not a matter of tolerating it," she said. "Much of strife in this system was caused by someone attempting to destroy it on an island south of here. Nuclear devices. The attempt failed miserably, and *c'naatat* survives."

Kiir was still staring at the water as if he expected to see bezeri. "Why have you not eradicated the risk in hosts, then?"

"Such as?"

"The soldier. Bennett. It's disgusting. One day, they'll all be like the isenj on Umeh."

"Wess'har managed to avoid that." Perhaps it was foolish to tell him, but he wasn't stupid, and he had to come to terms with it if the Skavu were to remain on Bezer'ej for any time. Nevyan Tan Mestin regarded the Skavu as a threat; Ade's observation that the Eqbas had introduced a dangerous alien superpower to the system had definitely taken root in her. "They used *c'naatat* hosts as troops to fight the isenj. It canceled out the isenj's great numerical advantage, and wess'har didn't succumb to the urge to spread it throughout their population. Without it, Bezer'ej would be another Umeh in the making."

"But Bennett is *human,* and you have Rayat—human— and Shan Frankland—human." Kiir turned very sharply, a perfect 90 degrees, and faced her. "Even Frankland believes *c'naatat* is a threat if humans acquire it."

"Yes, but they *haven't*. Deep space travel is still very difficult for them."

"I think you should eradicate all the hosts, and quarantine the planet."

"I've made my decision on the bezeri very clear, and the two humans and the wess'har male are *not* a risk."

"You know too little about *c'naatat* to assess it safely, and I think you should err on the side of caution."

Esganikan wasn't accustomed to having subordinate males lecture her on environmental hazard policy. The Skavu provoked her worst prejudices based on bitter memory, but nothing Kiir said was actually unreasonable. She simply didn't want to exterminate a almost vanished species on the possibility that they might one day become a risk.

"Avoid them," said Esganikan. "The bezeri, anyway. You'll meet Shan Frankland shortly. You worry too much."

"If you had seen this soldier healing in seconds, you might change your mind. Seeing it strengthens my opinion. As long as *c'naatat* exists, it's a threat to all natural life, which has to obey the cycle of life and death."

"I think *I* taught your people that," said Esganikan. She began walking up the beach back to the Temporary City. "Concentrate on your Umeh tasks."

"Where are the bezeri?"

"I forbid you to go after them."

"I wasn't suggesting that I would."

"The Ouzhari remediation team has located them on an island in that chain. You're confined to this camp. Is that clear?"

"Yes, Commander."

Kiir followed behind her, a tangible brooding cloud of disbelief and disapproval. The more he found *c'naatat* an anathema, the more Esganikan looked to the wess'har experience of *c'naatat* and how they'd made it work for them.

They didn't even have an antidote for it, and yet they used it sparingly to survive, and had the courage and discipline to end their lives when they felt they became too unnatural.

We can do this too. We can learn to manage c'naatat.

Shapakti had removed it from some organisms, so it could be done. It developed resistance mechanisms, but Shapakti *had* cracked the basic code. In time, he—or a biologist yet to be born—would develop a reliable way of removing the contamination.

Esganikan planned to protect *c'naatat*. If Kiir got in the way of that plan, she wouldn't hesitate to remove him.

Jejeno: Umeh Station

"They've left the dome operational, Minister," said Ralassi. "This would be an excellent place to raise plants."

Rit, head of state of the Northern Assembly, stood in the deserted dome, the largest single open space with a roof that she had ever seen. It gave her a glimpse of what other worlds might be like. It alarmed her because it was so very empty, far more empty even than her office chambers. Physicians said the appeal of large chambers harked back to the ancestors of the isenj who built large airy brood chambers. This was much larger than her primitive instincts told her was *airy*.

"I'm already being asked to make this into accommodation," said Rit. "And I'm minded not to."

"I think the humans say start as you mean to go on."

"And I will." Rit wandered around the impossibly large floor and stood looking up at the vine that covered much of the faceted dome. "This is our last chance as a species."

Jejeno was quiet. The streets outside were nowhere near as packed as usual, and her groundcar made its way back to the government offices without the usual delays of pedestrian gridlocks. Fighting had stopped, but to call it peace was optimistic. Isenj fell back and repaired damage and dealt with their dead. With no history of this kind of civil war, Rit had no precedence or genetic memory to draw on for what might happen next.

"I have bioweapons," she said. "In theory, I can wipe out most of the remaining population of Umeh. In practice, I have no delivery system, no air assets, and so no way of using them."

Ralassi gazed out of the window as the vehicle edged past workers clearing rubble and repairing water conduits. In a side road at a junction, a barrier caught Rit's eye: the road had been closed, and it was packed with isenj trying to make temporary shelters out of anything they could salvage—furnishings, awnings torn from buildings, whatever came to hand. The air felt different to her, and she made a note to check how much of the climate control infrastructure had been destroyed in the fighting.

It was hard to avoid the aftermath of damage in a city so densely populated, however far you were from the destruction, just as damage to state-run climate-control systems affected the whole planet in some way. There were no real boundaries.

"Citizens may simply be too busy to carry on fighting," said Ralassi. "Let's hope they've simply decided to get on with life."

"What about Pareg, Tivskur and Sil? They don't appear to be getting on with life." Rit looked at the back of the driver seated in front of them, and noted that his quills were ever so slightly raised. She reached out and closed the partition. "They're getting on with rearmament."

"But are you more afraid of them or the Skavu?"

Rit had some measure of the Skavu now, and they wouldn't be as clinical and logical as the Eqbas—or her long-standing wess'har neighbors. They would bring ruin, she knew, and the last thing the Nir system—Cavanagh's Star, Ceret—needed was another militarily capable species resident for any period of time.

"When I see Skavu troops patrolling Jejeno," she said, "I'll tell you."

Rit saw total disaster. If the wess'har had any sense, they would too. They wanted isolation. They wanted peace. It was only Bezer'ej that had ever been a cause of conflict between them and the isenj.

Her husband, Ual, had seen the obvious solution right from the start, and it needed no troops from beyond the system. In fact, it excluded them by its nature.

"I need to visit F'nar," said Rit. "This can't be done by link."

"If you leave, Minister, you may face a counter-coup."

"I'll risk that."

It was astonishing how effective thousands of troops could be when they had unthinkably superior technology. A replicating pathogen . . . it was possible not to use ground troops at all. Rit hoped Earth was taking notice. Without Eddie Michallat around, she doubted they were even aware.

"You need to make this fast, then," Ralassi said at last. "And return before anyone realizes you've left."

"I need to talk to Nevyan Tan Mestin. To see if the wess'har have any sense."

"Very well."

Rit thought of the *dalf* tree, which—by luck or design, and it didn't matter which—still stood intact. She would check on its well-being again before she left. It had become a symbol of how impossible things could happen, and in its ludicrous, fragile way, it reminded her she had children still relatively safe on Tasir Var.

Sooner or later, the Skavu would turn their attention there. When the Eqbas left for Earth, there would be nobody to control them, and Rit put little faith in orders.

If the *dalf* tree could survive the war, then so could she.

14

I'm reluctant to attempt removing c'naatat from a live subject, but Dr. Rayat is remarkably cooperative and has suggestions for growing cell cultures from various organs. He has a theory that when isolated from the human endocrine system, c'naatat may not be able to detect threats to itself as effectively. I agree with him that it is almost certainly not sentient, but that it acts remarkably like a planetary ecology, a complex feedback system.

DA SHAPAKTI,
updating Esganikan Gai on his progress

F'nar Plain, Wess'ej: Skavu landing area

An almost-familiar bronze cigar of a ship, a castoff of the Eqbas fleet, settled on the plain and kicked dust into the air. Ade could feel the faint vibration of its drives in his teeth and jaw as they shut down.

"Obsolete or not," said Nevyan, "those ships are still superior to ours."

"Better make sure we never have to test that," said Shan.

A hatch opened in the side of vessel, a ramp formed, and Shan got her first glimpse of a live Skavu.

"He looks like a laugh a minute."

"That's my chum Commander Kiir, Fourth To Die," said Ade. "It's okay, Boss, I won't remind him that he's a dead man. Best behavior."

"People who go in for this death-and-glory shit really bother me." A dozen or so Skavu disembarked with Esganikan, and they all had those long flat swords strapped to their backs along with Eqbas weapons. Shan glanced over her shoulder and Ade knew she was checking. Aras had one hand on his *tilgir,* the harvesting knife he always carried. "You're not going to use that, are you?"

"I would have to have a very good reason," he said.

Esganikan shepherded Kiir and his troops from the ship. Ade still wasn't sure what happy looked like on a Skavu, but he knew more or less what was going on with Esganikan, and she was an unhappy *isan*. He could smell her acid from here. So could Nevyan.

"Esganikan doesn't like this any more than we do," said Nevyan. She inhaled with a hiss of air. "I have to wonder what I would do in her situation."

"Never mind," said Shan. "Let's give it a go."

Nevyan had what looked like a small distorted brass bugle on her belt. Ade remembered now. The wess'har troops who threw them out of Constantine the first time had weapons that looked like musical instruments: Christ, Nevyan was carrying. He couldn't recall seeing her with a hand weapon before. She smelled of that faint mango scent, and Shan gave her a warning glance again and shook her head.

"I can deal with this, Shan," Nevyan said. "This isn't your business."

"It's going to be, I think."

Esganikan walked towards Shan and Nevyan with that casual, loping gait that belied her brisk and thoroughly lethal approach. Nevyan didn't move: she waited for the commander and the Skavu contingent to come to her. The troops halted ten meters away and Kiir walked forward when Esganikan beckoned.

"This is *Nevyan Chail*," she said. She was every inch the angry mother making her kid apologize for breaking a neighbor's window. "She wants reassurance that you won't disturb their way of life. They're followers of Targassat."

Kiir obviously knew who Targassat was. He did a little deferential nod, or at least Ade interpreted it as that. "Kiir, Fourth To Die." His focus on Nevyan wandered briefly to Ade, and then to Shan. "We're here to restore Umeh and ensure the isenj change their habits. They will never pose a threat to you again." He stared into Nevyan's face, utterly transfixed. Maybe he wanted to know why she looked so different to Esganikan. "When our task is complete, we'll return home to Garav. You needn't fear us."

"I found your behavior on Umeh unnecessarily brutal, Commander." Nevyan had decided it was gloves off from the start, then. Wess'har really didn't do tact. Ade watched Shan stiffen. "I'm reluctant to have your garrison on Bezer'ej, but I won't interfere with you as long as you respect our approach to maintaining the balance of ecology." She indicated Shan with a long multijointed finger. "This is Shan Frankland, a respected *isan* of F'nar, and her males—"

"We've met," Ade interrupted.

" –are Aras and Ade."

Kiir turned to focus intently on Shan. "You're the *c'naatat* host who survived spacing," he said. "I would not have allowed you to return."

Shan paused for a beat. "Pleased to meet you, too."

Fourth To Die or whatever his rank denoted was asking to be First To Be Smacked In The Mouth, and it was a toss-up between Nevyan and Shan as to who he was pissing off most. He seemed blissfully unaware of it. "*C'naatat* has spread to the bezeri. Did humans do this?"

"It's a long story, and you don't need to know," Shan said. "If we're going to be neighbors for a while, I think we need to loosen up and get to understand each other."

"But this is unnatural," said Kiir. Aras made a low rumble in his throat and moved to stand next to Ade, wafting citrus, ready for any aggravation. "The parasite is a threat we must control."

"I worked that out," said Shan.

But Kiir was talking past Shan, addressing Nevyan. "I mean that this human shouldn't be here. She's an affront to nature. This other male is infected too. What is *he*?"

Shan stared at Kiir and Ade watched her shoulders pull back and brace. The Skavu didn't have a clue about human body language, and Kiir carried on talking past her. Shit, she looked really big when she did that; *scary* big. She was six feet of lean muscle and a bad temper. She was back in full Superintendent Frankland mode now, and fucking *furious*.

"*He* was cleaning up planets when you were still destroying yours. He's got a name. *Aras*." Her pupils dilated and the ice gray irises almost vanished. Set against the sudden pallor of her face, the contrast made her look the stranger she sometimes became. "Maybe it's a good idea if we avoid each other in future. For your own good."

Perhaps it was the translation he was getting from his kit, but Kiir missed all the cues to back down. "*C'naatat* should be confined on Bezer'ej. No human should carry the parasite. Or any species, in fact. We need to deal with this contamination before it spreads further."

"Oh." Shan wore a convincing frown of concern. She smoothed her gloves over her hands like a nervous gesture and then stood with fists on hips, head slightly on one side. "Well, I'll take that under advisement, *arsehole*."

That phrase seemed to miss the transcast by a mile. Kiir was a meter or so away from her when he started to take a step forward, with the slightest twitch of muscle, and then Shan lunged. Her right fist caught him hard in the face. It was so fast that Ade didn't even see her square up. She just punched Kiir flat; no pissing about, no preamble, no *nothing*. The rest of the Skavu froze for a moment and Ade raised his rifle and flicked it to automatic a full second before they raised their weapons. Aras drew his *tilgir*.

So what if they shoot? She can't die and neither can we. It'll just hurt.

C'naatat was starting to change twenty-four years of drill and experience. It was about time.

Kiir tried to get up and Shan reached behind her back, pulled her ancient 9mm pistol and held it in the commander's face. It looked as if she'd done it so many times that she didn't even think about it. The Skavu party didn't lower their weapons.

"This is my turf." The 9mm made a comforting metallic click. Ade wasn't sure if she was going to kill him for the hell of it. "You want to fuck with me? Try it." The commander was frozen on one knee, not quite looking at the gun as if pretending it wasn't there might save him. His transcast probably hadn't made much sense of the interpretation. Shan looked up at the rest of the Skavu for a moment. "And you lot—you can open up with your fucking pop-guns and that might knock me over for a second, but I'll get up again and I'll be *fine*. And then I'll blow your fucking brains out and you will *not* get up again. I hope we understand each other. Do we?"

Ade moved round in front of her and stood between the Skavu party and their boss; without a translation that made any sense, the reality of opening fire on a *c'naatat* had been lost on them. Nevyan and Esganikan made no effort to intervene, but that seemed to be what Shan wanted, and Ade thought it might be a good instructive session in teaching the Skavu who they were dealing with.

"Disarm," Ade said. "Go on. Drop 'em. Now. Put 'em on the floor." He let the ESF's auto-targeting whirr. It was usually a sobering noise for anyone staring down the barrel. "I said *now.*"

They just didn't listen. Ade dipped the muzzle and put a burst of fire down at their feet, sending soil pluming. They stood their ground. *Stupid bastards.* If he didn't make the point now, he'd lost: no choice. He took a breath and leveled the rifle.

"Lower your weapons," said Esganikan. "Do it."

There was a frozen second that could have flipped over into shooting but they fell back, letting their weapons hang in their hands. Ade had been trained to talk down trouble and avoid confrontations like that, but Skavu weren't negotiable. He wondered why they hadn't opened fire on him; maybe they were afraid of blood spatter. Aras's faint rumbling sound died away and he sheathed the *tilgir.*

Esganikan, red plume bobbing, put Ade more in mind of an angry parrot than ever before. "I thought I might let you find out the most memorable way," she said, and for a moment Ade thought she was talking to Shan. "You're not to interfere with *Shan Chail* or her *jurej've*, Kiir. I'll kill you if you do."

Shan wasn't amused or placated. "You get them out of my face right *now* or I'll slot the fucking lot of them. Understand?"

Her 9mm was still held rock-steady on the commander and she looked like she wanted any excuse to pull the trigger. Esganikan considered the Skavu with a few tilts of her head.

"Has she infected me?" The commander got to his feet and put his stubby hands to his face. It was clear that nobody had ever decked him from a cold start before. "Will I be an abomination too?"

"Let me test that for you," said Shan. "If I put one through you and you stay dead, you're in the clear."

"No more trouble." Esganikan said. "I ask it of you. You'll treat *Shan Chail* with due respect, and also her *jurej've,* because both of them would kill you too, and lose no sleep over it." She turned to Shan and Nevyan, and Ade could have sworn she was apologetic. "We'll resume this familiarization when you're more calm."

Nevyan cut in. "We will not," she said. "Don't bring them back here. I want no Skavu on my world. Wess'ej is now barred to them."

"Your attitude to balance troubles me, *Chail,*" Kiir said.

Esganikan paused. Ade couldn't tell if she was offended, surprised, or just realized she was having a bad day. "Kiir," she said at last. "Take your troops back to the ship and wait for me."

Shan was still visibly pumping adrenaline: chalk-white, hyperalert and pulse throbbing in her throat. She stood and watched Kiir all the way back up the ramp, and waited until the hatch closed.

"You're improving with the anger management," said Ade. "You only hit him once."

She flexed her hand ruefully. "Even with *c'naatat,* that still hurts."

"You okay?"

"Fine. You know, he's only saying what I've said about *c'naatat,* but somehow it's harder to swallow." Shan turned to Esganikan, who was watching the conversation with apparent lack of interest as if her mind was on other things. "Is that all you came here for? To see if they could play nicely with others?"

"Partly." The Eqbas commander ambled off in the direction of the city. Shan followed and Nevyan fell in beside her, leaving Aras and Ade to do what wess'har males usually did: to walk behind. "And partly to talk about identifying potential allies on Earth."

Ade left enough of a gap to follow the conversation while he spoke to Aras.

"I can see why your lot left Eqbas Vorhi."

"The Skavu's right."

"What?"

"The bezeri, at least. The risk is too high."

Aras had taken the revelations about the bezeri worse than Ade had realized. "Yeah, but they still look like a bunch of psychos to me."

"The bezeri won't change, Ade."

"If you think nobody changes, why are we bothering to send the gene bank home?"

Aras gave him a look that told him he'd used the word *home* the wrong way. "I think," he said, "that I long for a tidier past, and can see no way back to it other than drastic measures."

Ade had expected Aras to return from Umeh a little more at ease with his past. But he was never ashamed of it to begin with: and it took one dispassionate killer to know another. Ade wished that absence of guilt could find its way into him, and tuned back in to the conversation going on a couple of meters ahead.

"What exactly passed between you and Helen Marchant?" Shan asked Esganikan. "Did she approach you?"

"I asked the Australian Matsoukis who would be receptive to the adjustment of Earth, and he gave me a great deal of information. Marchant seemed prominent in your green community."

"But you do know she was what we call a terrorist, don't you? Using violence and fear to achieve political ends."

"Yes, I did. We do similar things. And we discussed you."

"When I helped them, I was breaking the law I took an oath to uphold. Just remember to ask her what *she* wants out of all this."

"I told her what *we* wanted, which was the punishment of

those responsible for the order to destroy Ouzhari. She said she would make every effort to achieve that."

Ade had another unpleasant thought. He was getting a lot of those. Shan evidently had the same one. "Did she say how? Unless she specified bringing war crimes charges in the international courts, she's probably got pals who could do the job unofficially."

"How it's achieved is irrelevant," said Esganikan. "With the forces Eqbas Vorhi can commit to Earth, the terrorists as you call them are another asset. The planet will be for humans who can live responsibly upon it. Do you disapprove?"

"That'd make me a hypocrite, wouldn't it? I used them myself when the law wasn't sufficient."

"Do you have useful advice on those groups?"

"Nearly eighty years later? I've told you I haven't. Just be aware they range from highly organized and professional to the frankly insane."

"Do I need to distinguish between them to get the job done?"

Shan looked taken aback for a split second. Sometimes Esganikan sounded a lot like her. Ade got the feeling she looked at the Eqbas and had a sense of going there but for the grace of God.

"Probably," said Shan. "Or you'll get something worse than the Skavu. At least they look like they can take orders."

"And when will the Skavu find Wess'ej wanting?" asked Nevyan. Wess'har didn't ask rhetorical questions. She wanted an answer. "When will *we* be a threat to the balance?"

Esganikan jiggled her head side to side, annoyed. "They think you are now. They're absolutists. The technique of handling Skavu is to know what orders will moderate that into pragmatism. They lose sight of outcomes."

Ade understood perfectly. Earth was riddled with ideological wars fueled by crazed zealots, and he'd lost too many good mates in them. He walked along behind the boss women on the route back to F'nar and wondered what life would be like in Baral, where it was so bloody cold that most wess'har wouldn't live there, just Aras's people. Ade was an arctic survival specialist. He'd fit in fine, and Shan would be a long way from the distractions of F'nar, and Aras would be home. He liked the sound of that. A bit of peace and quiet.

Shan and Esganikan were still locked in an argument about relying on radical greens to prepare Earth for adjustment when they got into F'nar. "We'll leave you to it, then," said Ade.

Nevyan looked forlorn and the women headed off towards her home to continue wrangling. Shan turned around and walked backwards for a few paces. "I'll be back for dinner, I promise," she called. "If I'm not, come and get me."

Ade and Aras ambled in the opposite direction. F'nar was staggeringly pretty in any weather, any light. You couldn't go wrong with iridescence. Ade wondered if there was a variety of *tem* fly that laid down abalone-colored nacre, all the rich blues and greens. There were apparently lots of cities coated in pearl shit all along the migration route of the drab brown flies. It was a bloody shame F'nar didn't encourage tourism.

"I know where the bezeri are," said Aras.

He always had a knack of dropping bombshells. "What? Who says?"

"Shapakti sent me a message. They're living on Chad Island."

"*On* it. Ashore?"

"Yes."

"With Lindsay?"

"Yes."

"I know wess'har aren't secretive, but I don't think they've told Shan, then. And *you* haven't, have you?"

It was obvious why: Esganikan didn't trust Shan not to go after Lindsay Neville, and neither did Aras.

"Ade, if it was just Lindsay, I would leave Shan to do what she felt was necessary. But the problem is wider now, and not one that can be solved piecemeal."

"I don't get that. What are you on about?"

"It's not her job to take responsibility for the bezeri. It's mine. If anyone has to kill them, it should be me."

Ade stopped dead and grabbed Aras's arm to bring him to a halt. "Whoa, mate. That means you're going head on with Esganikan."

"Perhaps. I want to see for myself. I want to assess them."

"They told you to sod off."

"That's irrelevant. I've seen Bezer'ej nearly fall to *c'naatat* once. Nobody else has." Aras started walking again and Ade speeded up to match his pace. "I plan to see them."

"Are you asking me to come?"

"No. Shan will be angry enough with me. We promised her no more *half-arsed missions* without telling her."

"You *tell* her, or I will."

"She'll do it herself. She might not get it right."

"You *tell* her."

Aras lapsed into silence and walked so fast that Ade had to break into an jog from time to time to keep up. He wasn't sure if he'd disappointed or angered Aras, but he wasn't happy. When they reached the house, Aras started making dinner with that fixed concentration that said he was wrestling with an idea. Wess'har didn't sulk.

"Okay," said Ade, chopping sweet potatoes and *evem* into bright orange and gold cubes that looked color-coordinated. "If we all went, then Shan would be placated, and nobody has to hide it from her."

"I'm going alone," said Aras. "And I'll tell her when she gets back."

"Better get on her good side with the bananas, then." The haul from Umeh Station yielded two ripe bananas, and the dwarf tree was sitting on the terrace awaiting transfer to the tropical habitat chamber that Shapakti had originally created for the macaws. "That's the good thing about hardship. Puts the basic joys of life in perspective."

The fruit took some stretching with more sweet potato and a syrup flavored with local spices. There was a blissful hour that evening when the scent of the spice and baking bananas filled the house while Ade stretched out on the sofa, arms folded over his eyes, and managed to blank out a world where the rules of morality were now incomprehensible to him most days. Aras seemed to be satisfied too, because he made his *urrring* noises while he cooked. Maybe it was having a plan again that cheered him up.

There was always a warning of Shan's approach, the thud of the riggers' boots Ade had found for her. The door eased open and she took an audible breath.

"Oh, that smells divine," she said. "I don't care what it is. Just slap it on a plate."

Aras looked up from the flatbread dough he was dropping in lumps onto the hot range and peeling off in puffed skeins. Ade braced. Aras had his earnest expression on, the one that said he was prepping to blurt out something.

"They've found the bezeri," he said. "I'm going to see them."

Shan had a way of nodding once that said she wanted to shout at someone but thought better of it. "Lovely. Are you expecting the fight about this before or after dinner?"

"I have to do this."

Shan looked at Ade for support, spread her arms, and shrugged. "Okay," she said. "This isn't some daft sacrificial shit like last time, is it?"

"Of course not."

"Okay, then, go. Just tell me where they are."

"Ashore, on one of the islands."

"With Lin. Land-dwelling?"

"Yes."

"And what do you plan to do?"

"Assess the risk, because I have to know for myself."

Shan considered him with an unreadable expression and then half smiled. "Okay, but the deal is that you tell me what you find. Now feed me."

"I'll report back," Aras said, not asking what she'd do by way of the deal if he didn't.

The banana bake was strange but wonderful. Ade's taste buds remembered they were human and for a while the intensity of the flavor was enough to distract him. They talked about crazy Skavu, and how Nevyan had taken a strong dislike to them, and how Esganikan seemed torn between force and persuasion to sort out Earth.

"Funny to talk about it that dispassionately," said Ade. "Like we never came from there."

"We'll always feel the draw," said Shan. "That's why I can't get too angry with you, Aras. I'd react the same." She reached out and ruffled his hair, then tapped her glass fork against the bowl of banana mix. "This is delicious."

There were always blessings to count, even if you weren't Deborah Garrod. Ade counted himself lucky for having a family, and not being an isenj, or Eddie Michallat, or Lindsay Neville.

Shan hadn't raged about her. The placatory effect of bananas after long abstinence was stronger than he thought.

F'nar: tropical habitat, underground storage area

Shan straightened up from the tub of soil and wiped her hands on her pants before answering her swiss.

"I've given Minister Rit permission to land," said Nevyan's voice. No greeting, no identification, no preamble: she was firmly back in wess'har matriarch mode, all veneer of human compromise shed for the moment. "She's come to ask for a treaty."

"Bit late for that." Shan didn't get it at all. She laid the swiss carefully on a crate to free both hands and went on transplanting the dwarf banana. "But we're not involved."

"We are now."

Wess'har weren't good at surprises. They were good at blurting out shock news, Shan thought, but dramatic concealment was irrelevant to them. "What can she offer anyone now?"

"Nothing," said Nevyan, "except a common goal. I need your help."

"Advice?"

"Help. To remove the Skavu."

That got Shan's vote. She bedded in the tree with her heel and rinsed her hands clean under the irrigation spigot. "As long as it doesn't involve fighting them. Hasn't she had enough?"

"She doesn't seem to be asking for military aid."

"Okay, I'll clean up and come straight over."

It was a measure of the pace and frequency of events that Shan took this in her stride. Only months earlier, the arrival of Minister Ual was a sensation, or at least as much as wess'har could manage; the enemy had come to talk at last, to ask for aid. In the end they got destruction. Shan rinsed her face in the running water and tried hard to feel the shock she knew she ought to experience at the carnage on Umeh. It wouldn't come. It was a grim dark weight in her chest that wouldn't reveal itself. She needed to know that she could feel for the lives of piranha-faced spiders as much as she did for any species. It scared her that, after all these years, she was starting to show signs of anthropocentric bias.

Or maybe a failsafe had tripped in her mind to protect her from the full impact of the deaths of millions.

Could I have averted that? Should I have died myself?

Shan rapped on Nevyan's door. She didn't like giving anyone a surprise either, or getting one when she walked in unannounced. The air outside was growing thick with *tem* flies, who were shitting away happily on every smooth warm surface and making fairy-tale magic from their crap, if only all of life progressed in that direction, and didn't move from beauty to shit.

The door opened and she shot inside to avoid letting the flies get a pearly foothold in the house.

Livaor, Nevyan's most technically adept husband, ushered her down the passage into the main room. "Do you want food? Good." He didn't wait for her answer. "*Netun jay.* Go in, *Chail.* They're waiting."

And there she was. Perched on a large cushion with Ralassi at her side, talking to Nevyan in a strange mix of occasional English gasped out through air holes and that nail-scraping isenj language, was Minister Rit.

Giyadas knelt beside her mother, watching, absorbing every lesson. She was going to be formidable when she grew up, and Shan felt inappropriately and maternally proud of her.

Nevyan looked up. "I believe we have an agreement."

"That was fast." *Why do you need me, then?* "Talk me through it."

Ralassi—rather too like poor dead Vijissi for her comfort—motioned her to sit. "Minister Rit is asking for a permanent agreement with Wess'ej that isenj will give up all claims to Bezer'ej, and agree peace with wess'har in exchange for calling off the Skavu deployment and helping restore Umeh."

Shan had an immediate response and it ended in *off,* but this wasn't her decision. She filtered her comments through a fine sieve. "That sounds like a heavy commitment from Wess'ej in exchange for . . . nothing. Because Bezer'ej is already beyond isenj reach."

"I won't have the Skavu remaining in this system, Shan," said Nevyan. "Our long-term interests are about stability everywhere."

"I still don't see a fully mutual benefit here."

"Esganikan's universal pathogen."

"F'nar developed that anyway."

"And Esganikan turned it into a much *better* weapon."

Shan felt bad about raining on Nevyan's peace parade, but there had to be more than this. She'd invited Shan here, so that meant she'd invited her opinion and involvement too. "Okay, Ralassi, ask Rit what happens with no troops on Umeh, because Wess'ej sure as hell can't conjure up the ground forces needed to do that. The Northern Assembly will be overrun when the other continental states get their fleet and air arm built again."

Rit and Ralassi chittered. "She says she has the targeted pathogens."

"In know, but she's got no bloody air force. She's reliant on Eqbas or Skavu to deliver the pathogen. So Esganikan still has control of it in the end."

"I'm prepared to commit wess'har pilots," said Nevyan.

"You said no military action."

"Pre-emptive."

"Jesus, Nev, you're going to do a bit of freelance genocide to shore up a coup? Because that's what it is."

"The problem of isenj expansion will always be there." Nevyan gave her a look that said Shan didn't understand the stakes. "And one day we may not be able to deal with it, and we don't want to have to call in Eqbas Vorhi again. I want the Skavu gone, and I want the Eqbas gone."

Shan perched her backside on the edge of the table. Livaor, utterly unimpressed by the ladies gossiping over mass slaughter and long-term foreign policy, placed exquisite lavender glass plates of syrup-filled cakes by her. Shan had to step outside herself for a moment: this wasn't her little funny alien pal. This was Nevyan Tan Mestin, a warlord, drafted leader of a city-state that might have been bucolic and primitive to the city-slicker Eqbas, but that was still enough to reduce human armies to a greasy smear. She wasn't human. Her logic wasn't human. She wasn't even wrong. She was doing what made perfect sense in the context of the survival of her species and many others; she was being responsible and . . . humane.

And it was Shan Frankland who was the funny alien pal whose morality—and she'd rewritten that book a few times—was the novelty here.

Accept that this isn't your manor. It's Nevyan's.

"Okay," said Shan. And if she thought it was wrong, could she stop it? It was another event she'd agonize over. "Okay, so Umeh is drastically depopulated. That's a lovely phrase for it. What, three, four billion dead? Then it's a case of tally ho, nanites away, clear the land, replant. Or whatever. And the isenj still standing after all that change into some kind of Jain or Buddhist stay-at-homes, and everyone lives happily ever after, or else Wess'ej presses the button and gets rid of every last one of them."

And then we terraform the place.

Shan had no idea whatsoever where that last thought came from, and she slapped it away.

"Succinct," said Ralassi. "What is *tally ho?*"

"Never mind." Shan looked for some reaction from Nevyan, but she seemed satisfied. She had that happy, scent of powdery contentment, but there was just the edge of *jask* on it. Shan was still curious to find out what she'd feel if a matriarch unleashed a full blast of the pheromone at her, but it would have to stay academic curiosity for now. "I'm not advocating this, but if you want the Skavu gone, you could skip the targeted pathogen stage and go straight to Armageddon."

Ralassi chittered. Rit did her impression of a gaudy chandelier in an earthquake. They seemed to understand the inference. "They would stay, though, to start a new ecosystem."

"There's one other consideration," said Nevyan. "I have no interest in wiping out the isenj species. It's wrong. We never interfered with them in their own territory—which doesn't include Bezer'ej, of course."

Shan decided she must have been getting slow. "You want me to influence Esganikan with you, don't you? Lean on her with a bit of jask."

"Yes."

It was Nevyan's world. She was bred to lead, groomed for it, and it wasn't the job of a human copper to decide what was best for F'nar and for Wess'ej in general. If the other city states were content to let F'nar handle off-world relations, then it had to be good enough for her.

"I'll do it," she said.

"We have an agreement, then," said Nevyan. "Now Shan and I have to see Esganikan, and I will contact you when it's settled."

Of course she needed Shan: she needed more *jask*. Ralassi and Rit left, and Shan was left with the certain knowledge that she was back to being the hired muscle, a role she hadn't played for many years. She was happier with that than she could ever imagine.

"So, we put the deal to Esganikan and give her a burst of the old mango persuader if she looks balky," said Shan. She took one of the cakes and bit into it: the fragrant syrupy filling squirted against the roof of her mouth. "Okay. Let's set something up. Gives me a reason to be on Bezer'ej when Aras is."

Nevyan beckoned Giyadas to her lap and wrapped her arms around the kid. "I didn't know if you would support me in this, my friend."

"You should know me by now."

"I've never doubted your wisdom."

"It's not about wisdom. It's about pragmatism."

"Is there a difference?"

"I think so." Shan needed a plan B. Throwing your weight around with a bit of *jask* was fine, but it wasn't a science like ballistics: she couldn't calculate how much it would take to get the result. "What if we get it wrong and one of us ends up dominating the game?"

"This isn't a confrontation between two matriarchs like the time you deposed Chayyas."

"Reminding me of that makes me a lot more confident." Shit, she'd lost her temper with Chayyas and challenged her—wess'har *never* bluffed—by pulling the pin from a grenade. No bastard was going to punish Aras for infecting her, not God almighty and certainly not Chayyas. She had no idea it would trigger her to cede power. "Thanks a bunch."

"Esganikan will cede. There is a collective will."

"What if we've read her wrong? We've never tested her limits."

Shan had no idea what being crushed by *jask* felt like. She knew it made her irritable and punchy when she smelled it, and it took a conscious effort not to succumb to the instinct to challenge. It scared her: wess'har might believe that if you acted wess'har then you *were* wess'har regardless of origins, but she knew she was a substantially human template with wess'har and other alien modifications, and that meant the competitive ape within her was still there.

Nevyan fidgeted with the collar of her *dhren*. "You fear ousting her rather than being subdued yourself, don't you?"

"I don't want her job."

"What would you do if it happened?"

"Do what I did when I out-scented Chayyas," she said. "Hand the command over to someone else. I'm not leading some armada with no idea what to do with it. I'm just a copper. It's all I've ever been."

Shan pulled out her swiss and let it dangle on its lanyard as if she could hypnotize herself with it. No, she wasn't hypnotist's material. Then she thumbed the keys and scrolled for Esganikan's ITX terminal. She got the Temporary City operations center.

"This is Shan Frankland," she said. "Tell Esganikan that Nevyan and I are coming to see her."

Giyadas watched them both intently, gaze going from one to the other. "What happens to Bezer'ej?" she asked. "Will the Skavu leave there too?"

It was a good question: there was nothing to make them, except Esganikan's command. They didn't like the idea of infected bezeri, but they didn't seem likely to have the means to do anything about it beyond destruction, and that wasn't easy with the elusive bezeri. *C'naatat* was a mystery to them, beyond their technology.

"Let's add it to the shopping list," said Shan.

15

"Parcere subjectos et debellare superbos."
Spare the conquered, and war down the proud.

VIRGIL

Bezer'ej: Nazel, also known as Chad Island

Lindsay didn't see the boat come ashore: none of them did. But Keet spotted the intruder walking along the boundary of the marshes, and came thudding into the settlement to raise the alarm.

"The one I spoke to is here," said Keet. "The one who used to protect Bezer'ej. He comes."

It took Lindsay a few moments to work out that he meant Aras. She looked up at the woven nests strung in the trees, and the mud plaster drying on the newly built huts, and decided there was no point pretending their location could have remained a secret much longer. But Aras had no greater powers now than they did—unless he had a grenade launcher. There was no reason for one *c'naatat* to fear another.

"Well, then," said Lindsay. "Let's be hospitable and show him what we've achieved."

She laid the shell trowel across the top of the tightly woven container of mud daub and almost went to tidy herself, but Aras wasn't human, and she barely qualified now. What did appearance matter, for either of them? When he'd arrived with armed wess'har troops to expel the *Thetis* crew from Constantine, she'd feared and resented him; she'd feared his technology and weapons, and resented the fact that Shan Frankland's life was deemed worthy of saving with *c'naatat* while her baby's wasn't.

No, Shan made the decision. Aras saved who he loved, just like I would.

She found it hard to resent him, and his technology was only relevant as something to acquire.

"How does he know where we are?" asked Keet.

Bezeri still had a lot to learn about life above water. "There are devices up there." She pointed skyward. "In space. They watch this planet to keep it safe. There are many ways of finding things from a long way away."

"He would never have found us in the sea."

"The Eqbas found you, by testing water samples. It's hard to hide anywhere." She prodded Keet's mantle; he was warm and firm, like a beach ball left in the sun. "But it might be a good idea to stay clear of him. Just in case."

Saib lumbered across the clearing and stood amid the gathering group, reminding everyone that he was still the patriarch. "He would never harm us."

"He is angry," said Keet. "He thinks we did wrong."

"*We* have done nothing, and he knows that."

Lindsay wondered how far Aras might go. He'd executed Surendra Parekh, and he was no stranger to genocide himself. She tried to understand wess'har ethics and failed, seeing only the intersecting lines that cut across her own.

Hang on. I did this too. I didn't intend to, but I killed bezeri. And I saved them too, like he saved Shan. We're as bad as each other. Or the same.

"Don't take anything for granted with Aras," she warned. "Be careful. Just shut up and let me deal with him."

Half of the bezeri had gathered around her. The others had gone to explore Clare island again. They waited silently, with no exchange of lights or sound, just the occasional crack of vegetation as they shifted position. A few lounged in their treetop vantage points, tentacles dangling like tails.

"He is coming," one of them called.

Aras covered the ground fast. He strode into the clearing, almost human if it hadn't been for that strikingly angular half-animal face, and looked up. If it was possible to gauge astonishment in an alien whose expressions she didn't understand, then he hadn't expected to see bezeri in trees.

"Aras," said Lindsay. "I'd say welcome, but I'm not sure why you're here."

He froze and stared at her, which wasn't surprising under the circumstances. She'd been a normal woman when he last saw her. Now she was only vaguely humanoid in shape, and not the flesh and blood either wess'har or human recognized. After a few long seconds, he turned his head and his gaze tracked across the gathering of cephalopods transformed into land animals.

"I came to see if you're the threat to the Bezer'ej ecology that the Skavu dread," he said.

"Usually, *hello* works best." Lindsay couldn't hate him. She had no reason, although she'd never had a close relationship with him and some of their interaction had been tense and hostile. "Who are the Skavu?"

"Allies of the Eqbas. More fanatical, you might say, than we are. Shan calls them *eco-jihadim*." He'd said the dreaded name and summoned the Devil from the pit; Lindsay genuinely expected to see Shan emerge from the bushes with a grenade to settle the score once and for all. She glanced around as discreetly as she could, but Aras knew her preoccupation. "No, Shan didn't come. So, are you a risk? Should the Skavu balance you?"

"It's the Skavu calling the shots, then, not you."

"Perhaps, but I still want to assess the situation."

"There's just forty-four of them left, Aras. That's all." They'd put paid to the *sheven* on Chad, though. They complained that they found none when they plunged into the depths of the bogs and marshes. She decided not to tell him. "They're not the isenj."

"I know how many there are." Aras ambled around the clearing, gazing at the huts and the tree nests. "Rayat told us."

Oh God. What the hell is that slimeball up to now? "Ah, so you got him. I bet Shan—"

"He's alive and well."

And scheming. "I'm surprised. He must have some use to you, then, or he wouldn't be."

Aras simply stared back at her. She noted his sidearm, a wess'har device about thirty centimeters long, and the knife he always carried, like a machete with a notched tip. "Have you infected any other creature, to your knowledge?"

It was impossible to know, but the bezeri hadn't infected anything they hunted. Nothing escaped alive.

"As far as I can tell, no," she said.

"I want to look around?"

"Why?"

"To find a reason to tell Esganikan Gai that this colony isn't a threat, won't spread across the planet like the isenj nearly did, and won't repeat the actions of its forebears." Aras stopped as he caught sight of Keet, and—astonishingly—he seemed to recognize him. "You said you weren't sorry last time I met you. Remember?"

"I remember," said Keet. "And I am still not sorry."

"I don't need your repentance. That was my human element getting the better of me." Aras walked on a little further, hands clasped behind his back. "I need to know if you have learned and changed."

Lindsay thought of the *sheven*. No: the bezeri mentality hadn't changed at all, and she still didn't know how she might handle that. But if their physiology could change, so might their mentality.

Saib edged forward from the group of bezeri watching Aras. He swung forward and reared up into a sitting position, settling a good deal taller than Aras and—knowing Saib—showing him who was boss. Aras, never visibly intimidated, simply looked up at him as if admiring a building.

"We have returned to what we were," Saib said. "In a different place, in a different shape, but the people we once were—that is what we are again."

Shut up, Saib. He could never resist having his say. Lindsay tried to judge the right time to cut in.

"What do you eat?" Aras asked.

Saib rumbled with exhaled air. "Everything."

Aras turned around and continued his stroll through the camp, apparently unconcerned. Lindsay went after him, trying to think what might look like incriminating evidence to a wess'har, and remembered that if Aras had known the bezeri for five centuries, then—even if their history came as a

shock—he knew how they fed. He walked over to a hut and
peered inside. Then he turned in the direction of the open
wetlands.

"I can't smell sea creatures," he said. "You always smelled
of the sea. Now I smell something else."

Lindsay had forgotten a lot about wess'har, including
their sensitivity to smell. They also had no patience with lies,
and now, willing Saib and Keet to keep quiet, she debated
whether to tell Aras the truth. What could he do? What could
these Skavu do, come to that, or Esganikan, or any of them?
All the bezeri had to do was vanish into the sea again and
wait, but that wasn't the plan, *that wasn't what she wanted
for them*. She wanted them to be able to repel invaders.

"Commander Neville," said Aras, glancing over his shoulder, head cocked on one side. "Why did you give *c'naatat*
to the bezeri?"

"Because it was their only hope of survival. Rayat must
have told you that the survivors couldn't breed."

"He did." Aras caught his braid with one hand and centered it down his back, unselfconscious. "Perhaps it was the
element of me in *c'naatat* that drove you to do such a foolish
thing. My mission to protect the bezeri, and my inability to
resist using *c'naatat* to save a life that mattered to me more
than the balance of planets."

He said it as if it was just a speculative thought. It probably was: wess'har, according to Shan, weren't spiteful or
devious. They either killed you or they didn't. They spoke
their minds, unfiltered and unedited.

But motives didn't matter to them either, and the idea still
punched Lindsay in the face, a fresh pain. Her mind and her
motives were not her own. She had no way of knowing if it
was her idea or an echo of Aras in her genetic memory that
made her take that final step of infecting one bezeri.

Was that him?

She wondered how much longer she could hang on to the
core of Commander Lindsay Neville, naval officer, bereaved
mother, pilot, raised in a dale that the Vikings once invaded.
No sense of self still mattered. Loss of that was real death.

Aras walked on and she followed him automatically. Saib

went to follow too, but Lindsay turned and shoved him as hard as she could, bezeri-style.

"No, you stay where you are, Saib. You leave this to me."

"But I am the patriarch."

"And I'm the boss when it comes to dealing with things you don't understand." Maybe he *did* understand, though. If Shan's memories and impulses were in him, Aras's might surface too. "Just stay clear of him."

She trailed a few paces behind Aras, enough to maintain an appearance of being on hand to answer questions rather than stalking him. It reminded her of following a captain through her ship during a dreaded inspection. The sense of impending doom for the discovery of something neglected was as strong as ever.

"Tell me about the Skavu," she said. "I'm guessing that you regard them as a threat."

"I do. They reacted very badly when they realized what *c'naatat* does."

"Have they met Shan?"

"Yes. Quite emphatically."

"Ah, I get it. Our problem is your problem. They don't just think we're a risk, they think *you* are as well."

Aras never seemed to be troubled by comments that would put a human on the defensive. "Yes. They do."

"It occurs to me that you might be looking for an ally, then. They can die. We can't."

"We."

"Don't deny it."

"I hadn't considered it. I have now."

Suddenly Lindsay felt a lot better about life; she *understood*. Aras lapsed back into silence and she let him set the pace, following him patiently while he inspected the ground they'd cleared and the structures they'd built. He shielded his eyes against the sun as he looked up into the trees.

"They were always very skilled architects," he said. "And now they climb trees."

"They glide, too."

Aras did that instant freeze, more still than a human could

ever be, but it was gone in a moment. He examined plants and peered in the undergrowth, pausing from time to time to cock his head and stare at something. He froze, riveted by something unknown, for a full five seconds at one point. But it was the tree nests that kept drawing his eye.

"I find it interesting that they embrace so much change when many of their ideas are so utterly fixed."

Lindsay smiled, but he probably couldn't tell. "Sounds like humans."

"You went back to Constantine, then."

"Rayat's obviously been very communicative."

"I saw David's grave, actually. You took some of the glass."

Ah. The memory felt cushioned now, not quite as raw, more a flat dull ache. "Yes. Do you understand human grief?"

"You think we don't feel it? Shan may be back from the dead, but I lost the most precious thing in my existence, and I had no idea how to face the next moment in each day without her."

It was as good a description of grief as any. "How's the detachment?"

"Your marines are well. Hungry much of the time, bitter about being dismissed, anxious about their future on Earth. But they find things to be happy about, and they stay busy. They have an end in sight."

Lindsay understood that perfectly. Goals kept her going and erased all distraction, all unhappiness. This was as close to friendly conversation as she'd ever come with Aras. They were in the wetland north of the settlement now, still within sight of the nests and huts but looking out onto levels dotted with islands of vegetation and hills rising in the distance. Aras skirted the edges, apparently able to see the boggier ground.

Then he jerked his head up. "Listen."

She heard it now. The noise had become so much a part of the backdrop of her world that she hadn't noticed it, but there it was: the sporadic splashing of something in the bog.

She hoped, for once, that it was a *sheven:* but it wasn't. As she picked her way across the saturated ground, she moved clear of bushlike vegetation clinging to a solid patch and saw Pili plunging into the bog, easing herself out again and diving back in.

Aras grabbed her arm. "Be careful. You can't have forgotten there are *sheven* on these islands."

Pili pulled out of the bog with a loud liquid slop and shook herself, sending mud and scraps of vegetation flying. Then she spotted Lindsay. "Leenz!" she called. "Who is that?"

Oh God. Pili was hunting. No *sheven* had been found for a while, but she wasn't giving up.

"The wess'har who looked after you all these years," Lindsay called back. *Shut up, Pili, shut up . . .* "It's Aras. Go back to the camp. Saib will explain."

"I found *nothing*. No *sheven*. They're gone."

"It's okay. Go home."

Pili took it as a rebuke. "I only *look* for them. I promise not to eat this time."

However much her body had changed, Lindsay could still feel her stomach churn. Pili splashed onto more solid ground and made her way out of the bog, pausing to look at Aras before making a loud *thwap* of air and bounding kangaroo-style towards the settlement, jinking between bushes.

Aras hung his head for a moment. It was an incongruously human gesture. "So this is why you don't fear the *sheven* any longer."

"I'm sorry, Aras."

"The bezeri said they were gone."

What could she say? Could you even lie to a wess'har, who seemed to see every twitch of muscle, every dilating vessel, every change of temperature? *Yeah, the bezeri reverted right back to type and wiped out the native* sheven *here. They didn't learn a damn thing, Aras. You're right to blame them.*

"They found they could hunt them," Lindsay said at last. "Bezeri are compulsive hunters."

"I know that now. And *sheven* are the top of the food chain in the wetlands. They're predators. No natural enemies, until now."

"I've stopped them, Aras."

"What about the other islands? Clare, for instance?" He was getting angry now and she could see it in his human body language of tensed muscles and braced shoulders. She could also smell something that warned her at a primeval level, some scrap of wess'har in her that recognized his sharp acid scent as a warning. "You have to confine them. How many *sheven* are left? No, you would have no idea. You don't have the means to monitor them."

Aras turned on his heel and headed back to the settlement with alarming speed, zigzagging from one patch of firm ground to the next, then almost breaking into a run when he hit hard earth. Lindsay chased after him. He was bent on retribution: she had to stop him. "Aras!" she yelled. "Aras, don't do this."

She couldn't match his pace. He was nearly two meters tall, with a prodigious stride, and she couldn't keep up with him. He reached the settlement, but instead of going into the clearing and wreaking the havoc she feared, he carried straight on.

He was heading for the shore.

"Aras!"

He slowed and then stopped to turn around. "This is your duty now, Lindsay Neville. You created them. Do you want to resolve this yourself, or do you want to leave it to me? Or the Skavu?"

"What's to resolve? Are you asking me to kill them? I can't. I don't have the means. Even if I wanted to."

He raised his hand and stabbed his forefinger at her in a gesture of accusation that was pure Ade Bennett. "That," he said, "was something that you should have thought about before you infected them."

She stood exhausted by realization. Aras disappeared into the distance, no doubt rushing back to Shan to tell her she was right—that Lindsay Neville was a useless and dangerous idiot, just as she always said.

Aras had looked like an ally. Now he'd almost certainly turned into an enemy. He had a weapon, though, and he knew exactly what it took to kill *c'naatat,* so either he had something else in mind or the next visit would be from these Skavu.

We can retreat to the sea.

It's only because of me that the bezeri are on land anyway.

And maybe I can salvage something.

She ran into the clearing at the center of the settlement. "Keet, Saib, get the others back from Clare. Now."

"Things did not go well," Saib observed.

"No, and they'll go a lot worse if you don't get everyone back here now. No more hunting. No more killing *sheven*, anyway. You heard me—go."

Saib was a patriarch, used to giving orders, not taking them. He stood his ground for several long moments and then made an imperious flick of a tentacle at Keet, sending him on his mission.

"We should have stayed in the sea."

Lindsay wondered if he'd been right all along.

Outside the Temporary City, Bezerej: Esganikan Gai's cabin

"I thought you might want to see this," said Eddie Michallat. "The Australian premier is taking some flak about the gene bank."

Eddie's face had lost something of its animation. Esganikan couldn't pin it down, but the image in the bulkhead was a different Eddie, a man with some of the light gone out of him. She had no other way of describing it; there was a light in Rayat, and Shan, and even in the marines, but Eddie's had vanished. He was tired, perhaps, and he'd lost a source of stories. Earth didn't care about Umeh now the humans had been evacuated. Nobody cared how many isenj died.

"I haven't spoken to him recently," she said.

"Here you go." Eddie looked down, his hands working outside the frame, and a text panel appeared to one side of his image. "That's the BBChan 547 summary of what he's been saying to the media. If it helps, I can put you in touch with the BBChan bureau in Kamberra."

"Why?"

"He might give you a perspective that the government won't."

"I meant why can't *you* tell me what's going on." Eddie guarded his contacts carefully. Esganikan knew this was his sole source of motivation, the one thing that mattered to him: he was the only journalist here, and, as humans prized the control of information, that gave him status and power. "But if you insist I speak to this bureau, then I will. I thought you wanted to keep this contact to yourself."

Eddie looked down for a second and licked his lips quickly, a barely perceptible flick of the tongue. "I'm flattered that you trust me." His voice had changed subtly, a different tone to one he used with the marines or the voice he adopted for his reports. This was altogether more breathy, as if he was talking to himself. "I'm glad someone does."

"I would like to know what's happening in Australia that the premier isn't telling me. Anything that would indicate that his country—or his region generally—isn't fully in support of his invitation, or might resist us."

Eddie's eyes widened slightly and he became more alert again. "I'll assemble a digest for you."

"Thank you."

"Might I talk to you about your planning for the Earth mission?"

"I'm awaiting Shan and Nevyan at the moment."

"Okay." Eddie nodded to himself, listening to some inner voice. She could see it on his face. "Later, then."

Esganikan shut the link. She was used to Eddie now, and knew his way of filtering and changing information. She also wanted his skills. When he went back to Earth, he'd be ordinary again, and he would want to keep what had made him special; his alien contacts. And he knew how to do something that she couldn't: he could make humans listen and shape how they thought, all with words. Shan might have been best at advising on how to deal with humans, but Eddie could make them *want* to listen.

There was no point using military resources if a man's words could do the same job. Esganikan knelt pondering the extraordinary power of a willingly shared illusion, her cabin's bulkheads set to opaque, until the hatch opened and Aitassi peered through.

"Nevyan is here, Commander. With Shan Frankland."

Esganikan could smell the *jask* from here. They were coming to *lay down the law,* as Eddie put it. She felt annoyance and was instantly ready.

"Are the Skavu confined to their camp?"

"I ensured that they were," said Aitassi. "The patrols back from Umeh are sufficiently tired not to want to argue environmental policy with your visitors."

Esganikan could guess what Nevyan wanted: reassurance that the Skavu would stay clear of Wess'ej, and Shan's household. These Targassati were isolationist. They lost their nerve when the military support they begged for got its hands dirty. Esganikan turned, composed but ready, and faced them as they came into her cabin. Shan folded her arms and stood a little behind Nevyan, as if she was making sure her fists didn't let her down again. Esganikan wondered if she'd always been prone to instant retribution or if her wess'har genes had made her more liable to attack. Nevyan's daughter stood close at her mother's side. Did the child get formal instruction? Wess'ej appeared to have no education system. Everything their ancestors had known on Eqbas Vorhi seemed to have been abandoned. They'd reverted to a more primitive age.

"I realize we're now troublesome guests," Esganikan said. "And you seem to have a problem."

Nevyan was wearing the *dhren,* the white robe the F'nar matriarchs treated almost as a uniform. Esganikan's lasting memory of her brief time in F'nar would be the *isan've* in white robes shot with faint and shifting colors set against the pearl wall of the city.

"I have a treaty with Minister Rit that I can enforce," said Nevyan. "It means you can remove the Skavu from Umeh."

"I knew you might want that," Esganikan said wearily. "What are the terms?"

"If isenj confine themselves to Umeh and Tasir Var, and drop their claim on Bezer'ej, Wess'ej will provide the delivery systems for the targeted pathogens, and if and when Minister Rit chooses to deploy them, our pilots will aid her. If you leave us with the universal pathogen, we'll use that if the treaty doesn't hold."

"You'll end up wiping the planet clean of them. Was that all you wanted? I would have given you that anyway."

"No," said Nevyan. "It means there's no need for the Skavu to remain in this system. Wess'ej will provide the restoration support."

"You don't have the technology on that scale."

"We restored *this* planet."

Shan said nothing. She simply stood there, watching Esganikan, and unfolded her arms to place a gloved hand on the child's head. She seemed to take no chances with her parasite, even if it took body fluids to transmit it.

"And you would put aside your principles that you would never attack the isenj on their home territory," said Esganikan.

"To see the Skavu gone, yes."

"All to ensure they don't turn on your *c'naatat* friends and the infected creatures here?" Esganikan had underestimated the bond between Shan and Nevyan, then. "This is a massive commitment for your world."

"The Skavu," said Nevyan, "regard us as lacking their rigorous standards, and I fear that it's only a matter of time before they would want to interfere with us once you were no longer here to control them."

Shan scratched her neck thoughtfully. "Judging by the reaction to me, your supposed grip on their discipline seemed less than absolute."

Esganikan could taste the *jask* at the back of her throat. It even seemed to be emanating in some small way from the little *isanket*. She felt less inclined to stand her ground—Wess'ej would be sorely stretched, she knew—but Nevyan seemed adamant she would resort to total destruction of the isenj if the treaty collapsed.

Shan Frankland certainly would. She might have found

warfare distasteful, an odd thing for such a violent individual, but her instant reaction to a threat was proven. *Threat is now.* Shan seemed to have taken that wess'har attitude to heart.

It seemed sensible.

Esganikan felt no further desire to argue: the outcome from this course of action was balance, so if the wess'har here could make it happen, she had no dispute with them. She felt herself relaxing and the taste of released *jask* in her mouth was oddly pleasant and reassuring.

"So I'll stand down the Skavu," she said. "We'll arrange a handover period between my crew on Umeh and yourselves. Is that all?"

"I think so."

Shan looked slightly baffled. Humans—even her, even this chimera, this strange *isan*—had a habit of parting their lips when surprised. Perhaps they inhaled scent to assess the situation: perhaps they were frozen on the edge of a question that they couldn't frame. And perhaps they were taken aback to see matters resolved quickly and without violence.

Gethes seem to think we're violent just because we don't engage in ritual warfare. They like rules for their killing.

It was another thing she would have to work out before she reached Earth. It was a pity that Shan Frankland refused to accompany her.

Esganikan watched them leave, then waited for Aitassi to reappear. The ussissi would be watching for their departure. But there was no sign of her, so Esganikan tidied her cabin and took a slow walk across to the Temporary City. It was one problem removed, as long as Nevyan and the rest of the Wess'ej matriarchs didn't lose their nerve if the ultimate sanction was needed.

She walked into the command center. The duty crew were clustered around a projection that showed them a striking live view of a hurricane lashing a shore fringed with square white buildings. They glanced up when she entered, and she realized she must have had the faint trace of *jask* clinging to her.

"Problems, Commander?"

"Call Sarmatakian Ve's office for me." Hayin looked anxious: he didn't care much for Skavu support either. "We no longer need the Skavu."

"What happened?"

"Nevyan Tan Mestin has agreed to a treaty with Minister Rit to drop all claims on Bezer'ej in exchange for help with restoration. If they break the terms, she releases the universal pathogen. That's how badly they want the Skavu to leave."

"You're satisfied they can handle this?"

"I am, but I'd still prefer to transfer some more current technology to them." For a moment the ferocity and beauty of the storm reproduced in front of her was hypnotic. "Where's Joluti? Let's detach a large enough section of ship for F'nar to use as a template craft. They still have nanoconstruction systems. They could copy whatever we give them."

"Those systems are ten thousand years old."

"They're not incapable of working from a template craft. In time, as they create more vessels, they can use the coalescent function and see how they adapt to it."

"Surang can give them instructions."

Esganikan's last uneasiness was soothed. She'd give the matriarchs of F'nar what they needed to make the treaty stick. They could cope with updated technology.

"Hayin, send a message to Sarmatakian that I'm withdrawing the Skavu. She can explain that to the Garav authorities. And tell her I'd like to speak to her about what assets she can now release for the Earth mission."

The hurricane in front of Esganikan ripped a building to pieces and sent its roof crashing into the houses behind it. For all its violence, there was a majesty to it that she found compelling.

"Their storms are spectacular," said one of the crew. "And they have so many of them."

Esganikan was happy to focus on Earth and its problems again. She hadn't felt comfortable with the Skavu either.

Now she could concentrate on the matter in hand.

Constantine island: former home of the human colony

From the sea, the island looked as it always had since it has recovered from the isenj occupation; a rocky coastline, a smoky haze of blue, gray and pale mauve grass, and a fringe of orange-topped trees where an inlet cut deep into the island and formed a natural harbor.

Aras knew every inch of it. He took the boat at half speed, cutting close to the shore, expecting to see bezeri even though he was sure they hadn't reached this far north. He thought of the years he'd spent there. His infinite future had stretched ahead of him and he'd wondered how he would stand the isolation, but it was still better than going back to Wess'ej and living there unable to share the basic elements of wess'har life: an *isan*, housebrothers and children to raise.

Besides, the isenj might have come back. Bezer'ej had needed a guardian.

Now it needed to be protected from its own inhabitants.

Aras circled the island slowly, trying to make sense of bezeri that had now decimated the *sheven* population on at least one island. They'd been *c'naatat* for how long, weeks? Yes, just weeks, no more. Already they were fulfilling his worst nightmares. He ran the images through his mind over and over again.

Climbing trees.
Walking. Talking.
Could Lindsay Neville contain them? He had his doubts.

There were only forty-four of them, hardly an isenj plague of billions. But that was now, and he had to think in the longest possible term. He'd still be around when the worst happened.

Something was still nagging at him. Something specific was bothering him and demanding an answer, as if he'd been given one of Shan's Suppressed Briefings and with it the frustrating knowledge that there was something he had to remember.

I started this. I started it five centuries ago, when I first gave c'naatat *to my comrades. I should have learned, but*

I did it again with Shan, and now look where the chain of consequence has led me.

Aras wondered how he'd tell Shan about the *sheven*. Ade would be mortified; he'd blame himself. It was up to Aras to solve the problem for good.

Wess'har didn't lie, but he'd learned not to tell everything that he knew. The Skavu didn't have to be told about the *sheven*, and neither did Esganikan.

He saw the undergrowth of Chad Island in his minds eye.

Eggs.

The thought hit him and for a moment he wasn't sure where it came from, and then he realized what had been simmering away in his memory.

Among the bushes circling the huts, he'd seen something he thought was fruit. Now he knew where he'd seen something similar, and he knew what the fruits were, and they weren't from plants at all.

They were eggs. *Bezeri eggs.*

The few he'd seen underwater were a lighter color, anchored to the stalks of weed. The ones he'd seen clustered around the stem of a bush on Chad were darker, and slightly ribbed, but they were . . . *eggs.*

The bezeri were breeding again. In another time, under other circumstances, it would have been welcome news. Now it was the beginning of a disaster.

He knew what he had to do. And it seemed more terrible to him than the bombardment of Mjat and the other isenj cities, in which he was responsible for the deaths of millions. He searched his own conscience to make sure he wasn't punishing the bezeri for daring to have offspring, something he could never have.

But he knew what Shan would say. She had already taken an identical decision.

16

*Australian Prime Minister Canh Pho today announced the
creation of a global genome project to manage the return of
the Christopher gene bank in twenty-nine years' time. "This
is a global resource, and a second chance at common sense,
so we won't squander it or surrender to the greed of pressure
groups," he said. "And Australia and her allies don't cave in
to corporations or their lawyers. You might have noticed the
Eqbas are coming."*

BBChan 547

Bezer'ej: landing area, outside the Temporary City

Shan sat cross-legged in the grass, eyes closed, enjoying
something she couldn't recall savoring in years. It was the
simple warmth of sun on her face and a relative absence of
thought.

*I don't have to be the boss all the time. It's Nevyan's turf.
Restoring Umeh isn't my part of ship.*

She'd be Nevyan's bagman, the reliable sidekick, like
Rob McEvoy had once been to her in EnHaz. She thought
of the young inspector occasionally and wished she'd
thought of him a lot more, but time and space had put
him beyond reach. At least she now knew his police career had been a successful one. There was something of
a parental pride in the feeling, a knowledge that she'd
contributed something to the man, even if it was only
giving him a few steers to help him get his next promotion. You had to leave something behind you or you
hadn't lived.

Rob had left grandchildren with happy memories of him,
and a Wessex Regional Constabulary with much better col-
lation and accounting systems than he'd inherited. It wasn't
bad for one life.

I really ought to get my paperwork sorted. Still haven't resigned formally or closed off my pension.

She'd find a deserving recipient for her Earth-locked funds. The marines, maybe. They had their own nest eggs that had grown bigger than they realized, but it never hurt to have more. *Poor bastards.*

"Aras is taking his time," said Nevyan. "You should have gone to Chad with him."

Shan opened her eyes, the reverie shattered. "He wanted to do it alone. He's had five centuries' experience of bezeri, and I need to respect that." She took out her swiss and paged Ade, her mind still finding loose ends to tie up. "I never had any warning that my uterus had regenerated, you know. No bleeding or anything."

"You bleed?"

"Well, if you're not medicated to suppress it, yes. Women bleed once a month if they're not pregnant. Normally, anyway."

Nevyan's head cocked on one side. "Bleed? How?"

Shan realized how much Nevyan still didn't know about humans, and that she didn't need to. "I'll explain it when we get back." Ade didn't answer his link; she'd try later. She needed to hear his voice, not leave terse messages for him. "Must be nice to have control of your reproduction without involving doctors."

"If humans had that, I doubt they would use it wisely."

"But you choose if you conceive or not."

"And how many embryos we produce."

"Really?"

"Yes."

"Shit, I've been living here what seems like forever and I've never seen a multiple birth."

"When the population requires adjustment, you'll see many twins. Even triplets."

"But you don't choose gender."

"No."

"The Eqbas must have got around that."

"This is what I mean. Some things are fundamental to our culture." Nevyan rose a little from her kneeling position to look around, and then settled back again. "I have to take another husband when I choose to have my own child."

That was one of the downsides of taking on an instant family. All Nevyan's males, widowed and taken into her household, had already fathered children. They couldn't breed again.

"Where's Giyadas?" Shan asked.

"Serrimissani is showing her how to navigate."

"She's a terrific kid."

"Does this pain you, this talk of children?"

"Not if I don't let it."

Nevyan dropped the subject. Shan preferred wess'har when they were brutally outspoken: Nevyan was learning tact a little too thoroughly and Shan missed the time when she could blister paint with her directness. She went back to soaking up the sun, unafraid of skin damage, until a dark dot in the heat haze of the plain resolved into a shimmering outline that became Aras.

Shan nudged Nevyan, then licked her forefinger and held it up in the breeze—yes, it really did work—to confirm they were downwind. She expected to pick up his scent of anxiety any time soon.

"I knew it wouldn't go well," she said, inhaling.

Aras walked in the way of a man who knew he was being stared at expectantly but couldn't bring himself to break into a run; head down, a little embarrassed. It took him a few minutes to cover the ground. Shan stood up to offer him a kiss, but he didn't seem to be expecting one and dipped his head awkwardly.

"Okay, spit it out," Shan said.

"I found them. I inspected their camp."

"They have a *camp*?"

"They're competent builders, *isan,* and now they've started to recreate their civilization ashore. They walk, they climb and they can even glide."

"Jesus H. Christ, those things weigh a ton. How can the hell can they glide?"

"They're considerably lighter than that."

Nevyan cut in, impatient. "Their aerodynamics aren't what's made you distressed, Aras."

"No."

Shan decided to say the name. "Lin, then? What's the daft cow done this time?"

"Not her." This was definitely not like Aras. He was struggling with something painful. "There are things I have to keep from the Skavu. From Esganikan, too, if we're to be left in peace here."

Wess'har didn't have much of an idea about secrecy. It explained a lot. Failing to share important information had consequences, and this was the first time Aras had been faced with this dilemma in a long time, maybe ever.

"Tell me, then."

"It's begun already. The bezeri have hunted the *sheven* population of Chad to extinction, and . . . they're breeding. I found eggs."

Nevyan let out a low hiss. Shan plunged into an all-too-human sequence, thinking that there were just forty-four of them, and that it was just one island and one population of *sheven,* and how bad could it be—

She knew how bad. She could think in worst scenarios, and the combination of a careless predator and a limitless life had an inevitable outcome. Changing the path of that was the imponderable, and the years it would take for the disaster to develop didn't matter. All she could see was the point at which it could be averted relatively easily.

There would be no more Umehs, no more Mjats, not if she had anything to do with it. It had to be controlled.

"Do they understand the consequences?" Nevyan asked. Giyadas and Serrimissani, drawn by the scents and sounds of anxiety, came running towards them. "Are they able to limit their lives as you do, and contain the risk?"

"They've laid eggs," Shan said sharply. "Obviously not. And they're back to their old ways. Can you locate the eggs? How many? We need to deal with that first."

Her reaction appalled her in the very next breath. *Would I be thinking of destroying them if the word had been* children, *not eggs?* Surendra Parekh had killed a bezeri infant by careless arrogance, and she'd paid for it with her life. Shan had made sure of that, because that was the law here. The bezeri, like the wess'har, wanted balance, a life for a life.

And here she was overriding the law of the native species, and treating them the way most humans treated animals.

There was no such division for the wess'har between people and animals. There should have been no such division for her now, either, just a list of who could enforce their will on those beneath them in the power league.

But I took that choice.

I aborted my own child. Different reasons, and more about the life she would have lived than the risk she posed, but I did it. Motives don't matter.

"First thing is to destroy the eggs," Shan said.

Nevyan jiggled her head in annoyance and Shan wondered if she was going to forbid her, and try to enforce it with *jask.* But she simply went quiet for a moment.

"If we tell the Skavu, they'll destroy the bezeri."

"If they can," said Shan. "And they haven't a clue how to deal with *c'naatat.* Besides, all the bezeri have to do to escape them is go back into the sea. Esganikan wasn't too fussed about the risk, but once she knows they've started wiping out other species and breeding, she might well assess that differently. Either way, we'll have a mess on our hands and the two armies hanging around here far longer than they need to. So we sort it ourselves. That's what you wanted, Aras, isn't it?"

He looked wretched. Shan wondered how much of it was the realization that five centuries of careful, sometimes agonizing guardianship had gone for a proverbial ball of chalk in a matter of a few weeks.

"I feel we have few options left," he said.

"I reckon we should consider finishing them now, then," Shan said. "If we don't do it while they're easily located, we might never get the chance again."

"It would take seconds to lose one, and one is all it takes to spread the parasite."

"I think we should seek an agreement with them," said Nevyan.

"I fear they're not in a negotiating mood." Aras looked to Serrimissani, and Shan wasn't sure if he'd paused because he thought better of discussing the problem in front of her, given the speed of the ussissi grapevine, or if he wanted her opinion. "Would you be, after being almost totally wiped out?"

And this was the mire of wess'har ethics, human morality, and the pragmatism of protecting the environment. What the bezeri had suffered became irrelevant in one, and paramount in another.

"The eggs have to go, whatever happens," said Shan.

"The bezeri might just disappear and lay more."

"If they can."

Nevyan cut in again. "Instead of guessing their reaction, I'll go and talk to them."

She had a talent for common-sense rebukes. Shan, not sure if she should have been ashamed of her own knee-jerk reaction or not, squirmed at having such a discussion in front of Giyadas. Serrimissani compressed her lips in an expression that said she wasn't impressed, but it was hard to tell if it was imminent destruction or the hesitation to do it that earned her disapproval.

"I suggest we take the shuttle," she said. "Better we deal with this as soon as we can."

Nevyan walked off, hands clasped in front of her; if wess'har shook their heads in disbelief, she would have been doing that right then. Shan reached for Aras's hand and squeezed it to her chest.

"I'm so sorry, sweetheart. I'll deal with the eggs. Let me do it."

"The bezeri are my responsibility."

"I thought we said no more macho-duty shit."

"I'll do it. The whole situation began with me, many years ago." He looked at her hands locked tight around his as if he'd seen them for the first time. The lights were putting on a great display right now, as if they were trying desperately to say something and were frustrated at not being heard. "When you make exceptions, the fabric of the world unravels."

"You made an exception for me. You regret that, don't you? Things would have been very different if you'd let me die when my number was up."

Aras looked into her face. "I don't regret it at all, and not only because I love you. You were never the risk. I was."

Fifty meters away, three Skavu walked past the cluster of ship bubbles that made up the accommodation for crews, and stared. Shan let go of Aras and stood hands on hips, staring back. They knew exactly what they'd get if they started any shit with her now. She waited until they looked away again, and when she was satisfied that they'd got the message, she turned and made for the shuttle. Aras was way ahead of her.

He sat with his head in his hands as Serrimissani lifted the craft clear of the ground and the blue grasses dwindled beneath in a faint haze of heat and swirling debris. The most she could do was put her arm around him.

What have I come to?

Why can I take mass murder in my stride now? What happened to the Shan Frankland who'd have cheerfully gone to war over one genocide, let alone repeated ones?

She had no idea. She was back in the maze, looking for a line that told her where it was okay to be *c'naatat*, still breathing, and where it was a threat to life across the system and beyond. Being willing to die once didn't relieve her of the obligation to keep asking the question: it made it more pressing.

Her only answer was that she was now more steeped in wess'har thinking than human, and that was the line she had crossed.

F'nar: the Frankland clan home, upper terraces

"You don't have to knock, Eddie."

Eddie stuck his head around the door just to be on the safe side. "I didn't know if you'd be swinging from the chandeliers or whatever it is you get up to together."

Ade showed him two contemptuous fingers, grinned, and

beckoned him in. He was indulging in the unmarinelike activity of making something out of dough. "Shan and Aras are on Bezer'ej."

"And you're baking cakes."

"Bread. After a fashion." Ade paused mid-knead, forearms displaying formidable muscle. "You're not yourself, mate. What's wrong?"

"Still in the shit with News Desk."

"Shan feels bad about that, mate. She knows she shouldn't have barged in and let them know she wasn't dead."

"Doesn't matter in the global scheme of things, one journo versus a few million dead isenj." Eddie decided to stop there. He wanted to confide in Ade but that was too close to looking for sympathy for his noble sacrifice, and that was wrong. "I came to tell you that your pet brigadier has been on the UN portal asking after you."

"Shit." Ade punched down the dough and tore it into three parts, slapping each down in turn and kneading two at a time, one with each hand. It was quite impressive. "I never got back to her on Rayat."

"Academic, mate. They want him back. They can't have him. And you can't make them honor a deal to restore your lot to full Cub Scout membership."

"I know. But old habit and all that. Officer says jump, you jump."

It was easier to tell them Rayat was dead. He was, in any sense of the word. "No trouble patching you through from here."

Ade twirled the dough into skeins and began plaiting them. "Got to talk to the Boss first. Not my call."

Eddie dumped his jacket on the sofa. The upholstery still looked white to him, even if a *c'naatat* saw it as peacock blue. Sometimes this cave of a house felt like home, and sometimes it felt like alien territory, but he missed those months when he was part of the family here even if it had been one in mourning.

"So what's the business on Bezer'ej, then?"

"Getting the Skavu to fuck off home."

"Really?"

"Yeah," Ade said. "Nevyan's done a deal with Rit to keep the peace if they leave."

"Well, count me in for waving a few flags when that happens. They're as bad as I think, aren't they?"

"Worse. Total fucking savages." Ade was relatively mild in his dismissal of enemy forces, considering what he'd seen in his career. But the Skavu had hit a nerve in him. "I'd kill the lot of them without a second thought."

"It'll be bad enough thinking that they'll still be out there somewhere."

"The good thing," said Ade, "is that a round to the head kills them like any other arsehole."

He laid the plaited loaf on a sheet of mottled gold glass to rise, and the two of them went out onto the terrace, perched on the broad wall overlooking the city beneath and shared a beer. The brew was getting worse each time. Ade needed Eddie's expert hand in the process. But it was a beer shared with a friend, and that was all that mattered.

"So what you doing?" asked Ade.

"Getting stuff together for Esganikan about Australia."

"Ooh, she's made you her spin-weasel, then?"

"Just analysis. Like reporting, only with an audience of one."

"Like BBChan 88."

"Hah bloody hah."

"Well, when you get home, you won't be Our Man-In-F'nar, will you? You'll be grubbing around in the dirt with the rest of the hacks if you don't grab your advantage with Attila the Parrot."

Eddie hated the reminder. *Home.* There were things back on Earth that were hard to get or nonexistent here—food beyond the basics, sex, and a sense of permanence—but the thought of walking away from it almost panicked him. It wasn't like leaving Turkey or any of the other countries where he'd worked. Once he left Wess'ej, he couldn't just hop on a flight and visit the place again, catching up with old friends and tutting about how much the place had changed. He couldn't even call them, not easily anyway.

It was twenty-five years' separation, and 150 trillion miles. As soon as he landed on Earth, thinking he'd been gone a few months in the bizarre squeezing of time at near-light speed, anyone he called back here would have lived a generation's worth of experiences.

They might even have forgotten him.

"I thought you'd be spending time with the detachment," said Eddie. "I know they're on Mar'an'cas, but you could get up there a few times a week for a hand of cards."

"I know," said Ade. "I'm practicing not having them around. Getting used to not having them there."

"Ah."

"I'm going to miss them."

"Or you could make the most of the time you have with them. You've still got a few years, if they don't decide to go back with *Thetis*."

"Eddie," he said gently, "what about the hundreds of years after that? Maybe thousands."

Ade didn't say much after that. It seemed like he was thinking for the first time about what being immortal for all intents and purposes actually meant.

"If they could remove *c'naatat* from you," Eddie asked, "would you take the option?"

Ade chewed the idea visibly. "Not until I've had the life I should have had."

"Do you think they can do it?"

Ade swung his legs off the wall and stood up, stretching his arms behind his back.

"I think they can. Shapakti did, once. But the bloody thing learns."

"That's bugs for you," said Eddie.

It took him a matter of seconds to think through the implications of a countermeasure for *c'naatat* and the impact it would have. He added it to the list of stories that were five star, but not worth the shit.

The list of those grew longer. He had another beer instead.

The Temporary City, Bezer'ej: command center

"We have exactly the same pressures here as when we last spoke," said Sarmatakian Ve. "Except now you have ten thousand competent Skavu at your disposal that you didn't have before."

Esganikan took the return call from Surang in front of the duty crew as usual. There was nothing an Eqbas commander would keep from her comrades. Nor did she feel any compulsion not to argue with the senior matriarch's adviser in front of them.

"Skavu are a liability. They've already given me cause for concern here. I can't risk deploying them on Earth."

"Can you command them or not?"

"You know I can."

"Then those are your extra resource."

Esganikan had been under fire, and she was deterred by nothing; but the idea of Skavu troops on Earth filled her with a dismay so powerful that she couldn't take it in her stride at that moment. And this couldn't be solved by *jask*. So she argued.

"I can't allow a fleet of Skavu to wait on Bezer'ej for several years with nothing to occupy them, and I strongly advise against using them on a mission like Earth."

"They're all you have if you want a task force inside of six or seven years."

Six or seven years. In the context of the time she'd spent in suspension, and the displacement of light-years, it was a short time. *But I don't have this time. I'm older than the rest of the crew. I need to start my life, however late. And for Earth—every year counts too.*

"I'll ask you one more time to reconsider, Sarmatakian. The mission is under-resourced as it is. Adding unsuitable troops to the situation will compromise it."

"I don't have a choice. You can accept the Skavu, or reject them and carry out the mission understrength. Or abort it, and I know you won't do that. We want Earth restored before it becomes a much bigger task."

The gene bank had waited generations. It could wait lon-

ger. But Earth couldn't, and even the delay between leaving
Bezer'ej and planet fall would be marked by deterioration
and new problems. Some things were better done sooner
than later.

"If I accept the Skavu, then I still face having them hanging around this system longer than they're welcome. This
isn't one of our project worlds, *Chail*. This is our own people.
However different, however unlike us they are in many ways,
they're wess'har, and we have a duty to them."

"Then," said Sarmatakian, "you had better leave for Earth
as soon as you can."

"But what about the rest of the specialists and the remaining assets you promised me?"

"We still commit them. They're in transit. As there's no
need now to assemble at Bezer'ej, we can deploy them direct from their current locations, which means they'll start
arriving in the Earth system approximately a year after you
do, and at intervals thereafter. Purely from my memory, that
should give you nearly a full fleet on station within four
years of arrival."

There was no argument. She was right: the resources
added up, and all Esganikan had to offer by way of counter-
argument was that she didn't like Skavu troops. If she didn't
take them, another commander would have to.

Earth needed intervention: and because of the distances
and delays involved, this almost-accidentally assembled task
force was the best hope it had. It was *her* problem to solve.

"Very well," she said. "I'll prepare the mission for early
departure."

The operations room staff were quiet, but their scents
didn't seem as agitated as hers. Perhaps it was relief to be
getting on with the job, having been denied an opportunity
to be useful on Umeh.

"That means rushing through the planning," said Hayin.
"We can leave a clean-up crew on Ouzhari, though, can't
we?"

"Yes," said Esganikan, crushed. She envied Shan's ability
to conceal her scent. She felt obliged to explain her anxiety
to all who detected it. "You know I would have liked more

time to prepare, and I don't like Skavu, but I work with what I'm given, because that's my duty."

"The sooner we deal with Earth," said Hayin, "the sooner we're back on Eqbas Vorhi."

There was a general murmur of satisfaction from the crew and a pleasant scent to underscore it. Esganikan desperately wanted to share it, and failed. She went back to her cabin in the detached section of her ship, asked Aitassi not to disturb her, and knelt down to think.

She'd run out of time. She didn't have troop strength on her side. She had a *c'naatat* host as a prisoner, insufficient preparation work done, little liaison established, and a fear that if she had overestimated Wess'ej's capacity to handle the isenj, then she would have another clean-up task on her hands when she passed this way in—how many years' time? Fifty, sixty, a hundred?

She couldn't yet tell how long the Earth mission would take. Most missions took five to ten years to stabilize a planet and leave crews in place with the native population. Earth was too far from the core worlds to expect any wess'har or ussissi to want to remain there.

For a moment, she thought the unthinkable.

It was an *if only* thought, the kind humans had.

The one difference was that this wasn't an impossible wish to erase events and live a different set of consequences. This was a calculated gamble forming in her head.

Shapakti was a brilliant biologist. Back home, there were many more like him. He would find a lasting solution to removing *c'naatat*, or they would, but someone would find it, and all she needed was time.

Time could be bought, at a price.

If the Targassati wess'har here could make *c'naatat* work for them in a crisis, and not be destroyed by it, then so could she.

17

Police are investigating a third killing in Brussels after a senior FEU civil servant was shot dead at his home. He's not been named, but the FEU has denied claims that he was an intelligence officer. Earlier this week, a junior minister in the Foreign Office and a Treasury official were also found dead in what police have described as a "professional assassination."

BBChan 557

Chad Island, Bezer'ej

"Hi, Lin," said Shan. "You've let yourself go a bit, haven't you?"

Aras's heart pounded with dread, and Shan went into what Ade called her *smart-arse mode*. That was how each reacted to a tense situation. Hands on hips, Shan appeared ready to reach behind her back to pull a weapon that wouldn't do a *c'naatat*-infected creature any damage at all. Nevyan watched in grim silence.

Aras had a cluster of small charges, enough to reduce a few eggs to fragments. That was his priority, and it broke his heart. Shan nudged him, and he called on his human part, the dishonest and destructive monkey, to get him through the next hour. He was sure he was doing it for the right reasons, irrelevant as motive was to Wess'har.

"We're here to do a deal," Shan said. "Me and Nevyan. It's for your own good."

"It always is," said Lindsay.

Nevyan studied the assembled bezeri with fully dilated pupils. Most of them were here now—no, all of them, Aras counted—and they seemed at a loss; they made no attempt to repel Shan. They simply studied what was studying them.

Bezeri hadn't had enemies in hundreds of generations,

at least not enemies who confronted them directly. Their enemy was invisible, the by-product of the ambitions of surface-dwelling animals, but it killed them just the same. They didn't look ready to die quietly again.

"What's the deal?" asked Lindsay.

"Stop the bezeri destroying other species," said Shan. "Teach them to manage their resources. And stop them breeding."

"What's in it for . . . us?" Lindsay asked. She stood her ground, a glassy figure shot with lights, and Aras barely recognized her now. "Under the circumstances, being nearly extinct and all that, your proposition sounds a little one-sided."

"Remember how they got in this mess?" Shan said quietly. "*Two* twenty-four-carat decisions by you, Commander I-Know-What-I'm-Doing Neville. One more bad call doesn't undo the damage."

Lindsay looked at Nevyan. "So what have you got to say for yourself? Or do you do everything Shan tells you?"

"If the Eqbas or their Skavu troops knew what was happening, they'd eradicate you all." Nevyan might have looked quiet and compliant to a human, but she was pure steel. Aras calculated the route he would need to take to find the eggs nestled in the foliage. "When the Eqbas leave, we take over again, and if I feel you're a hazard to this planet, I'll eradicate you myself."

"Okay, I see the threat," said Lindsay. "But I'm having trouble spotting the deal."

"Keep the bezeri in check, both in their habits and their population, and we leave you alone."

"So, they're frozen like museum exhibits. Proud remnant of a mighty culture. Roll up and see the living fossils." Lindsay had adopted Shan's hands-on-hips stance, a clear indication of who she thought she was arguing with. "We have no incentive, then." She turned to Aras. "You're awfully quiet."

Of course I am. I'm about to take lives that have done nothing wrong, that can't have done anything wrong, not yet. But if I can't have children, then neither must these bezeri.

"Your incentive is a sustainable planet," he said. "Because even *c'naatat* can't live indefinitely if the planet is overrun. Sooner or later, you end up like Umeh, nothing but yourselves filling the world. At some point, you need to stop."

"Forty-four isn't that point," said Lindsay. She was looking around the clearing; some bezeri were up in the trees, keeping watch. Her eyes were visible in that gel face, and her darting glance suggested it might have already occurred to her that this was an ambush of sorts. "No deal."

Shan looked down at her boots, the brown riggers' boots that Ade had gone to so much effort to find for her. "I killed my own kid," she said. "I aborted her. If I'd kill my own flesh and blood, Ade's child, to stop *c'naatat* hosts proliferating, I won't have any trouble finishing off this whole colony. Will I?"

Her. Aras hadn't known that. An *isanket.* That hurt.

Shan could always silence Lindsay. She had now. Lindsay's shock, however altered her body had become, was obvious. She took a long time to find words again.

"You're not lying, are you?"

"I wish I were."

"You. Of all people. At least you've experienced what I've been through now. You understand, then."

Shan let out a dismissive snort. "Cut the shit, Lin. Don't pull the we're-all-grieving-mothers-together crap. I've not come here to fucking well bond with you like some support group. Get the bezeri to shape up, or I'll finish the job you started."

Shan's brutally worded ultimatum told Aras that she was still hurting a great deal more about the abortion than she let on. The more crude her dismissal, the deeper the wound. Lindsay lapsed into brief silence. The two woman handled their assorted ills and pains in very different ways.

Lindsay seemed to be struggling with Shan's revelation. "There's still nothing in it for them."

"If the Eqbas succeed in finding a way to remove *c'naatat* from hosts, then there *is* a solution," said Nevyan. "In time, when the solution is found, the bezeri can breed, restore their numbers, and then the parasite can be removed. But until that happens, they must stop."

Lindsay stood silent for a long time. Aras judged this was the point to wander off. He heard her say, "Let me discuss this with Saib and the others," before her voice faded and was swept away by the breeze. In the foliage, clustered on a stalk in the cool moist shadow, a clutch of eggs that couldn't be allowed to hatch did indeed look like exotic fruits. As he dug out a pit and laid the small charge, it occurred to him that grinding or mincing would have done the fragmentation job a lot more tidily. But he only had explosives to hand, and that would do the job. He set the fuse and withdrew to squat in the shelter of a tree.

The blast deafened him for a moment and in the seconds of absolute silence that followed, he saw movement and sparkling light. A couple of bezeri were rushing towards the detonation, bounding on limblike tentacles, clearing the bushes in great leaps. The nearest they had ever come to encountering explosives was—if they could detect it at all— the distant sound of wess'har skirmishes during the abortive attempt at an isenj landing. The bezeri had no idea what had happened.

Aras recognized one of the bezeri heading his way as the one who'd been searching for *sheven* in the bog. It was only when the creature rushed to the exact spot where the eggs had been that Aras realized this might be the mother.

He felt he guessed correctly. She thrashed around the bushes, making an incoherent bubbling growl, and saw only a shallow crater where her eggs had been. Her mantle lit instantly with the most vivid green light, no other color at all. She became an emerald beacon.

Aras no longer had his signal lamp, and so he couldn't interpret the language of bioluminescence. But he'd seen that green light before, and he needed no lamp to interpret it. He'd seen it when the bezeri were dying in the shallows after Mohan Rayat, Lindsay Neville, Josh Garrod and Jonathan Burgh had detonated cobalt-slated nuclear devices on Ouzhari island.

It was a scream of agony.

Now, perhaps, a deal might be discussed. Aras stumbled far from the green-screaming mother, bent double, and vomited.

"You're going to regret that," said Lindsay Neville's voice.

The Temporary City, Bezer'ej

Shapakti and Rayat were hunched over an examination tray whose magnified image was now a familiar one: the radial brush pattern of *c'naatat*. In he corner, behind a loose mesh, were the two blue and gold macaws.

"You don't allow them to fly free now," Esganikan said. Shapakti looked up, startled. When engrossed in work, he didn't even smell her coming. Not even the noise of the macaws distracted him.

"It's for their own safety," Shapakti explained. "They like having company, but they seem to get bored . . . and then they become disruptive."

Rayat looked up at nothing in particular as if he was listening. Esganikan thought about his insinuating human trick of planting ideas in minds with apparently casual statements, and realized that she'd learned a valuable lesson that would stand her in good stead on Earth.

"You missed my conversation with Sarmatakian in the command center," she said. "We're leaving for Earth as soon as we can make arrangements. A few weeks at most. The Skavu are making up the shortfall in the fleet."

Shapakti took the news in stunned silence.

"Some of your people have very lurid descriptions of their . . . environmental correctness," said Rayat.

"Nothing we say is lurid," Esganikan explained. "It is accurate."

"They massacre populations for the smallest infringement, I hear."

"Their own as well as their neighbors', yes."

"Right." Rayat nodded to himself a few times, as if distracted. The color of his face changed—blood diminishing, a more yellow tone—and his pupils dilated. "Well, I can predict the outcome, I think."

"What about my research?" Shapakti said at last. "I can't complete it in weeks, and probably not even months. I thought I had at least four years."

Rayat appeared to take great interest in that. He showed some agitation or excitement: she wasn't sure which. But his blinking became rapid. "So what happens to me? Does that mean you're taking me with you?"

Esganikan read his reaction. Now she was sure how he operated. He'd got her thinking about the benefits of *c'naatat*. He was now hoping he might go home to Earth as her prisoner. Shan Frankland had been right: he was still set on getting the parasite back to Earth for his government by one vector or another.

It would reach Earth, but not as he intended. And when it did, it would remain beyond the reach and use of his masters.

Esganikan leaned over to look at Shapakti's images of the parasite—or symbiont, depending on how benign its host felt towards it—that had caused so much grief. Shapakti held the microscope tray so she could see the enlarged image better. Shan called it a fractal hairbrush.

"Few biological problems have ever defeated you, Shapakti." Esganikan found herself considering delivery systems for agents to counter *c'naatat* infection. They would have been a great deal more efficient than the obliteration bombing the wess'har had been forced to use on this planet. "Do you lack resources here?"

"Yes—for this project, anyway."

"You return home now, then. When we can manage *c'naatat*, it opens up many possibilities."

"*Gai Chail*, I do believe that same thought was what started this cascade of problems here in the wess'har wars."

"F'nar is a culture from history, Shapakti. They live a carefully preserved agrarian lifestyle that we didn't even live centuries ago. They don't have the technology. We stand the best chance of understanding this organism."

The macaws started a noisy destruction of something metallic in their temporary prison. Shapakti glanced at Rayat as if seeking a reaction. "And then what do we do with that understanding, other than having a way of removing it from its host in the event of contamination?"

"That alone would solve most of the problems it presents."

"My friend Rayat says that makes it *more* dangerous, because of its potential then to be used at will as a military enhancement."

Esganikan noted the word *friend,* which wasn't ironic. "It's only dangerous if others like the *gethes* have that technology, and they don't, and they never will. But consider what flexibility it would offer us for missions."

"Don't you think I haven't?" Shapakti made a gesture towards the far wall of his laboratory, where he had an image of his home in real time, linked by the instantaneous communications system. "My family is in a conscious phase now. I can talk to them. Then when I embark on the next journey, they go into suspension again. I spend a great deal of time thinking how life extension might work with the time-displaced like us. But I doubt if being able to live consciously through centuries of separation from loved ones is any advantage at all."

It was inevitable: he had a family waiting for him, and the painful difficulty of managing that was the main reason why mission crew were almost always single, either the very young or those—like her—who had delayed bonding and children for the duration of their career.

There was only so much time you could buy with a combination of cryo-suspension and time dilation. Sooner or later, the days and months you lived in the conscious now added up to become a spent life. Esganikan counted them with increasing anxiety that had now reached the point where she had to take a calculated risk.

I need to buy myself time.

I have a small force, a long way from home, and I might need to manage casualties.

If the wess'har here could use c'naatat and not be controlled by it, even with their obsolete technology, then so can we.

"If we could manage *c'naatat,* we could enhance our military capability," she said.

"Do we even need to?"

"And families would have an alternative to cryo-suspension."

"We could, of course, just be more strict about who crews missions."

"And that means we never deploy the experienced and the mature, and we need to do that, Shapakti." Esganikan paused and looked Rayat up and down. His hair was streaked with gray, which indicated maturity in a human. He was utterly alone and everyone he held dear on his homeworld—if he held anyone dear at all—was dead. She saw her future in him. "I want to suggest something to you."

"Chail, I know what you're thinking."

"Send your data back to your colleagues on Eqbas Vorhi now, and take your bonded team members home with this *gethes.* In the five years of dilation, they'll have made progress on modeling, and you can begin work on a removal method with the best facilities as soon as you arrive home."

Shapakti exuded relief, a faint burst of musk, and his muscles relaxed. "I thought you were going to suggest an experiment that I would find ill-advised."

It was her life, and if things went wrong, then she knew how to bring the experiment to an end. "I'm going to do it. Do you have live tissue samples from Shan Frankland?"

"Yes. But don't do this. You can't be serious."

Rayat had been watching the exchange with interest. It seemed that he'd suddenly realized the implications of what was being discussed. "Hang on, that's insane. You can't do that. You're going to infect yourself?"

"Each host adds something to the next, if only memories. I wonder if it might be worth having yours, Dr. Rayat."

Shan had warned her he was slippery and manipulative, but understanding that way of thinking would make a difference in how she handled the Earth mission. Not all *gethes* were the loyal Ade Bennett or rigorously moral Shan Frankland. A normal, selfish, deceptive human psyche would be a valuable reference.

"Give me an infectious sample from this man," she said.

"Don't do this," said Rayat. "Don't take this to Earth. I'm begging you. You can't take the risk."

"But I thought that was your mission," she said. "And why you seeded that idea in me. So your government could find a way of harvesting it once we get to Earth, whether it comes from me . . . or you."

"I swear I didn't." It was the first time she'd seen Rayat react so violently. His scent had changed; if he could hide it like Shan, he'd abandoned that now, maybe to make his point. "It absolutely mustn't get into human hands. This isn't a game. I mean it."

She'd misread him, then. He was as distressed as any human she'd seen. A lesson learned; humans often gave out misleading signals to each other, so it wasn't surprising that he'd sent the wrong ones to her. But that didn't matter now.

Shapakti wasn't happy about it either. "And what if we never manage to find a removal method?" His scent was acid and anxious now, even afraid. "Close isn't good enough. We came close before."

"Then I have explosive ordnance, which I understand as well as you understand anatomy. I will do what so many wess'har troops did if it becomes clear we'll never be able to remove it."

"You have to warn the crew you're a biohazard, and the wess'har, too."

And I'll have to tell Shan Frankland. And that will be . . . interesting.

"Prepare to go home, Shapakti, and give me the infectious material in a form that I can use."

"I strongly advise against this."

"And then you can have infected Eqbas samples to take home for your research."

Shapakti's expression changed. "Ah, and *gethes* say we know nothing about trade."

"An infusion of blood."

"That would be simplest."

Hard decisions were only ones that you hadn't yet made, and Esganikan had made hers. It felt easy now. She looked into Rayat's face and wondered what she would find in his mind.

"Do you want to visit Surang, Doctor? On Eqbas Vorhi?"

Rayat's face was increasingly readable. He was far less expressive than men like Ade or Barencoin, but the muscle movement, dilation of blood vessels and skin changes were still visible to a wess'har. Rayat went from a flash of alarm—the *eyes,* those were the indicators in humans, she decided—to something like excitement. She'd seen that in youngsters and in Shapakti when offered new learning.

"You're sending me to Surang for safe keeping and further investigation," he said. "Fine. Do that. Keep me out of the hands of my own people. But don't give *c'naatat* to them gift-wrapped. You don't understand humans at all."

"Do you *want* to go?"

"I would love to go. I'd love to see your world. But I beg you, don't take *c'naatat* to Earth."

"Shapakti," she said, "do this."

"Oh God, no . . ." said Rayat.

Shapakti took a plain white metal tube that was cool to the touch and had a subcutaneous injector on one end. It didn't even need Rayat's cooperation. There were samples of his blood and tissue in conservation. Esganikan looked at the tube, and somehow it didn't look like the most dangerous thing she had ever attempted.

C'naatat had shifted from being a risky experiment to something she now thought she would actually need. She *had* to assume the Earth mission would take longer than planned. She *had* to plan for the Skavu compromising her, and possibly leaving her short of personnel. She *had* to assume the worst, and hope that Shapakti and the team he would work with eventually could remove the parasite from her system in time. Shan would have said her faith in providence was just like the *god-botherers.*

"You really don't get it, do you?" said Rayat, a sob in his voice.

Time was what she didn't have. *Threat is now.* Esganikan rolled up her sleeve, and took the step into a world of other people's memories, and a wholly uncertain and deathless future.

Landing area, outside the Temporary City, Bezer'ej

"Lin can rant as much as she wants," Shan said, "but she's got more sense than to mess with Wess'ej. Or give the Skavu an excuse to go after her little squid gang."

Shan was more worried about Aras right then than about Lindsay's reaction to the destruction of the eggs, and the ultimatum she'd been given. Only a wess'har could understand his self-loathing at taking a life that had genuinely done nothing, something as repugnant to him as eating flesh. He didn't discuss it, but destroying the eggs must have had a particularly painful significance for him.

"She knows what must happen if she fails to keep the bezeri in check," said Nevyan. "If she doesn't, at least our choice is clear. She understands the stakes very well."

Giyadas clung to Nevyan's side, annoyed that she hadn't been allowed into the bezeri camp, and wanting to know what had happened. Serrimissani, ever the little ray of sunshine, was pacing around impatiently, anxious to return to Wess'ej.

"You'd make a lousy taxi driver," Shan observed. "Stick it on the meter."

"Esganikan Gai is late."

"Wess'har don't care about late, so why do you?" Shan wanted to get Aras home, but a little while longer wouldn't make any difference. "Relax. We've all had a shitty few weeks and now we might get a little respite."

Shan passed the time waiting for the Eqbas commander to come by examining some vivid pink blooms on a flat rosette of vegetation. They looked like physalis husks, papery and fragile, but when she touched them they had the moist, fleshy feel of orchid petals.

Yeah, Esganikan was taking her time.

"You adapt to so much," said Nevyan. "And yet you still find it hard to accept that disputes can be resolved between wess'har without violence, consultation or long negotiations. Either something is resolvable or it isn't."

"Has there ever been an *isn't*?"

"Yes, and it's Wess'ej. The followers of Targassat left."

"Ah, we'd have taken entrenched positions, embarked on a long and fruitless ideological war, killed millions, and poisoned half the planet."

"You see my point."

"I'll just swing from the trees, scratch a bit and keep quiet, eh?" At least Nevyan understood what human jokes looked like now. "Ade and Aras will be proud of me. I managed to walk away from another ruck without belting anyone."

Nevyan let out a breath of impatience. She was a teenager who ran a superpower as far as humans were concerned. No, wess'har were not like *gethes*. They ran on a different clock and a different world view. Shan still felt happier among them.

"Here she comes," said Nevyan.

Esganikan covered the ground like a race-walker. She was a big woman. As she got closer, Shan could see—and smell—something wasn't quite right. "Shit, she's had a row with the boss. Look. Maybe she's had some flak for sending the Skavu home after they bothered to come all this way."

If anything, Esganikan looked hot and flustered. And that was just *not* Eqbas. She might have been unwell; Shan was used to permanent rude health now and it had become a habit to blanket everyone with the expectation that they were as bulletproof as her.

"What's wrong?" Nevyan asked, inhaling with a sharp sniff.

"I've been ordered to divert the Skavu fleet to Earth," said Esganikan.

Shan's gut flipped over. She thought she'd misheard in her preoccupation with the confrontation with the bezeri, but she'd heard right. The first thing she did was consciously batten down the *jask*. No, she wasn't going to get caught that way, not now. But the news appalled her. She felt her scalp prickle and tighten with anger.

"You can't seriously send those bastards to Earth. Whatever happened to your mighty million-year-old civilization? Overstretch?"

"Yes."

"Jesus Christ. And now you're going to unleash them on *my* bloody planet?"

"Wess'ej is your planet now."

"You'll just have to pardon my sentimentality, then. Look, Earth might have its problems, but it's not a wall-to-wall ecological disaster that you can sort with shocktroops."

"I told Sarmatakian that I didn't think Skavu were suitable. But either we accept them, or we operate understrength."

"Can you control them? And what the hell are they going to get up to hanging around here for a few years first? They're nutters. You know it."

Esganikan didn't look right somehow. She'd loosened the neck of her tunic, and she'd never done that before. "We'll embark as soon as we can. I don't want them idle here any more than you do, and that might mean some preparation for the Earth mission doesn't take place."

Nevyan was now totally pushed aside. Shan saw her gather up Giyadas out of the corner of her eye and usher the child to the waiting ship.

"What preparation?" Shan demanded.

"Consultation."

"You mean telling people what they need to do before you arrive."

"Yes."

"Oh, shit."

"We have a few weeks, perhaps. Once in transit, we can talk to the government of the day." She leaned forward a little as if explaining to an idiot. "The time dilation means that each time we contact Earth by ITX, time there will have moved on faster than we experience it."

"Oh, negotiate with a new government every day? Well, good luck, sister."

"Is that any less convenient than dealing with one government for a few years and then arriving on Earth to find it twenty-five years in the past and a new regime in its place? In the end, it makes little difference. Most of the action we need to take will be determined on arrival. That's one of the vagaries of interstellar operations."

"I'm still not happy."

"It's not your mission, so your happiness is irrelevant," said Esganikan. "And it's not your world any longer. You did your duty in recovering the gene bank, and you declined the option of accompanying us. Go home and attend to your city and your *jurej've.*"

Few people ever told Shan to fuck off and got away with it. Esganikan had managed it twice. Shan almost lost her struggle to control her anger—and with it her *jask*—but swallowed hard, compressing her wess'har scent glands.

"I'll just go home and get my old man's dinner on the table, then, like a good little wife," she said. "And you can ride out with the green jihad. Fine."

Shan turned and strode away to the ship, trying not to stalk off and show how close Esganikan had come to really getting to her. She was a wess'har, and none of it was designed to goad Shan. It was simply a statement of what she thought, largely impersonal and wholly for the common good.

But she was right. Earth was none of Shan's business now, and she'd agreed that Ade and Aras, the double act of her conscience, the safe pairs of hands who always got her back on course even when they did insanely stupid things out of blind love, could give her a hundred reasons for her to stay out of it. This was football-club mentality, supporting a team long after you'd left the city because it just happened to be the place you were born, and it held you in some irrational tribal thrall.

Rayat. The thought of him stopped her in her tracks. She turned around, put the tip of her thumb and forefinger between her lips, and let out a piercing whistle. It usually did the trick in getting *anyone's* attention. Esganikan turned, paused, and then ambled back to meet Shan halfway.

"Okay," she said. "I know you're capable of running a planet. Primitive reaction. Earth needs a short sharp shock, and if I thought it didn't, I've already gone too far in helping it get one to be squeamish now. I'll shut up. But what about Rayat?"

"I'm sending him back to Surang with Shapakti for further study. For a removal method."

Shapakti was homesick and had taken the diversion that extended his tour of duty with grim reluctance. Shan really liked him: poor sod. And now he was on his way home, and she might not get a chance to say goodbye.

"You could have told me," Shan said. "I'd have liked to have seen him off. And you're right, it makes more sense to use that bastard Rayat for something useful than for me to get a bit of revenge out of my system by making hamburger out of him."

"We are, as you say, *done,* then."

"We are."

It was one thing off her mind, anyway. Her pulse was still pounding in her ears when she got to the ship. Earth wasn't her problem any longer, and she'd lost count of the times she'd said that over recent weeks. She wasn't, as she'd told Aras and Ade, going to be the green movement's El Cid, a dead hero used as a rallying point. She'd done her bit. She didn't care, and she wasn't worried about the Skavu.

You bloody liar. You're horrified. You don't want those zealots waging jihad on your world, and not because you're squeamish but because you know that if you got up off your arse and did your job, you'd make a difference back there. Guilt, professional conceit, and a refusal to accept this is a bigger league than you ever played in.

She was about fifteen strides from the hatch when her swiss *eeped* loudly. She took it out without thinking, flicked the key and had one boot on the coaming of the hatch before she read the source code.

She knew that one, even if it didn't have a name on it.

Rayat.

Rayat was trying to call her. There was no message, no indication of what he wanted. It just said CONTACT RAYAT URGENT. How had he managed to get a message out? They'd taken his handheld ages ago. She still had it. But he was a spook, and spooks could do that kind of thing. It bothered her that she didn't know how.

She paused, one hand gripping the rail. She didn't like

loose ends. But this was Rayat, and he didn't make social calls. He was after something; she was damned if she was going to give him the chance to get it. All that mattered was that he was heading a long way from human reach, and if she couldn't trust Eqbas wess'har with *c'naatat*, then she could trust nobody.

CONTACT RAYAT URGENT

She looked at the text flashing against the dark red body of the swiss. He never let up: he always had one last trick left.

"Fuck you," she said, and erased the message.

18

Responsibility is the bedrock of society, and the duty of the powerful to the weak. We can never turn our back on it; it is part of choice, and can never be separated from it. Choice, as we have said before, must be made. The art of knowing when responsibility is ours, though, is more difficult, and judgment is needed to determine if a responsibility is indeed ours, or something we have snatched from another because of our own overconfidence and arrogance.

TARGASSAT of Surang: On Interventionist Policy

F'nar, Wess'ej

"A month? Oh Christ, no."

Aras watched Ade's face fall. Mart Barencoin, Ismat Qureshi, Bulwant Singh Chahal, Jon Becken, and Susan Webster stood awkwardly in front of their former sergeant on the terrace overlooking F'nar. They looked like they were expecting a dressing-down, not a farewell.

"We might as well go now," said Barencoin. "Otherwise we have to wait for *Thetis,* and then that crate's going to take seventy-five years to get home. Then it's another four years or whatever for the next bus to turn up. If Esganikan's slinging her hook now, we might as well go."

Webster nodded, rosy-cheeked and still looking sturdy despite the inadequate diet. "From where we stand, it'll feel like being home in weeks." She pursed her lips, defocused, and did a quick calculation. "Okay, maybe a few months. But home."

Aras watched, wondering if it wasn't better that the parting happened fast. Those who stayed behind on Wess'ej had to face the separation sooner or later, and it was probably kinder than building up to it for four years. But Ade's face said otherwise.

It had been a painful, harrowing few days. Shan was scrubbing the floor with a ferocity he hadn't seen since she first arrived on Bezer'ej. She had to spend her angry adrenaline somehow. Aras relived his shame—necessary, but shame nonetheless—at destroying unlived and blameless life. Shan told him he'd get used to it.

"Waste of bloody time getting the shit generator going on Mar'an'cas," said Webster. Aras was jerked back to the here and now. "But it's only sweat and blood."

"You can come and give us a tearful farewell when we embark," said Barencoin, winking at Ade. "I'll even let you kiss me goodbye, but no tongues, okay?"

"Piss off, Mart." Ade had tears in his eyes. Aras didn't even need to smell his distress, even if it filled the room. He was openly distraught. "You'll get a kick up the arse and like it."

"Yeah, but we can always call you when we get home, right? I mean, you're a permanent fixture in the universe now."

"You bloody better."

It was the worst afternoon Aras could recall spending since the terrible days after he was told Shan was dead. And it felt like a bereavement again, too: for all the beer that had been found to mark the occasion, it was funereal. Eddie showed up and stood looking at the marines with an oddly detached expression on his face. He'd been quiet and largely absent since they'd returned from Umeh Station, as if he knew something terrible was coming. He wasn't the bulletproof, emotionally undentable, resilient Eddie of old. Aras handed him a small glass of beer that he'd kept aside specially, and gripped his shoulder hard.

"I'd better let the bee cam loose," Eddie said. "Might be one of the last times we'll all be together like this. You'll be wanting some footage for the family album, Ade."

Nobody said they'd miss each other, and nobody talked about old times. Aras made a point of staying in the background and not attempting humor, because the ribbing and joking that was going on had an edge to it that he'd never seen before in humans. He'd never seen them facing permanent separation, and realizing what twenty-five light-years actually meant.

The last time they left, they left together. They were all people who weren't tied to Earth by relationships, even Eddie. A culture and a world was far, far easier to leave behind for a long time—or even forever—than the people you'd grown to love.

Aras was going to miss Eddie more than the marines. He leaned against the pearl-smooth wall, warmed by the sun, and recalled how Eddie had been the one who came to be with him when Shan died: Eddie had been the one who cooked and made him eat: and Eddie had hidden the grenades Aras had been set on using to end his life, even when Aras had physically threatened him to make him give them up. Eddie had very nearly been as close as a brother.

Aras walked over and sat beside him on the broad, low perimeter wall. He seemed very focused on the marines.

"You'll be a celebrity when you get back," said Aras. "Will you remain with BBChan?"

"Ah, I probably need a change." Eddie wasn't even sipping the beer, let alone swigging it back. "I'm such an adrenaline junkie now. I'll look for something more exciting."

"I never thought you would actually leave."

"Neither did I."

"Shan will be out soon. She's not avoiding you."

Eddie seemed not to hear. "You realize you lot are my family."

"I do, Eddie. As you are ours."

"I'm not a pretty sight when I get weepy."

"I know. We wept together, remember?"

"At least I'll still have some non-human company."

Aras didn't know what else to say.

"So what happened to Rayat?" said Barencoin. "Did Shan finally frag him?"

Ade took a steadying breath. He was on that sentimental edge that he often was, the odd counterweight to his other persona that switched off and became a professional soldier. "He's been taken back to Eqbas Vorhi for tests to work out how to remove *c'naatat* from him."

A small mocking cheer went up from the marines. The barracking started.

"Bloody good job," said Becken. "Makes me think that vivisection isn't such a bad thing after all. I hope they start with his balls."

"Nah, Shan had those made into earrings."

"You could have sold tickets for fragging him, mate."

"We should have slotted him when he started getting arsey in *Thetis* camp and saved a lot of paperwork."

Aras supposed that a display of aggression was easier than weeping. Walking away fast was the best option, Shan said, but Aras wasn't sure when she'd ever done that.

Barencoin was quieter and more thoughtful than Aras had seen him before. "Where's Lindsay Neville, then? She went with him?"

Ade opened his mouth to speak and then froze, looking to one side in slight defocus as if gathering his thoughts.

"She's a squid now," he said.

The marines held their breath for a second and then all burst out laughing at once.

"You're not taking the piss, are you, Ade?" said Qureshi.

"No. *C'naatat* changes you. She's adapted to a marine environment, you could say."

"Funny, you never did," said Barencoin, and the banter degenerated into playful insults and speculation about tattooed genitals, how squid had sex, and why Lindsay Neville probably liked having tentacles. It was all a useful diversion from saying what they all felt and what they all knew anyway: that they'd been through the unthinkable together, and that parting was the worst thing they could imagine.

Then Eddie looked up and past Aras, and said: "How long have you been there?"

"Long enough," said Shan.

She ambled across the terrace, sat down between Qureshi and Ade, and gave him a sad reluctant smile that Aras recognized.

"I can't do this," she said.

"What can't you do, Boss?" Ade was instantly focused on her, and so was Aras. "What's wrong?"

"I can't sit back and wait twenty-five years to see Esganikan and that fucking mob of fanatics unleashed on Earth."

"The Skavu or the colony?" said Becken. Quite a few people had asked to go back with the Skavu and Esganikan's ship rather than wait, both Umeh Station crew and colonists. "It's not going to be a laugh a minute when the Christians land in Australia with the way the religious shit's going."

"You're just convincing me," said Shan.

"You're a copper," said Qureshi. "They'll need someone who can break up riots, won't they?"

Laughter broke out again, strained and nervous. Then the terrace was completely silent except for the ticking of insects on the roof and the echoes from the city. Aras looked at Ade, and he could see sudden and instant hope on his face; it was unguarded, and it was *there,* and it told Aras that his brother really did want to go back to Earth for whatever mix of reasons—homesickness, comrades he couldn't bear to say goodbye to, loyalty, unfinished business, duty, and maybe all those things. And Shan . . . Shan was never, ever going to believe that she didn't have some responsibility for her homeworld. If that hadn't been an inextricable part of her, then she would never have come this far without even consciously knowing why.

Where Ade and Shan went, Aras went too. This was the price of having a human family, as well as having a human component in himself; he was curious about Earth, and a feeling in his chest said *home* just as an unwanted isenj voice had told him Jejeno was a city he loved.

Aras began working out a mental list of who would look after his plants when they were gone.

"I'm sorry," said Shan. "I'm sorry to do this to you. I've got to go. We've got to go. Me and Ade and Aras— we'll come back, but we have to at least go." Aras could have sworn she was going to cry. He smelled the faintest of changes in her scent, this time from her skin and mouth. Ade must have caught it too, because he wrapped his arms around her and buried her face in his shoulder in a fierce and boisterous embrace that seemed designed to block her from his comrades' view.

"It's better than listening to you crabbing on about Esganikan for the next few decades, you daft tart," he said, forcing a laugh and giving her an excessively noisy kiss on the head. "Okay, let's do it."

"One problem, Boss," said Qureshi. It sounded odd to hear her call Shan that, but she used it generically, without any of the sentimental endearment that Ade did. "You've got *c'naatat*. You were bloody set on not letting it reach Earth. How are you going to deal with that?"

There was an awkward silence. Shan extricated herself from Ade's arms—if she'd been close to tears, there was no sign now—and reached in her pocket to take out the ball of gel. She tapped it on her hand and it coated her as far as he elbow, giving her skin and sleeve a slight sheen and nothing more.

"This is how we're going to deal with the accidental contamination risk," said Shan. "It was the condom that gave me the idea. You can coat yourself in this, head to toe. It's amazing stuff. Complete barrier."

"Condom—"

Ade cut in. "Yeah, condom." Marines were savage pisstakers, Eddie said. Ade would never live this down. "Had to get a special one made because the regular varieties were too bloody small."

He got the raucous mocking communal laughter he seemed to aim for. "Yeah, yours is so small you needed lights on it to find it." Barencoin balled up a piece of hemp paper from his pocket and threw it at him with impressive accuracy. "You'll never be out of work as a novelty act, Ade."

Chahal didn't join in. It didn't seem to be a reluctance to barrack Ade and discuss his genitals, but that he was working out something.

"Bugger me," he said. "That means you won't see Nevyan for fifty-odd years. Giyadas will be a grannie. Shit."

Eddie stared down into his beer, and Shan muttered, "Yeah," and seemed very preoccupied with removing the gel from her hand. The marines played with it for a while until Becken asked if Ade had laundered it first. It was interesting to note what they found hilarious after a glass of weak beer.

Eddie didn't seem as amused as usual. Aras wondered who the separation from F'nar would be harder for, Shan or Eddie.

F'nar: Nevyan Tan Mestin's home

"I knew you would have to do this," said Nevyan.

"You think I'm running out on you."

"No, Shan." Nevyan had Fulaor on her lap, her baby son adopted with his father Dijuas. It was the first time Shan had seen her cradling one of the boys. "This is inevitable. You're a matriarch. I did what I had to protect my home, and you still feel a duty to do the same for Earth. We both see the Skavu as the same threat, so how can I criticize you for that?"

Nevyan never disappointed Shan. She took the news with regret, but no recrimination. Wess'har never hid their feelings. Nevyan understood what it was to feel compelled. It was what matriarchs did, not out of ambition but out of necessity.

"I swear I didn't mislead you, and Esganikan didn't lean on me," said Shan. "I have to see this through. You know why."

Nevyan held her hand splayed so that Fulaor could grip her fingers. He seemed to be getting very independent, now very much a miniature wess'har male and not a stick insect with a downy head. "It's the time and distance that makes this hard."

"I'm going to be back, though."

"How can you say that?"

"Because I can't keep Aras from his home forever, and because this is my home too." Shan had found a way of suppressing her scent, but the weeping reflex still required clenched jaws and pressing her tongue to the top of her palate to keep under control. "You'll be around when I get back, and Giyadas will be a matriarch herself by then."

Giyadas stood staring at Shan, and if Shan hadn't know wess'har better, she'd have thought her expression was

one of being betrayed by the trust she'd foolishly placed
in adults.

"I knew Eddie would leave," she said, "but I thought I
would have more time with him. Will he forget me, do you
think?"

It was the kind of thing bereaved adults said, and so typi-
cally Giyadas that Shan bitterly regretted she wouldn't be
around to see her grow up. It made her all the more determined to come back to F'nar.

"You go find him, sweetheart," said Shan. "He's at my
place with the marines."

"Go on," said Nevyan. "And try not to make it hard for
him."

Shan listened carefully for sounds in the house. There
was loud trilling echoing from another room down one of the
passages; it was the two other boys and their fathers, playing. It was sometimes hard to work out where the sound was
coming from in these warren homes. "I never really got to
know your sons."

"You have a few weeks. We can spend time together."

"You must hate me at least a little for leaving when you've
got Umeh to worry about."

"Shan, had this been Earth, and Wess'ej had faced what
Earth faces, I'd have done the same. And you're coming
back, although I won't hold you to that, because not even
you can look that far ahead and know what's coming."

"ITX. We can talk. Every day."

"It's indeed a valuable thing, and now I know why."

"I swear to God I'm coming back."

"You don't believe in a God."

"I swear to you, then, because I do believe in you." It
was too much for Shan this time, and she allowed herself the
luxury of hugging Nevyan fiercely. "You came to find me
when everyone thought I was dead, mate, and if you thought
I was worth bringing home, then it's worth my coming home
when the job's done."

"Go keep your males happy," Nevyan said, without a
trace of irony. "And make sure we spend some time together
each day from now on."

Shan didn't go straight back to the house. She stopped halfway along the terrace and soaked up the early evening glow of the city reflecting a sunset. There were other pearl cities, and she'd live long enough to come back and see them and a thousand like them.

But people didn't hang around that long. In the end, the pain was leaving Nevyan and Giyadas. By the time she got back, more than fifty years would have elapsed for them. For her, it would be just months.

On Mara'na'cas, the colony was grabbing what it could and leaving the rest for the few who chose to wait for the return of *Thetis* in a few months, with all the added time-exile of a journey that would take three times as long. At least the Umeh Station personnel had hardly unpacked from the evacuation. But today Shan didn't give a damn about anyone's pain but her own, and allowed herself the rare luxury of feeling it.

She took the swiss out and recorded the cityscape until the dusk finally swallowed the pink pearl and the terraces were dotted with pinpoints and pools of soft yellow light, and the night air was full of sounds that had once been alien and now were just the background noise of her city.

Shan knew she'd play that recording a lot to get to sleep in the years to come. In the sky above her, Bezer'ej was a crescent moon. She wondered if it was possible to spot vessels taking off and landing from here. She'd never wondered about that before.

Her swiss *eeped* and she turned it over to look at the message.

CALL RAYAT URGENT AGAIN

He was persistent, she'd give him that.

"Bon voyage, arsehole," she said, and hit the delete key.

Nazel, also known as Chad Island: Bezer'ej

Pili still raged.

The bezeri crashed around the island, smashing through undergrowth, and apart from the sound of snapping branches and the occasional thudding when she came close enough to the village to be heard, she was oddly silent.

A human might have interpreted this rampage as an animal looking in vain for its lost young. But Pili knew her eggs had been destroyed. She was simply expressing impotent grief and anger, destroying anything in her path, and unable to settle.

Yeah, I know that stage. Been there, Pili.

Lindsay was still enough of a human to expect to hear sobbing and screaming. But then Pili was doing just that. Her lights flared green, sometimes bright, sometimes just a faint flickering. Then she'd settle into a deep lobelia blue that was hard to distinguish from black in some light conditions. She grieved.

"Your fault!" she said to Lindsay. "You bring them here, and they kill us *again*. Everyone kills us."

"But you can have more eggs, sometime in the future." Lindsay hated herself for trotting out that line. It was what truly stupid and well-meaning people said to those who'd lost babies, as if they were easily replaceable as long as you filed the right insurance claim, not unique individuals who'd been lost forever. "I know it's hard, but one thing you all have that no other bezeri has ever had is *time*. Lots of it."

It was hard to give something they never expected to have and then snatch it away from them again. It was a double bereavement in a way, and Lindsay knew how Pili felt despite the gulf that still existed between their original species. Shan might have been able to pass through the loss of a child unscathed except for laying down an extra layer of titanium plating, but normal mothers grieved. But then Shan was less human than any of these bloody squid. She evaluated. She took decisions. She implemented. She never wept or loved. And if that meant aborting her own kid because it was a potential threat to the balance of ecology, she'd do it. She *had*.

Lindsay had more in common with this alien cephalopod than she ever had with Shan Frankland.

"If you have babies before the Eqbas have found a way of removing *c'naatat*, and. . . ." Lindsay tried to find a way of saying *overbreed* without sounding insulting, but the semantics were probably lost on Pili anyway. "If there become too many of you, then the Eqbas will come back and destroy you all. They're very near. You might not know what five light years means yet, but it's close. Far closer than Earth. Close enough to come here and wipe you all out, if Nevyan calls them in again."

Pili seemed to lapse into a quiet sulk. "How will they know? We will be many before they even see us."

"They'll know," Lindsay said.

She didn't understand Eqbas technology or even what the wess'har had left in place by way of satellite monitoring. Whatever it was, she had no way of countering it even if she knew every last component. She was a stone-age woman overseen by space-faring aliens. She couldn't even contact them unless they decided to visit. This was as helpless and as one-way as it got.

She walked along the shoreline, wondering how she would hold this community together now. The violent intrusion had made the bezeri restless and wary. She couldn't find Guurs and Essil, or their two daughters.

"They went back to the sea," Saib said. "They fear for their young ones."

They'd been the last to be persuaded ashore. Lindsay could understand their anxieties and knew there was no point assuring them they were safe. She couldn't guarantee a damn thing.

"And you, Saib? Are you going to give up and go back below?"

He ambled beside her, swinging between what was now a pair of forelegs. "This is my domain. I will not hide."

"Glad to hear it."

"I can wait. I have patience. I can wait until we can hold this world ourselves."

The next day, Pili had gone. So had Loc, her mate, and a dozen of the other bezeri. Lindsay assumed they'd gone hunting, and expected them to come back at sunset for what was now the regular communal meal. But they didn't.

She waited on the shore, looking for their lights. But they didn't return.

Their evolution had progressed at an impossibly break-neck speed, and now so had their political and social development. In short weeks, Lindsay had turned victims into captors into some kind of friends, and now they'd moved on to create a schism and become what she feared might be enemies.

There were now two camps of bezeri. Maybe Pili and her comrades would come back when she'd done her grieving, but Saib seemed to think they'd gone their separate ways, back beneath the sea.

"We search," he said. "But they are in none of the places we once were."

There were now two bezeri nations, in a way. It wasn't what Lindsay had in mind when she planned to save them and unite them against invaders.

She was glad Shan wasn't here to say that she'd told her so.

19

*We realize this is irregular, but we'd like to take our chances
and stay. If we went back now after coming this far, we'd
have lost a unique chance to catalogue the natural world of
Wess'ej. And no human is going to be allowed to come here
again, right? If we can go back one day, fine. If not—then
we'll die here. It's a risk explorers have always taken.*

OLIVIER CHAMPCIAUX,
on behalf of the remnant of
the *Actaeon/Thetis* survey team

F'nar

"I'm glad you decided to come," said Esganikan.

Shan simply listened to the audio on her swiss. She wasn't
keen to see Esganikan's face, nor for hers to be seen. This
wasn't how she'd planned to go back to Earth. She hadn't
planned to go back at all.

She sat on her terrace with Nevyan, cramming in every
available moment to gaze at F'nar's beautiful pearl terraces
and store up memories and motivation. It wasn't as if she'd
be aware of the fifty-year separation, but she'd know the real
distance between her and home—this home, her Wess'ej
home—and she could guess how strong the pull of her former homeworld would be. She could predict what her gut
would do when she saw that blue and white disc again. But
she was going to ignore it.

*I'm coming back here, as soon as it's under control on
Earth. I must.*

"I swore I'd never let *c'naatat* anywhere near Earth,"
Shan said. "But you leave me no choice. I can't just sit back
and watch while your Skavu berserkers fuck my planet."

"As long as you abide by the contamination proce-
dures, and stay with the task force, *c'naatat* can be as

secure there as it is here," Esganikan said, a faint peevishness in her tone. "Any contamination would have to be deliberate."

Oh yeah. Don't I know it. "We've got a few weeks left. I'll talk to the Australians for you. Maybe even some of the sensible greens. Shit, they know I'm alive now. Nothing to lose."

Shan closed the link and found herself rubbing her face with one hand, realizing that all she could do was maybe talk Esganikan out of certain actions. That was all. She had no power beyond influence over the greens, and sod all sway with the governments of the day, whoever they turned out to be in the fullness of time.

"Ah, sod it." She'd have plenty of time to talk to Esganikan. But she had precious little left to spend with Nevyan, and that hurt more with every day that she counted down. The two matriarchs sipped tea, and Aras kept the cups topped up. "Push comes to shove . . ."

"You're going to use *jask*, aren't you?" said Nevyan.

It had certainly crossed Shan's mind. "If things get out of hand and there's something I feel I absolutely need to stop her doing, then I'm pretty sure I can outscent her, yes."

Nevyan simply cocked her head and said nothing.

We're both acting way out of character. She's discovered tact, and I've discovered that I can get attached to people. Who'd have thought it?

Aras seemed remarkably chipper about it all. Shan thought that perhaps a life that spanned centuries gave him a different perspective to her, someone who was still in double figures. It was just another trip to him. What mattered and what constituted home for him was going on that same journey—her and Ade.

"I won't see Giyadas grow up," said Shan.

"You'll see her *grown* up," said Aras.

The hardest thing Shan had to do was simply to turn her back in a few weeks' time and let a silent liquid-metal hatch close behind her. It was an act of separation that would take a second.

Like stepping out of the airlock, it was something she would simply tell herself to do. And she would.

F'nar

Eddie sat on the wall outside the Exchange of Surplus Things and finally held a perfect double-voiced note. Giyadas applauded. There was a bitter irony to achieving it now he was close to going home.

"Now, all I have to do is keep that up all day, plus learn an alien language that my brain is hopelessly unsuited to handle," he said. "And I'll be talking wess'u like a native."

"We know ordinary humans can't manage this," Giyadas said. "So we'll speak your languages instead."

Maybe it was easy not to be fiercely nationalistic when you knew you could zap the shit out of humans any time. Speaking English was a small concession for the wess'har. All they cared about was getting a job done.

"I won't have any wess'har to talk to," he said.

"There's Aras. And there's the ITX."

That wasn't what he meant, he realized. "Not the same."

"You want to go home, don't you?"

"One day, yes."

But this was too soon. Desperately lonely as he could be, desperate for simple sex and a glass of decent beer as he was, Eddie knew he wasn't going to leave Wess'ej gladly. He had too much unfinished business. His days of covering momentous events and going home for dinner, unchanged, were over. He was ripped in half now.

"Some of the Umeh Station crew have asked to stay," said Giyadas. "Five of them. They said they have too many things they still want to see."

"And is Giyadas going to let them?"

"Yes. She can always kill them if they become a problem."

It didn't seem to bother Giyadas one bit. *That's my little matriarch, all right.* "Well, then . . ."

"I will miss you."

Eddie wished she hadn't said it. He'd tried to avoid it. But as the days ticked away, he did the maths and looked at the distances, and knew that he'd feel nothing but regret for a lost opportunity—an unknown opportunity—if he walked away now and became just another human back on Earth again, even one with an extraordinary experience behind him.

They always said that walking on the Moon changed the early astronauts. Nothing was the same again for them, apparently.

And if you'd lived among aliens, and learned to love them—

Eddie only had one brief human life. Making this kind of choice was a lot harder for him than it was for Shan and Ade, with all their infinity stretching ahead of them.

"Well, I'll stay, too, then."

Oh God. That's it. I just did it.

Giyadas blinked. "This is good news."

He'd never see Earth again. He knew that. He'd always known it, really. "How could I not stick around to keep an eye on you, doll?"

"But you'll be dead by the time Shan gets back."

"Well, very old . . ." No, probably dead. She was right, and he didn't care. "But that's okay. Shan won't miss me at all."

Giyadas grabbed his hand with a grip that belied her fragile fingers.

"Besides," she said, "we don't want any other *bastard* getting all your stories, do we?"

No, she had a point there. Eddie was far from done with Wess'ej.

There'd be women in the Umeh Station remnant, and he could live without beer. That was a small price to pay for not looking up at the Earth sky each night, and wondering what had become of his little *isanket*.

He'd break the news to Shan later. He never did like long goodbyes.

FEU Fleet Ops
Status update
January 5, 2399

Eqbas Vorhi fleet: inbound for Pacific Rim Space Center.
Thetis: inbound for FEU Mars Orbital for Earth transfer.
Personnel: six FEU passport holders still remain in Ca-vanagh's Star system. All others embarked.